CRIMSON QUEEN

THE BLOOD & FLAME SAGA
BOOK 4

E.A. WINTERS

To my husband, who, the first time I really got down on myself about a one star review, told me they'd probably been dropped on the head as a child.

You certainly weren't gracious to that poor soul, but you're gracious to me, and I love you for it.

SOCIAL MEDIA

Connect with me on social media! [1]

- Website and newsletter: https://www.eawinters.com
- Facebook: https://www.facebook.com/eawintersnovels
- TikTok: @eawinters
- Instagram: @e.a.winters

---

1. Warning: connecting on social media may lead to exclusive content, behind the scenes snapshots, and joining a community that is way more fun than your daily to-do list. Engage with caution.

Mount Hara
Haizlin
Kalma
Carfus
Qalea
Ryden
Camar
Pillerae
N
E
S
W

Boan
Pilall
Ellix
Kinlock
Surion
Strip
Seddon
Horen
nor
elera

1

THE DUNGEON

Windowless dungeons are dark, cold, and accompanied only by the saddest of rats—the ones that haven't found their way into warmer accommodations. Certainly the place provided little in terms of food to pillage, but the quick padding of footfalls and the rattle of tin echoing down the hall reminded him that the rats had occasional opportunities for foraging.

A hooded figure came into view, lit only by the meager flickering light of a candle so stubby it barely deserved the name. The figure slid the tin plate under the lowest bar of the dungeon cell, an inch-and-a-half slot the candle and rations fit under with no difficulty. Mystery Figure placed a small tin cup through the bars for good measure, and then disappeared.

The man in the cell crept forward, less like a disheveled cur snatching fallen crumbs and more like a panther on the prowl. His movements were lithe and graceful, smooth and deliberate. His callous fingertips ran across the smooth surface of the plate, then explored the porous bread, pulling apart the pieces and deconstructing it piece by piece. The first slice of bread, the slice of old cheese, a slender steel key, a barely detectable sliver of meat, and a thin slip of paper.

A ripple of what might have been excitement ran up his spine. He unfolded the paper and lifted the stub of candle to examine it. The warm light caught a plate of opal-like stone embedded on his temple, casting a rainbow of color across the strip of parchment:

Her Majesty the Queen formally invites you to dine with her at
9:30 p.m.

Hot wax ran down his thumb, but he hardly noticed, only rubbing it between his thumb and forefinger thoughtfully before snuffing out the flame and relishing the soft *hsss* that emanated from the wick. He dropped the parchment into his cup, swirled it twice, and downed the beverage in a single gulp.

2

"I'd be happier if it were a barred cage, but Madensig Fortress isn't much better. Let her rot."

Semra sucked in a breath. Count Darbune often gave tactless comments, but suggesting that their young king let his sister *rot* just two months after his father's assassination seemed a little much.

The members of the high court filled eight chairs around a large oak table—seven men, and then Semra. The lower throne room was much smaller and far less ornate than the one upstairs, exchanging marble floors and gold inlaid pillars for dark woods and onyx-accented pieces. Zephan sat on a carved throne with mahogany dragon wings folded behind him and an array of mahogany spears fanned out above them. His eyes fixed on the map in front of him.

Darbune rapped his knuckles on the table. "*Queen* Avaya, as I am loathe to call her, has the loyalty of a toad and the heart of her Belvidorian predecessors. We saw how they slaughtered each other for the throne. I'd sooner marry a pig than send a delegation to her in Belvidore."

General Soldan set his goblet on the table. "That's quite

enough, count. Anger at her betrayal does not solve the problem—and she is still a Shamaran."

Semra darted a glance in Zephan's direction. Shadows darkened his face, less by the torchlight and more by the limited sleep he'd had in the weeks since his coronation. Not that he'd had much before that either. His finger traced the route. Semra bit her lip. Someone's chair creaked.

Zephan let out a long sigh, but when he looked up at Semra, a mischievous glint flickered in his eyes. She'd always thought they were amber, but today they were sweet, soft honey. Like molten gold mixed with sorrel. She loved nothing more than to be lost in them.

A slow smile crept across his face. "Semra?"

She startled. "What?"

"I asked what your thoughts were on sending a delegation."

"Right." Semra's cheeks flushed scarlet. She cleared her throat. "I agree with Duke Villir that we need to set a clear expectation for how we are going to deal with Belvidore. I think sending a delegation is the wrong way to do it. Madensig is a kill box. Send no one."

"I stand with Lady Myansara on this," General Soldan said.

Semra cringed at the noble title. Before his death, King Turian had pardoned all her assassin-related activity, due to her indoctrinated childhood under Azi's thumb, and praised her as a hero to Jannemar for her actions over the past few months. She had hoped for a pardon, but never expected Turian to elevate her from the nothingness of her birth to nobility, signing over to her the earldom of Pilall. It wasn't right.

Part of her wanted it, of course. She had no idea what she was doing when it came to being an earl, but having a qualification that allowed her to work with Zephan was a dream. It felt good, even though it seemed like a sham.

But it had also felt good to be purging the world of evil, when Azi handed out missions of who needed to die. Semra knew better than anyone that just because a thought was comforting, it didn't mean it was true.

"Excellent." Zephan leaned back in his chair. "We will not respond to Avaya's request to visit. We have nothing to say to her and will send no delegation. Meanwhile, we will strengthen our position south of the strip and grant as much aid as we can afford to rebuilding the area."

Darbune's lip curled, and he shot Semra a withering glare. The count despised her with every fiber of his being. He had since before Turian was killed, before Avaya faked her own kidnapping to Belvidore. Why did he hate her so?

Semra's stomach twisted into knots. Maybe it was power. She had a dragon, after all. Maybe it was fear. The last dragonlord murdered the queen, framed Semra, and nearly took over the kingdom before he was defeated and thrown into the dungeons.

Or maybe it was truth. Maybe Darbune saw the fakeness of Semra's tenuous position, the farce of nobility, like a ball gown on a sewer rat, and knew she'd never be right for it. It wasn't fair for her to be given military responsibilities and prestige without the elite upbringing the likes of him had endured for many years. Maybe Darbune knew what she felt in her core—*you belong to ditches and caves, Semra. Not castles.*

It was one thing to be forgiven for unspeakable crimes. It was another to go from the meekness of a convicted killer under grace, to the authority of a military strategist and peer to the highest advisers in the kingdom.

Zephan scanned the room. "General Tallem, I want updates on the recovery of our men and the situation along the Surion Strip as soon as you have them. Earl Lundoon, I need everything you can find out about substances that could have poisoned Semra by inhalation at close range, but not harmed Avaya, who was right on top of her at the time. I've not heard of anything like it, and we've ruled out konnolan. Belvidore has a new weapon, and we need to know what it is and assume they plan to use it on a larger scale. This could have been a test run."

The general and earl dipped their heads.

"Of course, Your Majesty."

"Right away."

Zephan continued: "General Soldan, brief Captain Firfell of our security concerns and change up the guard shifts. Avaya knows everything about operations here at home. If she tries something stupid, I want her as cocky as possible, so make sure no information leaks. Have Saeb briefed as well, and let all guards and staff know that anyone who shares logistical information on the changing of the guard outside these walls, whether with friends or family, will be relieved of their duties effective immediately."

More nods, more assent.

"That's all, gentlemen."

Chairs scraped the floor as the council pushed away from the table. Semra turned her body away from Darbune and fixed her eyes on the double doors. She could feel his gaze boring into her back. Council meetings always set her on edge, and after getting distracted by Zephan's beautiful face in a professional setting, she needed a dragon ride. Or maybe a visit with Zephan's little sister, Aviama.

"Lady Myansara, please stay to go over plans for your visit to Pilall."

Semra froze, and Darbune bumped into her. He recoiled from their touch, as if mere contact would contaminate his noble blood, and let out a disapproving grunt. Semra muttered an apology under her breath, that she half-hoped the count wouldn't hear, and angled around him back toward her seat.

The doors shut, and Zephan leaped off his throne to block her path to her chair. Semra opened her mouth to protest, but all resistance wilted as his lips met hers. A tingling thrill ran through her body, and she reached for him. Her hands ran up his chest and draped around his neck, and he pulled her in.

He lifted her off her feet and a short gasp escaped her. She felt his smile beneath their kiss as he carried her toward the largest chair in the room. A warning bell rang in her mind, and Semra pulled back.

"No, not there. It's illegal for anyone but the monarch to sit on the throne."

Zephan lowered her into the seat of his throne and bent over her. He kissed her neck. "Well then, we'd better not tell the king."

Goosebumps sprang up and down her arms. Zephan noticed and grinned. He kissed her again and ran his hand along the curve of her hip and thigh. "How are you liking the new wardrobe?"

Semra laughed. She'd never put much thought into what she wore while growing up. All the mission readies in the mountain had worn fitted trousers with built-in sheaths for their throwing knives, and a cheap rough-spun tunic. She had to wear a wrap skirt on top when on missions, since pants were unusual for women in Jannemar, but it was designed for easy removal. She hated missions that required actual dresses and had always planned her ops to avoid them whenever possible.

Since being made an earl and lady of the court, Aviama had redoubled her efforts in trying to stuff Semra into velvets and silks and various pretentious gowns. Semra staunchly refused and said she needed to feel comfortable and have easy access to her knives. Zephan proposed a compromise that would make her more suitable for formal court attire and keep her in trousers—sort of.

The result was a minimally ornamented bodice belted at the waist and flowing out into a billowing skirt behind her but cutting away in the front. From the back it looked like a gown, but in the front, her trousers and knives were visible, and her belt was both stylish enough to please Aviama, and sturdy enough to support wearing a sword or dagger.

Semra glanced down and ran a hand over the smooth, rich materials of her new clothing. "It'll take some getting used to, but I think it works. I know military uniforms are important, and I feel like this is sort of my uniform now that I officially work for Jannemar. And I like that I don't have to figure out what sidesaddle looks like on a dragon."

Zephan laughed. "It's more appropriate for court than your typical, but still a little scandalous—still you. I like it." He kissed her again. "You'd be stunning in a burlap sack, but I do love seeing you in this."

She kissed him back, and a single curl of smoke escaped her fingertips and wrapped around them. She waved it away, and it dissipated throughout the room. Zephan propped himself on the arm of the throne and straightened, watching the last of the smoke disappear.

"You're getting better at that."

"What?"

"Two months ago, we were in a pitch-black cloud every time I kissed you. Now, you have more control."

Semra's chest swelled with pride. It was true. She could feel the energy swirling inside her when they kissed, like frenetic fireflies in a jar bursting to show themselves. Their connection gave her an easy access point to whatever smoke magic she'd somehow wound up with through the mark of the dragon's kiss. But she could keep the lid on it if she wanted to.

It wasn't foolproof. Sometimes nervousness would let a whisp escape, but by and large, she was containing the smoke. Sometimes she felt heat building and building inside her, and she went to the cleft beneath the catacombs, or took a ride with her dragon, Zezura, and released pent-up heat into the air through smoke and a little shower of sparks—far less embarrassing than smoke leaking under every door and out every window where Zephan and Semra were alone together. They'd had to be judicious about when and where they kissed until she got a handle on things.

Semra slipped off the throne and perched on the table instead. *Much better,* she said to herself. *Sitting on tables is frowned upon, but not illegal.* She swung her legs and changed the subject. "So am I really going to Pilall?"

"You've been earl for two months. You need to lay eyes on your land and your people and start a relationship with them. When he went off to war, Earl Libric put a steward in charge of the estate, and he seems to be doing a decent job. But you can't let him stay in limbo there forever."

Semra's heart sank. "Is it stupid that I don't want to leave?"

Zephan cocked his head. "It makes perfect sense to me. You've never been a noble before. You do your best public speaking when everyone you're talking to is facing imminent death. And you'd miss my incredibly handsome face while you were gone."

She rolled her eyes, then swallowed. "I would. And also, I don't have the faintest idea what I'm doing."

Zephan would know what to do. He could take her by the hand and walk her through every step. But with his coronation so fresh, his list of to-dos was simply too long. He wouldn't be able to justify a trip to Pilall.

"I'll coach you. You'll be fine."

Semra hopped off the table and kissed him. "If you insist."

"I do."

Zephan took her hand and drew it to his lips, his fiery amber gaze never leaving her face.

Crack.

Pop.

Pop.

"Ouch!"

Semra yanked her hand free and stumbled backward, staring at the embers falling from her fingertips. They were the strongest sparks she'd ever produced, and the surge of heat had been too sudden to stop. She tripped over the hem of her skirt and knocked over a chair; Zephan caught her around the waist just as Semra seized the back of the chair before it hit the ground.

The double doors to the lower throne room opened. Captain Firfell stood in the opening, flanked by two guards. He opened his mouth, then shut it. He licked his lips and tried again.

"Your Majesty. You have a visitor."

Semra's chest tightened, and her heart threatened to beat right out of it. Firfell glowered at the strange sight before him, and she could hardly blame him: the young king, he was sworn to protect with his arms around the assassin woman as if they'd just been caught in a deep dip of the waltz. One of Semra's arms was thrown around Zephan's shoulders, and the other, inexplicably, gripped the back of a half-fallen chair.

Zephan shot upright and set Semra on her feet. She straightened the chair and stepped to one side. A squirmy feeling roiled through her insides. She clenched her jaw.

"Shafii Rinab is here with urgent news of Lady Myansara's condition. And Queen Avaya has been sighted in Kinlock. She should be here in ten days. Our men have surrounded the coach and are escorting her as we speak."

Zephan smoothed his jacket. "She's across the river?"

"I'm afraid so, Your Majesty."

Zephan furrowed his eyebrows. "Impossible. How could she appear out of thin air?"

"We aren't sure what happened. Our guard posts have been interviewed, but none saw anything out of the ordinary. They gave report on everyone at the crossings, and nothing like it passed them. The coach is Belvidorian, the woman inside meets her description, and its Belvidorian escort befits royalty."

"Scourge." Zephan plucked at the edges of his sleeves and let out an exasperated sigh. "Let her come. We'll meet her at the gate. She is not to be permitted inside the castle until a written statement of purpose is in our hands. I want to know how she got across the Surion River and into Kinlock without being seen, and I want details on her entourage."

Firfell bowed. "I'll see it done. And Shafii Rinab?"

"We will meet him in the conservatory. He's a friend, and I'm sick of being cooped up in formal rooms this morning."

"Of course."

Firfell receded down the hall, leaving Semra and Zephan standing together in the lower throne room with the double doors open wide to the guards posted outside.

Zephan swept his hand toward the door. "After you, Lady Myansara."

"Thank you—err ... mhmm." Semra strode from the room and down the hall; Zephan's deep chuckle followed her. She'd never quite been able to call him *Your Majesty,* but she didn't want to be insulting either, so she did her best to avoid addressing him in public at all.

Two guards fell in behind them, leaving as tasteful a distance as they deemed appropriate as their monarch and his totally-believably-platonic earl swept down the corridor. Semra clenched her hands into fists, opened them again, and stared at her fingertips as they walked. They looked so innocent, her hands, as if they'd spent their time on flower picking and embroidery rather than knifework and combat.

But today they betrayed her. Today they revealed they had a secret. She ran her thumbs over her fingertips on both hands, but the heat she'd felt earlier was gone. No smoke. And certainly no sparks.

It was a good thing Shafii was here. Maybe he had answers.

"Lady Myansara!"

Semra and Zephan paused and turned toward a guard running in their direction. He paused, panting, and bowed. The man was young, perhaps twenty. His helmet was slightly askew, his face red, and his breastplate loosely fastened.

"Get ahold of yourself, soldier," Zephan said.

Red Face nodded and bowed. "Forgive me, Your Majesty. I was told to pass a message to her ladyship as a matter of urgency."

"Is someone dead or dying?" Semra asked.

"I—I don't think so," the guard replied. "The healer Coanor has sent for you. It's something about your illness. She said it was *latent,* that it hasn't gone away."

Semra and Zephan exchanged glances. Her stomach flipped. It had all started with konnolan poisoning in Belvidore, which had awoken magical essence in Semra's blood. Elemental magic had been destroyed in The Crumbling six hundred years ago, but a few select species retained it—like dragons. After Semra saved her dragon, Zezura's, life, Zezura had sealed their bond with the mark of the dragon's kiss on her chest. When Semra's old commander tried to kill her with venomous snakes, the mark expanded and seemed to swallow up the poison, and when it did, the magic inside the mark broke into her bloodstream and made her ill.

Eventually, the burning heat inside her found a way to release through smoke and the occasional spark from her fingers, and the sickness abated. Semra shuddered at the thought of returning to that weak, feverish state. It had been nearly unbearable.

"Shafii could have answers for whatever it is," Semra said. She turned to Zephan. "He and Coanor are both healers—why don't we invite Coanor to join us in the conservatory?"

The guard shook his head. "Coanor has something to show you, in person, at her place on the outer ward."

Zephan studied him for a moment. He pursed his lips, but Semra held up a hand. "It's okay. I'm sure it's not as bad as it sounds. I'll go see what she wants, and I'll come up as soon as I can."

Zephan nodded. "Fine. Harun, please accompany Lady Myansara and our flighty friend here to Coanor's house."

Semra arched an eyebrow. "As if I can't defend myself?"

"The point is that you shouldn't *have* to defend yourself. And yes, I like it when you have someone with you. Even if you could beat them, they're well-trained men and formidable to most everyone else." *And obviously this fresh-meat fellow wouldn't do the trick.*

Semra wondered how exactly Red Face had made it through training. She spread her hands and bowed, then spun back down the hall.

"Ladies curtsy," Zephan called out behind her.

"If I see one, I'll let her know!" Semra was rewarded with another laugh, and she smiled to herself as she exited the keep and cut across the open courtyard.

Harun and Red Face walked with Semra at a clipped pace past the gardens and courtyard, through the east wing of the keep, and into the outer ward. The granary and storage barns greeted them on the far side, and the faithful clang of the blacksmith sounded from around the curve. Semra quickened her step, turned the corner of a long, low building hugging the inner wall, and flung the door open.

Beds lined the wall to her right, and a table filled with beakers, herbs, handwritten notes, and half a pot of stew stood to her left. Two doors led to bedrooms beyond it, the nearest of which Semra had spent far too much time in during her illness. Although perhaps *illness* was not the right description.

A gray-haired woman emerged from the second door, holding three potatoes and a sprig of rosemary in one hand and a bulb of garlic and small pot in the other.

"Semra! What a surprise! Come, darling, why don't you take this here for the soup and set it down for me—not that one; the garlic and honey are for a poultice!—yes, very good, thank you. Tell the guards to kindly leave you alone, and come sit and tell me what's on your mind."

Semra set the potatoes and rosemary on the table next to the pot and tilted her head. "Coanor, it's great to see you, but I received urgent word that it was *you* who needed to see *me*."

Coanor frowned. "Urgent word? From whom?"

Something in Semra's stomach churned. She leveled a glare at Red Face, who was once again living up to the name she'd given him. "Who gave you the message?"

His eyes grew to saucers, and he swallowed. "I ... the healer's apprentice. I was late to my shift, and she found me in the guard room, and told me if I didn't get to you right away, anything that happened to you would be my fault."

"Darling, I haven't had an apprentice for three seasons."

Semra felt the blood drain from her face. *Zephan.*

Her feet moved before she could blink. She rocketed out of Coanor's and screamed over her shoulder as she ran, "Harun! Don't let Red Face leave your sight!"

She was out of the house, through the door to the keep, and down the corridor before she realized she'd said the guard's nickname out loud. She didn't recognize him from Mount Hara, and he was too young to be one of Azi's sleeper assassins. He likely really was a nervous new guard off his game, but they couldn't take any chances.

Who had posed as the apprentice?

Someone wanted to draw Semra away from Zephan. Someone who knew enough about her history to make a believable message. Not to mention Zephan was now short a guard.

The opal-like mark on her chest burned as she reached out to the dragon in her mind. *I need your eyes in the sky, Zez. There's an enemy in the castle.*

A deep roar answered from somewhere far away, and Semra felt the dragon bank against the wind and wheel back toward Shamaran Castle. Semra sprinted up the stairs through Ancestry Hall, up the next flight of stairs past the paintings of an endless royal lineage, past the family portrait of the current monarchy mocking her—King Turian, dead; Queen Sharsi, dead; Princess Avaya, traitorous; Prince Zephan, made king, and up against some faceless danger even now.

Her fingers itched as they brushed against the hilts of the throwing knives strapped to her thighs. *Not yet. Don't cause a panic.*

"Stop her."

The guards at the top of Ancestry Hall blocked Semra's passage, and she let out a guttural cry. An image flashed through her mind: Shafii aspirated on his own blood on the marble floor of the conservatory, his lifeless eyes staring up at her. Zephan, sword in hand, stabbed through the gut. He strained to form the sound of her name on his lips, the blade still protruding out his back.

All because she couldn't get to him fast enough.

She whirled toward the voice. Captain Firfell strode

forward and motioned her to step back. "The king has expressly commanded no one disturb him."

Semra ground her teeth. "He's expecting me. He's meeting with Shafii Rinab."

Firfell clasped his hands behind his back. "I'm afraid the king was explicit."

"When exactly? Is he *not* meeting with Shafii? I need to know anything that changed, and I need to know it *now*."

"You're not cleared to know."

"Aurin's Spear! Scourge, you know I am! Let me pass!"

Firfell jutted his chin forward and puffed out his chest. "Maybe you're taking your closeness to the king a little too far. Spending time with him is one thing, but being privy to all matters of state is quite another."

Semra groaned. "He's in danger. You can come, just hurry up."

Firfell scowled. "I'm not permitted either."

Her knives burned at her thighs, begging to be drawn. But as much as she hated Firfell, he was a decent captain, and loyal to his king. And the bigger scene she made now, the more resources would be drawn away from Zephan to deal with Semra.

Harun and Red Face bounded up the stairs behind her so that two guards blocked her entry over the Grand Hall, two hemmed her in from behind, and Firfell stood between them.

Semra gestured at Harun and Red Face. "Tell the good captain what happened. I need to get through."

Red Face hung his head. "Someone claiming to be Coanor's apprentice gave me a message from Coanor to Lady Myansara on urgent business. It turns out Coanor didn't send any message."

Firfell crossed his arms. "Coanor doesn't have an apprentice."

Semra rolled her eyes. "Catch up, would you?"

"If there is a mole in the castle, I'll launch an investigation and a search party. I'll send a pair of guards to confirm the king's safety, but you're known for taking a rather ... extreme approach."

Semra gritted her teeth. "It's not extreme if there's a credible threat and you hope to keep two kings from dying in the same year."

Firfell gripped her arm and yanked her to the side. He leaned down, his face inches from her nose. "Just because you're a good fighter doesn't mean our entire security team is worthless. Let me do my job. It's time you started to respect me."

Semra's eyes flashed, and her lip curled. "So this is what it's about. Your ego."

"It's about diplomacy. A skill you lack entirely. What do you know of repairing national relationships? I'll call you if we need a bloodbath, but for anything that requires a more delicate touch, I'll thank you to stay as far away as possible."

"I'm more than a sharp sword."

"Yes, I know. You've got a sharp tongue too. But when it comes to problem solving, you tend to dispatch anyone inconvenient."

Anger burned in Semra's chest. She opened her mouth to retort, but a singsong silky voice cut her off.

"Care to make a bet?"

Semra froze. It couldn't be. But that tenor, that honey dripping with danger—she'd only heard one person with a voice like that.

Firfell bowed.

"A gentleman does not make a bet with a lady, Your Highness."

A golden-haired young woman leaned against the door

frame leading into the royal family residence hall—the one where Zephan, Avaya, and Aviama had all lived until a few months ago. The king and queen's quarters were on the opposite wing across the U-shaped keep, where Zephan had taken up residence after his coronation.

The woman was slender, languid in her movements, and objectively gorgeous. Perfect ringlets flowed down her back and over one shoulder. Semra blinked at her. She was the spitting image of Avaya. But something about her face was rounder and her eyes a hint softer.

"Then it's a good thing I know you're not a gentleman."

It was Aviama, the baby of the family and Semra's good friend. She knew it was. But the uncanny likeness to her older, capricious sister just now was hard to shake.

"I beg your pardon, Your Highness! I've never shown myself the least bit untoward."

"So says the gentleman in the presence of a lady. It's what the gentleman does in the presence of only other gentlemen that makes them uncouth. You've made a few wagers in your day, haven't you, Captain?"

Semra glanced between them and arched an eyebrow.

Firfell cast a look over his shoulder at the other guards, then dragged Semra over to Aviama and lowered his voice. "Stop shouting, Your Highness, and tell me what you want."

"Semra and I are going to the library. We may visit the conservatory while we are there, as I often did when my father was king. You're going to allow it, and by and by we may check on my dearest brother while we are there. If Zephan wants to see Semra, you get to be my personal bodyguard for a day. If he doesn't, you can toss Semra into the dungeons for a day as penance for insubordination or something. Even though she outranks you now. But she'll go without a fuss."

"No I won't," Semra said.

Aviama waved her off. "Yes she will. Firfell?"

4

Captain Firfell pursed his lips. "You can't bribe me to break protocol."

Aviama gasped and clutched at her chest. "I wouldn't dream of it! But I would certainly be appreciative. I'll give you one of my gemstone bracelets. You can pawn it and pay your debts."

Semra's jaw dropped. Aviama caught her eye and grinned.

Firfell eyed the princess, then lifted his chin and sniffed. "You can't cross here. But I can't keep you from visiting the library or the conservatory, as you've always done, I suppose."

"Launch your investigation. And start with *him*." Semra jerked her head toward Red Face, and Firfell gave a curt nod.

Aviama took Semra by the arm and dragged her down the spiral staircase to the second floor.

"That was ..." Semra shook her head. "When did you learn to do that?"

Aviama shrugged. "I've watched Avaya. It's the kind of thing she would do."

Semra laughed. "No kidding. For a minute there, I thought you were her."

Aviama couldn't help the smile bursting across her face. "Really?"

Semra nodded. "Absolutely terrifying."

"Thank you! It was *so* exhilarating! Is this why you do risky things? I feel fantastic. Oh, but what's the matter? You sounded bad, and when *you* sound bad, things are usually a hop and a skip from total disaster."

"Yes, well, I wish your risky things wouldn't involve landing me in the dungeons, but I congratulate you on your adventurousness."

"Oh, Zephan wouldn't let it happen. He'll want to see you, and on the off chance he doesn't, he'll overrule my wager before you land in a cell. Firfell should never have accepted my bet."

The corner of Semra's mouth twitched. "I never knew you were so devious."

"My brother picked *me* to hide you in a trunk and make you into Axelia Berinon for the gala, thank you very much," Aviama said with a sniff. But her eyes twinkled. The two of them exited the stairwell at the second floor, left Ancestry Hall behind them, and crossed the empty expanse of the Grand Hall.

Aviama lowered her voice as their footsteps echoed up to the lofted ceilings above them. "What's going on?"

"Zephan and I were on our way to meet Shafii when I was called away on urgent business to Coanor. I was supposed to rejoin him with Shafii after that, only Coanor never sent for me, and the message was a ruse. Someone wanted to get me away from Zephan. And now he has demanded no one disturb him? Please. I think he's in danger."

Aviama's face paled, but her face never faltered. "What do you need?"

"We need to find Zephan and make sure he's safe. And we need to get him and Shafii to a secure location."

"What about his security?"

Semra scoffed. "You mean the security Firfell is supposed to be running point on?"

"Ah."

They exited the Grand Hall to the anteroom and passed into the library. Semra went to the third stack of books and ran her fingers over the spines. Where was it?

"Gaulen or Monac should be head of Zephan's security. I know Monac is at the strip, but if we see Gaulen, we need him to know what's going on. I don't trust anyone else."

"He's a stickler for the rules. If he's under orders to keep distractions away from the king's wing, he'll do it. We don't have much to go on, and I think he reads protocols to fall asleep at night."

Semra's hands flew across the books, and she yanked two from the shelves. "There's a first time for everything. Let's go."

"Conservatory?"

"Yes. I'm less threatening when I'm with you—you give me innocuous reasons to be places. We don't know a thing about restrictions to the west wing. We're just two friends on a stroll from the library, headed to visit brother dearest."

Semra heard Aviama's breathing quicken as they passed two guards and entered the stairwell. Semra looped her arm through Aviama's and slowed her pace just as they reached the top. "Take a breath. Nothing unusual about today. We're just typical friends, you know—the sort that meet under false pretenses in a stuffy trunk and a royal bedroom."

Aviama snorted, and Semra laughed. The two of them giggled right up to two guards posted outside the conservatory.

The guard on the left stepped into their path and bowed

his head. "Your Highness. Your Ladyship. Are you looking for Shafii Rinab?"

"Oh, no, we just came to drop off some books for our reading time this evening!" Semra said, waving the books in her arms. "We wanted to ask the king what he thought of our selections. Why? Is Shafii in there?"

"No, I'm afraid he's been sent home. The meeting is postponed, and the king is unavailable."

Semra glanced behind them at the mention of the guest rooms, as if imagining the east wing behind them instead of the west. Six guards stood post outside the king's chambers. Zephan wasn't in the conservatory.

Aviama's arm trembled in Semra's, but she kept her voice light as she turned to Semra. "Oh! Let's surprise him then, what do you think? Should we leave the books in Mother's room?"

"Great idea," Semra gushed. "You wanted your mother's favorite perfume bottle too, didn't you? For the glass blowers to replicate."

Aviama opened her mouth, but for a moment no sound came. "Yes," she stammered. "For the glass blowers to replicate." She bit her lip.

Semra's stomach soured. It was a beautiful idea, an item Aviama would love to have, but had not yet thought to ask for. It was a sentimental enough request to challenge the guard's restrictions, and only next door to where Zephan must be hiding, or whatever mysterious meeting he was in.

The guards exchanged a glance and turned to them again. "Be quick about it, and keep your voices down. No one is supposed to be in the royal residences until this evening."

Aviama drew herself up tall and lifted her chin. "My father *never* kept me from mother's chambers when I needed to be with her. And my brother has never kept me from her either."

The princess wiped a tear from her eye, and the guard blanched. "I never denied you access, Your Highness. It's the *king's* chambers that are off limits right now. Like I said, be quick about it, and keep your voices down."

Semra tugged Aviama away, and the guard at the conservatory gestured to the guards down the hall. The six guards stood at attention outside the king's chambers, giving no acknowledgment of their existence as they passed. Semra slowed a tick outside the doors, but there was no sound she could detect.

They passed the doors to the king's valet, the queen's chambermaid, and finally the queen's quarters. Aviama slipped a key from a chain around her neck and let them inside.

Semra sucked in a breath. She'd never been in the queen's rooms before. Gold leaf shimmered on the walls, and royal-blue couches, chairs, and pillows beckoned for company after setting so long in idleness. Queens of old observed their entry from frames lining the wall on either side of a large fireplace. On one side, several steps led into a window seat alcove, and on the other, two black marble pillars signaled a shift from entertainment to secluded privacy.

Aviama marched to the doors beyond the pillars. Semra shook off her awe and hurried after the young princess. It had been a long time since Semra had been taken aback by anything opulent, but there was something different about the grandness of the queen's receiving room paired with the sacredness of a bereaved space.

The doors to the queen's bedchamber opened, but for a moment Semra saw the Great Hall, decked out for a gala and filled with beautiful people, the king and queen talking together with Belvidorian guests. The queen's laugh sounded like birdsong, and the music begged for a dance.

The smell of garlic. The arc of a juggler's colorful spheres. Cold, hard marble.

Blood.

Queen Sharsi of Jannemar, the first of the Shamaran family to fall at the Framatar's hand. Lying in a crimson puddle on the floor.

The Framatar, Azi, dragonlord of Mount Hara, brother of King Turian. The man responsible for kidnapping Semra as a child and raising her as an assassin, for making her what she was, for building his army of brainwashed killers.

A chill ran down her spine.

The dungeons were too good for him.

"Semra," Aviama hissed. She waved Semra inside and shut the doors behind them. "I think I can get us into Wurik's room, but if they're in the king's chambers—"

"They're in there."

"—then they've probably locked the door from the valet's room to the bedchamber."

Semra nodded. She scanned the bedchamber. It was beautiful, but surprisingly simple after the lavish sitting room. Instead of purified marble and gold, good old-fashioned, honest cedar formed the bed, writing desk, and vanity. Nezil Myansara flowers were carved tastefully into the grains. The vanity held a little village scene at one end, and Shamaran Castle on the other. A tribute to her humble upbringing, Semra thought.

She crossed to the vanity, set down the library books, and opened a drawer. Aviama sucked in a breath, and Semra paused. "What?"

"No one has opened it since she died."

Semra grimaced and stared at an ivory hair comb gathering dust on the vanity. Her stomach twisted. *It's been left out on purpose. She'd left it out, before the gala.* "I need a hair pin or some other thin thing. The locks are simple, but I need something to rotate the actuator with. Do you want to get it?"

Aviama spun one of the rings on her fingers and swallowed. She stepped up to the vanity and slowly opened first one drawer, then another. She produced two sapphire hairpins and handed them to Semra. Something in her eyes shimmered, but she blinked twice, and it was gone.

Semra dipped her head. "How do we get to the valet's room from here?"

"Through the chambermaid's room. They say that years ago, the queen's chambermaid and the king's valet were in love. Forbidden to court, they created a secret door between their rooms and carried on their relationship in secret." Her voice dropped to a barely audible whisper. "I always loved that story."

The sort of story a mother might tell a daughter at bedtime. Semra cleared her throat. "Right. Okay, show me. And from here on out, no more talking. They could hear us."

"Is Zezura close?"

Semra closed her eyes and reached through her consciousness for the dragon. *Did you have to go so far away to hunt, Zez?* She opened her eyes. "She's close. Almost here."

Hurry up, Zez.

Aviama took a deep breath and led the way to the opposite end of the queen's bedroom, through the door to the queen's chambermaid's room—uninhabited since the queen's death—and across the small space. The princess dropped to the floor, hooked her finger in a divot of floorboard, and removed it from the floor with practiced ease. She reached into the hole and under the wainscot paneling, and a moment later a portion of the paneling swung outward.

Semra's eyes widened, and a smug smile crept across Aviama's face. Semra smiled and followed Aviama from the chambermaid's room to the room of the king's valet. Wurik was very much alive, which made the move somewhat riskier, but luckily the room was vacant.

The door to the king's chambers stood on the opposite side of Wurik's room. Semra pressed her ear to the wood, but it was deathly silent. Maybe she was wrong.

If Zephan isn't here, then why is the conservatory empty? And why are there six guards in the hall?

Semra froze. *It's all for you, idiot. The fake apprentice. The command to stay away from the west wing.* Her heart dropped like a hammer on an anvil. *He's been taken somewhere else, with perfect breadcrumbs to lead you away from him and then divert you here. And you gobbled them up like a little puppet.*

She'd fallen for distractions at the gala when the queen was murdered. Tymetin had wafted garlic under her nose, and she'd been so sure it was arsenic. The redirect had worked like a charm then, and it worked just as swimmingly now. Was Zephan even in the castle?

Who was doing this?

Semra took out the queen's sapphire hairpins and inserted them into the lock. Aviama leaned into her back, watching closely. Tension thickened the air. She felt the actuator catch, and began to turn it.

She got just halfway through when the lock spun of its own accord and the door opened. Semra jerked her hands back and lost her balance, and Aviama yelped and fell into her, spilling the two of them onto the floor of the king's room.

A voice smooth and cool as the Shalladin river prickled Semra's memory and stood every hair on end.

"If you wanted to join us, why didn't you just say so?"

5

―――――

An invisible force hit Semra in the chest, and she collapsed under its weight. No one had touched her, but the impact felt real enough. Panic seized her.

The door clicked shut behind them, and the voice of her childhood floated over her. "My dear"—he clucked his tongue—"Oh, how deluded you've become without my tutelage! What's this trash you're wearing? You can't be an assassin *and* a noblewoman. It isn't decent."

No. No, it can't be ...

The pressure against her body released, and Semra lifted her gaze from the ground to meet the ice-cold nonchalance of evil personified. Azi Shamaran, dragonlord of Mount Hara, kidnapper of children. The sun glinted off the opaline mark of the dragon's kiss on his temple, the same mark Semra had on her chest after she'd saved Zezura's life. The binding of a dragonlord.

Azi plucked lint off the shoulder of stone-gray robes embroidered with emerald, amethyst, and onyx. Black cord epaulets formed in the shape of a dragon's head at each shoulder. He leveled a fiery glare at her.

"You were not made to be decent, Semra. You were made to purge evil from the world, to set wrongs to right. And you failed."

The rustle of velvet caught her attention, and Semra snapped her head to the side. An older version of Aviama stepped up beside Azi. Her supple frame was draped in decadent cherry red silk, her lips stained to match, and the golden rivulets of her hair were caught up in twists at the base of her neck.

Scourge. Semra's lip curled. *And she's wearing a crown.*

Queen of Belvidore indeed.

A soft whimper came from Aviama, and Semra reached a hand behind her. She found Aviama's wrist, and gripped it. The princess's other hand clamped down on Semra's as if her touch were the lifeline she needed to be dragged from a raging sea.

"Sem."

Semra's heart broke at the sound of her favorite voice in the world. Except today it was urgent, and raspy, as if it had been screaming for hours and hours on end.

She turned. Zephan stood plastered against the wall, his arms and legs pinned by nothing at all. He had no bruises, but his shoulders sagged. If he'd been beaten, Azi had been careful to avoid his face.

Which meant he had a reason to keep Zephan alive and looking like the king, at least for a little while longer. A thin thread of hope clung to the thought.

"What's happening?" Semra half-whispered. "Why aren't the guards rushing in?"

"I think they're controlling the sound in the room. They have magic."

"That's not possible," Aviama said. "Magic was destroyed six hundred years ago."

"You must be one of my queen's weaknesses," Azi crooned. "Delighted, I'm sure. You have no idea what is possible, Highness. But I intend to show you."

Aviama shrank back, and Semra stood and yanked Aviama to her feet next to her. Semra squeezed her hand and caught her eye. She held Aviama's gaze, and lifted her chin. The fear in the princess's eyes flickered, and she took a deep breath and followed Semra's example.

She seemed to get the message. *No sniveling, princess. This is a political negotiation, like a thousand others you've sat through. Just a little more honest.*

Azi walked to a table on one side of the room and pulled out three stuffed chairs, one on the far side, and two on the near side. He swept his arm toward them. "Our distinguished pretender, on this side, please. And the traitor with her poppet on the other. We have a proposal."

The force holding Zephan dropped away, and he stumbled into the room. Semra's chest tightened. She ran forward, but a blast of air shot her backward.

"No need," Azi said, wagging his finger. "Let the pretender king walk it off."

Semra clenched her jaw, but Zephan held up a hand. "I'm fine. Let's be hospitable, shall we?"

He strode to the table—stiffly, Semra thought—and waited at his chair for the rest of the party to join him. Semra glanced back at Azi. He hadn't moved a muscle when the wind came and went. *How was he controlling the wind?*

Azi clapped his hands. "Finally, a decent host!"

Semra stepped to the table and took the opportunity to survey the room. Light blue, gold leaf, and red and white accents decorated the archways and molding of the room, dancing over four pillars dividing the room in half. Murals on the walls reached floor to ceiling, the ceiling made of wooden beams inlaid with gold. But her attention was drawn to the gently swaying chandelier.The windows were closed, and there was no wind.

Semra jutted her chin at Avaya. "Red is your color now, I see. Does it stand for all the soldiers you killed in the war, for the two kings of Belvidore you had assassinated, or for the wedding tradition of brides in your country?"

"There is no better memorial for my husband than to continue his dream of our union," Avaya said. "Our wedding is the hope of peace, the promise of a brighter future. Of Jannemar and Belvidore coming together at last."

Zephan pulled out a chair for his sister at the table beside him. "A wedding is much less work than a marriage, isn't it?"

"I suppose I wouldn't know." Avaya ignored the offer and seated herself at the head of the table instead.

Azi took a chair next to her on Zephan's side of the table, two seats down from the rest of them. They took their seats, and Semra's heart sank. She could no longer watch Azi's hands.

"So." Semra spread her hands on the table and looked at Azi. "You call King Zephan a pretender. You're still going with your claim to the throne? Your defeat last year, the obliteration of your child assassin network, your time in the dungeons ... none of these outrageous failures made you rethink your approach?"

Azi clutched at his chest in mock dismay. "You misunderstand me! I am merely a guest in the king's house, not your enemy. Oh, but how rude of me. I know I came on strong, what with lockpicking intruders and such—"

"The assault seemed rather hostile too, if we're pointing out red flags," Zephan said.

Azi held his hands up. "To be sure, I understand your confusion. You see me as the evil man whom you've had stashed in your dungeon. Not so. Let me introduce myself. I am Azi, prime vizier to Queen Avaya of Belvidore, and it is only at her request that I am present today."

Zephan leaned forward, his glare shifting to Avaya. "And why does the queen of Belvidore sneak into a neighboring kingdom's castle and release a criminal responsible for the murders of countless people, including our mother?"

"We are here to pay our respects to the late king," Avaya said.

Aviama's lip quivered and curled into disgust. "You mean you're here to capitalize on the death of our father, which is your fault."

Avaya reached across the table toward her sister, hesitated, and withdrew. "No, Avs. I'm here to make things right."

Her tone was soft, and Aviama eyed her suspiciously. Semra squirmed in her seat. The interaction reminded her of the intimacy she saw between the sisters after Sharsi's death—Aviama in Avaya's lap, Avaya stroking her hair and holding her close. Before Avaya blamed Semra and paid Siler to kidnap her to Belvidore.

Semra wondered where Siler was now. A homing pigeon had returned to the dovecote with his signature a couple weeks after Semra had mustered the Mount Hara assassins and rescued Siler at Axis and Avaya's wedding.

Thanks for coming back for me. I've since turned my life around and become an ordinary basket weaver.
Your most recent Lesala says hi. She says I have to say hello to princey.
See you around.

Avaya straightened. "I want what I've always wanted. To honor our commitments as a kingdom, to provide peace to the land, and to ... to have my family back. I want to come to an understanding. I just won't be overlooked any longer. I was born to lead."

"Honest negotiations tend to break down under duress," Semra said.

"Would you have invited me in?" Avaya arched an eyebrow and let the resounding silence enunciate her point. "I didn't think so."

"It's unwise to ransack the dungeons of nations whose trust you want," Zephan said. "Not to mention the lunacy of your particular choice."

"My vizier has been nothing but a friend. Misunderstood, as I am."

The table shook, and black scales obscured the light from the window. Avaya jumped. A roar shook the air.

Thud. Scraaaaaaape.

THUD.

Screams and shouts went up from the hall outside and the floor below. Whatever sound barrier Azi had in place seemed to have shaken, but a moment later, the sounds beyond the walls cut off again.

A blue tail thrashed against the window and disappeared.

Semra reached out to Zezura in a panic, and the dragon's experience overtook her vision. Zezura's blue scales were entwined with black ones, two enormous beasts locked in a duel of fire and teeth. Heat broiled in Zezura's throat and burst forth in a blaze. The black dragon unleashed great flame of its own, meeting Zezura's fire.

A ghastly scar ran across one of the black dragon's eyes, the damaged eye permanently closed. Semra had sunk a knife into it some months ago. She hadn't seen or heard of Rotokas since.

Rotokas lunged beneath the stream of fire and caught

Zezura by the throat. Zezura reeled back and rotated as she flew, dragging Rotokas away from the castle and over the cliff to the Shalladin. Semra's heart dropped.

The king's chambers snapped back into focus, and Semra gasped at the abruptness of being ripped from the vision of dragons and back into her chair.

Azi cocked his head at her, but said nothing.

Avaya cleared her throat. "Perspective. It's what we need most when we're stuck on a problem, the thing that shifts us from one, ineffective mindset to a new, more functional one. Azi has a perspective different from any I've ever experienced."

"Because killers think differently than regular people," Aviama snapped.

Semra clutched the girl's knee under the table and squeezed, hard. *Shut up.* Azi glanced at Aviama and smiled.

"Yes, they do," Avaya said. "But it's a mistake to judge a person by their being acquainted with the business of killing. A monarch too soft for dirty work doesn't deserve the title. Our father killed plenty of people. Most of them deserved it. A few didn't. Being king is a dangerous business, which necessitates dangerous people."

"Being strong always makes a person dangerous," Zephan said. "But to retain our humanity, we must be principled and restrained—ruled by something larger than ourselves. That is the difference between unscrupulous murderers and judicious rulers."

"Don't preach father's lessons to me," Avaya snarled. "He may not have valued me as a successor, but he spouted the same lines to me as he did to you. The only truly safe people are inept weaklings. They're safe because they are incapable of anything worthy of fear. They are nothings.

"Perhaps that is why you and Father and everyone else only saw me as a pretty thing to come out at parties—you didn't think me strong enough to be dangerous. Semra is dangerous, and you welcome her. Now, for the first time, I have real power. A chance of an alliance our forefathers only dreamed of. And you reject me."

Avaya sighed. She twisted a ring on her finger and adjusted the two pendants hanging from the chain around her neck. "I had no tutor, no one to guide me. I needed someone with a fresh perspective on Jannemar, an understanding of political negotiation, and knowledge on how to get what we need to form an effective empire. I made him a proposal, and he accepted. Did you know he knew our mother when she was a girl? Father never did."

Zephan stilled. "Did you just say empire?"

"It's just an idea. If you're open to it, we could combine forces. Work together. No need to fight over the strip if it's as much yours as it is ours, and benefits us both."

Silence settled over the room. With noise blocked from beyond the king's chambers, the only sound was the rustle of the chandelier chain as it swung gently overhead. Semra's chest tightened. Aviama shifted in her chair.

Semra scanned the chairs across from her. Avaya drilled Zephan with a cool stare. Azi eyed them lazily, bored from his momentary step away from the spotlight. Zephan took a deep breath and let it out. He fiddled with the end of his sleeve and looked at Semra.

The ends of her mouth tugged toward the floor in a slight frown. *Avaya's got no clue what she's in for. Azi's always two steps ahead, and he'll kill her as soon as her usefulness expires. Don't let him in.* She could only hope her eyes carried as much of a dissenting sentiment as was reasonable without tipping the scales too far. Azi was no fool. He knew they wouldn't agree. What was his end game?

Zephan studied her for a long moment, then turned back to his older sister. "What happens if we say yes?"

"There's no need for hostility moving forward," Avaya said. "You agree to host us and be amicable. We stay and get to know each other. You've lived two doors down from me all our lives, but you don't know me. Not really. So we reconnect and discuss a future between Jannemar and Belvidore."

Semra opened her mouth and shut it again. This wasn't her negotiation.

Zephan pursed his lips. "And if we say no?"

"If we can't work out a proposal"—Avaya shrugged and leaned back in her chair—"we go our separate ways, and at least we can communicate. I take my vizier and my guards, and you decide how many more soldiers you want to die before things get rockier. But I think we can avoid that."

Semra could contain herself no longer. She jutted her chin at Azi. "And you? What do you want?"

Azi met her gaze evenly. "Family."

6

———————

Semra's lips parted, and the air left her lungs as if she'd been slugged. *You told us we were your family. And you used us.*

The dragonlord who raised her, the Framatar she'd both loved and feared as a child, turned to Avaya and softened. He looked at her tenderly. With warmth. Like a father would. Semra felt sick.

"My parents sent me off as a child," he continued. "My brother took the throne meant for me, and kept me so far away from the family that I never got the chance to know my nieces and nephew. You three were poisoned against me before I got the chance to explain the truth. So I created a family, the best I knew how. A way to prove myself, my capacity for rule. And I did it well."

Semra's heartbeat hammered in her ears. Who was this man? She'd never seen Azi—the Framatar, as she'd known him—to be gentle. He was always cold, always calculating.

And never vulnerable.

Yet here and now, for *her,* he was everything Semra had craved and nothing she'd experienced. Avaya smiled, and Azi smiled back. Jealousy sprang from an abyss deep within to clutch at her throat. Semra despised herself for it. He was lying. Of course he was.

It's all he ever did.

"You destroyed our home, killed our guards, and tried to murder my father and brother, all to get to know us better?"

Semra jumped. She'd all but forgotten Aviama sitting beside her. The princess leaped to her feet.

Azi tensed, and a steely resolve materialized in his eyes. *Ahh, there he is,* Semra thought grimly. *Someone familiar.*

The hair on the back of her neck stood on end, and Semra yanked Aviama back down. Aviama's cheeks flushed, and her eyes flashed. She stayed in her chair, but she rolled her shoulders back and set her jaw.

"I understand your confusion," Azi said. Honey dripped into his voice. Semra had found it almost comforting as a child, but it was patronizing now. Azi shook his head and ran a hand over his face. Another gesture foreign to the man. "There's more to it than that. Belvidore is not the only kingdom your father insulted over the years. He was good with people. They always loved him on the tours. And that made it easy to distract them from his more ... distasteful activities."

"Watch yourself," Zephan growled.

Azi held up a defensive hand, but the corner of his mouth twitched. Zephan's threat was empty, and everyone knew it. "I had no choice when I saw my kingdom being ripped to shreds. It wouldn't fall to pieces right away, of course. The consequences of his decisions are only now slowly being realized. When I learned what he was doing, I confronted him by letter —the only communication I was permitted. He covered his tracks for the worst of it, but he admitted to me what he did."

Semra edged forward in spite of herself. Beside her,

Aviama held her breath. Zephan gritted his teeth, and Avaya nodded along dutifully to a story she'd no doubt heard several times before.

"Turian's tactics may have bought him friends in Jovan, but it isolated him on the north and south. Years ago, Radha sought Jannemar's aid in their war against Tomos, and Jannemar refused. When Radha sought alliance through marriage, Jannemar refused again. Their friendship would have meant security and stability in the north, and perhaps they would have come to help Jannemar in their hour of need against Belvidore. Instead, you are alone."

Avaya pressed her lips and shook her head, as if Jannemar were a small child to be pitied. She turned to Zephan. "Even if you are too angry to care about me, about our family, the war has crippled Jannemar. You need allies. You need money. And if Radha or Tomos make a move, you'll need more power than you have. We can solve all your problems."

Anxiety gripped Semra's throat as the dragon's kiss on her chest burned with the pain of Zezura, hit again and again. While Semra did nothing. She ran a hand along her thigh under the table and slipped a knife from its sheath.

"Everyone knows about Rhada's civil war," Aviama said. Semra hadn't known, but now wasn't the time to confess her ignorance. "We get reports of the latest bombings every month."

Azi shrugged. "Did you know they've been faking the last six months of bombings, targeting unoccupied spaces, and covering the sound of developing new quarries?"

"Impossible," Zephan said. But he looked unsure. Semra wondered what kind of position Jannemar would be in if caught between Belvidore and Radha. What were relations like with Tomos, the nation to the northeast?

"I have proof," Azi said. "I'll show you if you host us properly."

Zephan stilled.

A chill ran up Semra's spine. He was considering this. He eyed her with an unreadable expression, and fear washed over her like an icy wind.

"Snakes don't make bargains," she said. "They make debts."

They were Azi's words once. Mount Hara assassins gathered debtors and bloodstains, not friends.

"Please don't be dramatic, Semra," Azi said. He examined his nails in feigned disinterest. "Snakes are reactive. I am proactive. Snakes also make ineffective assassination plans, as it turns out; they are tools of lesser men. I don't make such mistakes."

Azi raised his dark, steely gaze to lock onto her face, and all breath left her body. She could almost hear his voice in her head. *Ramas failed to kill you, but he was a fool. I am no fool.*

Goosebumps fled across her skin like an arrow from the string. Her muscles tensed. Her vision blurred. A single thought formed as her heartbeat rose to a thundering roar:

I'm already dead.

"Azi." Zephan pulled the dragonlord's attention away, but Semra only sat, a statue gripping the handle of her blade.

Avaya cleared her throat, and Zephan dipped his head a hair in her direction. "Avaya." He took a deep breath. "I accept."

Aviama leaped to her feet, shouting. Avaya smiled, and Azi patted her hand and inclined his head at Zephan. Semra only stared ahead, seeing everything as through a daze.

Zephan held up a hand. "I have conditions."

Aviama sat.

Avaya leaned forward, eyes bright with anticipation.

Azi leaned back. "Naturally."

"I'll write a formal invitation for you both to be here, and a release for Azi Shamaran. We'll say you came subtly and without fanfare out of respect for Jannemar's grieving over the late king, and to prevent unrest that anti-Belvidore sentiment would bring in light of the war.

"I will formally release Azi from the dungeons to Avaya as her vizier. Avaya, you will accept all responsibility for his actions, and will sign to it. You will also sign acknowledging that I warned you of his malicious, conniving nature."

Zephan's voice calmed her, and Semra focused hard on his words to shake off the sense of doom. He'd done a thorough job coming up with explanations for the situation on the fly, and tying Avaya to Azi rather than himself would mean Azi's actions would be attributed to Belvidore rather than Jannemar. Azi's inevitable future evils would be a blight on her reign, not his.

Zephan folded his hands on the table.

"After you sign, it will be official—neither of you live here, and you will be guests, and act accordingly. You will remain on the east wing and northern halls. The west wing will be strictly off limits."

Azi opened his mouth, then closed it. He patted Avaya's hand again.

Avaya glanced at her uncle, and tilted her head at her brother. "Drop the warning of my vizier's malicious nature."

Azi squeezed her hand.

"And I would like to have the second floor of the west wing, and access to the conservatory."

Semra and Zephan exchanged glances, and she knew they were thinking the same thing. *The library.* They were looking for something.

"I'll drop the warning," Zephan said. "And any reading

entertainment you request will be delivered to your guest rooms."

Azi withdrew his hand from Avaya's, and Avaya gave a curt nod. "Done."

"Bring me my writing set."

Aviama's foot bounced incessantly underneath the table, her hands shaking in her lap next to Semra, but she remained silent. Avaya pushed back her chair, and Semra rose to mirror the Belvidorian *queen*—Semra nearly gagged at the thought—standing as Avaya stood. She pulled Aviama after her to round the table toward Zephan as Avaya stepped behind him toward the writing desk.

Semra expected the unnatural wind to hit her at any moment, but none came. Azi's glare followed Semra from his seat. Semra knew that look. *Why doesn't he kill me here and now?* But the answer smacked her in the face. It was obvious. *Image.* Everything had to look right, and her death in a room alone with four Shamarans would not serve.

Avaya brought the writing set on Zephan's right, and Semra edged toward Zephan's other side.

"That's far enough," Azi warned.

Semra dropped the knife back into its sheath, hidden from their view, and spread her hands. "Tell your puppet to back off, and I'll do the same."

"Says the vagrant mooching off my family," Avaya said with a sneer. She placed the set on the table in front of her brother and took two steps back. "I'm no puppet. By the way, congratulations on your sham nobility, Semra. A sewer rat in a ballgown is still a sewer rat, but it's nice to try something new once in a while."

Semra's skin flushed red, and her fingers itched against the blade on her leg. It would take less than a second to drop the pretentious tart to the floor. Avaya, the venomous traitor responsible for escalating the war, ripping the Shamaran family apart, and getting King Turian killed. The privileged power monger who had released the most dangerous person Semra had ever known, the man from her nightmares, the man who slaughtered her parents and turned her into a deplorable killing machine.

Avaya, the woman who had Semra captured and beaten before her eyes, who used Siler and strung him up to the wall as a trophy for her political wedding. The wedding where she killed her new husband and took his throne. The wedding where she tried to kill Semra again, and almost succeeded.

Semra could feel Zephan's eyes on her, but she couldn't tear herself away from Avaya's insufferable face. In her peripheral vision, Zephan opened the writing set, removed a stack of stationary, ink, and wax, and set pen to paper.

Heavy footsteps and the clink of armor of patrolling guards passed by in the hall, and somewhere the sound of silver platters rattled. Semra's stomach grumbled, but the sound cut off again before the realization hit—for a moment, outside sounds had come through.

Aviama took shallow breaths behind her, and Avaya bored emerald eyes into Semra's skull. No, not emerald—malachite, that sparkling green mineral that turned black as pitch under heat. And nothing could fuel that fire like the dragonlord of Semra's childhood.

Just past Avaya's shoulder, Azi caught her eye and arched an eyebrow. The corner of his mouth twitched in an amused dare. *Kill her. You know you want to. Such a delicate touch, a quick flick of the wrist ...*

Semra's gut twisted. She flexed her fingers as they brushed the knife blade, but she did not draw. Firfell's voice replayed in her mind. *When it comes to problem solving, you tend to dispatch anyone inconvenient.*

Azi's soft rumble cut to her core like a spear to the heart: "Once a Bandaka, always a Bandaka."

Always Bandaka. Because she always wanted to kill, because that would forever be the easiest solution? Or because she was always bound to him? *Bondservant …*

She clenched her jaw and forced her taut muscles to relax.

Azi clucked his tongue. "Pity."

Uncle dearest, so sweet on his niece, Semra thought wryly. How long would it take him to deconstruct Avaya's defiance and enslave her to him forever?

Semra almost pitied her. Almost.

Minutes ticked by, with nothing but the scratch of Zephan's quill on the parchment to keep them company. Azi drummed his fingers on the table. Avaya chewed on her nail. Aviama leaned on a chair. Semra stood stock still, her fingers relaxed but never moving from their position against the butt of her throwing knife.

A long scrape broke the silence as Zephan pushed back his chair. A gust of wind hit him square in the chest and sent him flying back into his seat. Semra lurched halfway to Zephan before she realized it was Avaya's hand, not Azi's, that was outstretched.

Avaya has magic.

In a world where magic was destroyed.

7

———————

Semra dropped to the floor behind Zephan's chair, sprang up right before Avaya, and twisted her arms behind her back. She doubled over with a cry, and the wind disappeared. Semra secured both of Avaya's arms with one of hers, and pressed her blade to Avaya's throat with the other.

"Any jerking movement," Semra said into Avaya's ear, "even to push me off, and this major artery"—she pressed the blade into Avaya's flesh—"will empty onto your father's table."

A small piece of paper floated to the floor from Avaya's sleeve, and Semra glanced up just long enough to catch Aviama's eye. She'd seen it too.

Semra whipped Avaya around to face Azi, their backs to the paper and to Zephan. Azi was on his feet, every muscle tense, forcing himself to move slowly toward Semra.

"Seal the documents, boy," Azi growled at Zephan. "Semra, my dear, don't be a fool."

Semra glanced over her shoulder. Aviama ran forward and lit the candle from the writing set to melt wax for Zephan's seal, stepping over the parchment and obscuring it from view.

She knocked the quill to the floor and Semra yanked Avaya backward to block Azi's visual as the little sister retrieved the quill and returned it to the table. When Aviama hurried back behind Zephan, the paper was gone.

Well done, Avs.

Zephan reached around Semra's waist and snatched a spare throwing knife from her thigh. "Stay where you are, Azi, with your hands where I can see them. I'll seal the documents, but if you take another step, I burn them."

"No need for that," Azi said. He sidestepped away from the table, examining Semra's hold on Avaya. His queen was doubled over toward the floor, her necklace and hair dangling in front of her, her chest heaving in fury as she struggled in Semra's grasp.

Zephan brushed Semra's arm with his and the small touch reminded her to breathe. *Your brain is on fire. Shhh.*

"He'll never let me live if he's in the castle," Semra said, her eyes never leaving Azi's face. "He'll play pretty until the setup is right to spin his narrative, and have me dead by sundown."

He poured melted wax in perfect circles at the base of the documents on the table and adjusted the signet ring on his finger. "I know."

Avaya straightened, and a coil of air whispered up to Semra's nose. It was the same sickly-sweet smell she remembered from Avaya's wedding. Avaya wore the same seashell and pearl necklace as she had that day, chemicals wafting out from the open pearl locket. Semra's head swam and her muscles weakened. She dropped the knife.

Semra staggered backward and away from the chemicals, dragging Avaya with her and breathing in clean air. She jerked the chain of the necklace tight against Avaya's neck until she heard her sputter and gag, then she reached around and shoved the locket against Avaya's nose. Avaya dropped to her knees.

Pain exploded in Semra's jaw, and her head snapped back; an arm twice the size of her own slithered into the open space around her throat and cinched tight. Her brain went foggy, and she knew the world was about to go dark. Semra swung her elbow into Azi's torso behind her and pulled at the arm around her throat with both hands, a whisper of a prayer for room to breathe.

His grip only tightened. "You did fine against your playmates in the mountain, my dear, but you've never been a match for me."

Semra lifted herself off the ground and kicked Avaya to the floor with both feet. Aviama squealed, and somewhere a door opened. Zephan flew at Azi with a powerful jab to the eyes and slashed at Azi with the knife. Semra fell to the ground, coughing, and gasping for air. She dragged Avaya off to the side and Azi abandoned his fight with Zephan, barreling after her.

Semra dove toward Zephan and Aviama, but Azi reached for Avaya instead. Zephan caught Semra around the waist and Aviama by the wrist, lifted Semra off her feet, and sprinted for the valet's door. Semra's head cleared only an instant before Zephan pressed his lips to hers.

Swirling heat flooded her body and smoke poured from her fingers. Crackling sparks cut through the dark, and the last thing Semra saw was Azi looking up from Avaya with unbridled rage.

Black smoke swallowed them. Wind whipped the smoke into a frenzied moving mass of shadow, and Semra, Zephan, and Aviama were plastered against the wall and door. Zephan gripped her by the back of the neck, and his breath tickled her ear. "Take Aviama."

Semra's mouth went dry. "I can't—"

"Don't fight me. I will not abandon the castle, and you can't stay. Take Aviama and go." Zephan pressed something hard and cold into Semra's palm and closed her fingers around it. "This isn't the one I wanted to give you." He threw Aviama into Semra's arms, strained against the wind to open the door to the valet's room, and kicked them both off the wall and through the opening. The gust of Avaya's magic hurtled them through the valet's room to the far wall; Semra dropped to the floor, rolled to one side, pushed the panel open to the queen's chambermaid, and shoved Aviama through.

Six months ago, Semra would have stayed, and likely died, to stay by Zephan's side. But she wasn't a one-woman show anymore, and it would be damaging not to trust Zephan now. They'd figure this out *together*—even if they were apart.

Semra clutched Aviama's wrist and they hurtled through the chambermaid's room, the queen's chambers, out into the hall, past the receiving room, and through the double doors of the grand formal throne room. Semra hardly noticed the grandeur of the sparkling marble floors, the pillars as they leaped up the steps, the smudge of rust-colored stain where her friend Brens' blood had never quite been purged from the stone. Gold leaf winked at them from the columns as they sprinted toward the back of the room, breathing hard.

"It's a dead end," Aviama said. "There's no guard stair here."

A single golden throne sat on a cobalt-blue carpet matching the back of the rounded end of the room. Windows lined both sides, pouring light on the spectacle of their escape attempt.

"Wow, Zephan really played things close to the vest on this," Semra muttered. She leaped up the dais and dropped down behind the throne.

Aviama slid into the narrow space next to her. "I think you've grossly underestimated our size in comparison to this single-person chair."

Semra's hands flew along the backing of the chair, its carved edges, its smooth gilded feet. "Thank you, Avs. When they were teaching me how to break into high-profile villas, murder people, and escape without a trace, they did neglect to inform me that two people cannot hide behind one chair."

"Really?"

Semra gave her a look, and a sheepish expression overtook the panic on Aviama's face.

"Oh."

Swords and the swish of chainmail rang out down the hall. Aviama pressed into Semra's back as the sound of the guards' footsteps went from a rhythmic muffled thudding to an echoey, harsh pounding. They were through the throne room doors, at the base of the stairs.

At last Semra's fingers found what she'd been looking for; she depressed a lever in the bottom of the throne, and the portion of floor and wall swiveled around, depositing them into a narrow space between the false wall and exterior wall—and away from the guards.

"What?"

Semra shook her head and placed a finger to her lips. She glanced down, but where the floor should have been seamless until she released the hidden handle, it was cracked open a half inch.

Her head screamed the truth: *Not safe, not safe, not safe.*

But if Azi and Avaya knew about this passage, the guards they sent after them would know it in moments.

Semra found the divot in the floor, pulled the handle, and gripped Aviama's wrist as half the floor in the small space slid away. She walked Aviama down the staircase, released the pulley, and the floor above shut them into the dark.

They descended the stair in silence. Semra drew another throwing knife and slipped whatever small object Zephan had given her into its sheath for safekeeping. Semra had dropped a knife, and Zephan had drawn one. She had three left, after the one in her hand.

"Can you at least hold my hand instead of my wrist?" Aviama whispered. "I feel like you're capturing me or something."

"Sorry," Semra said. But she didn't let go. "I hold your wrist so we can stay connected, but I can have my hand free as soon as I need it. If I held your hand, and I reacted to a threat before you realized you needed to let go, I'd lose time trying to get out of your grip before engaging an attacker."

"Oh."

Their footsteps padded softly down the rough-cut stone. Semra counted the stairs in her head. *Second floor. First floor.*

They were underground before Aviama spoke again.

"So you're saying you know how many people fit behind a chair. Among other things."

Semra grinned in the dark. "Something like that."

The mark on her chest burned, and Semra paused. *Where are you?*

A flash of color surged into view. Black scales. An aquamarine tail. Water. Blood. The two dragons tumbled through the water. A wingtip escaped the surface, and a glimpse of the cliff wavered above them through the chill river. They were in the Shalladin.

Get out of there, Semra urged. *You don't have to kill Rotokas. Just get out of there.*

Semra could feel the heat, the warm glow in Zezura's throat as she worked up to a release of flame. She held it in, brighter, brighter, until even the serpent felt the burn of it. Rotokas' razor teeth skidded along Zezura's neck, seeking purchase between the airtight scales.

Zezura launched the attack, the water boiling between them, searing the open gash on Rotokas' belly. He roared and released her, and Zezura spun toward the surface. She crested the river, turned, and dove back down.

Snakebrain! You don't know when to quit!

Rotokas buckled beneath the impact, then hooked the talon of his wyvern wing between her eyes and raked down her face. Nothing had the chance to penetrate dragon scales like dragon talons and teeth. Zezura's blood swirled in the river around her, and Semra's heart broke at the sight of it.

Her dragon's answer came clearer than ever before.

Neither do you.

Zezura kicked Semra out of her head and back into the secret passage of Shamaran Castle. Her lips parted and her breaths came in anxious gasps. *Stubborn.*

Zez would ultimately follow Semra's instruction, but she was committed to saving Semra, and Rotokas was the greatest threat. Just one more hit, one more try.

A mindset Semra knew well. If it weren't for Zephan, Semra would likely be on her way to an undignified funeral even now, courtesy of his darling dragonlord uncle and her own refusal to back down when it made sense.

"Are you sure you never heard about this tunnel before?" Semra asked.

"Never."

Semra pursed her lips. "Either Avaya or Azi used it recently. They've got their claws on far too many important people. They're looking for something, which is good and bad."

Aviama took a deep breath. "How is it good?"

"It buys us time. They'll never settle for alliance with Jannemar. Azi wants to rule, and Avaya thinks she can be empress. For such a devious person, she's acting an awful lot like a naive idiot. But they aren't ready to make their final move, or they would have done it already."

"That makes sense. And the bad?"

"If they get whatever they're looking for, everyone dies and the kingdom falls."

8

It was past lunch by the time they reached the end of the passage, judging by Semra's clamoring stomach. Semra bumped straight into the dirt wall at the end. She rubbed her nose with her hand, felt along the wall in the dark, and tugged Aviama back into the passage several paces.

"There are rungs to climb up, and a hatch that opens on the ground in the woods. I'll poke my head out and look around, and then come back for you. Stay here."

Semra turned to go, then paused. *Four knives. That's all you've got.* She grimaced, but pulled one from her leg sheath and held it out handle-first to Aviama. She felt for Aviama's hand and placed it on the hilt.

"Do you know how to use this?"

"Will I have to?" Aviama squeaked.

Semra pressed her lips together. *She'll be useless in a fight.* "Probably not. Just a precaution. If anything *does* happen, don't just stab and stab, okay? Stab and *slash.*"

"I don't even know what that means."

"Stab into the person, keep your knife in, and drag like

this." Semra guided Aviama's hand through a stab-slash motion. "And don't throw up."

Semra stepped to the end of the passage and drew another knife into her palm. An anxious flutter tightened her stomach, and her mind argued with itself over arming Aviama.

At least I didn't leave her defenseless.

Giving her a knife is just wasting a knife. And now you only have three.

Semra shook her head and climbed the rungs. She'd only been in this passage once before. Was it just six months ago that Zephan had led her through this same tunnel to escape the guards? Just shy of that, really. Back when he was Dahyu. Back when life was simpler.

It felt like a lifetime ago.

The air was dank and clammy underground, entirely sealed off from the light of the world above. Even so, it didn't take long to reach the hatch overhead in the dark. Semra held a rung and a knife in one hand and pressed up on the hatch with the other. It cracked open a hair, and the smell of soil and grass greeted her.

Twigs, rocks, and crunchy leaves blocked her view of the forest, but that was no surprise. The hatch was hidden among shrubbery, and Semra remembered Zephan had arranged more brush about the opening after they'd exited the tunnel before. Semra pushed the hatch open several more inches, scanned the woods, and shook her head.

Zephan's stuck in the castle with your murderous mentor, and Rotokas could be ripping Zezura apart while you stare at a forest full of dead leaves. You're a coward and you never should have left him.

She planted her hands on the ground to hoist herself up, the knife still cupped in her palm.

No, Zephan told you to go. He wasn't just being gallant—he has a reason. He wouldn't send me away from danger just because it's dangerous. Not anymore. We do things together now.

Semra's heart sank as she thought the word. *Together.* But they weren't, were they? And what if Azi killed him? What if—

SNAP.

Crunch, crunch.

SNAP. CRACK.

Semra spun toward the sound but saw only a blur of motion before the blow came. She threw her elbow up to protect her head just before she was knocked to the forest floor, her body still half in, half out of the tunnel. Her mind swirled with the data, two steps behind what her body already knew: the *snap*, a heavy landing on twigs and sticks; the *crunch*, running footfalls over dry leaves.

The subsequent sounds—he wasn't alone. And they were dropping from the trees.

The knobby circle of a kneecap dropped on Semra's spine, and the game was up. She was an easy kill from this position. The man's weight fell forward as he misjudged his landing, and his mistake was all she needed. Semra twisted just enough to swing the knife in her right hand over her left shoulder and into her attacker's torso.

The man grunted and fell to one side. Semra kicked the hatch open the rest of the way, squirmed out of the opening, and rolled to her back. Three more men charged her, wearing the blue, red, and gold of Belvidore and armed with swords.

Semra threw the knife; it sailed a hair beneath the jawline into the soft of the second guard's neck. She rocked her feet up into the air and rotated into a kip up. She landed upright before the second guard hit the ground and dodged the third guard's sword thrust. The first guard clutched his side and struggled to stand. He lifted his sword and swung at her side.

Line them up. It doesn't matter how many there are if you go one by one. A basic instruction. It was both sickening and ironic that it was Azi's voice fluttering up from her memory to save her now.

Semra ducked under the first guard's swing as he teetered at the edge of the hatch opening. She whirled behind him, leaped on his back, and slit his throat. The remaining two guards were blocked by the body of their companion. They split off in opposite directions, and Semra shoved her latest kill down the open hatch of the passage.

Thud.

A terrified shriek emanated from the tunnel below, and Semra cursed. The men froze. Semra swallowed. She couldn't leave the opening unattended, not now that they knew someone else was in the tunnel. But facing them both at once over a giant hole wouldn't do either.

Semra leaped to the other side of the opening, placing both men and the hatch in front of her. She adjusted the grip on her blade. *Two knives left.* The guard on the left flung himself over the hatch; Semra evaded his sword swing and burst in close. She seized him by the neck and sword arm, but he tossed his sword to his free hand and Semra settled for slicing her knife across his arm as she slid under it and danced away from him.

The guard on the right closed in, and the man on her left arced his sword and brought it down hard from above. His footwork was good—but his stance was too tight. Semra ran forward into a flying kick. The broadside of his sword struck her forearms, protecting her face, its edge making a superficial slice along her arm. Her foot connected with the man's kneecap.

Crunch.

The man screamed. Maybe next time he'd remember to keep his limbs loose. It was too easy to hyperextend the joint and crush the bone at the knee. Semra landed on the ground and flicked her knife up into the man's trachea.

"Semra! Are you still alive?" The question came as a high-pitched yell echoing up from the tunnel.

Semra drew her final blade and lunged to her feet. "Would you shut up? I'm trying to *stay* alive, thank you very much!"

The last guard let out a guttural snarl and barreled toward her. Semra threw her knife, but the man knocked it from the air with his sword without slowing down. Her chest tightened. She scooped up the fallen sword of the guard at her feet and raised it to the resounding *clang* of metal.

Her muscles strained, and her face flushed with the effort. Brute strength would never be her saving grace against a broad-shouldered man twice her size. His eyes gleamed fire, his lips pulled back, the veins in his neck bulging.

Change the game.

Semra reached for the heat in the swirling cauldron of her body, the heat that spilled out of her fingers as smoke and spewed glowing embers up into the air. She felt warmth of it, the pull of its power, but it did not come.

The guard knocked her backward and struck again, and again. Semra stumbled to catch up as her focus ripped from her failed attempts at the smoke and back to steel. She parried each blow, but each hit pushed her backward. Semra's foot caught on the corpse behind her. Her heart lurched into her throat and she struck out at her adversary as she fell.

He blocked her blow, wrenched the sword from her hands, and tossed it aside. Semra kicked his out of his grip, and her cheek lit up with pain as the guard's knuckles connected with her face.

She clapped her hands into the guard's ears on either side of his head and dug her thumbs into the man's eyes. The guard reared back and dove for his sword.

"Semra?"

Aviama's head poked out of the hatch, and she held the knife up into the open.

"Throw it!"

Aviama tossed the knife, and Semra caught it by the handle. The guard snatched the sword off the ground and Semra threw the knife into the man's sword arm. He dropped the sword and clutched at his arm, then left the knife in his arm and held it close to his body. He grimaced, but scooped up the sword in his non dominant hand.

"We don't have to do this," Semra said. "Go."

"I don't take orders from you, dragon witch!"

The guard leaped forward. Semra rolled to one side, snatched her fallen sword and sprang to her feet again.

"You're already taking orders from a dragon demon," Semra said. "And your queen is putty in his hands."

They danced in and out, exchanging blows. Strike, parry, thrust, strike. But he was weaker on his nondominant side, and it showed. Semra brought her sword around, knocked the blade free, and lunged forward. She clubbed him in the head with the butt of her sword, and he dropped to the ground in a heap.

Semra's chest heaved from exertion, and she scanned the area. Three bodies lay scattered on the forest floor, two lifeless, one unconscious but breathing. Her knife still protruded from one of the guards' necks, and another was half-buried in leaves on the ground several paces away.

Aviama peered out from her place, her head only a foot above ground level. Bulging round eyes seemed to take up half of her ashen face as the young princess surveyed the scene.

Semra stared at the Belvidorian guard at her feet—dead to the world, but certainly more alive than his companions. For now. Leaving him free to chase them wouldn't do.

"Climb out, Aviama," she said, her gaze still fixed on the guard. "Close the hatch and cover it with brush like we found it."

"What about the guy in the tunnel?"

"Dead. Leave him. We don't have time to clean up, and they knew we would come this way anyway."

A soft *clink* behind her told Semra the hatch was closed, and leaves rustled as Aviama followed her instructions the best she could.

"Are they all dead?"

"Not yet."

"Do ... do you have to?"

Semra sighed. Killing was quick. It solved multiple problems—him chasing them, waking while they bound him, or calling for reinforcements, for example. It would be humane.

Do you have *to?*

Her stomach twisted. *You've gone soft,* a voice whispered in her mind. *Soft is weak, and weak is stupid.* No, that was Azi talking. Memories of a time when she cared what he thought.

Aviama's round green eyes searched Semra's face, concern and confusion written all across the princess's features. Semra sighed.

"We'll have to be quick. Get the belts off the other two and bring them, fast. There's no way Avaya only brought four guards."

Semra retrieved three of her four knives and cleaned them on the grass. She abandoned the one in the guard down the tunnel, plucked one from the forest floor, extracted another from the dead guard's neck, and removed the last from the surviving guard's arm. He stirred, and she hit him again on the head. He slumped.

"Any chance yarrow grows around here?"

Aviama furrowed her brows and shrugged. "No idea."

"Right." *Three seconds ago you were planning on killing him. He's fine.* Semra tied him with two of the belts and made a tourniquet for the guard's arm above the elbow with the third. She packed the wound with moss, threw the swords down the tunnel, and covered up the hatch again.

"Let's go."

Semra led Aviama through the woods in a round-about way, doubling back, covering footfalls, and zig-zagging through the forest toward the city. They were an hour in, lost in their own thoughts, when Aviama finally spoke.

"Thank you."

Semra started. "For what?"

"For not sending me away when it was time to go to the king's chambers. For trusting me to stay. Everyone sends me away when danger comes. Do you know where I was when you and Father and Zephan fought Azi in the throne room?"

Semra thought back. The princesses had been secured ... "Locked in your room?"

"Exactly. Locked in my room. Do you know what I did when Avaya was kidnapped, and you and Zephan went off to find her, and Father spent every waking moment beside himself over Avaya or in meetings with his military strategists?"

"Um ..."

"I cried. A lot. A fat lot of good that did me, too, but then, I had nothing else helpful to do, did I? I don't have the faintest idea how to fight. I'm the baby of the family, so I'll never be asked to lead a country. Good thing too; it looks like a terrible occupation if you ask me.

"At least when you were framed for murder, I got to help you escape. And then what did I do? I twiddled my thumbs. I twiddled and twiddled, and wondered if you and Zephan had died yet, or found the real killer yet, or if I passed an assassin every day without knowing it.

"And where was I when Father was killed? In the hall. Watching, in slow motion, as Annais' body blew up. There was—there was pink mist, Semra. *Pink mist.* You ran off in the other direction, and Pidge and I ran to Father, and I fell—I tripped—over an arm. Just an arm, lying there, by itself. I thought I was going to be sick.

"But more than anything, I'm sick of being told to shut up and stay safe and not *do* anything."

Leaves crunched softly underfoot as they padded through the woods. How long had it been since Semra had been shocked or disgusted by the grizzly realities of violence? It was a beautiful privilege to be so protected. Nobody should be as desensitized to all of it as she was.

Though the nightmares she had up until recently might have suggested otherwise—maybe she never totally came to terms with it. Maybe she stuffed it, compartmentalized it as best she could, and moved on without considering how much of her still wanted to scream with the horror and insanity of it all.

Aviama broke the silence again. "Is the guard going to be okay?"

Semra raised an eyebrow. "Quick reminder, he was *just* trying to kill us. But yes, he'll probably be fine. If it gets infected bad enough, he might lose the arm below the elbow, but he'll be fine if he gets help. I'm sure another guard or someone will be along."

"What if no one comes?"

"He'll probably free himself."

"What if he can't?"

Semra shrugged. "Then he lives to try to kill us another day."

There were far more pressing concerns than what would happen to one of Avaya's murderous pawns. Like what Azi and Avaya were looking for in the library of Shamaran Castle, and what they hoped to do with it. Like whether Zephan would live out the week, and how long the charade of their being guests would last. Like whether she'd ever see him again, and if leaving him was a mistake.

A lump lodged in her throat, and she blinked back tears. A taut, strained feeling gripped her chest like a dam about to break, as if the weight of a thousand tons of water bore down on her rib cage.

Zephan's face floated before her in her mind's eye, the memory of his voice through the smoke at their parting, his insistent, urgent tone playing again and again: *I will not abandon the castle, and you can't stay. Take Aviama and go.*

He'd said something else too, before he unceremoniously kicked them through the open door. What was it?

Semra searched her memory, and the answer came clear as crystal.

She was asking all the wrong questions.

What was in her pocket?

9

GAULEN

Gaulen scanned the queen's chambers, his gaze sweeping the cedar furniture, the colors of spring dotting the decor in tasteful hints. The servants had already been through here after the scuffle. What did he expect to find?

It was important that Semra visit her new earldom and establish herself there. Gaulen knew it would be happening soon, but her sudden disappearance in the wake of Avaya's arrival? Ridiculous.

She was an impulsive little thing, savage, plucky, and uncouth, but he'd spent enough time with her tracking down Mount Hara assassins and watching her with Prince Zephan —well, *King* Zephan, now—to know there was more to the story. The trip could have waited.

Princess Aviama accompanying her was less surprising. Her grief over the loss of both parents, and her anger toward her older sister for making matters worse, was no secret in the castle. But then, maybe the trip wasn't for Semra so much as an excuse to get Princess Aviama away from Avaya. Maybe that was all there was to it.

Avaya. As a distinguished member of the royal guard, Gaulen would never have dreamed of addressing a member of the royal family without their title, even in the privacy of his own thoughts. But he couldn't bring himself to call her queen.

Gaulen tapped his thumb on the hilt of the sword in his sheath, running his fingers over the soothing, familiar grooves of its handle. The queen's bed was made up and smoothed with precision, the vanity well tidied except for an ivory hair comb and a couple of books. That, too, was usual; he'd heard the room was kept just as the queen left it before her death. She likely left those out on the night of the gala, and the servants hoped to return the room to that state.

He made a mental note to ask Saeb which servants had straightened the chambers. What had it looked like when they arrived? How long after the incident were they ushered in to set things right? Had anyone else been in the room since?

Why was anybody in the queen's chambers to begin with? What sort of scuffle would Semra have gotten into with King Zephan, Princess Aviama, Avaya, and her adviser?

Scuffle. Gaulen rolled his eyes. They'd made it sound like there was a mild disagreement that Semra had gotten dramatically angry over, like she'd tossed things around to make a point. But Semra didn't stumble in the queen's chambers by accident; she didn't trip and knock a few things over, and she didn't throw a tantrum.

It was obvious. She fought.

She certainly didn't fight the king or Princess Aviama, and if Semra had fought Avaya, Avaya would likely be dead. Semra must have fought the adviser, who was none other than Azi Shamaran. There weren't enough dragonlords in the world to throw that into reasonable doubt; he had only known of two in his lifetime, and they had both been in the castle together that very morning.

And now one of them was on the run.

But why? *And why was anyone in the queen's chambers?*

Gaulen walked from one end of the room to the other, and back again. He squatted down and peered under the bed, then rocked back on his heels. A blue glimmer in the corner caught his eye. Gaulen crossed to it and picked up a slender sapphire hairpin from behind the lantern on the floor.

He ran a finger over the surface of the gemstone as it sparkled in the light from the window, then caught himself. *Stop touching the queen's things.* He wiped it clean on the hem of his shirt and walked to the vanity. Gaulen pulled open a drawer and set the hairpin inside, but the title of the book laying out caught his eye.

The Art of Secrecy by Kernig Navello. His pulse ticked up a notch. The queen didn't read military strategists or treatises on government discretion. He lifted the book to read the title of the second one underneath: *All the King's Chariots* by Hermon Toronel.

Gaulen's muscles tensed, and his lunch soured in his stomach.

The king was in danger. And Semra was not at the earldom.

10

This isn't the one I wanted to give you.

Those were Zephan's last words to her before he flung them from the room. He'd pressed something small and hard into her palm and she'd slid it into the knife sheath pocket of her trousers for safekeeping as she fled with Aviama.

Semra's breath caught, and her fingers trembled as they ran down her leg, searching the sheath. Empty. It was gone. In the chaos of the battle, it must have—no, wait, here it was. She reached inside and drew it out.

Aviama gasped and the two of them stared down at it, hardly noticing the trees passing as they walked.

"Is that—"

Semra nodded, gaping at the golden circle with its familiar emblem engraved on top. "Zephan's signet ring."

"He thinks they're going to force him to write more documents."

"He *knows* they're going to force him to write more documents," Semra corrected. "He's gambling for time. If Azi is mad enough, he'll move up his timeline and kill Zephan sooner rather than later over this. It all depends on what the next steps of his plan are."

Aviama took a moment to absorb the information, and they walked on through the woods. What *were* Azi's next steps? Have Zephan declare him king, and facilitate a peaceful transition of power? Have him declare Avaya empress, and set himself up as successor, and kill her? It was so elementary, so obvious. So overdone, for Belvidore, at least. Surely he had a more artful, subtle plan. The dramatic flair of his plan would only be revealed later ...

Aviama clapped her hands and squealed. "He's going to propose!"

Semra wrinkled her nose. "Eww, he's her uncle! And twice her age."

"Not Azi, dummy," Aviama said, practically bouncing along beside her. "Zephan. He's going to ask you to marry him. He basically already did. You're going to be queen!"

Semra opened her mouth and closed it. Her heart flip-flopped, and a nervous warmth fluttered through her body. *This isn't the one I wanted to give you.* He had a ring.

Her cheeks flushed, and the corner of her mouth twitched. Sham or not, she was nobility now. King Turian had removed an obstacle to their marriage, first with her full pardon, and second with the earldom, turning no-name Semra into Lady Myansara. Had he hoped for this? He too had married a commoner. But Semra was nothing like Queen Sharsi.

She was not poised, elegant, or softspoken. Her laugh didn't sound like bluebirds, and she didn't garner awe and respect wherever she went—only fear, suspicion, and an ever-climbing body count.

"You're excited; I can tell," Aviama gushed. "You love him; you *love* him! Look, you're *smoking* over it."

Panic seized Semra's chest, but the tendril of smoke rising

from her fingers was small enough to dissipate into the air with a wave. Semra breathed in the sweetness of a hopeful future with Zephan, but the cold dampness of reality settled over her as she exhaled. "Yes, I love him," she said softly. "But it won't matter if he's dead."

Aviama clamped her mouth shut and swallowed. Her eyes glistened, but she blinked hard, and nothing came of it.

Semra bit her lip, then changed the subject. "Wait. He gave you something too, didn't he? Parchment, documents? And the scrap of paper Avaya dropped from her sleeve—do you have it?"

Aviama brightened. "Yes, yes! Let me see ..."

"Nice work, by the way. Grabbing that little slip of paper off the floor. I'm not even sure Avaya saw it."

The princess beamed and produced rolled up papers from the bodice of her dress. "Thank you! I hoped you would be proud. If we hadn't been running, I would have asked you to compliment me earlier."

Semra grinned, and Aviama laughed. She unrolled the documents Zephan had shoved into her hands and held them out between the two of them. Semra raised her eyebrows. The contents weren't short.

"There's no way he had the time to write all of this with Azi and Avaya watching," she said. "He must have prewritten them and snuck them out of the writing set when he got out fresh paper."

Aviama handed two documents to Semra and squinted at the other two. "Azi is removed from the line of succession, on grounds of *'high treason and unfit mental stability.'*"

"Who's next in line?" Semra asked, scanning the introduction of the document in her hands.

"Nobody, after Zephan. Only males can inherit the throne in Jannemar, so I guess some distant relative somewhere, since

Father died and Azi is now unfit. Zephan declared him no longer a Shamaran family member."

Semra's lips parted and she jabbed her finger at the paper in her hands. "Not anymore. Zephan overturned the law that only males can rule, right here."

"But that—that doesn't make sense. That makes Avaya next in line, and he would never do that."

Semra drew her brows together and scanned the other document in her hands. "No, not Avaya. He's removed her from the line of succession too, for high treason and acts of aggression against the kingdom of Jannemar, and conflicting interests as the monarch of another nation demonstrating a" —Semra's eyes widened, and she leaned in to ensure she read it correctly—"'lack of care to the welfare of the Jannemari people, a failure to keep the interests of Jannemar a first prior- ity, or indeed any priority at all, and defecting to an enemy nation to the detriment of her family and allegiance of birth.'"

Aviama's hand flew to her mouth. "Wow. Well, he's not wrong."

Semra nudged Aviama. "What does your last document say?"

Aviama looked down and shifted the papers in her hands. "It says ... it ..." She swallowed. "It's me. Not only does the line of succession naturally fall to me after instituting law of women in rule, and removing Avaya, but he specifically endorses me as heir to the throne 'in the absence of produc- tion of a biological child' at the time of his death."

Her hands shook, and she twisted the rings on her fingers. "I was never ... I'm not ... it can't be me."

Semra's heart sank for Aviama, even as pride for Zephan filled her chest. He was strategic and smart. He hadn't quite gotten everything passed in time. Maybe he wanted to look over the wording, to proof the documents another time or two before making an official release, but he'd figured it all out.

Azi could not be permitted to reign. It was high time for Jannemar to overturn the ancient tradition of only males ruling the kingdom, but his pernicious elder sister could not be allowed to reign either. Zephan wasn't married and had no children. He needed a living heir he could trust, someone with Shamaran blood to love Jannemar as much as he did.

Aviama was the perfect choice. The only choice. She wasn't educated or prepared for rule as he had been, but she would have help. General Soldan would hold her hand and walk her through it as she learned. If she took wise counsel, she'd do better than half of her predecessors, in the event that Zephan followed his parents' footsteps in a grizzly, untimely death.

Semra wrapped her arm around Aviama's shoulders. "He made the right choice. You wouldn't be alone, and we don't even know it'll come to that. But when he sent us out of the castle, he wasn't just keeping me safe from my childhood nightmare, and watching out for his sister. He was protecting Jannemar's only hope to escape Azi and Avaya's destruction."

Semra steeled herself to say the next thing, to remind herself as much as Aviama that their priorities must be altered for the sake of Jannemar. It was not enough that they try to protect their loved ones. There was a greater purpose here.

The weight of the crown.

"Nothing is more important to Jannemar's safety and security now than these documents, and *you*, the only living rightful heir to the throne."

Realization hit Aviama's like a punch in the face. Her skin paled. "We can't go back and help him."

Semra worried her lip and let out a heavy sigh. She shook

her head. "No. It's too risky. We can't expose the king's edicts, or the crown princess, to that kind of risk."

Aviama's eyes filled with tears. "We can't sit back and do nothing."

Semra let her mind recede into itself, flowing out across the bond of the dragon's kiss. *Where are you?*

A flash of the Shalladin broke into her consciousness, a series of images cycling through in lightning speed: the waterfall in the cliff beneath the castle, blood in the shimmering waters of the river, fields, grass, and a dark crevice in some deep fissure where she'd sought refuge to recover.

Semra let out a breath. She was safe. *Rotokas?*

Alive. Gone. Free.

Semra sent her own meager calm to the dragon, as best she could. *Recover. Be safe. Keep an eye on the castle as best you can—you are my link to Zephan. We have business in Qalea. I'll call you when the time is right.*

The dragon's assent came strong. She wanted to fight. She had tasted blood, and she wanted more. Rotokas' blood, in particular.

Semra's vision returned to the world around her, and she looked at Aviama. "We're not going to do nothing. But we're not going to be stupid either. What was on the slip of paper, the one Avaya dropped?"

Aviama dug into her bodice once more and pulled out a small scrap of paper. The two of them huddled over it to read:

Great the dangers that are loosed when rise what laid to rest;
None but seed of flower planted could restrain it best.
Crimson queen shall open door protecting all from shame,
Then guarding it forevermore, he of the same great name.

"It's an old prophecy," Aviama said. "There's more, but I don't remember it."

"*When rise what laid to rest,*" Semra repeated, scrunching her face up tight. "What is rising, and why does it need restrained?"

"This prophecy. It's ancient. Could it really be about ..." Aviama's voice trailed off, and she stared at the paper in disbelief.

"Crimson queen," Semra said. "A queen in red. A queen come to power through blood."

"And ... guarding it forevermore? He of the same great name?"

Semra's stomach dropped. "What name do Avaya and Azi share? What *great* name?"

Aviama's face drained of all color. "Shamaran."

"Whatever this prophecy is, it's about them. And they're following it to the letter."

11

———

AVAYA

"Why would he do that? Why would he keep her from me? I've never harmed her."

Avaya's hands balled into fists on the table of her guest quarters' sitting room. Books and notes were strewn before her, but her view of them blurred with tears.

Her uncle patted her softly on the shoulder and leaned in, dropping his voice low. "Your brother doesn't understand you. He doesn't respect you. But he does *fear* you, and with fear we can demand respect. With respect, we can demand time. And in time, he can come to understand you."

Azi jabbed his finger at the parchment in front of her. "*You* were meant to rule. *I* was meant to help you, to be by your side through it all. If there is nothing else you know for sure, know that this truth of our partnership was established hundreds of years ago. No matter the struggles we encounter, we know how the story ends. We just need to see it through."

He was right, of course. He always was. How had she made it so long without him? How could her father have robbed her of an uncle like him?

They were scarce on family connections as it was, and

her father had lied about Azi. And now, both her parents were in the grave, the little nobody assassin girl had poisoned her brother against her, and Zephan had sent her one remaining family bond away. Aviama was gone. With *her.*

Avaya sniffed and nodded. She wiped her face and took a steadying breath. Azi hated it when she cried. She rolled her shoulders back and sat straighter in her chair.

"There now, that's my girl," he crooned.

"Zephan would be wise to make me a friend," Avaya said. "Despite the slander, despite the ash they throw upon my name, we have a higher purpose. And we will rise."

Azi smiled. "We will rise."

"There's no reason for Zephan to die. He'll do what he must when the time comes. He *will.*" Avaya swallowed hard and blinked back a second round of tears. She fingered the pearl on her necklace. "He'll have no choice."

Azi leaned back in his chair. "Your people, your network, you trust them? They won't break under pressure?"

Avaya shook her head. "They will serve me. I'm sure of it. Several of them have been doing it this whole time."

Azi pursed his lips, considering, then dipped his head. "Good. And your goldsmith?"

"I can get word to him. He'll duplicate the signet ring when he makes Zephan's replacement."

"Good. It was a fine move, his sending the signet ring away. It slows things down, but not by much. It'll take time to make a new one, but if we get our copy before he gets his, things could work themselves out better this way than we even imagined."

A rush of power flowed through Avaya's body, and she sent a light gust to buoy Azi's wine goblet up off the table and into his hands. "To us."

Azi swirled the glass and lifted an eyebrow. "You know you shouldn't waste it."

A pinch of guilt almost dampened her mood, but the thrill of using magic would never get old. She waved her hand. "Oh, we're in the castle, Semra is gone, and we're close to finding our missing piece. Live a little."

12

It was late evening by the time Semra and Aviama neared Qalea. Semra wound this way and that, covering their trail, doubling back, and taking twice as long to get anywhere. It didn't matter though. A princess and a noblewoman with a pants-dress situation going on weren't exactly what they needed to blend in inside the city.

"But if we wait until it's late at night, and dark, won't we get mugged?" Aviama asked.

"Maybe. That would be great. Muggers might have money on them, and we can take it."

"Do you really just go through life totally fearless? Do you have normal person fears—like the dark? Or spiders?"

Semra pursed her lips. "I grew up in the dark. Spiders are usually harmless. Most criminals are unskilled cowards."

Aviama's brows soared, and her eyes glittered with admiration. A sadness climbed up Semra's body like a vine and planted itself firmly in her heart. Aviama thought much higher of her than she should. There was nothing in Semra's life that she would recommend for others. She cleared her throat. "I'm afraid every day. I'm afraid for missions to end, and to be left alone with my thoughts. I'm afraid that without adrenaline, without distraction, I would find myself aimless and alone in the world. I used to be afraid to go to sleep, but the nightmares have mostly gone away."

The princess gaped at her, and Semra's cheeks flushed. Her insides squirmed. It felt weird saying that stuff out loud. But somehow, as innocent and naive as Aviama sometimes seemed, she was also safe. Aviama was better at the emotional side of things than Semra.

"You're not alone." Her voice, gentle and calm, swept over Semra like a balm.

Semra bit her lip. "I know that now. At least, I know it more than ever before. But I haven't had a real home in all my life, not that I remember anyway. When Turian gave me the earldom, that was my first opportunity for something stable, something legitimate to *do* to sustain me and keep me around Shamaran Castle. I'm not sure it's for me, but it means a lot and I want to honor his memory and do a good job. If Azi and Avaya don't destroy the kingdom, that is."

Aviama nudged her in the arm as they walked. "If the kingdom isn't destroyed, I'll be happy to watch you become queen instead of me."

Semra laughed. "I'm not sure an assassin is worthy to call herself a queen and lead a whole country. But if it happened, I'd probably need your coaching. I'm not known for ... propriety."

Aviama giggled. "Not exactly." She paused, then looked at Semra again. "The nightmares—what were they of?"

Semra lifted one shoulder. "I haven't had one since the battle at Surion Strip, when Zephan risked his life for mine *again*. He told me to jump off the explosives wagon, and I did. Zezura shielded us, and he carried me off the field.

"For a while before that I'd felt crazy, hearing Commander

Ramas' and Azi's voices in my head. Not *hearing* them, hearing them, but memories of what they'd said, or imaginings of what they would say, kept pushing into my mind. They told me how worthless I was, how much they hated me, how weak I was and how no one would ever stay. No one ever *had* stayed, really, before now.

"My nightmares were more of that, or reliving old missions, killing people. Rotokas snatching me from my village when I was four. Blood—mine, other people's. That sort of thing."

"Oh."

Semra's gut twisted. She turned the signet ring on her thumb again and again. It had fit on Zephan's pinky finger. She missed holding his hand. Had she really been in his arms just that morning?

A niggling thought popped into her head, and Semra turned to Aviama. "When we were with the guard outside the conservatory, trying to get into your mother's rooms—how'd you do that? Cry on the spot, I mean. I've always struggled with that."

Aviama shrugged. "It's not hard. I didn't manufacture it; I cry *off* the spot rather often. Anytime I think of her too long, if I haven't had a good cry in a while, it comes up. I feel like a flayed fish. All my protective scales are off, and I'm sensitive to all the world."

A deep ache set into Semra's heart, and a lump lodged in her throat. Semra hardly remembered her parents, but she did remember sobbing over them for weeks and weeks when she was first brought to the mountain. Sometimes she wondered if she was broken, or inhuman somehow, when she didn't remember or miss them enough. Other times the emptiness inside screamed so loud she wished she was a little less human so she wouldn't have to feel it.

Darkness descended, and Semra angled out of the forest and through the outskirts of Qalea at last. The outline of shops and houses stood against a crescent moon, and a soft wind lifted Semra's hair off her shoulders. Her stomach competed with Aviama's for loudest grumbling.

"What do we do now?" Aviama whispered.

"We need to get out of castle clothes, or everyone will remember us wherever we go. And we need to find Garbane's beeswax merchant in the morning—a beekeeper. Need to get word to Garbane somehow, but I'm not sure where he lives, and they'll probably have guards on him anyway. He's a known friend of mine."

"How are we going to find peasant clothes by morning?"

Semra snorted. "A good first step is to avoid calling them *peasant clothes.*"

Aviama bit her lip. "Right."

"We need to go somewhere surprising. But we don't want someone who's going to raise the alarm right away, so I'd rather not chance it breaking into a stranger's house. Anyway, if you become queen, it won't look good to have your people remembering the time you were an intruder and thief."

"So ... where are we going?"

"We're almost there."

Semra led them through a series of streets and back alleys. *What if she moved? What if she's been tipped off?*

It didn't matter now. It would have to do. The stupidity of leading the only legitimate heir so close to the castle raked on Semra's conscience. Hiding in plain sight was one of those things that brought praise as bravery if it worked, and judgment and death if it failed.

Semra drew a knife and spun it in her hands. She pulled Aviama into the shadows of the house, circled to the rear, and pulled back the curtain to the bedroom window. Semra jerked her hand back. A pinprick of blood ran down her thumb. Thorny brambles had been fastened across the window from the inside.

Aviama's eyes widened to saucers. Semra put a finger to her lips, cut away the thorns, and pushed them inward. She hopped through the opening and dropped to the floor of a modest bedroom. A bucket, scrap of needlework, and tattered shawl lay scattered across the bench on the far wall. A large trunk and small bed stood against the wall to Semra's left, and locks of golden hair poked out of covers pulled up high over someone's head.

Semra watched the bed for a long moment. The lumpy blankets shifted slightly, then lay still. Aviama poked her head into the room and raised her eyebrows. Semra nodded and gestured her inside, flipping her knife from forward grip to rear grip and back again as she waited.

Aviama slipped and landed with a grunt. "Ouch!"

Semra's heart lurched at the unwelcome sound. She cut Aviama through with a dirty look, and the princess's mouth turned down in a bashful frown. Semra jerked her head toward the trunk, and Aviama shuffled over to it.

Rats and rot, were all princesses so *loud?*

Aviama lifted the latch. The covers on the bed tore to one side and their occupant lurched upright. A long wooden object sailed through the air at Aviama's head.

Semra snatched the object from the air and lunged at the bed. The woman cowered into the corner, and a thousand options flew through Semra's brain. The object in her hands, as it turned out, was a rolling pin. From her elevated position, Semra could swing it down hard and crack the girl's skull, club her with the pin and slit her throat with the knife, or drop the pin on the bed and restrain her from there with any number of holds or chokes.

Instead, Semra passed the rolling pin back to Aviama and waved her knife in the blonde's face.

"Some little girls sleep with dolls."

The woman bristled with whatever was left of her pride, and lifted her chin. "Dragons and daylilies! I'm no kid no more, and not everybody's been broken into before. Least of all us with nothin' to steal."

"You're not friends, I suppose?" Aviama asked.

Semra grinned. "I've had the pleasure of breaking into this house before. Polerma here took a bribe to impersonate Avaya for her kidnapping."

"Name's *Polena,* thank you, and I've not been sleeping well since."

"So I gathered." Semra gestured to the window. "The thorns were a nice touch."

Polena's anger almost gave way to her curiosity. "They were?"

"Sure. They were cute."

Polena scowled. She folded her arms. "I don't need no trouble. I learned my lesson, and I'm done, hear? Get out. Out!"

Aviama glanced uncertainly between them. Semra sighed and shook her head. "It's a nice thought, but I don't think you've learned anything at all. I wouldn't say you have a knack for trouble, because I don't think you're very good at it. But you've certainly got a penchant for it."

Polena's eyes narrowed. "I don't got pendants of any kind, not but the cheap thing my mother gave me, and you don't want nothin' to do with that!"

Semra hopped off the bed and lifted her knife in Polena's direction. "Play nice over there, and we'll leave just as easily as we came. And you might be richer for it." She crossed to the bench and lifted the ratty shawl from the bench. A half-sewn purple silk bodice lay underneath. Semra cocked an eyebrow. "This isn't yours."

"Don't make no difference," Polena said with a sniff. "I work for a tailor, not that it's any of your business. Perfectly legal."

Something about the way she said it didn't sit right. Semra picked up the bodice. Polena flinched. Semra ran her fingers along its seams, and found a tube hidden in the unfinished boning. If it hadn't been for the unfinished detailing over its edges, she never would have noticed it.

"Who's this for?"

"Not for you to know."

"You might be the smartest idiot I've met. If only you were a serviceable liar, you might be incredibly useful."

"Yeah, well, like I'd work for you anyhow!"

Aviama held up a hand. "What's going on?"

Semra replaced the silk and the shawl on top. "She probably does work for the tailor, but she's making specialized clothing with hidden compartments. Probably small-time smugglers, cartels, that sort of thing."

Aviama's jaw dropped. Polena glared, but said nothing.

Semra spread her hands. "We've got a deal for you, Polerma."

"Polena."

"Bless you. We're going to take two sets of clothes, you're going to stay in bed until the sun is high in the sky tomorrow, and then you're going to wear the dress my friend is wearing across the city and into Boralin Square."

"Dragons and daylilies, what a big ask you've got," Polena exclaimed.

"You get to keep the dress, but you've got to be seen wearing it first. If my contact doesn't see you *in* that dress in

Boralin Square tomorrow, a farm in Pillerae will have an unfortunate accident."

Polena gasped. "How?—Who?—You wouldn't."

"Really? The dragon lady who broke into your house wouldn't do something unseemly? My, how trusting you are! But if you do what we ask, you'll get two things in return: the considerable value of the clothes we'll be leaving with you, and our promise not to turn you in for your black-market dabblings." Semra tilted her head at Polena and twirled her blade again.

Polena glared at her. Her lips pulled back into a hint of a snarl, then she nodded. "Deal."

13

GAULEN

The morning was bright, but it felt like a mockery as Gaulen walked the cold halls of power and betrayal toward the rooms of the pretenders. He flinched as a flash of onyx scales swept by the windows, for a moment granting the darkness the day deserved. The black dragon flew as an ominous reminder that though in his experience all dragonlords were violent and unpredictable, blue was kinder than black.

Blue would protect.

Black would destroy.

"Saeb hates the dragons." The voice came in a whisper from a woman on housekeeping staff, bundling sheets with another woman as Gaulen passed. "She says it's never been so hard to hire good gardeners."

"Yes, but we've never been so close to unifying with Belvidore before," said the other. "Imagine it—not just forging a peace treaty with a rival kingdom, but having two royal siblings working together! Perhaps this is what we've been waiting for. If that takes a dragon, well, so be it."

Ire burned in Gaulen's chest. *If they only knew. If they only knew it was all a farce.*

Semra knew. She was as skeptical, as realistic, as he was himself at times. As much as he'd questioned her methods in the past, no one knew the lord of the black dragon better than Semra. And with that knowledge, she'd gotten as far away from him as possible.

Gaulen quickened his pace past the women and down the corridor to the door of what he'd mentally begun calling The Pretender Suite. He rapped on the door and stepped back.

"Who is it?"

The sickening singsong of her venomous voice boiled his blood. He steeled himself to his usual professional calm, and raised his voice to carry through the door. "Gaulen, Your ... Majesty." No need to boil *her* blood until the time was right. "I've brought your latest library requests, and Coanor's recommended brew for your headache."

Footsteps padded to the door, and the heavy oak swung inward. Avaya put a hand on her hip and glanced around him down the hall. "I thought she was coming to assess me herself."

"No, Your Majesty. She said she has served the Shamaran children long enough to know what soothes their ailments, and sent along her best wishes to recover quickly."

It wasn't exactly true. The healer had looked Gaulen dead in the eyes and said "send my regards to the princess I used to know, if she's still in there. And tell her to come to her senses—I've got no herbs to cure whatever's in that girl's head."

Gaulen liked Coanor.

Avaya took the tray from Gaulen at the door and set it on the table in the sitting room. She lifted the teacup and sniffed it, and her shoulders relaxed to its warmth. "She's not wrong.

All the same, I'd like her to assess me in person if my headaches persist."

"Of course."

Avaya shuffled through the books and paused. "We—*I*—requested *The Essence of Herbology*, not *The Essence of Crater Wood*. This is one of Mox's children's stories."

Gaulen swallowed. "It seems *The Essence of Herbology* was damaged along with a number of other titles in the west-wing fire two months back. King Zephan suggested perhaps this one would suit your needs."

Gaulen liked his young king too.

Though petty digs of family drama could end in a bloodbath with so much ill will and power between them.

Avaya's hands on the book clenched into claws, and a vein in her neck threatened to pop. She took a slow breath through flared nostrils and let it out. She smoothed the soft velvet of her skirts, lifted her chin, and handed the book out to Gaulen. "Please return this book to him. Tell him thank you for his consideration, but I know he must struggle to sleep at night, and perhaps it would do more for him than for me."

Gaulen took the book and bowed. "Right away, Your Majesty."

"That's all, Gaulen."

Her snobbish voice reverberated in his head as he turned on his heel and made his escape. *That's all, Gaulen.* He clenched his jaw.

Gaulen wound his way through the castle to the library, but it was empty. He checked the conservatory, knocked at the king's chambers, and did a sweep of the courtyard. Three Belvidorian guards and two Jannemari ones roamed the gardens, avoiding each other and making poor attempts at looking casual. He picked up his pace. *What have they done?*

"They're pitiful, aren't they?"

Gaulen spun. The gravelly voice belonged to a gruff-looking man in an apron, leaning against the wall of the courtyard. The chandler.

"Excuse me?"

"A man can use time alone. Anybody can see how badly he's needed it." The chandler dipped his head and disappeared into the keep.

Gaulen pursed his lips and rapped his knuckles against the cover of *The Essence of Crater Wood.* He turned away from the courtyard, receded back through the keep, down the stair, and out into the west outer ward.

Where does a king hide in his own house?

It took half an hour, but the answer came with a soft nicker and a grunt in the back of the stables. Gaulen paused and retraced his steps, following the sound to the back of the stable. He leaned over the stall door and found his king sitting on the hay with his back against the wall, his father's old stallion pressing its large head into his chest.

King Zephan patted the stallion on the neck and scratched behind the animal's ears. The horse dropped to the ground with a huff and rolled in the hay, finally laying its head in the man's lap.

Gaulen watched the tender moment for a stretch before Zephan glanced up at him. Gaulen dipped his head. "Your Majesty. I'm sorry to disturb you."

"Don't *Your Majesty* me," Zephan said softly. "Come in, keep your voice down, and close the door behind you."

Gaulen did as instructed and squatted down next to the stall door.

The king gestured to the book in the guard's hands. "Doing some light reading, Gaulen?"

"For you, I'm afraid. Our esteemed guest says it will help you sleep at night."

Zephan nodded, and his mouth quirked up at the side. "How'd she look?"

Gaulen couldn't help his own small smile in return. "I believe she nearly combusted on the spot, Your Majesty."

The king's eyes glittered with mischief. He looked more a boy than a man in that moment. "You liked that, didn't you?"

"I did," Gaulen admitted. "Though perhaps I shouldn't. And she's hiding something. She took the tray from me at the door."

"What's so suspicious about that?"

"It wouldn't have been suspicious if it was you or Princess Aviama. Normally your older sister wouldn't extend herself with such menial labors. She would have me make the harrowing trek to the table and dismiss me from there."

Zephan's mouth twitched. "Careful, Gaulen."

Gaulen's cheeks flushed. "Forgive me. I forget myself."

"Nonsense. I'll be requiring you to remember quite a bit. But you'll need to do it with more tact. The walls have ears, more now than ever, and I need you to start acting like it."

The horse nickered and nosed the king, and he ran his hands along its mane. Zephan looked up and arched an eyebrow. "A *jemari* for your thoughts, Gaulen."

"Permission to speak freely, Your Majesty?"

"More trustworthy words than the captive kind."

Gaulen took a breath. "I question the wisdom of toying with a madwoman. Like with the book."

Zephan stroked the stallion's head. "I want her mad enough to fixate on me and my disrespect—rather than on what else I may be doing—but not so unsteady that she tears everything apart prematurely. It's all about balance." The young ruler shifted under the horse and looked dead in Gaulen's eyes, his golden eyes lit with fire. "Are you willing to die for your king?"

Gaulen dipped his head. "I am sworn to it. It is my duty."

"I'm glad you found me here. We will not speak this openly or at such length again. There are few I trust as much as you, and fewer still that Semra trusts as well. Speak nothing of what I am about to tell you, or you will be guilty of treason. Do you understand?"

Gaulen's heart raced, and he swallowed. "Yes."

Zephan leaned forward. "As you've probably guessed, because you're not an idiot, my sister is not here for a family reunion. I'm building an underground network, and you're part of it. If at any point I become ... unavailable, I want you to comply with whatever they say and send word to me.

"Be Azi and Avaya's most trusted guard. Give no red flags, no reason to question you. Coanor needs to get out. She's too firmly supportive of my father, and too free with her opinions. Avaya knows it, and Coanor will be the first to go when the slaughter starts. She needs to slowly get any important documents out of the castle and somewhere safe, and I want her gone by the end of the week. Give her as little information as possible before she's out. You'll both receive more instructions soon."

"Are you planning on leaving, Your Majesty?"

"I'll never run. I think when they find what they're looking for, they're going to force a transition of power, and they're going to make a lot of threats to do it. I will not capitulate, and I will force their hand to show their true colors.

"The king's guard dies for their king, but a king is only worthy of their sacrifice if he is willing to die for his kingdom in return. It's only a matter of time before they kill or exile me. I have a contingency plan for both eventualities, and I want a system in place before that happens."

Gaulen's sovereign grew older before his eyes, transforming from the adolescent youth the guard remembered so well to a king with the wisdom of his father. Zephan held his head high and spoke in a hushed rasp. "Azi and Avaya will never rule Jannemar."

Gaulen stared at the king.

Zephan Shamaran was no fool.

14

———

"You didn't have to be so mean to Polena."

Semra bit off a chunk of stolen roll from the bakery down the street and sighed. "I wasn't trying to be mean. I was trying to be threatening."

Aviama frowned. "What's the difference?"

"I don't know. I think *mean* is just making people feel bad for no reason. *Threatening* is purposeful. We had a very good reason."

"Which was?"

"Go somewhere unexpected, keep the heir safe, and get clothes to blend in. If we fail, the kingdom could fall."

Aviama pursed her lips. "Why did you pick her?"

"She's worked for Avaya before, or at least Siler, when he was in her pocket, though Polena never knew it. Polena is out for a quick *jemari* and doesn't care how she gets it. She's motivated by money, easily bought, easily threatened, and a coward. Most common criminals are."

"How did you know she had family in Pillerae?"

Semra shrugged. "I didn't, but you know that phrase she says, 'dragons and daylilies'? Pidge says it too, and she picked it up in Pillerae. Polena's diction isn't from around here. Besides, she's a terrible liar, so if I was wrong, she'd show it, and I'd be able to play it off."

Semra scanned the square. It was early, but merchants were already setting up their booths for the morning. Shopkeepers arranged ribbons, silks, and shawls. Beads and jewelry sparkled in the soft light. The bakery threw open its doors, beckoning passersby with the aroma of steaming, fresh-baked bread, and flies already gathered around hanging meats across the way.

But the beekeepers weren't there.

Aviama shifted from one foot to the other beside Semra, her gaze darting in every direction. An older woman nodded at the two of them as she passed with her basket. Semra nodded back, but Aviama stared after her, frozen.

The woman did a double take over her shoulder, and Semra didn't blame her. The princess's gawking was disconcerting. Semra looped her arm through Aviama's and leaned in toward her.

"Stop acting weird. Don't be nervous. Just be normal."

"Nothing about this is normal."

Semra's heart went out to her friend. *She's usually stuffed in a corner for dangerous things, but this time she's been kicked out of her home.* Aviama moved to twist a ring on her finger, then dropped her hands when she found them empty. They'd hidden the princess's rings and hairpieces in Semra's drab satchel, or Aviama's stained sash. Such extravagancies were far too dangerous to leave exposed.

"Just relax," Semra said. "We don't want to be remembered, and that means not being overly rude, and not being creepy. Don't stare at people. When someone says good morning, be polite, but minimal. Don't add to conversation or be too interesting. Be forgettable."

Aviama dipped her head in a stiff nod, but her expression was stony.

She's probably never even anywhere without an entourage. Semra groaned. "Okay. New plan. You're at a gala, and you're meeting a line of dignitaries. You have to be polite, but the line is impossibly long, and you're bored beyond belief."

A gentle smile pulled at the corner of her mouth. "I can do that."

The sun's rays peeked over the houses, and the earliest shoppers receded with their goods. Morning regulars shuffled in to replace them, and the familiar murmur of voices, greetings, complaints, and haggling brought a balm to the anxiety bearing down on Semra's chest.

The swirling worries of Zephan in the castle with Azi faded to the background and the focus of the task at hand took hold.

A mission. A crowd. Yes, this is what she needed.

Semra tugged Aviama out into the stream of people. A soldier dressed for duty stopped at a fruit stand, and Semra angled away from him, pausing to admire a useless carved nick-nack. The man behind the booth busied himself with the coin of a customer, and a young boy sat next to him on an overturned bucket, whittling a dragon of all things. He gaped at Aviama.

"I like your hair," the boy said.

"Thank you," Aviama answered.

The man behind the booth set his money bag aside and glanced at Aviama. Semra started to pull her away when the boy spoke again.

"Did you know I saw a princess once? I did. Last year."

"That's nice," Semra said.

The boy's gaze was fixed on Aviama. "You remind me of her."

The soldier's head swiveled in their direction. Semra's heart leaped into her throat.

"You're too kind," Aviama mumbled, and Semra steered her away from the figurines.

Another soldier appeared on the fringes. Semra felt the eyes of the boy and his father boring into their backs. Her mouth went dry.

A window opened in the sea of people on the far side of the square, and a box fell from a booth. Someone cursed. Two men rushed to right it and set it among jars and crates on the table. A bee symbol was engraved on each one.

Semra weaved Aviama through the marketplace, past the beekeepers' table, and ducked up behind them when they were out of sight of the soldiers. Semra extracted her arm from Aviama's and gave her a gentle nudge toward the neighboring table. The soldiers were looking for *two* women. Aviama busied herself with a potter's bowl, but Semra knew she was listening.

The beekeeper's donkey and cart stood to one side, and Semra gave the donkey a pat and tapped the older man on the shoulder from behind. He jumped.

"Good morning," she said.

"It's certainly *a* morning. Not sure how good it is yet." He looked her up and down. "We've got the finest honey this side of the river, but if you're buying, you should be on *that* side of the booth."

Semra sidestepped further behind the booth toward a stack of crates set aside. Several had slips of paper attached, reserving them for particular buyers. "Which river?"

His eyes narrowed. "Any river."

She scanned the list of names: *H. Horin, B.T. Morrel, G. Yaskir.* What was Garbane's last name?

"Garbane couldn't come today. I'm picking up his order of wax."

The man folded his arms. "Are you, now?"

Semra nodded. "I'm his apprentice."

"Yaskir doesn't take apprentices. Never has. Hates 'em."

The man knew Garbane decently. She could use that—so she did. Semra leaned in. "It was easier to say I was his apprentice, but perhaps I should clarify. You know where he works, right?"

The man scoffed. "I've been his primary supplier for fifteen years, little lady."

Semra held up her hands. "All right, all right. He lost a bet to Saeb a while back, and she got me a temporary job with him. He hated every minute of it, but when I started running errands for him so he didn't have to interact with people as much, he decided I wasn't so bad. Once in a while he still pays me to do a few things."

Three soldiers broke into Semra's eyeline, scattered across the square but pressing steadily toward her. She eased to one side and let the broad-shouldered beekeeper's body block her from their view. Aviama set down the bowl at the table beside them and picked up a serving plate. Her fingers trembled.

Semra bit the inside of her lip. *I just need to know where Garbane lives. Tell me where he lives.* She glanced up at the oncoming soldiers. One spied Aviama, and changed course in her direction.

The beekeeper laughed, a low rumbling sound deep in his throat. "That sounds like him. But you must have done something stupid for him to send you out here with nothing but your skinny arms to carry his order back to the castle. He's not above petty revenge, that one."

The keeper gestured at not one, but five crates of beeswax

stacked to one side, plus the single crate she'd noticed earlier with G. Yaskir's name on it. "You won't budge it an inch."

Semra's eyes bulged. But maybe ...

She jerked her head up from the crates and fixed her face into horrified shock. "Please, I have to get these to him today! Where does he live? I'll come back with a cart and take them there. The castle gates aren't open in the middle of the day anymore, and by the time I come back, I'll miss my chance."

Aviama turned the plate over in her hands and edged to the end of the table toward Semra and the beekeeper. Her ear was to their conversation, but her back was to the entirety of the square. The soldier nearest to Aviama disappeared, and the other two eased toward Semra's side of the marketplace. The girl was clueless. Semra clenched her jaw. Protecting people was so much more *complicated* than killing them, however wrong it may be.

Semra's four knives burned in the sheaths on her thighs, as she became suddenly intensely aware of how much skirt fabric was between her fingers and her blades. *You can't just kill people in a square. They don't even know they're not serving their king.*

Unless Azi and Avaya had the soldiers in their pocket. But they really only needed a captain or two issuing orders. Soldiers were not meant to question or think, but to obey.

The beekeeper grunted, then rolled his eyes. "I've not seen a little lady so tortured as you since I brought my wife home cabbage instead of lettuce. I've no desire to go to the castle, but I'll take you to Garbane's." The man clapped his associate on the shoulder and spoke to him briefly before turning back toward Semra. He loaded the six crates of beeswax on the donkey cart and waved her on. "Come along. The sooner we go, the sooner we're back, and you won't have to go find a cart of your own. I have a delivery that way anyway."

"Oh, thank you, sir! Thank you ever so much," Semra gushed. "Just one more thing ..."

Semra slipped to one side, snatched Aviama, yanked her into a low crouch, and shoved her toward the cart. She pulled Aviama up with her, and the beekeeper cocked an eyebrow.

"Another errand?"

"Cousin," Semra muttered. "She's visiting from out of town, and remarkably horrible at directions, so I have to keep her with me or there's no telling where she'll end up."

"True," Aviama said. She grimaced, then looked back over her shoulder.

Oh, now *she cares who's following us,* Semra thought. She adored Aviama, but traveling with Zephan was easier. Or Siler. Or Pidge. Anyone with survival skills, really.

Not to mention Aviama's perfect ringlet hair and familiar face were not exactly assets in melting away from attention.

The beekeeper snorted and gave the donkey a gentle snap with the reins. The cart lurched into an ambling pace. Behind them, two of the three soldiers turned this way and that in the marketplace. The third was gone.

And then the cart passed into an alley, and the square was cut off from view.

15

The cart bumped along the cobbled streets, the donkey's long ears twitching this way and that, its head bobbing up and down as it walked. They followed the alley to its end and progressed through a series of winding streets. The raucous of the main road drifted toward them from two streets over, but the beekeeper stayed to the side roads.

Semra didn't have much experience with donkeys, but it was hard not to find the animal's fuzzy coat and big brown eyes endearing. The donkey slowed by the window of a house to the left, eyeing it with interest from underneath impossibly long lashes. It let out a comical wheezing grunt and snatched a mouthful of flowers from the window box.

"Honey! Get out of there!"

Semra could have fallen over at the relief of hearing that familiar gruff voice. Aviama straightened beside her, craning her neck for a peek through the window. Did Garbane have a lady? He never spoke of one, but he was a private man. She didn't want to intrude on any domestic dispute, but they had little choice.

The beekeeper chuckled and dropped the reins. "Yaskir! Come get your shipment. I expect a nice tip for the delivery."

The chandler opened the door to his modest dwelling and gave the donkey a good-natured swat on the nose. "Does he not feed you, Honey? Hmm?"

Semra nearly laughed aloud. Garbane didn't have a lady. He'd been talking to the beekeeper's donkey.

Aviama popped her head over the crates in the cart. "You named your donkey Honey? Doesn't that get confusing, what with all the bees and honey making and such?"

"I've never accidentally slathered him on a sourdough, if that's what you mean." The beekeeper grinned.

Garbane's gaze snapped to the back of the cart, and he frowned. "What in the name of Aurin's—"

Semra jumped down and tugged at a crate. The beekeeper hadn't been joking. It was heavy. "I tried to pick up the delivery, just like you said. But you knew I wouldn't be able to transport it, didn't you?"

The beekeeper swatted her hands away and hefted the crate up against his chest. "I'm surprised at you, Yaskir. You sent a twig to do your hauling for you, eh?"

Garbane pressed his lips together. "Two twigs, apparently." He stepped up to the cart and picked up another crate. He dipped his head down as he passed Semra. "Get inside. Now. And don't get comfortable."

Semra winced at his tone, but caught Aviama's eye and jerked her head toward the house. Garbane glanced down the street in both directions as Semra ushered the princess inside. Ladles, mugs, and baskets hung by hooks along one wall, and a table stood to one side, holding a stack of books, a basin of dirty dishes, and a rag that Semra supposed might have been white once upon a time. A sitting area comprised of a low table and several chairs surrounded a fireplace in the room beyond, and a bubbling kettle hissed over the flames.

Outside, the beekeeper prattled on to Garbane as the two of them unloaded the rest of the crates. "What are you doing lazing around at home? Does the castle not need any new candles today?"

"The castle always needs candles. I was about to head to the market for the shipment, and after that I was *supposed* to be off today."

The beekeeper set the last crate just inside the door and headed back to Honey with a wave at Semra and Aviama through the window. "That's what you get for working with an apprentice! Ha!"

Garbane grunted and closed the door. "Indeed." He shot a dark glare in Aviama's direction, and Semra twisted to follow his gaze. She'd plopped down on one of the chairs and was leafing through a book. Garbane gave a sharp whistle and jerked his finger to one side, making his desire unmistakably clear.

Aviama snapped the book shut and tripped over her feet in an effort to flee the forbidden chair. She bit her lip, dropped the book on the chair, and swallowed.

Semra had never seen Aviama so uncomfortable. She'd seen the princess giddy, and she'd seen her grieving, but their time together up until today had been spent strictly within the castle's walls. What an experience this must be, without the guards, resources, and respect afforded her station. To her credit, Aviama did not expect Garbane to offer her any partiality. She simply hadn't a clue how to handle herself in a manner that would please the owner of the house.

It was unfortunate that Garbane was her first experience of hospitality from a commoner.

Garbane peered out the window, barred the door, and shook his head. "I thought I told you not to get comfortable."

Semra cleared her throat. "I'm sorry to come to you like this. I didn't know where you lived, and we're short on trustworthy friends. We're in trouble."

"Next you're going to tell me the sky is blue." Garbane reached into a basket hanging on the wall, retrieved a clean cloth, and began rummaging in jars and vases on the shelves. "I already know the sky is blue, the grass is green, and the older princess has lost her mind, so if you're going to endanger my life, you could at least start with some new information."

Guilt needled at her, and Semra grimaced. Garbane was one of the first places soldiers would be sent to look for Semra and Aviama. Garbane had been a confidant of hers since she first ran into his chandlery six months ago. He was quiet, calm, and curmudgeonly, which felt honest and safe to her. The fact that Garbane's prickly exterior kept the bulk of the castle staff away from the chandlery had been an added perk.

But she usually got the sense that he didn't mind her intrusions, and even secretly enjoyed them. She did not get that sense today.

Garbane stuffed whatever he found in the jars and vases into the cloth and folded it. He pulled a string from a tangle of twine and fussed with the bundle in his hands. The frown on his face deepened, and his forehead creased. "If you're out here with her, something went south in a big way. A life and death way. So who is about to die? You, or someone else?"

Semra's throat constricted. It was so much worse than anyone could have imagined. "Garbane. They have magic."

Garbane's hands stilled. Slowly, he recaptured the ends of his string and worked them into a knot around the cloth. "Who is *they?*"

"Azi is out from the dungeon. He's working with Avaya.

They're in the castle masquerading as guests and black-mailing Zephan." Saying the words out loud broke the numbness of the mission, and all the emotions that she'd been holding at bay threatened to break through the dam. Azi, who kidnapped Semra, slaughtered her parents, and slit her best friend's throat before her eyes. The man whose voice haunted her nightmares, whose lust for blood knew no bounds, who was bent on the violent destruction of any obstacle in his path.

The fear of him had settled in her bones the moment she saw Azi in the king's chambers. It was not the fear of a trained assassin that had come over her, the thrill of the fight as an accomplished killer observed a worthy adversary whom she had defeated before. It had been the fear of a child staring into the face of death itself, the kind that killed slowly, tortuously, from the inside out until the raw terror of being alive held little reward.

And now Azi, the dragonlord of her stolen childhood, had set his sights on the throne with renewed vigor—and Zephan, the orphan king of Jannemar, the last loving ruler, was alone in the castle with him. Zephan was Azi's obstacle to claiming the throne for himself, no matter what lies he'd sold Avaya.

A lump lodged in Semra's throat. Zephan, the man who danced with her when the world was on fire, whose arms encircled her when the court called for her head, who believed she was more than her upbringing. He had once told her that perhaps her job, as she called it, was death, but her inclination was life. He'd seen through her before she'd believed it was true. Zephan, whose honeyed eyes searched her very soul. The man who wanted to marry her.

A king with a ticking clock counting down the minutes until death.

Semra cast a glance at Aviama, plucking lint off the plain cotton of her dress. Zephan had placed the hope of a nation on her shoulders. Without Zephan, she was the only chance Jannemar had for security. Semra stepped up to Garbane and put a hand on his, a gesture that shocked them both and instantly acquired the chandler's full attention. Semra dropped her voice low so that only he could hear.

"We have to get Aviama far away and safe before I can do anything else to help him. I don't know where to go, but every second I spend taking her to safety is a second I'm running the wrong direction, away from Zephan."

A flash of pain rocked her as her mind's eye created a waking nightmare—Azi, in the throne room, his hand on the back of Avaya's neck, guiding her forward. The steel in her hand glinted in the morning light and she floated forward, borne on an unnatural wind, toward her brother. A slight dip of Azi's head was all the signal it took. Avaya slit his throat and he crumpled to the ground. Semra opened her mouth in a silent scream, but as he fell, it was Semra's friend Brens she saw staring up at her. Would the people who loved Semra most always suffer?

"I think ... I think I will never see him again." Semra blinked back tears and stared down at her hands. Had her hand been on Garbane's this whole time? She snatched it back and looked at the floor. "I don't know how to fight this. How do you fight a magic that isn't supposed to exist?"

Black tendrils of obsidian mist poured from her fingertips. Semra raked a hand through her tangled hair, a cascade of smoke flowing after her every movement. She couldn't control it, and it was going to get them killed. It was bad enough to show up at Garbane's when soldiers were looking for them, but a smoke signal would virtually destroy any meager head start they had managed to gain.

Garbane looked at her solemnly, then nodded pointedly at her fingers. "With magic that isn't supposed to exist."

16

"**S**emra!"

Semra hardly registered Aviama's terrified cry. Somewhere in her mind, alarm bells rang—her smoke was a liability. A *big* one. Dragons held ancient magic in their blood, and some sort of magical hiccup had given her this strange ability when the mark of the dragon's kiss had broken apart to save her from venomous snakes. Whatever was in the mark had entered her bloodstream, and she'd been deathly sick for weeks before she felt better. And then the smoke had come.

But the smoke was chaos. How could an anomaly she was powerless to restrain compete with *actual* magic?

If the tales were true and the great elemental melder Aurin had destroyed magic six hundred years ago, how did Avaya have it?

And if she was nothing but a liability, how could she live with herself when she brought death not only to Zephan, but to Aviama as well? She couldn't carry out Zephan's desires and protect Aviama if her smoke revealed their location, not unless she took the princess to a deep dark uninhabited cave. It wasn't out of the question.

Her stomach dropped and all she could do was stare at Garbane, smoke still spilling from her fingertips in streams of inky black. Garbane took her by the shoulders, wheeled her around, and marched her to the fireplace. The chandler snatched the whistling kettle off the fire and doused the flames, then thrust Semra's hands into the chimney.

Whisps of black escaped out the window, but the rest of her smoke channeled up the chimney. The casual passerby might assume that the billowing ebony wafting over the house was merely from a clueless sot burning leaves, grasses, and wet wood rather than the result of a dragonlord's emotional meltdown with a side of magical accident.

"You can't keep anyone safe until you have that under control." Garbane shoved the cloth bundle into Aviama's hands and batted away the ebbing smoke from Semra's fingers.

Aviama clutched the bundle to her chest. "Can't we just take the dragon?"

"Because the lunatic in the castle has a dragon too," Garbane said. "And because everyone is scouring the skies for a sight of anything with wings, and your location would be in jeopardy."

Semra took a shaky breath and swiped tears from her cheeks. She'd hardly noticed them before. Semra inspected her fingers. The smoke was gone. "We can use her eventually, but not yet. Zezura is my eyes. I can't be with Zephan, but if she can, I can see what she sees. Once we're out of the city, I can send Zezura in the opposite direction under cover of night, and have her wheel around and find us. The mark of the dragon's kiss acts like a beacon—she can always sense my location."

Aviama sank into a chair, then caught a glimpse of Garbane and sprang back to her feet. "But the soldiers are going to look here first, aren't they? How are we going to get out without Zezura?"

"You're going to stop yelling names like *Semra* and *Zezura*, for one," Garbane grumbled.

"I would go to the Rinabs, but I can't put them in danger again. If I disappear to a cave somewhere nearby, Rotokas could still find us. If I go too far, Aviama won't—well, I can't go anywhere that takes months of travel." *If Zephan dies, the heir needs to be around to take the throne.* Not that it would matter, if Semra couldn't find a way to fight back against Avaya's new magic.

Semra pinched the bridge of her nose. "Tell me you know of a place with a library where I can figure out what's going on with the magic. Do you know of any a historian on the melders and on magic? Do you have a reclusive relative we could stay with, or just somebody you don't like that wouldn't turn us in? I'm afraid we haven't got any money for an inn."

The chandler pursed his lips. "Anything else?"

"Oh! Um, actually, yes." Semra grimaced. "We need the original prophecy about ... rats and rot, this sounds weird, but there's some old prophecy about a crimson queen. Avaya had it. We need the rest."

Garbane turned and disappeared into a back bedroom without a word. Semra rocked back on her heels and crossed her arms. Aviama worried her lip and shifted her weight. "Did ... did he just abandon us?"

Three minutes later the chandler returned with a small pouch and two envelopes. He arched an eyebrow at Aviama. "Patience isn't really your thing, is it?"

Aviama bristled. "Manners aren't really your *thing,* are they?"

"Get used to it. You don't live in the castle anymore, and you need to stop acting like you ever did." Garbane dropped the pouch into Semra's hand, the *clink* of jostled coins betraying its contents. "Coanor has been up to something the last couple months staring at old books and poems and things. She's a bit of a conspiracist, but when the conspiracies are real, those people go from loons to wise men."

He handed Semra the envelopes. "Here's a note Coanor wrote me about it. The other is a letter I just wrote. Don't break the seal, and give it directly to the person I tell you. I'm going to give you a name and a place. You're going to tell him I sent you, and you're going to stay there until he says you can leave. If you don't, you and the princess will die. And if you and the princess *do* die, Zephan isn't the only one that will be lost. All of us will be as good as dead in your wake."

Semra swallowed, but nodded. She slipped the pouch into her satchel. "I understand. Thank you."

"Don't thank me. Stay alive."

"That much money must have taken you a long time to save." Aviama reached into her sash and pulled out a sparkling gold and amethyst ring. Sunlight from the window cast ripples of radiant purple bouncing off the stone in every direction as she held it out. "Please take it. It's the least I could possibly do."

Garbane covered the gemstone with his hand and gently pushed the ring back toward Aviama. "Proof you were here and that I helped you? No thanks. Pay me back when things are set to rights again."

Aviama bit her lip and withdrew the ring.

Garbane sighed. "Don't worry, I'll keep an itemized list of all my sacrifices. Now come on. We don't have much time. Semra, if you would, now would be an excellent time for a dragon distraction."

Semra nodded and sent out the call through the mark on her chest. Zezura's answer came in an onslaught of anxious anticipation and pent-up energy. She was restless and eager. "Where are we headed?"

"Northeast side."

Semra reached back out to Zezura. *Do a sweep to the south. If Rotokas comes, can you outfly him?*

The dragon let out a throaty chuff that might have been a laugh. *He is a bird, but I am the wind.*

Semra looked up. "We're covered. Let's go."

Garbane disappeared once more and returned with a small wooden box and a mallet. Semra raised an eyebrow, and Garbane shook his head. "Don't bother about the box. The mallet is for anybody who stops us and won't let us pass. I like my life, so let's hurry and see that I don't have to use it."

The chandler tossed a scarf at Aviama and instructed her to wrap her shining golden tresses in it. "A drab dress won't hide that," he mumbled. Aviama dutifully laid the scarf over her head, tucked it in, and pulled the ends over the stray hairs at her forehead. Garbane snatched a mantle off the back of the door, but it did little to conceal his frame, or the way he walked—long, sturdy, purposeful strides, with a sort of plodding clunk to his gait.

The sun was high, business at its peak. Bustling people filled the streets, and Garbane led them from one street to the next, winding through the city at a clipped pace. Semra strode after him with Aviama half jogging to keep up. A flash of gold and blue caught her eye—soldiers. Semra gripped Aviama's arm and spun her away, and Garbane seamlessly angled toward the opposite side of the street. If it weren't for his deepening frown, Semra never would've known he'd seen them.

Aviama's stomach growled. "I used to wish I was out adventuring with you instead of cooped up in the—at home."

The princess stumbled as Semra dragged her forward, and her breathing quickened as she gathered her feet and hustled forward. "But if I'd known you spend so much time without hope of a meal, I might have reconsidered."

It would have been funny if they weren't in sight of soldiers. As it was, Semra hardly registered the comment until they made it to a side street. A roar thundered overhead, and the great blue dragon drew every eye upward as Zezura coursed across the sky, past Shamaran Castle and down over Qalea in broad daylight. Murmurs and cries rippled down cobblestones as people drew in their breath, some clutching at their children, and a few even sending up a cheer.

What must it be like to be so clueless on the reality of life, so ignorant of dragons and their lords, kings and assassins, danger passing them by every day? How long would it take Rotokas to pursue—or would Azi play a different card?

Semra, Aviama, and Garbane emptied into the stream of foot traffic on the far side of the block, and Semra breathed easier in the crowd. "Going hungry is the least of our worries."

Aviama's midsection rumbled in protest. "Maybe for *you*."

Garbane scanned the signposts of the shops, and Semra followed his gaze. What was he looking for? Weren't they getting out of the city?

Nothing in the row made sense to Semra. The signs ahead indicated a mercer, weaver, tavern, spicery, and scribe. She *was* hungry, and Aviama would certainly appreciate the tavern's food, but stopping someplace so visible—or at all, really—wouldn't be wise.

Semra glanced at Garbane, but his expression gave nothing away. Beside her, Aviama's pace quickened as they approached the tavern. A young woman with a box exited the tavern door, letting out the smell of fresh bread, roasted meats, and ale.

"Ohhh." Aviama leaned forward, sticking her nose into the crack of the door, and nearly got hit by it as it swung closed.

The woman made her way down the street, but something in her walk caught Semra off guard. In truth, several somethings caught her off guard.

She walked like a brick, and if it weren't for the clamor of the city, Semra was certain she would have sounded like an elephant rather than like a lady—and a slight lady, at that. Well-kept black hair fell down her back, and her dress placed her in middle class, but the pleats of her skirt were askew on one side. A new take on the wrap skirt?

A ball rolled out of an entryway straight at the woman from the tavern. The woman jerked her skirt up with one hand and kicked the ball into the stomach of a boy of about ten who had run after it.

"Dragons and daylilies! Watch yourself!"

The boy grumbled an apology and darted off.

The lady dropped her skirt back to the ground and adjusted her grip on the box in her hands, but not before Semra had caught sight of her shoes. Despite her nice clothes, muddied boots marched down the lane where stylish, polished footwear should have been.

Semra smiled. "Pidge."

She'd spoken softly, but the young woman whirled at the sound of her voice. A girl of about seventeen stared back at her, brown eyes wide, mouth agape. Her gaze flicked across their party.

Garbane held out the box in his hands and gave a curt nod. "I need that favor."

Pidge stacked Garbane's box on top of hers, and the corner of her mouth quirked up. "Oh, this oughta be good. Rats and rot, look at you lot! *You* coming to find *me.* I always thought it would be the other way around."

After the battle in Madensig Fortress, King Turian had pardoned Pidge from all her assassin dealings as a result of her work to aid Semra and Zephan. When Semra was sick and framed for the Belvidorian king's assassination, Pidge had wound up joining her. Together with Siler, they had gotten Semra to the healer Shafii Rinab and worked to gain evidence to clear her name.

Zephan had left the castle, found them at the Rinabs, and joined the group. After that, they'd failed to stop Avaya's wedding to Prince Axis, and in the battle, Avaya had ensured Axis's death and secured her position as queen and ruling monarch in Belvidore. But they managed to save Siler and get Zephan home safe, with enough evidence to clear Semra's name. Siler had disappeared after they'd escaped Belvidore safely, but Pidge had accompanied Semra back to Shamran Castle. Zephan's eyewitness testimony to Pidge's collaboration in storming Madensig was all Turian had needed to offer her clemency.

Pidge looped her arm through Semra's and for all her picking, she was nearly bouncing as they left the tavern behind and passed the spicery, Aviama and Garbane trailing them. Semra couldn't help but smile. She'd grown fond of Pidge from their adventures, and had hoped to discover what became of her after her pardon. Perhaps she took up the late king on his offer to apprentice for a legitimate trade.

The muddy boots under that fine dress begged the question—how could a girl like Pidge entirely abandon the familiarity of chaos? No, Pidge would entertain herself one way or another. The thrill of adrenaline was a lifeline to her, just as it was to Semra.

"It's good to see you." Semra squeezed Pidge's arm. "What have you been doing all this time? I'm surprised you're still in Qalea."

"Oh, this and that." Pidge stopped outside the scribe and glanced up at the signpost. "I've been working for a copyist. We do everything from duplicating documents, creating stationary, and formal invitations, to legal agreements and marriage certificates. The boss can even officiate, so it's a one-stop shop, as it were."

Pidge opened the door and ushered them inside. Several people bent over desks with a stand holding a book open for them to reference as they made copies, or an example of a particular stationary to fit a client's preferences as they worked. Varying types of parchment hung on the wall to one side, with models of clear concise printed programs next to announcements set in long elegant script. A few heads glanced up as the group entered, but after seeing Pidge, they continued without interruption.

Pidge paused by a young man in the front of the room. "Is he here?"

The man nodded and gestured to a door at the back. "Just got in."

Three interior doors broke up the walls of the room—two in the back, and one to the side. Pidge led them past the copyist's workers and knocked on the closest door along the rear wall. An assenting grunt bade them entry, and they filed into a small meeting room stacked with papers, books, and neatly organized boxes on large shelving across the entire back wall.

The boss was hardly two years older than Semra's eighteen years. Shaggy brown hair framed a handsome face adorned with stubble and set with a piercing set of silver eyes. Semra drew in a breath, and the figure straightened to take them in.

"Aurin's spear, look what the rookie dragged in."

17

AVAYA

"Murin. You know me." Avaya ran her thumb over her fingernails and leaned forward on the arm of her chair.

Her sister's lady-in-waiting was around the same age as Aviama, maybe a year older—perhaps seventeen. The girl sat in a cushioned chair in Avaya's guest chambers, hands folded tightly in her lap, head down.

Murin was as loyal to Aviama as Avaya's lady-in-waiting, Teriv, had always been to her. Teriv melted into the back of the room even now, but Avaya knew she was listening. Teriv was always listening. She had been Avaya's eyes and ears in the castle for weeks. She wasn't privy to everything, of course. Just what she needed to fulfill her purpose. And she fulfilled it gladly.

How much of Aviama's purposes had Murin carried out? How much of a purpose could her little sister have even had? Aviama was the youngest born royal, matters of politics never taking precedence over hobbies and little harmless distractions. As a woman in Jannemar, Aviama would never be queen; as the youngest with both an older brother and an older sister, her age pushed her so far down the line of accension that her gender hardly mattered.

Unless Zephan decided to marry her off to strengthen international relations. But Zephan was soft, like their father. Avaya doubted he had the stomach for it. But if not the royal family of another nation, was it really better to leave Aviama a spinster?

Zephan was ill-equipped to address so many things. He was too like Father. And his obsession with Semra proved his judgment had flown straight out the window. Unlike Aviama, Avaya had always paid attention to diplomatic dynamics and matters of state. She knew the members of court, and they'd been just as concerned over an assassin so close to Zephan as she had been herself. How did he not see the long con she was playing?

And even if she wasn't playing, did it matter? No. She was a commoner. Avaya's mother, Queen Sharsi, had been a commoner. But at least she wasn't a murderer. At least she wasn't responsible for breaking apart a family and setting fire to a delicately arranged, strained peace between age-old rival kingdoms.

"Your Highness, I do know you." Murin worried her lip. "I hope you would know me enough to know I am a terrible liar. Princess Aviama is headed to Pilall to help Semra establish her earldom, and reassure the people there."

Avaya pursed her lips. Murin seemed innocent enough, but a lot could happen over the course of six months. All one had to do was look at Avaya's own life to see it—an underestimated, supposed air-headed gossip of a princess could take over the monarchy of an enemy kingdom and become queen almost overnight. There had been no riots, no revolts. On the contrary, the Belvidorian people were happy to have her.

What had Zephan done in the past six months, besides

shirk his duties for chances to see Semra? How had he earned his kingdom, except by the death of their father? Avaya had earned hers, first in cunning, and then in blood.

In cunning, because as others dismissed her as a frivolous gossip, she had built an information network filled with willing volunteers of every station. As captains, guards, dukes, and earls considered her nothing but a beautiful chess piece pawn to be admired and played, she had reached the other side of the board and become the most powerful player in the game.

"And did she ... how long have they been planning the trip to the earldom? It seemed like our staff was pretty surprised by it. And she left her typical luggage. Perhaps we should send a party to catch up with them as they travel, and give her anything she left behind?"

"Oh, I don't know, Your Highness. I thought I'd be going with her on the trip to Pilall, but I suppose things change. I only know what I've been told."

Avaya squinted at Murin, then leaned back in her chair. She might have corrected the girl's use of *Your Highness* instead of *Your Majesty* in another setting, but it was an old habit for many in Jannemar who had known her before. And Murin required a delicate hand, and rapport was important if she wanted to win over the staff and learn anything important. But alas, it appeared Murin really was the most elemental of pawns. Not the sort that would ever make it to the other side of the board, but a run-of-the-mill, clueless one trusted with few responsibilities. A disappointment.

Still, perhaps Murin knew more than she thought. The girl was with Aviama constantly, waiting on her hand and foot every day, talking to other servants and staff. Avaya slipped from her chair and knelt on the floor next to Murin's chair. She peered up into Murin's face.

Murin squirmed in her chair, pressing herself against the backrest. Her eyes grew wide, and her cheeks flushed. Surely she'd never had a queen kneel beside her before. *And she never will again.*

Bangles and gem-studded bracelets jingled as Avaya rested her hand on Murin's knee. "You know I love her, don't you? In wartime, as in times of unrest and transition of power, people are prone to riot. It's not safe on the road right now. I only wish she could have stayed to visit with me longer while I am here, and I'm worried. If they had postponed the trip, and my brother had taken part in the tour of the country himself, in person, to secure his reign and connect with his people, he might have cleared the way for a safer mission to Pilall next summer."

Murin opened her mouth to respond, but paused as heavy footsteps traipsed down the hall outside. Avaya's stomach twisted and she rose and turned just as the doors were flung open and Zephan strode into her sitting room, six guards in tow.

Avaya lifted her chin and arched her eyebrows. *A little much for a pleasant host, hmm, brother?* She touched her hand to her chest, her fingers grazing the smooth shell of her necklace pendant. It had become a nervous habit, something comforting to hold onto as her world spun around her.

Zephan's fiery eyes bored into Avaya's as he marched forward and held up a fist, signaling his guards halt and stand at attention. "You dare detain someone without my knowledge?"

Avaya's heartbeat quickened, and she fought the urge to bite her nail. Instead she focused on the smooth curve of the shell necklace as her finger traced its edge, then drew herself up tall and clasped her hands behind her back. "I haven't detained anyone. I've only connected with an old friend."

Her brother's jaw clenched, and he spoke to Murin without taking his eyes off Avaya. "Murin, what questions has my sister asked you?"

Avaya held Zephan's gaze with steely resolve. *I am just as stubborn as you. I am just as smart as you. I will not be intimidated.*

How had they been born of the same parents, and yet become so different? Out of the corner of her eye, Murin shifted awkwardly.

"Her Highness asked me how I was, and how everyone was faring under the recent ... loss, and transition of power. She asked me about Princess Aviama and Countess Myansara, and their sudden departure."

"I'm sure she did." Zephan's tone soured, and his lip curled ever so slightly. "And did my sister share anything of her own, the way friends do with one another?"

Avaya ground her teeth. She'd known Murin all her life! She knew this castle and everyone in it. She was a queen, and still he treated her thus!

Murin dipped her head. "Only that she fears for the princess, Your Majesty."

A diplomatic answer. The girl's furtive gaze flicked between them. She dare not lie to the king, yet she hoped not to offend either of the monarchs in the room with her. Ah, but she had no idea of just how delicate a balance that might be.

"And how many old friends has my sister formally summoned since her arrival?"

Murin shook her head. "I don't know, Your Majesty."

Avaya held up a hand. "Zephan. Enough."

Zephan ignored her, turning instead to Teriv, quietly organizing books and papers on the nightstand. "Teriv, how long have you enjoyed employment here?"

Avaya's head snapped to Teriv. What was he doing?

Her lady-in-waiting curtsied low. "Nearly all my life, Your Majesty. It is my great honor, as it was my mother's."

Zephan gave a short nod. "And how many old friends has my sister summoned since her arrival?"

Teriv froze. Most of Avaya's meetings and interactions had been casual, but she'd called for a few in particular, the way she always had. Avaya's throat tightened. Her mouth went dry.

Teriv cleared her throat. "Only two. Coanor the healer, when Her Majesty was not feeling well, and Murin."

Zephan took in a deep breath and let it out. The angry older brother disappeared under the guise of what might've been mistaken for a composed, scolding parent. "Teriv. Forgive my temper—it is not aimed at you. You have always served our family well. But do not misunderstand me. I knew the answer before I asked the question. Do you think perhaps you have miscounted?"

Avaya's jaw dropped. "Zephan!"

How were they to negotiate under such hostility? Where was Azi? Would Zephan dare speak this way with *him* here?

He was toing the line on their agreement. If he broke the ruse of Avaya and Azi as invited guests, they would have to move up their timeline, and Zephan wasn't ready for that. He was too smart not to know they had a plan, but he was also smart enough to know he couldn't be ready yet for them to release it. And so they existed in a tense status quo, each waiting and watching, hoping they prepared to make a move better and earlier than the other.

"I ... I may have miscounted, Your Majesty. Perhaps I was not present for all of them. I am just now remembering there was also a summons for two others, for a total of four."

Avaya shot Teriv a withering glare, and she stared at her toes. Zephan might not have known the answer. It wouldn't have been hard to get, but Teriv could have evaded the question instead of snapping like a twig.

Zephan dipped his head. "Thank you, Teriv. Murin, you are dismissed. Is your father's health improving?"

Murin's face twisted, and the corners of her mouth tugged downward. "He's up and down, Your Majesty."

"With Aviama and Semra headed to Pilall, we can afford to give you a well-deserved break. There's much to do around here, but take the afternoon and next three days to be with your family. We'll see you back next week."

Murin lit like a fuse, a smile breaking across her face and her whole body animating as she dipped into three haphazard, unnecessary curtsies. "Thank you! Of course, yes!"

Avaya's chest tightened as Murin floated from the room. Zephan, the good and fair one. Zephan, beloved by all.

How did they not see his weakness the way that she did? But if only he would listen to her, if only he would realize he was following in the footsteps and pitfalls of their father instead of putting Turian on a pedestal, he could come to understand. They could work together. They could be a family again.

Zephan stepped toward her. "You will not summon staff, and these are not your servants. You are a guest in *my* house. You will inform your guard or your lady-in-waiting, and anything you require will be brought to you."

Anything you require. And who but Zephan would determine what was required? Was this her hostile takeover, or a hostage situation—with her as the hostage?

She pressed her lips together and lifted her chin. He wanted a power play. Well, if he wanted power, he would have it. What would it feel like to knock him off his feet right now, to blast him back along with his guards, with a great gale of wind …

A thrill ran up her spine at the thought. But no. Not yet. Soon.

But above all, one question drove her mad as she lay awake at night. Avaya reached out and nearly clutched her brother's sleeve, then drew back at the last moment. She lowered her voice for him alone to hear. "You told her to take Aviama. She's in no danger. Why would you tell her to do that?"

A question flickered across Zephan's face, and he looked at her a long time. "She is in great danger. And so are you."

The hair on the back of her neck prickled. "Is that a threat?"

"No. It's a statement of fact. You have no idea what you've gotten yourself into. Who you've thrown yourself into business with."

Heat flashed through Avaya's body. "You sent our baby sister off *alone* with a killer, a killer you have *no* control over! She was the start to it all. She got Mother killed. She started the war with Belvidore. Semra has been elbow-deep in blood for as long as anyone can remember, and she's been manipulative enough to have you all hoodwinked. Well, not me!"

"A killer? A killer who I have no control over?" Zephan arched his eyebrows and his tone oozed disdain. "Speak for yourself. If Semra is elbow-deep in blood like you say, Azi is wading through pools of it. And any blood on Semra's hands was poured by Azi himself."

"He's restoring order!" Avaya cursed under her breath as one of the guards shifted his weight. Her voice had risen. She lowered it again and hissed at Zephan in a sharp whisper. "He doesn't want the throne. He's willing to bring Belvidore and Jannemar to a peaceful place, the goal of our ancestors for generations, and he has the know-how to do it! Father wronged him, deeply, but here he is making up for lost time."

"You want so desperately to be in control—will you really forfeit common sense to get there?" Zephan shook his head and clenched his jaw. His eyes simmered with roiling anger, and he seemed to grow taller as he bent closer. "Before you lecture me on Semra, the only one of your mentor's students brave enough and smart enough to see through Azi's lies and stand up to him, take a hard look in the mirror. You're cavorting with the person responsible for the murder of *both* of our parents. If you don't see the problem with that, you're as dangerous as he is, and the safest place for Aviama is as far away from you as possible."

Avaya fell back a step, speechless. Tears burned in her eyes, but she blinked them back and ground her teeth. With a start, she realized her hands had balled into fists, her nails biting into the flesh of her palms. It wasn't a good image. She uncurled her fingers and smoothed her velvet skirts.

Clipped, measured footsteps fell in rhythmic time against the wooden floorboards, at once brisk yet unhurried. The tension in Avaya's shoulders eased as her uncle swept into the room with a quiet flair. It was his way—commanding attention without a word, exuding confidence like light from a candle.

"I do love a good family reunion. You learn so much about a person when you see them with their family, don't you think?"

His voice dripped like wax before a flame, slow but inevitable, eating away any resistance. Azi planted himself several paces away from Zephan and Avaya, ignoring Zephan's guards altogether, surveying the two of them with interest. "It's good to know my brother raised such emotionally resilient, stable young royals."

Even as his presence soothed her, Avaya's mouth went dry at his rebuke.

Zephan stiffened. His expression was stone, but Avaya knew her brother. He was nervous, and the vein in his neck betrayed him, straining against the skin as his heart pumped twice as fast. Good. *Be nervous. And one day perhaps you will respect me as much as you respect him.*

King Zephan, as he was so eager to appear, turned away from Azi and gestured to one of his guards.

"Kolorim, remove my sister's books. It seems she has tired of reading, and has entertained herself enough for today with the stimulating company of our staff."

The guard hesitated, and his gaze shifted from Zephan to Avaya, and came to rest on Azi. Azi locked eyes with the guard, a cool glare that seemed to drop the temperature of the room to ice.

Zephan snapped his fingers. "Kolorim."

Kolorim jerked away as if from a trance, and marched to the nightstand and desk to gather a dozen books from the room. Avaya pulled back her shoulders and ran a thumb over the smoothness of the shell pendant at her neck. Zephan would test his newfound muscles as king, Azi had said. It was to be expected. Their time would come, and until then, the fullness of their power must remain discrete.

Had it really come to this? Grief had plagued her dreams of late, as her parent's faces swam before her memory, and the searing pain of her siblings' rejection weighed upon her shoulders. Avaya stood stock still, the picture of elegance and indifference, her eyes following Zephan as he strode from the room with his entourage of swordsmen.

But even as she blinked back tears her uncle would find unsuitable, even as she swallowed hard against the lump lodged in her throat, the lines of the ancient prophecy brought her comfort.

Her solemn strength is weathered wild even as she grieves.

Who but she had experienced as great a grief? *Uprooted Myansara* ... the flower of old, named for its resilience and offered to the queens of Jannemar. Avaya had been ripped from her home. She had traveled to another kingdom to fight for both her own land and the lands of her neighbor.

She was indeed called to greater aims. The question now lay in whether Zephan would be wise, and make her a friend, or unwise. Avaya loved her siblings. But if her two naive siblings' favor were the sacrifices she must offer—the cost of a promise of nations, the cost of peace—she would gladly pay it.

Avaya stared into the void, the emptiness of her guest chamber doorway where Zephan had so self-righteously made his departure. They were close now, to the final piece of the puzzle. In the face of Zephan's foolishness, Avaya's true cunning would shine like a star. It was under *her* power, not his, that the kingdoms of Jannemar and Belvidore would unite, and peace would reign throughout the land.

One day, not far from now, he would see her for who she really was—who she was born to be. The ancients of old had foreseen it, though she herself had not realized the truth until recent times.

And who was she?

Her Majesty, Queen Avaya of Jannemar and Belvidore, empress of the lands south of the sea, born of adversity through her mother, and of royalty through her father. The bridal queen, dressed in red, bought with blood, the bridge between two kingdoms and the only person alive with a rightful claim to two thrones.

The crimson queen.

18

ZEPHAN

A roar shook the castle, and somewhere a servant screamed. Zezura never roared on the grounds, but then again, Zezura never used to prowl the outer wards or perch on the bastions. It was Rotokas haunting Shamaran Castle, and the shadow of his dark presence hovered in the thoughts of every man, woman, and child for miles around. Rotokas unfurled massive wings and took off toward Qalea. It was the first time he had set his sights on the city since taking up roost, as it were, at Shamaran.

What did it mean? What was really going on behind the curtain, in the castle on the cliff where Jannemar's young new king sat on a fragile throne?

But the question in Zephan's mind now was much more specific. Kolorim stood before him in the formal throne room, hands clasped behind his back, jaw and shoulders tense, mouth shut as he waited for his king to address him. Zephan had gone directly from Avaya's chambers to the throne room, explicitly for this purpose. A few key members of court were present, but it was an intimate affair.

Zephan had sent Kolorim away from his guard while he

conferred with his advisers, and had brought him in with a formal summons just moments prior. Staring at Kolorim now, Zephan wondered how honest the man would be in a setting like this. And was it really so bad, a moment of doubt, a moment of questioning, followed by obedience?

But he knew the answer already. In his training as a soldier, Zephan learned that a moment's indecision was all that it took. Men died in moments. Wars began with moments.

Gaulen would not have hesitated. Monac would not have hesitated. And who deserved to belong to the king's personal guard but the best of the best?

Zephan took a deep breath, but even as he let it out, the twisting in his gut did not ease. He clenched his jaw and looked up at the guard. "How long have you served in the king's service?"

"Seven years, Your Majesty."

"Longer than some. Shorter than many." Zephan pursed his lips. "And what oaths did you swear upon entering this prestigious position?"

"To serve my king, at any cost. To put the mission first. To press ever forward in the face of danger, and give my knowledge, my skill, and my life, for the sake of the crown."

Kolorim rattled it off with ease. But keeping such oaths was not so easy. Zephan leaned forward. "Whose crown?"

"The king."

"Which king?"

"The king of Jannemar, occupant of the throne you fill, Your Majesty." Kolorim swallowed, the only hint of discomfort from the practiced soldier.

"And yet you hesitated to carry out a direct, simple order from your king. One that was not dangerous at all."

Kolorim's jaw clenched again, and Zephan arched an eyebrow. "Do you disagree? Is obeying me so dangerous? Do you so fear our"—here Zephan nearly choked on bile at the word —"guests?"

The guard shifted his weight. "There are concerns named in your halls these last days, Your Majesty."

Zephan's eyes flashed. "There are always concerns in the halls of any monarch. Yours will do, at present."

"They take note ... they say ..." Kolorim stared at his boots, then raised his gaze once more to his king. "You do not have a dragon."

A murmur rolled through Zephan's courtiers. Count Darbune's face flushed beet red, and General Soldan's eyes turned to flint. Zephan took in his nobles' displeasure, and it matched the sourness of his own stomach. Things were delicate. He could not be so unfair as to lose the loyalty of his men. But he could not be so soft as to lose their respect.

He was king.

Zephan drew his sword and examined it, letting the sun from the tall windows lining the hall to glint off its perfect steel and bounce to the goldleaf covered pillars and polished marble floor. When he looked at Kolorim again, his eyes blazed like smelled in a molten furnace. Zephan slammed his blade home in its scabbard to the hilt, the ring of the steel emanating down the hall.

"I may not have a dragon. But you don't have a job. Get out."

The guard's composure faltered. He opened his mouth, but no sound came.

"Is hesitation your greatest skill? This ruling is better than treason. You leave with your head attached." Zephan's mouth flattened and his tone turned to ice. "Accept my mercy before it sours. Am I not still king?"

Kolorim bowed. "It has been an honor, my king." The guard's voice broke as he said the last word, and he fled from

Zephan's presence as swiftly as the decorum of that great hall allowed.

Zephan nodded at two of his guards, and they broke away from their formation to escort Kolorim out. The knot in Zephan's stomach doubled in size. Soldan gave him a reassuring nod. The nobles bowed and made their exits as he dismissed them, Zephan himself following as soon as the hall was emptied.

The echoes of heavy footwear on marble floors were left behind for the rhythmic *thud* of the same on wood. Zephan stormed down the corridor, borne on the urgency of an overwhelmed mind, and paused at last outside the king's chambers. *His* chambers. Had they really belonged to him for two months already?

Zephan turned the carved doorknob—a dragonhead framed with spears and nezil myansara flowers—and stepped into the room. He entered a receiving room of sofas, chairs, and comfortable reclining, the bedroom off to the side. But there, through the pillars, his private meeting room and its empty conference table plagued his every waking moment.

Every undistracted second, each miserable hour as the hostage king, he saw Azi and his capricious sister sitting at that table. He saw Semra and Aviama sitting across from him, Semra paralyzed by fear of the dragonlord who had slaughtered her parents and made her part of an assassin army when she was too young to have a choice. Her face, drained of blood, eyes wild, filled him with a sorrow that words could not articulate.

He'd never known a stronger woman than Semra. No one was so fearless, so bold—reckless, yes, but courageous too. No one had such spirit, such fire, as she did. To see it squashed had taken his breath away.

She had faced him before, in the very throne room he'd

just left. Somehow, in this setting where her knives would do her no good, she'd been flattened into the floor. The pain of sending her away, and the victory of getting Semra and Aviama out of Azi's reach, swirled in an endless battle battering his brain.

What was she doing now? Were they safe? Did the documents make it out with them?

Semra would want to come back for him. It was against her character not to. It was only a matter of time before Azi was in position to kill Zephan, and they both knew it. And with magic inexplicably on Azi's side, Semra didn't stand a chance.

Which is why Zephan had to be faster than either Azi or Semra.

Zephan retraced his steps to the door and called for Monac, his childhood friend and one of his most trusted guards and soldiers. Monac appeared, the door shut behind him, and they were alone. His friend stood at attention, the picture of professionalism. But it wasn't the soldier Zephan so desperately needed in that moment.

Two long strides was all it took to clasp the man in tight embrace. Monac stumbled back at his fervency, then crushed Zephan's ribs in a returning hug. They stood like that for several minutes. Zephan's chest heaved, and a sob shook his shoulders.

Monac clapped him on the back. "You made the right call."

Zephan drew back and ran a hand over his face. He nodded with a grunt. "I know. I think." He ran a hand through his hair and sighed.

A moment was all he could afford. The king must return to the forefront. "Azi and Avaya are looking for something. I can only assume the books left out for us to find were decoys, and nothing useful, but search them anyway, and then bring them to me. Inform the guard that Her Majesty Queen Avaya is the queen of another nation, not the princess they are used to gossiping in the halls. She is not in her old room, but in guest quarters, to highlight this fact. My sister is a visiting dignitary without authority in Jannemar."

Monac ran a hand across his nose and dipped his head in a curt nod. "Of course."

"Has our jeweler been approached?"

"Azi offered him a deal, yes. He's working on it, with the changes you requested."

Zephan nodded. "Good. If anything shows up with my signet ring symbol on it, alert me immediately."

19

A feather could have knocked Semra over. Siler gestured at two chairs opposite him at the table. Garbane grunted and leaned against the wall, leaving the chairs for Semra and Aviama. By the tenseness of his shoulders, Semra figured Garbane hadn't known about Siler being here. Maybe he knew where Pidge worked but had never gone inside.

Why had he come back to Qalea? He hadn't sought a pardon from the king as Pidge had, and therefore hadn't gotten any trade training arranged by the crown as part of the agreement. Then again, Siler would probably rather die than apprentice for a regular job. Not unless it was a cover.

Semra took her seat. "It's good to see you."

Siler stared at her for a long moment, but what his thoughts were, she couldn't hope to guess. There was a time when she thought the two of them were similar, but not so much anymore. Her stomach dropped.

He gave a small, earnest smile. "It's good to see you too. I guess you can't stay pent up in the castle even when you try. I'm glad."

Semra smiled back. "I'm surprised to see you."

An understatement. Complete and utter bamboozlement would have been a better description, though she wasn't about to say it out loud.

Pidge set down her boxes, slid the one from the tavern toward Siler, and walked around the table to sit in the chair next to him. Siler opened the box, and his eyes lit up. He plucked out a cherry pastry and slid the box back to Pidge. She selected a lemon cake and leaned back in her chair.

Aviama's stomach growled, and Semra glared at her. She hated to seem in need, even if the girl's body couldn't help but protest its lack of lunch. Besides, they *weren't* in need. Not for food anyway.

Garbane snatched the cloth bundle from Aviama's arms and set it on the table. "I thought you might need this on the road, but it looks like we'll be here long enough for you to eat a morsel. Go ahead."

Aviama dipped her head and untied the bundle. "Thank you."

Semra and Aviama tore into the provisions Garbane had packed, and Semra looked up at Siler as she swallowed her first bite of bread. "Business must be good to dine on desserts."

Siler shrugged. "People keep having events, and signing documents, and getting married. It's a good occupation to be in."

"Rats and rot, you really officiate?" Semra laughed. "And from there you learn what, exactly? Where the couple will live, how wealthy they are, and which aging family members have income they wouldn't miss?"

"Oh, it's all totally legitimate, I'll have you know," Siler said, waving the pastry in her direction. He took another bite, not bothering to swallow before continuing. "And very boring."

Pidge leaned forward and dropped her voice to a near whisper. "But with Rotokas up at the castle and you and a princess down here with us ... dragons and daylilies, yours is the story that needs telling!"

Semra and Aviama quickly filled them in on the events of the morning that led to their flight from the castle. By the time they finished, Pidge's eyes were wide as saucers. "I can't believe Azi's free. He'll take over Jannemar. He would never risk such exposure for anything else."

Siler eyed Semra. "Princey won't live long in there."

Semra's breath hitched. "I know. That's why I have to get Aviama out safe and figure out how to stop them, fast. I need someone who knows about magic. Ancient magic."

Garbane shook his head. "Leave that to me. I'm going to give you a name and location, remember? But these two can get you out of Qalea without a dragon, and I'll wager they'll take care of just about anything else you might need."

"You've already got clothes." Pidge licked the last of the lemon cake from her fingers. "What's left?"

Semra looked at Siler. He spread his hands. "Name it."

"I need help getting out of Qalea, wherever Garbane has in mind. And I need a prophecy. Avaya had a scrap of one—I know there's more to it, but I'm not sure where."

Semra nodded at Aviama, and the princess dug out the torn parchment and read it:

Great the dangers that are loosed when rise what laid to rest;
None but seed of flower planted could restrain it best.
Crimson queen shall open door protecting all from shame,
Then guarding it forevermore, he of the same great name.

"We think the crimson queen is Avaya, and Azi—another Shamaran, he of the same great name—is to guard it, whatever it is." Aviama folded the paper. "How do we foil a prophecy?"

Siler held out a hand. "Let me see that." He scanned the parchment. "If magic really is back, even just a little, that would be a great danger loosed, wouldn't it?"

Pidge dropped her chin into her palm. "If we can find out how they loosed magic, maybe we can ... I don't know, capture it again?"

"But they didn't release *magic*. If they had, wouldn't magic be popping up everywhere?" Semra grimaced. Maybe magic didn't return as widespread as it once was. Maybe it came back slowly. Maybe that's what was going on with her smoke. But who ever heard of a melder with powers of smoke? No, that had to be dragon related.

"There are remnants of magic in the world." Garbane stroked his beard. "But they're rarely recorded, even in the last several hundred years. I'll poke around and see what I can find. Coanor has verses of old things lying about—maybe she'll have an idea where the original prophecy is. If not, my friend that I'm sending you to knows much more about ancient things than I do. He can help."

Siler crossed his arms. "You also need a way to communicate with the castle. Secure messages that don't rely on the chandler here. We may have a lead on that."

Semra nodded, then paused. The scrap of paper wasn't the only thing Aviama had hidden in her bodice. And if anything happened to them, the hope of a nation would be lost. "We also need copies of documents."

Siler cocked his head. "Copies?"

"I use the word loosely. We need additional ... originals." She arched her eyebrows, and couldn't help the smile that crept over her face.

Pidge's hand flew to her chest and she gasped in mock

distress. "We are reformed, and our business is entirely legitimate!"

Aviama snorted. "Even I am not dumb enough to believe that."

"Catching on, are you?" Siler grinned. "Well then, let me teach you another rule about the world out here—we help you, you keep your mouth shut. You keep our secrets; we keep yours. It's a good deal too, because yours are far more dangerous than ours."

Pidge clapped her hands. "I've missed a good old-fashioned blackmail. It keeps people honest, don't you think?"

"How long does it take to work on high-caliber forgeries of the king's own hand?"

Siler sobered. "You wouldn't."

Semra needed a backup plan, to protect Zephan's edicts, but she couldn't leave them here with Siler and his crew. As much as she wished she could, she didn't entirely trust Siler, and his 'employees' even less so. "As long as I pay you, what does it matter?"

Siler pursed his lips. "I'm not saying *I* wouldn't. But *you* certainly wouldn't. You haven't stolen anything of his, and you wouldn't commit treason. You don't have it in you. Does he know?"

Garbane eyed her quizzically, and Aviama's eyes grew wide. Aviama knew the truth about the documents she was hiding, but she didn't know what Semra was up to.

Semra leaned forward. "How long?"

Siler sighed and leaned back in his chair. "The most important part is getting the right paper. If we have the originals on hand, and don't need to piece other handwriting samples together, that helps. But if these are official documents, that still leaves the signet ring."

"Can you do it?"

"Of course I can."

"Come with me. I'll pay you. I won't leave the documents with you, and I can't stay."

Siler spread his hands. "I can't leave my operation. I'm the copyist. Copyists don't get work, even to pass off to protégés, without a master to contract with customers."

Semra grimaced. "Forgery isn't my forte. Pidge?"

Pidge shook her head. "I'm learning, but I don't have the experience for a job of that level."

Siler set his palms down on the table. "You know I want to help, but what kind of salary have you been earning that you can pay for this?"

Ah, yes. The truest love of Siler's heart. It was a good heart, overall. Probably. But money whispered sweet nothings to it whenever it really threatened to turn a new leaf. Semra looked at Aviama, and she sighed. "You'll be paid."

Siler winced. "Not quite what I wanted to hear."

Semra rolled her eyes. "He needs a deposit. The ring you were going to give to Garbane will do. Siler isn't so honorable as Garbane, and it'll be gone by afternoon, so it won't be traceable."

Aviama's eyes narrowed, but she withdrew the ring and handed it over.

Siler tossed it in the air and caught it. He turned it over and smiled. "Brilliant."

"Prep the documents, and I'll give you the contents when you're ready." Semra took a deep breath. "Now, can you get us out of Qalea?"

20

The sound of horse cart wheels over cobbled streets had lulled Semra half asleep in the last two hours, but now the *clip-clop* of horse hooves on stone transitioned to a quiet plodding, the cart swaying this way and that over uneven terrain. Blankets, bundled around them and tossed over their heads, staved off the night chill, and crates of what Siler had sworn were carpenter's tools rattled on either side of them.

Semra shook her head. The driver must have been in a hurry when he packed the crates, because he'd done a poor enough job that the sound of iron sliding against iron caught her ear. They were in a weapons transport. She'd decided not to share that piece of information with Aviama, and the princess had been blissfully dead to the world for the last three hours of riding.

Garbane had snuck out of the copyist shop as soon as he could manage, and Siler and Pidge had hidden Semra and Aviama while they made arrangements for getting them out of the city by night. The driver had reluctantly agreed to the added cargo after Siler buttered him up with extra *jemari* lining his pockets, on condition that they bail once they were safely outside the city. He had insisted that he wouldn't stop the cart and that the stowaways jump off before he reached his destination.

Semra shook Aviama. It was almost time.

A tug niggled at her through the mark on her chest. Zezura flew over Shamaran Castle in the cover of night, in one of the rare pockets of time when Rotokas receded from the wall to loom over some other forsaken place. This would be Zezura's last patrol before meeting Semra and Aviama tonight.

Semra reached to move aside the blanket over her head, but the dragon's call came again. Urgent. Semra dropped her hand.

What do you see?

No sooner had she sent the message, than her world tipped over and her vision dropped into the consciousness of the great beast. The phenomenon had happened enough times by now for her to know when Zezura was pulling her in to see what the dragon saw, but it still left a lurch in her stomach.

Shamaran Castle was stunning in the moonlight, its bright sandstone and swirling carriage roads winding down from the three gates in soft curves and lines that delighted the eye. The cliffs on the north side dropped away to the Shalladin river below, and the city of Qalea winked with lanternlight and evening fires down the hill to its south.

I didn't mean this, Semra grumbled. *A quick update would have sufficed.*

Zezura tossed her head and dropped altitude to fly by the guest quarter windows. Avaya and Azi bent over a table of papers, too engrossed in their work to notice the silent flier outside. Zez rounded Ancestry Hall, dipped over the river, and skimmed the trees on the west side before ascending back up toward the king's chambers.

Semra's heart pounded. If she looked in his window, what would she find? What did Zezura want her to see?

Images flashed through her mind. Zephan, dead on the floor, poisoning. Zephan, slumped against the wall, arrow through the heart. A thousand scenarios cycled through her brain.

A rush of air fled from her lungs in relief as he came into view. The king sat at his desk pouring over parchments and books by lantern light. It struck her then how similar his activity was to Azi and Avaya on the other side of the castle keep. But where the two of them were more animated, Zephan sat with his head in his hands. His shoulders drooped; his sandy hair was disheveled, and his eyes were closed.

A deep pain seized Semra by the gullet, and she nearly choked on the lump in her throat. *He's alone. And he can't hope to win.* More than anything in that moment, Semra wished she could be there in person with him—to wrap her arms around him, bury her head in his chest, hold him. She wished she could dance with him the way they sometimes did when the world was aflame, to see the stress slide away as he grasped onto something familiar and lovely in the steps.

Zezura hovered outside Zephan's window and bumped her nose to the glass. Zephan jerked his head up, bleary eyes staring into the darkness. He squinted out the window, then slowly rose and crossed the room to it. With a soft *click* he unlatched the window and swung it open.

"Zez?"

The dragon beat its wings, holding space in the air outside the room of the man Semra so desperately wished to see with her own eyes. Would he know she was here, seeing him, when all he could see was reptilian eyes and scales?

Zephan furrowed his brow. "Aren't you supposed to be with Semra? Is she okay?"

More beating of wings. More silence.

"What are you doing here?"

Semra gritted her teeth. *Do something!*

But Zezura did nothing.

Semra wanted to throw her hands up—if she *had* hands in the dragon's body to move. She wanted to reach through that serpent's skull and open its mouth and speak for herself. She wanted so many things.

Zephan's eyes narrowed. He took three paces away, spun back, and approached the window. The tenseness of his shoulders, the tight lines of his face, mirrored the frustration in Semra's own chest.

He leaned his elbows on the windowsill. "I know you must understand what I'm saying. At least, you understand enough. I've been around you long enough to know that much."

The dragon dipped her head in a nod. A piercing jab struck Semra's chest through the mark like a sword. *Direct me.*

Zephan peered at her. "Is she safe?"

Semra sent the direction, and Zezura dipped her head again. *Yes.*

"And Aviama?"

Yes.

Zephan breathed a sigh and nodded. "Okay. Good. Okay." He stared down at his hands, then looked up again. "Did she read the documents? Are they out of Qalea? Why are you still here?"

Semra groaned, and Zezura let out a grunt. *Too many questions.*

Zephan got the hint. He grimaced. "Right, okay. No human voice. Wait a minute ..." He gazed into the dragon's eyes, amber pools boring into slitted blue. "Is she spying on me?"

Zezura chuffed a throaty laugh.

Semra pursed her lips at the dragon. *Hey!*

Zephan grinned. "The prize I most want to protect, and she's set on protecting *me*. Is she as stubborn with you as she is with me?"

Something in Semra's stomach twisted, and an ache settled in her chest at his words. Zephan was like no one she'd ever known. The world wasn't deserving of a man with as pure a heart and as dedicated a hand as his. How he had landed on holding her in such regard, she would never know.

The young king cocked his head. "Semra?"

Yes! Yes. The dragon puffed a curl of black smoke.

"Are you in there? You're doing that thing ... you see what she sees."

Semra nodded, and Zezura followed her lead. *Yes.*

Zephan clapped his hands and beat the air with one fist in victory. "Yes! Okay. Okay, yes or no questions. I don't want to know where you are. But are you out of Qalea?"

Semra bit her lip. He wouldn't be happy with her answer, but they were working on it. Almost? Zezura tilted her body back and forth on the air.

"What does that mean? You can't be serious. Are you going to stay in the city?"

Semra shook her head. *No.*

"Good. If you did, I would kill you. Provided Azi doesn't beat me to it." Zephan rapped his knuckles on the sill, thinking. He glanced up, eyes alight. "I have something to tell you."

He ran to the desk, shuffled several papers, and returned scanning a ripped piece of paper. "We confiscated books from Avaya's room, and they were mostly redirects, decoys, nothing of consequence. But this—I don't think she meant for it to be mixed in."

Zephan smoothed out the parchment and lifted it up. It

was a sketch of a spear, with serrated edges and engraved with symbols of water, wind, and earth arranged in a blazing circle of fire. Handwriting filled the margins, with lines drawn to indicate various measurements and aspects of the weapon.

"I've never seen this before. I've seen paintings of the spear, of course, but never a labeled diagram. It's made entirely of metal, but not just any metal. *Wyronite* metal. It doesn't conduct heat."

Semra stared at the sketch. Zezura beat her wings. A single curl of black smoke puffed from the dragon's nose. *So what?*

"It's Aurin's spear. Aurin, the fireblood, responsible for destroying magic six hundred years ago. He did it with this." Zephan waved the sketch in the air. "They're going to find it. I know it. They're after power, *magical* power, and how better to get it than to retrieve the one thing powerful enough to stop the flow of magical energy at the origin of the world? They might be able to win without it. But with it, they would be unstoppable. This is what they're after. This is what they're waiting for."

A chill ran up Semra's spine. The Origin Wellspring. The place in the eastern mountains from which the Dezapi and Surion rivers splintered, the source of the creation of the world and the birthplace of magic. And to think that it was Aurin, a fireblood, forbidden to exist much less enter the Tabeun Tournaments of the nations, who had destroyed magic once and for all when he plunged his spear into the spring at The Crumbling all those years ago.

Could it really have happened as the legends claimed? Could this really be the spear? Was some other power at work, or was there really magic in the weapon itself, to effect such change on the fabric of the world? And if magic was released again, into a world with no memory of its use, what devastation would the dragonlord and his minion queen work upon the world?

Zephan's voice pulled her focus back to his earnest face. "Semra. If Azi and Avaya get their hands on Aurin's spear, all we can hope for is the mercy of a swift death."

Her stomach dropped. Mercy was not in Azi's repertoire.

21

The glimpse of Zephan from outside the window vanished and Semra was plunged into darkness as her consciousness was yanked back into the wagon. Stuffy blankets itched against her nose, and she had half a mind to sneeze. Icy fingers clamped down around her arms and shook her, hard. Aviama. She was trembling.

Semra gasped as she came to herself, still wishing for one last look into those golden eyes that could pierce her soul, that could draw her in even from miles away through the eyes of a dragon. What was she thinking? Her only hope for seeing Zephan again was Aurin's spear. They had to keep Avaya and Azi from finding it. She had to get to it first.

If she found it, could she wield it to overpower Avaya's magic and take back the kingdom? What if the magic was too strong—would it kill her? Was it even visible, or had it been sucked down into the wellspring and lodged itself somewhere in the core of the world?

A deep raspy voice cut through the night, and Semra stilled. "I haven't got 'til daybreak. What's the hold up?"

The wagon creaked, and a voice rumbled from the seat up

front. "You're short three hundred *jemari*. You'll get what you asked for when you pay what you promised."

"You think I care two figs what I promised after what you pulled? I don't do meetings with newcomers. You knew that. What kind of operation you running? I gave myself a discount for the inconvenience. We had to kill the kid after he saw our faces."

Semra's chest tightened. Her encounter with Zezura had cost them time. Time they were supposed to use for jumping from the cart and running for the hills before the drop. Aviama's nails dug into Semra's arm, and she winced. Semra eased her hand down her own leg and up her skirt, resting her fingers on the hilt of a throwing knife.

Come to me.

Zezura wheeled away from the castle, but Semra and Aviama had been traveling for several hours. She wasn't close enough.

The blanket ripped away in a single smooth motion, and Aviama fell to one side. Semra's fingers slipped from the knife handle as Aviama's hands on Semra's arm jerked sideways, pulling her over. The cart had stopped in the outskirts of the woods. The late-night firelight of the city could still be seen dotting the hill beyond the tree line. Four men blinked back at the two women before them. The one in the front drew a dagger and grinned, revealing a chipped tooth.

"Looks like the next shipment will be free, or I'm sending the boss your head on a platter."

Semra tossed her mussed hair over her shoulder and straightened. "Don't look a gift horse in the mouth. Drivers are pawns for hire; he didn't even check his cargo. My employer wants to know if you're ready to level up."

Going for the knife off the bat was impulsive. If she was

quick enough with her wit, maybe she wouldn't have to be so quick with her blade.

Chipped Tooth sneered at her and licked his lips. "Want to know what I think, little missy? I think you look like a sewer rat. You're just trying to survive, but this game's too big for you."

Semra's heart hammered, but she plastered on an impish grin and hopped off the cart to stand just inches from Chipped Tooth's nose. "You know what rats are good at, bumpkin? They are at home in the dark. They patter through every forsaken cranny and are found among rich and poor alike. And they never seem to die."

Chipped Tooth leaned away from her, his smile shaken and uneasy, the whites of his eyes bright against the night. Semra snatched his dagger in one smooth motion and held it to his throat. "What about you? Are you a rat?"

A murmur ran through the watching men, and three blades surrounded her. Chipped Tooth laughed, but there was a chill to the sound. Semra smirked and spun the dagger, thrusting the handle into the man's stomach and patted him on the back. "The choice is yours. Take your little trinkets and toy swords. Keep bumbling on with the idiots you work with now. Or tell your boss he can make three times as much working with *my* boss."

Chipped Tooth arched an eyebrow. "Who's your boss?"

Semra backed away and shrugged. "Be back here in two days' time. If you accept the offer, you'll get a healthy advance on a deal. If not, well, you must not have the stones for this sort of job anyway."

The driver stared at her, mouth agape, and the four men stood in open shock. Semra caught Aviama's eye and jerked her head. *Let's go.*

Aviama scrambled off the cart with less grace than Semra

had hoped—it didn't exactly scream dangerous gangster—and Semra backed away from the group, eyes boring into Chipped Tooth as she went. "Two days. Same time, same place. Don't be late."

Semra backed away until they were out of sight, then gripped Aviama by the arm and strode away as swiftly and purposefully as she imagined an unpanicked person might go. As soon as they were far enough away for night sounds to cover their escape, Semra pulled Aviama in and dropped her voice low. "Run."

They ran. Leaves crunched underfoot, and a branch snapped against Semra's cheek as she turned to help Aviama over a fallen log. Goosebumps rose down her arms, but it wasn't just the chill of the air. Semra had been incapacitated during her episode with Zezura. Aviama could've been killed. If the arms dealers had been more experienced or less cowardly, they probably would've been. She couldn't take those kinds of risks. But Zezura had insisted, and once she'd seen Zephan, Semra had *needed* to be there with him at the castle.

And now she knew what Azi and Avaya wanted.

They ran until Aviama dragged behind, wheezing and puffing for air, and then pressed on at a brisk walk for another hour after that. When Semra was satisfied, they climbed a tree and rested there until the leaves around them shook abominably as if the sky itself was collapsing around them. Zezura descended to the forest floor, Semra and Aviama slid down from the tree and onto her back, and the final hours of darkness were spent climbing above the trees and pulling further and further away from Qalea.

Further from danger.

Further from Zephan.

For every breath that came easier, knowing Aviama was

out of harm's way, another one hitched in her chest because by following Zephan's directive, she abandoned him as the last sane member of his family in Shamaran Castle. Three Shamarans now slept under that famous roof, and Semra supposed each of the three considered themselves the rightful ruler.

There was only one thing left to do—run to the name and place Garbane had given her, learn about Aurin's spear, and keep it out of Azi and Avaya's hands. Maybe even use it against them to protect Zephan's life and reign. The faster she ran from Qalea, the faster she'd be running back.

Aviama did not travel well. She got hungry almost immediately after provisions were eaten, and she often talked when she should've been sleeping.

"Rats and rot, complaining about how tired you are isn't going to give you any more energy," Semra said one morning.

"Maybe not, but it staves off the mind-numbing boredom," Aviama grumbled. "You know you don't talk much when you travel? I thought you'd be having all these grand bonding adventures, but I think your greatest accomplishment on days like these are not feeling the rocks and roots in your back when you're trying to sleep."

Semra shrugged. "Maybe you should make sure you don't lie down where there are so many rocks."

"There are rocks *everywhere*."

"We're outdoors."

"Yes, well, being outdoors is overrated." Aviama slouched against a tree trunk, plucking dirt from underneath her fingernails. "Besides, the great outdoors might feed deer, and birds, and mice, and bugs, but there's not a single thing out here suitable for humans. I'm hungry."

It took a full seven days as the dragon flew to reach the other side of the mountains. Semra replayed Garbane's message in her mind for the thousandth time. "*Frigibar*

Curmody is hidden away within a day's journey to Ellix. The trees get larger and larger that direction ... visit the mammoth tree on the far side of the mountains, in the valley by the lake. And don't knock. Throw rocks at the windows—two high, one low."

What kind of insane man were they going to meet? Semra had had her fill of paranoia with King Arnevon, but he *had* been assassinated, after all. And she'd been called paranoid herself, which she'd deemed ridiculous since the threat to her life was real. There remained only two options: either the man was out of his mind, or dangerous people wanted him dead. If the first, how much help could he be? And if the second, how could she put the crown princess at risk of being caught in the crosshairs?

But then, why did Garbane send her here? He'd sent her off with nothing but a name, location, and quick letter that he'd demanded was for Frigibar's eyes only. And yet, there were few people Semra trusted as much as Garbane. Turian had made the list—before his death. Zephan. That was pretty much the end of the list.

She trusted Aviama, as far as that Aviama wanted good things to happen for Semra and would never purposefully harm her. She lacked any practical skill, but was a sweet friend, if not a bit naive. In contrast, Semra trusted Siler's skill, but not always his intentions. He didn't want to see Semra dead, but had aided in her capture and watched her be beaten.

Pidge was similar but had gone above and beyond for Semra, despite the fact Semra first ran into her while she was under contract to kill Turian. Zezura had plucked her off the castle wall and the two had fought, before Pidge abandoned her mission and followed Semra instead.

Semra had been betrayed by people close to her before. Almost everyone, really. But Zephan and Garbane had proved hearts of gold that left Semra wondering why they allowed her blood-soaked reputation to infiltrate their lives and be friends.

But they were friends, and Semra would choose to trust. And so she sent Zezura flying at night over the mountain and valley below, dropping into the vision of the dragon. Zezura would be too conspicuous during the day, and Semra's vision wasn't sharp enough at night, nor did she trust her ability to hold onto the dragon while sharing Zezura's eyesight. So she settled for the great reptile's night vision through the link of the dragon's kiss.

The tops of the mountains were bare, all rock and wind and craggy heights. Ellix was built into the mountainside down where trees six and ten feet wide cropped up here and there, and grass and moss softened the paths for men and animals alike to go about their business. Further still, in the valley, the circle of the surrounding mountains was inverted in the water of the lake, the moon and stars blinking up at her, interrupted only by the ripple of the water and the shadow of the dragon overhead.

There.

Zezura banked over the lake and caught a southward current of air, evening out over the water, sharp eyes intent on the trees ahead. A collection of the largest trees Semra had ever seen grew at the edge of the lake at the base of the mountain, putting the ones in Ellix to shame. They stretched along the bank and partway up the mountain before coming to an abrupt stop.

Semra scanned the tree line. Any one of them would be monstrous if it grew anywhere else. *Thanks, Garbane. They're all mammoth trees.* How was she supposed to find any one in particular?

If she were hiding away, where would she be? Semra

groaned. *Probably not in the most attention-grabbing trees known to man. In a valley. With low visibility of the land above.*

She was missing something.

Zezura coasted toward the towering boughs, pulled in her wings, and descended through *branches* as thick as the *trunk* of any respectable tree anywhere else. A flash of vibrant color, in the range of colors known only to dragons, snatched at her attention. In Semra's mind's eye, through her connection with Zezura, she could see them, though had she been there in person she would've been oblivious to its beauty.

Brilliant shades of an unknown hue painted the bark of a tree twenty to thirty feet across, and as Zezura stretched her neck toward it, movement flashed from above. The dragon puffed a curl of smoke and rose on her hind legs, stretching her enormous frame to its full height, a claw on the trunk of the tree. Invisible from a distance, Semra now saw windows embedded in the sides of the tree on three different levels.

Zezura lifted her snout and came nearly nose to nose with the silhouette of a man, dim light from the room beyond casting him in darkness. His eyes glinted from features shrouded in shadow, boring into the dragon with neither warmth nor fear.

Semra's mouth went dry. The man who held the key to finding Aurin's spear and saving the world from Azi's evil was a hostile hermit. Garbane's warning came to her again. *Don't knock.*

What unfortunate death awaited anyone who dared approach the front door?

The figure in the window vanished, and the light inside went out.

22

———

Mist rose over the lake as the dawn broke soft through emerald leaves. After Zezura's searching expedition last night, the dragon had returned to camp, picked up Semra and Aviama, and delivered them to the cover of the towering trees south of the lake just before daybreak. There would be no sleeping so close to the suspicious man in the tree.

Semra held her hand out to Aviama over a snarl of roots and a steep hill, but Aviama shook her head. The princess snatched up her skirts with one hand, steadied herself with the other on the ground, and slipped and skidded her way down the incline on her own.

Aviama tripped once, recovered, and smoothed out week old, dirt-stained skirts. "I'm not totally incompetent, you know."

"I never said you were." Semra resisted the urge to pull thorns away from snagging Aviama's dress. No need to be patronizing. She'd figure it out. Semra half ran down the next slope and stopped at the bottom to wait. *You do castle life just fine. It's the basic survival skills part that I question.*

"I know I can't fight. I'm dead weight for anything important. I guess it's a good thing I was left behind before, for all your adventures off saving the kingdom." She bit her lip, then jutted her chin forward.

Semra sighed. Couldn't she have waited to be insecure about all this until after they made it to Frigibar's alive? They were close now, though Semra wasn't sure how easily recognizable the place would be from the ground.

Zezura, who had been watching Aviama's progress with a keen eye, dropped to her belly and slid down the slope behind them. Her head hit a tree, spinning her sideways, and her tail snapped a sapling in two. The dragon shook her head and chuffed out a laugh. Semra smiled. They'd both missed the woods. What comforts did Aviama have at home that she was missing?

"You're not trained as a warrior, but you have a different kind of strength, I think. And for being raised in silks, you've adapted to dirt pretty well." Semra grimaced and glanced at the princess's downcast face, racking her brain for helpful things to say. "You're diplomatic, and kind, and honest."

Aviama pursed her lips. "Rulers of countries don't do a good job because they're *nice*. I'm a better option than Avaya, but I'm still not a *good* option. I don't have a clue what I'm doing. So Zephan can't die."

Semra sobered. She wasn't wrong. Aviama wasn't prepared to rule, and she cared too much about other people's opinions to stand up for herself as a queen must. But there was something about her that made everyone love her, and the way she'd jumped into character to play the guard outside the conservatory, and maintained most of her composure before Azi and Avaya in the king's chambers, and willingly put on rough-spun wool ... well, for Aviama, these were tremendous steps. Who knew but that she would rise to the occasion and become something great, if only given the chance?

"And you have to marry him." Aviama skipped once beside her, and Semra jerked her head toward her.

"What?"

"Yes. And have babies. And then *those* kids will be in line for the throne. And then I won't ever have to worry about being queen, and I can figure out something else to do with my pitiful life that's more realistic and doesn't give me way more responsibility than I can handle."

Semra's jaw dropped, and her insides squirmed in seven different directions. Zezura nudged her hand, and Semra stroked the slick, smooth scales of her nose. The signet ring of the king sat heavy on her finger, the imprint of Jannemar's emblem burning against the inside of her hand where she'd twisted it inward.

"Queens don't have to be fighters, Aviama." Semra's throat constricted, and she swallowed. "That's why the monarch has armies and bodyguards. Yes, kings are traditionally trained for war, but a queen's primary duty is to the kingdom's rule. You would preside over decisions of commerce, law, and diplomacy. You know the rules of elite circles, and your reputation is spotless.

"No, you wouldn't know everything when you start, if something happened and you had to take the throne. But you have a court of strategists and nobles to help you. General Soldan would be an invaluable tool for you. Surround yourself with the right people, and you'll make it. But me ..."

A twig snapped underfoot, and Semra winced. She'd been so consumed by the thought of kings and queens—how careless and heavy she'd been walking!

What if Zephan did survive, and he did propose? *This is not the ring I wanted to give you.* Her heart battered her rib cage, and her breathing quickened. To have a life with someone she trusted, even someone she loved, was more than she'd ever deemed possible. Scourge, there hadn't been hardly anyone *to* trust in her life before.

But she was unsuitable for rule, even as a queen standing behind her king. What would she do?

"I'm tainted, Avs. Your father pardoned me, but I'm an assassin. How could the people accept an assassin queen? How could other nations respect Jannemar with a murderer sitting on the judgment seat? What right have I to any authority over others?"

Spirals of black smoke seeped from her fingers. Zezura puffed at them, and the ebony swirled away, dissipating into the air overhead. Semra stared at her hands. "I can't even control my own body. I don't know what this is inside me or how to keep it in check. I'm a liability. So stay alive and keep your wits about you, because your country may need you yet."

Aviama tilted her chin to watch the last of the smoke disappear. "You said ruling isn't something I know, but can learn, with the right people around me. Well, maybe your weird magicness is like that. You didn't used to know you could see stuff Zezura sees, but now you can. Who knows what else you might learn?"

Semra mulled over her words, but her gut told her she had no right to rule. What hypocrisy would she have to have to take on that responsibility? If she could marry Dahyu, she would do it. But Zephan came with royal regulations and requirements. Pressures and threats of death that would never end. Could she ever give up looking over her shoulder?

Don't be a fool. You'll look over your shoulder every day for the rest of your life no matter where you are.

Aviama stubbed her toe on a root in the ground and yelped. Semra snapped her head sideways to check on her, and saw Aviama had been studying her face so carefully she'd forgotten to watch her own footing. The princess sighed. "Please just think about the queen thing. You're still a much better choice than I am. You're strong and brave. And what will you do if you don't? You'll break all our hearts if you leave, you know. No pressure."

It was more than she could think about right now. Semra ran a hand over her face. "You would do fine, and hopefully Zephan will live a long life, and you won't have to worry about it. Stop overthinking things. You'll feel better once you've had something to eat."

Aviama perked up. "You think the man in the tree will have food?"

"If he's been living out here, I do assume he eats food regularly."

Aviama rolled her eyes, and her shoulders deflated a little. A pang hit Semra's stomach. *Lighten up. She's an orphan with her siblings back home close to fighting to the death. She's not in the mood to take sarcasm well.*

Semra cleared her throat. "Sorry. I was just kidding. We can't know for sure if he'll offer us breakfast, but if he's willing to read Garbane's letter, I assume he'll receive us. Why else would Garbane have sent us here, if he didn't think Frigibar would help us?"

The wood thickened as they descended, and the lake grew nearer. Semra had never seen a grove like this one. What kind of soil or what kind of seeds grew a tree to such widths and heights? The closer they got to the water, the bigger and more wizened they looked, jutting out in harsh angles or reaching overhead to one another like old women meeting again at last after decades apart.

Semra turned to Zezura, who was sniffing the air and

popping up to compare herself to the pillars around them. It wasn't every day that a dragon felt small.

"Okay, Zez. Where is it? It's marked by some color we can't see, isn't it?"

Zezura bounded her fifty-foot body ahead of them, poking her snout this way and that.

Aviama giggled so hard she snorted. "I thought dragons were supposed to be scary! She's just so *big,* she's always scared me. But right now she looks like an oversized fluffy bunny."

Semra laughed. The light of day was good for the soul, and the adventure of meeting the mysterious tree man added a spring to her step. The best days were days like today, spent with people she cared about, laughing here and there as they went, with a decent dose of danger sprinkled in to get the blood pumping.

Zezura snorted and tossed her head, flashing her scales red and green before settling her color back to her usual aquamarine and rose quartz patterning. *I've found it.*

Aviama trudged forward, but Semra held out a hand. She lifted her skirt and drew a single throwing knife from her thigh, then dropped the ends of her stupid dress and hunted for three small, smooth stones. They circled the tree, and Semra again marveled at the size of it.

She'd known it was big when she saw it through Zezura's eyes last night, but from her human height down on the ground, it seemed even wider and taller. Several windows let in light on each broad side of the tree and seemed to be placed across three levels. Around the northern side, facing the lake, a gentle winding of branches and roots created an archway, and a rounded door was set three feet beyond, inside the trunk.

It looked like a painting, the elegance of it was so precise. The archway and the door were both too smooth to be carved, but too natural to be designed by any architect. Though made from the tree itself, it certainly couldn't have grown that way.

Semra cocked her head to scan the windows, but she saw no movement. She raised the three rocks and threw them against the glass of the windows according to Garbane's instructions: high, high, low. Third story twice, bottom level once.

She waited.

Nothing.

Aviama shuffled her feet, and Zezura stretched to peer into the second-story window. Semra whirled the knife in her hands, then second-guessed herself. A hermit expecting trouble wouldn't take kindly to people with weapons and a dragon. She sheathed her knife and straightened. If Semra ever managed to live somewhere alone, she would be equally suspicious. The whole scenario was highly unusual.

A light creak came from above. Semra scanned the windows for movement, but noticed the narrow slitted window hidden against the knobs of the tree a moment too late. A whisper of wind, a rustle of leaves, and the flash of an arrow tip—and the arrow left the string.

23

———

Semra yelled, and Aviama screamed. Zezura extended her wings in front of them, and the arrow hit the dragon in her well-armored chest and fell to the ground. Zezura opened her mouth and let out a rush of flame, white-hot fire licking the wood of the house.

"No! Stop!" Semra gave the dragon a hearty shove that the beast likely only barely felt. Even so, she sent a puff of smoke after the fire and snapped her jaws. Semra glanced nervously at the house in the tree, but nothing had caught fire. And no more arrows flew.

Semra climbed up on Zezura and stood on the spikes of her sides, bringing her closer to the second level where the arrow had come from. "Hey! I'm not sure who you're hiding from or who you think we are, but I'll have you know we're *trying* to come peacefully, and our friend Garbane Yaskir told us to come. I can't imagine there are two people as crazy as you living out here, so we must be in the right place—you must be Frigibar. I have a letter from Garbane. We don't want any trouble."

There was a beat of silence, then a window on the second

level cracked open and a low, husky voice called down to them. "This isn't my traditional way of collecting mail."

Semra spread her hands, lifting them high enough to prove they were empty. "This isn't our traditional way of asking for help, but here we are."

She craned her neck toward the window, but saw no one. Glancing down, she gestured Aviama to stand behind Zezura, and the princess hurried to obey.

"It's not every day that a dragonlord asks for help at all." A hand flung the window open wide, and a hooded figure stepped into view. The night before, through Zezura's vision, she'd only seen his silhouette and the light catching in hard, intense eyes. Now, his features were more apparent.

Flint-gray eyes set deep into the wrinkled, leathery skin of a man exposed to too many summers, with the solemn certainty of a man who had weathered too many winters. Bushy gray eyebrows matched a long gray beard streaked with white, but when he leaned his forearms on the windowsill, the strength of his pose and the cords of his forearms reminded Semra of a much younger man. Zephan had leaned out his window in just the same way just a week ago. She swallowed the lump in her throat.

The man cocked one eyebrow to a comically severe height and pursed thin lips under a shroud of impossibly long mustache. "You don't have to *want* any trouble to have found it."

He knew enough about dragons to know what a drag-onlord was, and to know that she was one. That was a good sign, at least. And he was cautious—a trait she shared with him, and maybe one she could use. Semra cleared her throat. "We're not looking for trouble with *you,* specifically. I think you and I both know that trouble can find us despite our best efforts."

The man straightened. "Indeed. Today is proof enough of that. But while you may think you need my help, I do not need yours, and nothing good can come of you wasting time here with an old man in his solitary retirement. Good day."

The window shut, and a latch clicked home from the inside. Semra blinked at the glass; branches and leaves reflected off its surface, tossing the light back just as the man had tossed her request back at her.

Aviama crossed her arms. "Did he ... did he just shut us out?"

"Better than shooting us," Semra mumbled. Why hadn't he reacted to Garbane's name? He'd neither acknowledged him as a friend, nor asked who Garbane was. A paranoid man would absolutely have wanted to know what stranger had sent two odd women and a dragon to his door. He knew the name. So why hadn't he let them in?

Semra dug in her satchel for the letter and held it out for Zezura. "Get him the letter, Zez."

The dragon arched her neck, swinging her head back around and clamping the envelope in her lips. Zezura bumped her nose against the window in gentle taps, one, two, three times.

"I'd open the window," Semra called.

Nothing.

Go ahead, girl.

Zezura pulled her head back and poked her nose straight through the glass. They were rewarded with a gruff shout, and Zezura dropped the envelope inside on top what must have been a bed of broken shards.

Aviama paced on the forest floor below. "Now what?"

Semra glared at the window and patted Zezura's neck. "Now we wait."

"How long?"

Semra slipped down from Zezura, strode twenty paces away from the tree residence door, and plopped down at the base of another tree. She crossed her ankles and leaned her head back against the smooth bark of the trunk. "However long it takes. He's stubborn, but after he reads whatever Garbane wrote, he'll soften. And he'll be curious."

Aviama came to stand in front of her, and Semra opened one eye to squint up at her. The princess pointed back at Frigibar's tree. "You've only just met the man. And I'd say *met* is grossly exaggerating things. How do you know what he might do? What if he shoots us instead, from the window Zezura bashed in?"

"Ah." Semra stifled a smile, but the corner of her lips still quirked up despite her. Aviama was as flighty as an Arrow Class, jumpy as those young children just learning the ropes back in Azi's program in the mountain where Semra grew up. If she ever went hunting, which Semra doubted, Aviama would probably wait five minutes and wonder why exactly no duck or deer had been by yet. She opened her eyes, lifted her chin, and hollered up at the window. "My friend is worried you're going to shoot us. Are you going to shoot us?"

Aviama's eyes bulged, and she smacked Semra on the arm. Semra held a hand up to defend herself and grinned. No response came. She had not expected one.

Semra shouted again. "If you do decide to shoot us, please have the decency to do it before we've waited long. My friend hates waiting. Thank you!"

Aviama threw her hands up. "Are you out of your mind?"

"Sometimes." It shouldn't have been funny. Really, it shouldn't. But it was.

"You're enjoying this."

"Maybe a little. But we have no other option than to wait

him out, so that's what I intend to do. If he was truly likely to murder us, I don't think Garbane would have sent us here."

In the end, they waited only a couple of hours before a rock hit the bark of the tree Semra and Aviama leaned against, smack in the space between the two women's heads. It hit Semra's shoulder and she caught it before it hit the ground. Her heart pounded as she raised her gaze to the second-story window.

Frigibar looked down his sharp nose and beckoned them inside. "Don't touch the door. Climb up your dragon and come through the window."

Semra and Aviama exchanged a glance and lurched to their feet. *Here we go.* A thrill ran up her spine as she patted Zezura, climbed up the spines on the dragon's back, and pulled Aviama up behind her. Zezura unfolded herself from the place she'd been coiled on the ground, blinked, and stretched. Aviama squealed and threw her arms around Semra's middle.

"Imagine you're riding a horse." Semra angled her body as the dragon stretched this way and that, then straightened. "Lean and balance out."

"This is *not* like riding a horse," Aviama grumbled. "It will never be like riding a horse."

Zezura raised herself up, and Semra led the way up the dragon's neck, planting one foot on the sturdy bones of the wing structure, and up onto the windowsill. Inside, wooden floors flowed through a space divided into two or three rooms per floor. Semra hopped down onto a single sturdy block—there were no floorboards. There was no need to harvest from the tree for lumber, but to simply to carve away unwanted bits for walking and breathing.

The room Semra found herself in held a ladder leading up into the ceiling to the next level, a rocking chair by the window, shelves of books, and a large area where the wood of the tree rolled up from the floor into the shape of a long table and chairs. Aviama landed with a *thud* and gasped from behind Semra.

Frigibar's eyes narrowed. He turned and walked through a circular opening leading to the adjoining room, ornamented by a furnace, fur rug, side-table, and two real, movable chairs. He plucked a teapot from the fire and snatched two mugs from hooks in the wall.

"Sit." The man's rough voice commanded the air in the room, and he seemed to grow taller even as he bent to pour.

Semra and Aviama sat dutifully in the chairs by the furnace, and Semra found herself wondering how exactly a fire in a tree was a good idea. She thought again of Zezura's flame against the sides of the house earlier, and the unknown substance Zezura had noticed in a color spectrum beyond human sight. Something flame-retardant, surely.

Frigibar handed them their mugs and stood back, folding his arms. Semra cupped the mug, reveling in the warmth of its smooth sides. "Thank you."

"What is it?" Aviama asked.

"Tea. The only sensible drink from a kettle."

"Oh, thank you. I do love tea, but I couldn't place this scent." Aviama tasted the drink and her whole face brightened. She took another sip, smiled, then sobered. She squirmed in her chair and chanced a sideways glance up at their host. "My favorite thing to have with tea is biscuits or honeycakes. What is yours?"

"Solitude."

Semra grimaced.

Aviama pursed her lips. "Well ... seeing as you don't have what you like best with your tea, do you have anything we might have along with ours?"

Semra's cheeks flushed and she cut Aviama a dark glare. "Shush!"

Aviama held her hands up and turned to Frigibar again. "Forgive me. I normally have far better manners, but it turns out my stomach makes me completely irreverent to tradition."

Frigibar grumbled something incoherent and turned on his heel. In a moment, he was gone.

Semra's chest tightened, and she leaned in toward Aviama, dropping her voice to a low hiss. "We need him not to hate us."

Aviama edged to the end of her chair. "That didn't seem true when you were chucking rocks at his window and begging him to kill us!"

Rats and rot, she had a point. Semra twisted her mouth into a frown, but almost let a smile slip through. "Fine. But he's already invited us in, so let's not push it, shall we?"

"I think you just like to be the one doing the pushing."

Another decent point, but not one Semra needed the princess to be making. Something slammed in the other room, and plates rattled with rough handling. Aviama arched her eyebrows at Semra over her tea. "See? And just imagine how much nicer we'll all be once we're not starving."

Semra rolled her eyes and let the warmth of a hot drink warm her down to her toes. "My mood isn't dictated by my stomach. I've been hungry half my life."

"Not to sound harsh, but you've also been killing people half your life, haven't you? Well, maybe if Azi had fed you a bit better, you would've got out sooner."

Semra's jaw dropped and her stomach flopped. Suddenly Aviama must have realized what she'd said, because all blood drained from her face and she clapped a hand over her mouth. "I'm so sorry. I didn't mean it, you know that, don't you? I didn't mean it! See, I wouldn't say stupid things like that if I weren't so empty inside!"

Frigibar strode back into the room and tossed two plates on the end table between them. "I doubt I can keep you from being stupid, but this'll help your stomach."

He had a keen ear. And a decent plate of food, as it turned out. Semra's mouth watered as she took in the cooked rabbit, cheese, and fruit arranged for them. She glanced up at the man in surprise. "Thank you."

Aviama lunged for the plate, hesitated, and followed Semra's lead. "Yes. Thank you ever so much for your kindness." She popped a grape in her mouth, followed by a chunk of rabbit and three slices of cheese.

Frigibar shrugged. "Seemed the easiest way to shut you up." He turned to Semra, feet planted a shoulder width apart, arms crossed once again. "So. You need training in a long lost art, from a man who could not possibly have had personal experience with it."

Semra swallowed a piece of meat. "Excuse me?"

"You need training. In magic."

"Is ... is that what Garbane said in his letter?" It was true—she needed to be able to control her smoke. If that was even possible. It was a liability, and controlling it would remove a dangerous unpredictability. But they also needed to understand how Azi and Avaya were using magic, and stop them. And find out about the prophecy.

What *had* Garbane told Frigibar? Did he actually think he could train her? Semra eyed the man with renewed interest. "Do you ... have magic?"

Frigibar laughed, but there was no amusement in his eyes. "Magic has been asleep for six hundred years. Why would I have magic?"

Semra leaned forward. "Why would you think I need training in magic if it doesn't exist?"

"I didn't say it didn't exist. I said it was *asleep.*"

Aviama popped another grape in her mouth. "That's the same thing, isn't it?"

Frigibar's mustache twitched. "If it were the same thing, there would be no point of you coming here. Now you tell me —what do you think you need?"

Semra set down her plate. "I need the rest of an old prophecy, because it's about powerful people who will destroy Jannemar. I need to stop them from using the magic they have, and keep them from getting more. And ... well, if you can tell me why I'm ... why I'm ..."

Frigibar waited. Semra's lips parted, but for a moment no words formed there. *Why you're what? A freak? Cursed with smoke after a dragon saved your life, and you were poisoned, and dragon stuff flooded your human body and totally messed you up?*

She winced. "If you can tell me why I'm different and how to stop it, that would be great."

"I'm not in the business of making people normal. Never succeeded with it myself, thank the stars." Frigibar tilted his head to one side, and Semra found herself fascinated by the steel of his eyes, a sort of suspicion challenged by curiosity. Or was that her own emotions she imposed on the stranger?

Frigibar let out a sigh long enough for Aviama to take three more bites of rabbit and drop a grape on the floor. "Come. You're going to tell me the whole story, and if I think you've told me the truth, we'll start with answering your only easy question—the prophecy of the architect."

24

ZEPHAN

Running feet thudded down the walkway over the Great Hall. Zephan jerked his head up from his seat in the conservatory to take in three soldiers headed his way. His hand flew to the hilt of his sword, but as the door burst open, the face of the first guard became clear. Monac.

Seven days had passed since that night with Zezura when Semra had dropped into the consciousness of the dragon, and he'd shown her the sketch of Aurin's spear. It had been difficult to pin down what else Azi and Avaya were looking into, with all the decoy books they requested from the library and any secret acquisitions they gained through underground means. Avaya had lived in Shamaran Castle a long time, and though Zephan doubted she had many friends, exactly, she certainly had allies.

Zephan had ordered all books on the legends of Aurin and the histories of The Crumbling be removed and counted against the most recent inventory of the royal libraries. It had been six years since the last inventory, so it was impossible to know for sure which books had been missing before now and which were in Azi's hands. Still, there were several missing titles related to The Crumbling, to the Origin Wellspring, and the Dezapi and Surion rivers.

They wanted the spear, and they were after its precise location. Had Semra figured it out? Was she headed there now, or did she get Aviama someplace safe? Zephan wasn't sure which he'd prefer. They *had* to get the spear before Azi and Avaya did, and if Rotokas provided transportation, there would be no hope of catching up on horse. In his experience with Zezura, dragons cut travel time by half.

Zephan dropped his hand from his sword and jumped to his feet as the three soldiers filed in and panted breathlessly just inside the door. "Monac?"

"He's gone." Monac shook his head in wonder. "The black dragon hasn't been seen in two days, and Azi is missing."

Zephan's heart fell like a stone to the bottom of his stomach. "Did you check the cellars? The dungeons, the dovecotes, the tunnels, every crevice in which he might hide?"

"We looked everywhere. Five times." Monac's eyes were wider than Zephan had ever seen them, but as he caught his breath, some of his composure returned. "Your Majesty, the ... your sister is refusing the checks on her room and has denied your invitation to meet."

His friend's stanch refusal to call Avaya by her Belvidorian royal title of queen was a balm to the ache in Zephan's chest. Gaulen was using it, and perfectly, at Zephan's own command, but he was assigned her detail. Monac would never leave assignment on Zephan's personal guard. Zephan looked out over the north bastion to the cliffs. "She's refused me three days in a row."

"Your Majesty, she has done nothing suitable for a guest in your house. And Teriv, though you dismissed her from your service after she was caught in restricted areas of the library and the north tower, has been seen again in the servant's quarters beneath the castle since your sister hired her as part of the Belvidorian envoy."

Zephan gritted his teeth. "Accompany me now to visit my darling sister. I want three teams with me, and another two teams to tear Azi's quarters apart. Do we have Firfell's report on the staff survey?"

Monac nodded. "We do, Your Majesty. Captain Firfell is scheduled to go over the results with you this afternoon."

"And we have confirmed that my sister has never formally denounced Jannemar as her citizenship, but only added Belvidore when she married into Axis's family, correct?"

"That's correct."

Resolve hardened in his chest, and Zephan dipped his head. "Good. Send word. Firfell will meet me at Avaya's chambers immediately."

Monac signaled one of the two guards with him, and the guard disappeared down the corridor. Zephan started down the walkway over the Great Hall, then paused. No, not yet. If Azi was gone, now was their best chance to show the castle who Avaya was. And remind everyone who their true king was.

Zephan spun and returned to his chambers. Twenty minutes later, a small, hunched older man exited the door of the king's valet, scurried down the hall, and disappeared into the servant's stair. Ten minutes after that, Zephan straightened his jacket and emerged from his rooms with a clearer head to accompany his thundering heart—wearing all the formal regalia befitting his station.

He lifted his chin and swept down the stairs and through the Great Hall itself, unseen by the guest hall windows but parading through every conspicuous indoor space on the way. *See your king. Not the boy that once played in these halls, not the brother once picked on by his older sister, but the monarch filling the shoes of his beloved father, King Turian, and protector of that great legacy. Keeper of Jannemar and its people.*

Servants ceased their work to bow as he passed, and guards backed away and stood sentry on either side. Whispers and murmurs faster than an executioner's ax flew from caretaker to watchkeeper to launderer, until at last Zephan came to a stop outside the double doors of the guest residence hall.

Captain Firfell waited there, bowed low, and gestured for private discussion with the king off to one side. Zephan nodded, inclining his ear to Firfell to receive the results of the recent survey of all the staff regarding Avaya and Azi's activity, suspicious movements or actions against regulation among the staff, and any unusual communications coming in and out of the castle.

Zephan's lip curled as he listened. One hand balled into a fist, rested on the hilt of his sword. Yes, that would do. He raised his voice just loud enough for those present in the room to hear, three teams of soldiers, and servants and staff poking their heads in from the rooms behind them.

"My sister Avaya has not been honest with the crown, and has acted against the nation of her birth, the homeland you and I share. In a time of mourning, she has broken faith. I think it's about time my sister reaped what she sowed, don't you?"

Adrenaline flooded his arms as he lifted his hand and the double doors swung open. He may never get this chance again. The chance to control the narrative.

It was now or never.

25

"So." Semra spread her hands. "You know far more about us than I had ever hoped to share, because Garbane trusts you. He knew we would be dodging each other's questions all day long if he didn't tell you who we were, and now you have the upper hand. We've told you our story. You know everything about us. It's your turn."

Semra had started out sharing bits and pieces of their story in generalities before Frigibar rolled his eyes and told them Garbane's letter had informed him the gist of the situation and that Semra was the dragonlord of Qalea, traveling with Princess Aviama. Of course, "the dragonlord of Qalea" didn't quite sound accurate, since Semra wasn't *from* Qalea, but it was natural for the city to give some sort of identifying name.

"It doesn't take a genius to figure out," Frigibar had said. "There are only two present-day dragons I've ever heard of, one with a female dragonlord and one with a male, and you are a woman. Friend of the king. And your lady companion carries herself like a noble, even if she eats like a half-starved street urchin."

They'd spent half the morning explaining the events of the last few months, finally ending with Avaya somehow getting Azi out of the dungeons and arriving from Belvidore and infiltrating the castle under the guise of a diplomatic guest. At Frigibar's request, she repeated three times—with frequent stops, clarifications, and retellings—the final moments in the castle, with Avaya's unnatural wind and Semra's unnatural smoke.

"Her hands—where were they when the wind came?" Frigibar asked. "And did she hold any trinkets, or weapons? Was there any glow or light?"

The answer to the last two questions was no. He paced, then asked again. "She *must* have an artifact. Nobody has natural magic, not now. And how did she *look*—was she healthy or gaunt? Did she look strained or effortless?"

Effortless. Cocky. Sucked in by the serpent's poison, but Azi was the serpent and Avaya was a plaything.

At last he asked for the scrap of prophecy Aviama had stolen from Avaya when it fell from her sleeve in the king's chambers. Aviama produced it, and flattened out its crumpled edges on the table.

Semra spun the gold signet ring on her finger beneath the table, twisted it inward toward her palm, and laced her fingers on the tabletop. Her mouth went dry, and her pulse sped up. "Frigibar Curmody. Who are you, and why did Garbane send us to you?"

Frigibar scanned the poetry fragment on the table again, then rose from his chair and crossed to the bookshelves running the entire height of the back wall. "I imagine there are three reasons my old friend sent you to me, despite his knowledge that I despise encounters with high-profile individuals, getting involved with politics, and having house guests."

He ran his fingers over the spines of the books, tenderly, as if each one was an old friend. He pulled one out, leafed through it, returned it to the shelf, and continued his search. "The first reason is he thinks you will remind me of someone from my past that will make me willing to help you. He's right that you have similarities with someone I used to know, but that does *not* make me more likely to help you, so he's out of luck on that count.

"The second reason is because I am somewhat off the grid, or was, before you got here and inevitably bring a swarm of undesirables to my door after you. I'm in a prime location for your needs, I've seen enough of political spheres to believe your crazy stories, and I'm motivated by my own selfishness to keep my mouth shut about you."

Frigibar's fingers paused on an old leatherbound book and drew it gingerly from the shelf. The edges were tattered and the pages browned. "The third reason is that I am the last of my kind, keeper of magic, scholar of ancient melders, and the most knowledgeable person alive when it comes to the inner workings of the magic that formed the world, fueled the world, was thrown out of balance and sickened the world, and finally was laid to rest by Aurin at the origin of the world."

The wealth of knowledge the man must have arrested Semra's attention. Old legends of keepers of magic had become something of a myth and hardly spoken of in recent generations. She could barely believe her luck that there were any surviving magic keepers, much less finding one willing to help her. All her efforts would be like fumbling in the dark without someone to guide her against Azi and Avaya—who clearly already knew a thing or two about magic themselves.

The old man drilled Semra with a cool stare, and she hardly breathed under his gaze. "I imagine Yaskir also wanted to warn me, because anyone seeking magic as the tool to over-throw the king will want to use or eliminate me, depending on my willingness. But my time in the courts of kings is over. I serve no king."

He set the book down on the table and slid it toward Aviama and Semra. "We'll start with your easiest question. You wanted to see the prophecy of the architect. Here it is, in full, as written hundreds of years ago."

Aviama and Semra leaped forward to look over the book, and their heads bumped together in their haste.

"Ouch!" Aviama rubbed her head, and Semra winced at the throb before pulling the book closer and hunching over it again.

Nezil Myansara lives ten-thousand feet at tops.
The wind and rain may batter, but its beauty never stops.
Resilient is the flame within the shoot that sprung of stone.
Harshness is her home, yet wise would make her friend of throne.

Blooming in adversity, nobility she claims;
Despite the soot upon her roots, she's called to greater aims.
Ashes, ashes, hail her coming, magic in her leaves,
Her solemn strength is weathered wild even as she grieves.

Home among the mountains, plucked and left to battle dread:
Uprooted Myansara must be planted, or be dead.
Roots of rock and roots of storm, wherever did you go?
Power dormant, wellspring locked, awake from long ago!

Spearhead of an ancient spring, blood and flame and smoke
Shall usher in the clash of kings, a dragon-blooded stroke.
Ho, what a peril, what a risk, unleashing what was sealed!
Be loathe to wield so far afield; let Aurin's wounds be healed.

Great the dangers that are loosed when rise what laid to rest;

None but seed of flower planted could restrain it best.
Crimson queen shall open door protecting all from shame,
Then guarding it forevermore, he of the same great name.

Aviama sat back and looked up at Frigibar. "So the crimson queen is Avaya, right? Because of the red that Belvidorian brides wear, and the ... the blood on her hands now?"

"That's a reasonable theory." Frigibar slid the verse Aviama had pinched off her sister down beside its corresponding section in the book, the verse about the queen. "And *she* certainly seems to think so."

Semra re-read the prophecy. "We thought the guard forevermore would be Azi, since he and Avaya are both Shamarans. And here ... in the second verse. Soot upon her roots. Sharsi was not noble born."

"All decent theories," Frigibar rumbled. "The prophecy speaks with knowledge of magic, as it indicates a *sleeping* magic to be awakened, rather than a dead one, like the clueless people of our time say these days."

Aviama squinted at the parchment. "Are there going to be more wars, or is the *clash of kings* Arnevon and my father, and it's already happened?"

Frigibar folded his arms. "Prophecies are not easy to interpret during the time they come about. Could be that it's happened ... could be that it hasn't."

"And the Nezil Myansara is the queen of Jannemar, correct?" Semra asked.

Frigibar shrugged. "Could be. Could not be."

Semra frowned. "I thought you were an expert."

"I am." The man arched a bushy eyebrow. "And as an expert, I'm telling you it's impossible to know for certain. But it does seem to indicate Avaya and Azi Shamaran. We will continue pouring over it and thinking on it. Now, on to more challenging tasks."

"Aren't we going to spend more time on the prophecy?" Aviama asked. "Can prophecies be broken? Are there loopholes?"

Frigibar let out an exasperated breath. "As I said, we'll keep working on it. But our next tasks are far more difficult, and will take far more time. And from the sound of it, time is not on your side."

Semra nodded. They had to get to the spear before Avaya did. "How do we find the spear, then? And how do we stop Avaya from using magic?"

Frigibar wagged a finger. "No. You must control your own magic if you hope to face theirs."

Semra's stomach soured. "I don't know how."

"Obviously." Frigibar rolled his eyes. "If you knew how, you wouldn't need my training, would you?"

Aviama cocked her head. "But magic has been gone for six hundred years, and you're definitely not six hundred years old. You've never used magic. How can you teach it? You're a historian, not a trainer."

Frigibar placed both hands on the table and leaned forward. He held their gazes for a full minute before speaking. "Manipulation."

Semra choked on her tea. "Excuse me?"

The older man's eyes flashed white fire under the dark shadows of his bushy brows. His lip curled into the first expression of true disdain she'd seen on his sharp features, and he rounded the table in four long strides and jabbed a finger into Semra's chest. "You're *weak*. That's why you can't control your magic."

Heat leaped into her chest, and Semra's throat tightened. She swallowed, but kept her voice level. "I'm not weak."

"You traipsed across the kingdom to beg at the door of a stranger. Some dragonlord you are. Ha!" Frigibar swept the book of the prophecy off the table and snapped it shut in her face, the wind of its closing blowing her hair back. "You cheat the rules of magic and expect it to bow to you. You see your failure prophesied, and decide it is not you, but the prophecy that must change."

He wants the smoke, but it doesn't work like that. Heat rolled under the surface, but it was muted and unreachable. Inaccessible. Semra twisted her mouth into a wry smile. "You're trying to get under my skin, but it doesn't work like that."

Frigibar's brows soared comically high. "What do we have here? A little girl traveling for days, sleeping in the dirt to seek out an expert, only to tell him she already knows how everything works?"

Semra gritted her teeth but softened her glare to what she hoped was an even gaze, at least half as intimidating as his. Aviama's soft, uncertain voice broke her concentration.

"Semra?"

Her glance flickered to Aviama, who had risen from her chair and was peering around Frigibar's large frame. Semra looked again at Frigibar. "It doesn't work like that. It's not that easy."

"Because if it *were* that easy, what would that mean about you? Hmm? That you were too stupid to figure it out?" Frigibar stooped to drop his face inches from hers, and Semra took a step back at his insistence.

Irritation seeped into her tone. "I've tried it. Yes, it seems to come out more at certain times, but it just ... comes."

Frigibar's eyes narrowed. "You've been trusted with the princess of Jannemar. Orphan girl, right? All alone in the world except for a brother who sent you both far away. Because he knew he was going to die."

Semra's hands itched for something to hold. A knife blade, if only to turn over and over in her hands. A friend. "He's not alone."

But it was a lie, wasn't it? Even with Monac, and Gaulen, and the rest of his staff. What were they against a dragonlord and a well-connected queen with magic? A queen and adviser who both had claims to the throne? Azi would have to prove or contrive proof that he was the elder twin brother of Turian. It wouldn't be hard for a man of his skillset to come up with something. And Avaya would need only a change in the law to allow female children into the line of succession.

A little blackmail, a little forgery, a little support to back their claims ... and either one could send Zephan scurrying for the hills.

Or send him to the gallows. Or the guillotine. The options were endless, really. But if Zephan wouldn't run, he would die.

And Zephan wouldn't run.

Semra's heart ticked up a notch, and her breathing quickened to match.

Frigibar shook his head. "He knows he's going to die. You know he's going to die. The only one who doesn't know is his baby sister."

"Semraaa?" Aviama's voice cracked from behind the keeper of magic, but even as the sound broke her heart, Semra found herself unable to tear her eyes away from the icy silver daggers of Frigibar's unyielding scrutiny.

Firigbar waved a hand dismissively at the princess's fear-torn call. "She's young. She's naive. There were only two people in the king's chambers that day, the last day you saw him, that really understood who Azi is. Avaya hasn't a clue, but you do. You do, and the king does. The king did what he does—he protected. Everybody but himself. And you ... you let him give himself up."

A lump lodged in Semra's throat. Something inside her broke. She'd been so afraid that day. Paralyzed in her chair before her childhood mentor, her twisted, depraved father figure. Zephan had seen her fear and responded to it by placing himself in harm's way and literally shoving Semra and Aviama out the doorway and across the room to make their escape.

"He would've hated me if I stayed. If Aviama got hurt. He would have hated ..." Her voice trailed off. Zephan could never hate her, could he? She'd done what he asked.

But she hadn't fought for him.

She had fled.

But wasn't fleeing the same as fighting for him? Didn't she flee so she could fight another day? For a chance to make things right, to stop Azi once and for all? Wasn't that what had brought them so far, and landed them in this ridiculous treehouse in the first place?

"You abandoned him to die just to protect his sister," Frigibar crooned. "And today, you fail them both."

The old man whirled, wrapped his enormous hand around Aviama's neck, and slammed her face down on the table between them. Her scream shook the air. The hairs on the back of Semra's neck stood on end, and she ripped her skirts out of the way to draw her knife when she heard Aviama's soft inhale and caught the glimmer of the magic keeper's own blade against the princess's tender skin.

Semra flipped the blade in her hands, nostrils flared, but as she stepped forward Frigibar dug the blade into Aviama's skin. She winced, and a drop of blood ran down her exposed neck.

Frigibar scanned Semra slowly from head to foot. "What do you think my privacy and freedom are worth, hmm? What do you think my life here is worth? What do you think *she* is worth?"

He couldn't mean it. He couldn't.

But if he did, Zephan would die, Aviama would die, Azi would reign, and magic would rule forever in the hands of the most evil man Semra had ever known.

Her chest burned, and fire roiled under the surface of her skin. In that moment, Semra's heart broke for Aviama and Zephan, whom she had failed again and again. First protecting their mother, then their father, and finally all three of those royal corpses' children who may in fact share the crypt with their parents too soon.

Because of her.

Again.

No. Let this never be. Semra lunged, and the trio were enveloped in a darkness as black as night. Onyx shadows filled the treehouse, and in seconds, Semra couldn't see past her own nose.

Semra's body ran into something solid and glanced off it. She heard a scraping and a cry. She twisted toward the sound, afraid to lash out for fear of hitting Aviama. Then, through the darkness, a gasp—a muffled scream—and a limp body was thrown at Semra's torso, knocking her to the floor.

26

Semra's chest burned wild fire, and sparks crackled at the tips of her fingers. The mark of the dragon's kiss tingled with electricity as she connected with Zezura.

Light it up.

Smoke fled from the flame of the dragon through the broken window, ushering it up the chimney and billowing overhead into the upper rooms. As the haze slowly cleared, Semra's gaze locked onto Frigibar, and surprise interrupted her fury.

He sat across the room in his chair by the furnace, holding out a pipe toward Zezura's fire in one hand, and his knife by the blade in the other. Frigibar caught her eye, leaned back as the dragon's flame receded, and offered the knife handle to her.

Aviama stirred in Semra's arms, and she looked down. Semra checked her fingers against her own face—warm, but not uncomfortably so. And no more smoke. She checked Aviama's pulse and helped her sit up.

"This is no trivial game you're playing." Frigibar's rough voice rumbled like thunder through the hazy remnants of smoke. "Based on Garbane's letter, you don't have time to waste. If we're going to be efficient, you need to stop telling me how magic works, because you haven't got a clue."

Semra's lip curled, her heart still hammering against her rib cage. She ran her hands over Aviama's face—a light abrasion and scrape colored the side of her face that had met the table, and the nick on the side of her neck was still red, but she was otherwise unharmed.

"Are you okay?"

Aviama winced, touched the mark on her face, and nodded. "I think so."

"If I wanted her dead, she'd be dead," Frigibar called again. "If I wanted *you* dead, you'd be dead. I let you in because I trust Garbane. Do you? Recall your dog."

It was all a test. He never would have released Aviama and given up his leverage otherwise. But it had gone too far. Semra shook her head, but still she sent word to the dragon. *Stay.* "You're insane. You could have killed her by accident."

The older man took a puff of his pipe. "Would you have killed her by accident, if you were in my shoes?"

Semra gritted her teeth. "No, but I know what I'm doing."

"I've lived much longer than you, and I know more than you think. Now, listen. Your lessons start now. I wasn't kidding when I said you're weak. We need to make you strong."

Semra gently shifted Aviama to one side and leaped to her feet. "I *am* strong. And you broke trust."

Frigibar took another puff on his pipe, stood, and pursed his lips. "You can't break what you haven't got, sparky. And if you were strong, I wouldn't have been able to manipulate you so easily. You are emotionally weak. You're insecure."

She opened her mouth to retort, but her response died on her lips. *It was still too far, even if it was true.*

He paced the room, paused, and turned. "Your weak

points, which I identified in minutes, are as follows: the king, who is nothing less than a boy loved by a girl; the princess, who is a vulnerable friend you love and feel responsible for; and finally your own guilt and fear of failure, which paralyzes you beyond comprehension."

Semra's gut twisted. Her love for Zephan and Aviama, her blood-soaked past, her nightmares and fears—all casually listed in the span of half a breath. To be read so quickly, poked and prodded so painfully, her anger drawn out when she *knew* what he was doing, when he'd *told* her what he was doing ... it was infuriating. He'd promised to manipulate her, and he had done it.

"My attempt to throw you into chaos was outrageously successful." Frigibar flipped the blade in his hands and dropped it into a sheath along his belt, hidden when he walked by the mantle he still wore. "Unfortunately, I then discovered that an assassin was preparing to murder me, and had little choice but to take advantage of the smoke you so kindly provided. Do forgive me. I've observed it's difficult to explain oneself from the grave, so I prioritized survival over exposition.

"But I was too unreasonable, extreme, risky in my approach, wasn't I? I scared you, and the fact that I could do it so easily terrified you to your core. Well, good. You *should* be scared. A lot more than you are now. Because when reckless killers gain magic, the stakes reach heights I dare not describe.

"My task, it seems, is to make you strong and less reckless. Garbane knows I've faced such a one as you before. So be scared. Be angry. And keep your heart rate a little unsteady. Scan your body. What do you feel, right now, in this moment?"

Semra's mind whirred at the speed of a thousand galloping war horses. Her chest still heaved with heavy breathing, adrenaline fueling every muscle. Rage, though giving way to reason, still lined each thought. "I'm angry."

He waved his hand dismissively. "Sensations, little spark, *sensations.*"

Semra glared at him, but paused and turned her focus inward. "Tingling. In my hands and chest. Heat. Light."

"Light? You *feel* light, do you?"

Semra threw her hands up. "I don't know. Maybe. Like a current underwater. It's bogged down. That might not even be what it is."

"No. That's what it is." Frigibar took three long pulls from his pipe and eyed her with interest. "There were sparks in the smoke. Your magic is dragon-derived, from the bond you share with the dragon's kiss. The magical essence entered your bloodstream when the mark broke apart and expanded to save your life from the poisonous snakes you told me about. And what is a dragon famous for?"

Semra blinked.

Aviama furrowed her brow, but gathered her wits about her again from her harrowing two minutes of unconsciousness and lifted a hand. "Um, breathing fire?"

"Yes. Fire. Five points to the fainting lily."

Aviama slumped into the chair at the table and dropped her chin into her hand. Did it count as fainting if he'd choked her out? Semra rather guessed that was what had happened, rather than a simple faint. She edged closer to Aviama, but did not sit.

Frigibar beckoned at them. "And what, pray tell, *causes* smoke?"

"Burning?" Aviama asked hopefully.

Understanding struck. Semra's lips parted. "Fire. Where there's smoke, there's fire."

Frigibar jabbed an exultant finger into the air. "Fire!

Because fire comes *first,* and smoke follows. Yet with you, we *see* only smoke, and pitiful little baby sparks on its fringes. But" —here Frigibar rounded the table and rapped Semra lightly on the chest where the opal mark now peeked out of her wrinkled dress—"in here. In here there is fire. The fire is first. You feel the heat of it. Your magic is derived of the dragon. And you must learn to control not only your anger, not only your smoke, but also the flame that causes it to burn."

27

ZEPHAN

Zephan tugged on the sleeves of his thick formal jacket and swallowed for the third time in a minute. The reverberation of his firm footsteps echoed down the hall as he led the three teams of soldiers along the corridor and burst into Avaya's guest chambers.

Avaya twisted from her place lounging on the sofa and sprang to her feet as he entered. "What's all this?"

Zephan nodded to team one's leader and set his feet in a broad stance, braced for impact. "Princess Avaya Shamaran, you are under arrest."

Avaya drew back, holding up her palms as if they might keep the team leader at bay as he advanced toward her. "That is *not* my highest title. You will address me as my station deserves, you will tell me precisely what I am charged with, and you will not lay a hand on the monarch of a foreign nation without risking war!"

The team leader gripped her by the arm and drew her back toward Zephan in the middle of the room. Avaya swatted at the man's arm and ripped herself free. "Don't touch me!"

Zephan gave a hand signal in response to the team leader's questioning glance, and the soldier gave a short nod. All signals had been changed. Avaya shouldn't understand a single one of them. She would learn soon enough.

Avaya looked between them, and her lips parted. The leader gestured to his men, and two came to stand on either side of Avaya. Team Leader One produced a set of wrist shackles and stood at the ready.

"My *rank* is *queen*," Avaya said through gritted teeth, "and you will tell me with what I am charged, dear brother."

Zephan scanned her posture—rigid, every muscle tense, chest heaving, nostrils flared. Wide eyes. She was angry, but she was scared. Yet even so, she remained controlled.

Show yourself.

"You contradict yourself even with such a simple sentence." Zephan clasped his arms behind him, then thought better of it and brought them in front. If Avaya threw him against the wall, he was going to need his hands free. "Are you queen, or am I your dear brother, and you my sister?"

Avaya laughed, but the sound was hollow. "Is that my crime? Being related to a family as warped as ours?"

"You claimed your *highest* title is queen, and it is customary to address a person with their highest title. But you still claim your Jannemari title, do you not?"

"I got married, Zephan. I didn't die." Avaya's lip curled and almost quivered. Was she supposed to look sad, or was it anger that made her tremble?

Avaya took a step toward him, and the guards thrust their swords in an X formation to block her path. She scowled, but returned her focus to Zephan. "I took on the responsibilities customary of a widowed queen in a nation crumbling with grief. What was I supposed to do?"

Such pretty words. How he despised the sound of them. Zephan swept his right arm to one side. "Queen of Belvidore!" He swept his left arm in the opposite direction. "Princess of Jannemar!"

Zephan brought his hands together in a clap. One of the guards jumped. "You never renounced your Jannemari title, as you should have done to honor the husband you killed and the people you pretend to shepherd there. Since coming as a *guest* to *my* kingdom and *my* house, you have broken every requirement we gave you."

"How dare—"

Zephan didn't care what useless words escaped her now. He raised his voice and spoke over her. "We allow you in to treat with us, and you free a war criminal from our dungeons and claim him as your adviser. We give you a room, and you summon servants and old connections as if you ran the castle yourself. We offer you access to the libraries, and we learn you blackmail and usurp servants to steal them from restricted areas instead. We—"

Avaya's eyes burned, and she half-screamed at him, "I've done nothing of the—"

"I wasn't finished!" Zephan's voice boomed in the air around them. A furious pounding pulsed in his ears, and power rippled through his muscles.

Avaya pulled back as if she'd been slapped, eyes wide, cheeks flushed. But she was still only angry that she'd been caught, that her dragonlord uncle wasn't there to sweep in and save her, that she wasn't getting what she wanted.

She had no remorse for her betrayal. And that lack of remorse ate at Zephan's soul. Avaya condemned Semra for her life of killing, blamed her for their parents' deaths, accused Zephan of spending time with a good for nothing. But when

Semra learned the truth about Azi, she had forsaken every-thing—risked everything—to stop him. She had devoted herself to freeing his victims and protecting his targets, the first of which being Zephan himself.

Avaya, when given the choice, had freed the same man, joined him, and steeped herself in the very guilt she claimed she hated Semra for. Her station might not always have required Avaya to get her own hands dirty, but the red of her wedding dress stank of iron and rust—the crimson blood of hundreds of Belvidorian and Jannemari soldiers in a war to fuel her own ambition, not to mention her own husband, whose death she had ensured on the day of matrimony.

In two long strides, he came nearly nose to nose with her across the barrier of swords.

"We find your old handmaid shirking assigned duties and sneaking around the guard towers, cellars, even the lower meeting rooms. In my mercy, I am gentle. I fire her. And you hire her. We extend a hand to you in friendship, and you conspire against us, against this crown, against Jannemar."

Avaya stared at him, for once caught off guard.

Zephan's chest tightened, and he took three steps backward.

Slowly, she shook her head, never moving her gaze from his face. When she spoke, her voice was small. "So this is what you think of me?"

Yes. Yes, this is exactly what I think of you. Zephan raised two fingers, and the second team moved into a defensive position, swords drawn.

Avaya swallowed and her chest moved with quick, shallow breaths. Her glance flicked from one guard to another and back to Zephan. A bead of sweat broke out on her forehead. "You cannot arrest the monarch of a foreign nation!"

Zephan squared his shoulders. "I do not arrest a foreign

dignitary. You never denounced your Jannemari citizenship or royal ties, which of course makes sense if you were planning to make a play for the throne. Therefore I do not arrest Her Majesty, Queen Avaya of Belvidore, but rather my sister, Her Royal Duplicitous Highness, *Princess* Avaya Shamaran of Jannemar, for theft and conspiracy to commit treason."

The guards on either side of Avaya took hold of her arms, and Team Leader One gripped her wrist and raised the shackles.

"On what evidence?"

She was shaken, her cheeks flushed, her eyes wild. Zephan could almost taste her diplomatic resolve dissolving, like sugar in a pot boiling over.

"We've done a survey, complete with individual interviews of the entire staff. It's been quite the undertaking. We will protect the identities of our sources, but believe you me, there will be plenty to hear at the trial."

"Which you will preside over."

Zephan spread his hands. "You will be tried in the highest court of our land. As your *station* demands."

The first shackle locked in place.

Avaya yanked her second hand away, but the guards held her fast. "Zephan. *Zephan!*"

The blood in his veins ran cold at the shrill cry of someone he used to love. Someone he should have been able to care for. Someone who should never have been capable of such evil.

When had the switch flipped? How long had she held her peace, reigning in a vengeful, raging ambition that would cost the royal family—*their* family—its parents, its bond, its goodness? How long had she spent laying her plans, devising her kidnapping, scheming for two thrones?

Zephan balled his hands to fists at his sides, clenching his jaw and relishing the bite of his short nails digging into the skin of his palms.

A flash of madness crossed her face like a shadow, and the facade fell as a crashing wave at the break of a dam. "NOOO!"

Her scream set a shiver down his spine, and the hairs on the back of his neck stood on end. No sooner had he registered the chill of that unhinged sound than a shock of air threw him back across the room.

Half of team two flew back scattered along the wall with broken crockery from the low table in front of the sofa, now skidding toward the door after a stray soldier grasping at nothing for a chance at a hand or foothold. Team Leader One still held the other half of Avaya's shackle, and his weight when he fell had tumbled her to the floor.

Instantly, the wind receded, but Zephan knew better than to trust the respite. Something was blocking her power. He glanced up just as her hand flew to her necklace, the shell and pearl dangling toward the floor as she struggled to pull herself up. Team Leader One, bless him, had managed to shackle the other chain to his own wrist.

Fear and admiration for the man mingled in Zephan's chest at the sight of it, but he didn't have long to think on it before the mighty gale picked up again. Crystal glasses became missiles and books became birds as the *woosh* of Avaya's wind filled his ears. He flattened his body to the ground and lifted one arm over his head. Something glanced off his forearm and flew over him to the wall with a crash.

How many of them did she have in her pocket? *Is this the queen you would support? Is this the kingdom you want?*

Zephan snatched a flying silver platter and held it in front of his face, a shield against the onslaught, protecting his eyes from the wind. He crawled forward on his forearms, body low to the ground, and across the room, he saw his soldiers following suit.

Avaya roared like a caged animal and slung a gust of air at him so strong he slid backward to the wall. His knees buckled against the pressure, his shoes kicking up against a fallen desk, broken chair legs, and shards of crystal. Avaya adjusted her pendant and threw both hands out, knocking three more soldiers to the floor.

The pearl on her necklace had held poison before. But now it must hold some source of magic. The answer came to him like a wick catching flame in the dark. *That's* why the wind had stopped when she fell. It dangled to the floor, instead of laying on her neck. It needed contact with her skin.

"The necklace!" Zephan waved frantically at the team lead attached to Avaya. "Get the necklace off her!"

Avaya's lip curled and she threw a gust at Zephan like an arrow. He lifted the platter over his face, but it tore from his hands and skittered along the floorboards. The team leader struck her in the ribs and reached for his sword, but even as he moved, Zephan knew he would be too late. A howl of pain ripped from his sister's throat and a short, powerful burst of wind snapped his neck sideways and dropped him to the floor.

"No!"

Zephan knew he was safer flat against the floor. He knew it lowered his chance of injury. But he also knew it made him slow, and Avaya was distracted dragging the body of one of Zephan's best soldiers backward toward the sofa and searching for a key to the shackles still binding them together. He sprang to his feet and lunged.

Two bodies slammed into him and tackled him to the ground. "You're not safe here, Your Majesty!" someone yelled in his ear.

Monac, who Zephan now recognized as the second body

who'd collided with him, held up a shield as Avaya threw another gust their way.

Zephan strained against the arms of his men. "I had her! *I had her!*"

Avaya tugged at the corpse in vain, and finally stepped behind him and threw a gust to slide them both across the floor toward the doors. Soldiers blocked her way as Zephan was half-carried, half-dragged backward into the hall.

Zephan's mouth went dry, and his eyes latched onto Avaya's fiery emerald glare. Her resemblance to Aviama was striking.

They were nothing alike.

Avaya lunged once more for the door and froze. Monac and the soldier on Zephan's other side drew him back, and he followed her gaze—castle guards and staff lining the halls. Launderers, cleaners, attendants, cooks. Soldiers with brandished weapons. Fear, anger, confusion.

Monac wasted no time. Her moment of hesitancy was an opportunity he could not miss. "The king is secure! Lock the door!"

Soldiers muscled the door closed and Avaya was shut off from view behind it. A man ran forward with a key and locked her in from the outside, and three more men slid a wardrobe and two trunks in front of the door. A deep ache set into Zephan's chest, and his shoulders dropped at last.

"He's gone," Monac said, for only him to hear. "You couldn't have saved him. And after you tackled her, she could have killed you too. We'll secure the room, regroup, and lay siege to the chamber if we have to. She can't stay in there forever."

Zephan nodded. He had known an aggressive move like an arrest could make her volatile, but he'd hoped it wouldn't come to this. But he must not make his team leader's death be in vain. He'd come to control the narrative, and he intended to do just that.

The lessons of today must be cemented in the minds of all the witnesses crowding around right now, in this moment. He could not afford to be the haggard defeated brother, or the mourning son.

Zephan drew himself up to his full height and tugged at the ends of his sleeve. For the first time, he noticed blood seeping out at its hem. He raised his chin and searched the terrified faces of the many people under his roof and in his care. He would do what he must to protect his kingdom. To keep his throne from falling into the hands of madmen.

To give Semra and Aviama more time before the end.

When at last he spoke, Zephan's voice was clear and strong. "Remember what you've seen today. Remember how we looked in the eyes of someone we once loved, a valued member of the royal family, and found them vacant. Today we mourn the sister I once had, as she has embraced insanity and rage over reason and love.

"What you saw today was not a ruler, not a uniter of kingdoms. She cannot bring peace to her own soul, and if even her own chambers turn to chaos, how could she bring security and prosperity to two entire nations?"

Zephan paused, half-expecting to hear screaming from the other side of the door, but as he scanned the faces of his staff and the soldiers under his command, all he could hear was his own pulse pounding in his ears. He took a breath, opened his mouth, and closed it.

They'd won the battle, but the war still raged, and Avaya was only a pawn in a bigger game. Where had Azi gone? Did he know where Semra was? Had he found Aurin's spear? Zephan shuddered at the thought of Avaya's necklace housing magic. If that little thing contained so much power, what chaos would ensue if Azi unleashed the weapon of The Crumbling, its tip embedded in the magic of the origin of the world?

"This hall is off limits effective immediately. Anyone with information on the conspiracy of Princess Avaya of Jannemar and the traitor war criminal, Azi Shamaran, have until dawn to provide it, at which time the last shreds of my clemency will have left me. Arrest Teriv on sight, and anyone who assists her will not escape their punishment."

Zephan jabbed his finger at the blockaded door and let his voice boom down the corridor. "The woman in this room is under house arrest for the use of *sifal* magic, along with theft and conspiracy to commit treason. Investigation is underway. Today I make one plea and one promise. My plea: remember. Remember the person you saw today, hiding under a facade of velvets and smooth talk. There may come a time when you choose a side. Remember.

"My promise: to serve the Jannemari people until breath leaves my body, willing to sacrifice myself, my life, all that I have in the service of the crown of this great kingdom and the security it deserves. I, King Zephan and ruler of Jannemar, will bring swift justice to anyone standing in the way of this cause."

Zephan set his face as flint and strode down the hall, out the double doors, and back through the Great Hall. His fingers shook. At least his voice had been steady.

He would not go quietly. He would not be held by blackmail. He would not entertain evil in his house, feeding it, serving it, treading lightly and treating it like soft soap. He was the king. And no matter what came, whether fire, blood, or stone, he would face it.

And pray that Semra and Aviama would make it on the other side.

This was it. Zephan had forced Avaya to show her hand,

and therefore Azi too would be forced to make a move, a big one, on his return. One that Zephan was not likely to survive.

Had it really come to this?

But the answer was as clear as the morning, and as certain as nightfall every evening. *This is only the beginning.*

28

—————

The days with Frigibar fell into regimented routine— Semra spent mornings and most afternoons exhausting herself trying and failing to access magic on command, and evenings were spent pouring over old books, Frigibar teaching the history of magic, and going over the prophecy of the architect in hopes of finding a loophole. Zezura lazed about or rolled in the leaves at the base of the tree, and lunches were often spent outside with her.

Avaya was assumed to be in possession of a housing artifact of some kind, for no better reason than because nothing else made any sense. How else could she have magic? Frigibar wanted to know how long she'd been capable of magic, but there was no answer. Semra and Aviama thought long and hard about any memory of her practicing, any glimmer of evidence of magic before the day they'd fled the castle, but came up empty.

Time spent outdoors brought hope to offset the disappointment of making no progress. Frigibar didn't seem concerned by Zezura at all except to wonder about the colors Semra had seen on his house through Zezura's vision, and he requested that the dragon not do anything to mark up the trees. Semra ditched the dress almost immediately, procuring one of Frigibar's too-large tunics by the morning of the first day and going about in her preferred trousers. The world's problems didn't seem as insurmountable when one wore trousers.

Frigibar's library was extensive, and Aviama spent her time reading and rereading the edicts Zephan had written and given to her possession, helping research magic and prophecy, and diving into books of strategy and kingdom rule. She hated reading the strategy books, but had announced early in their stay that her education as the youngest of three had been minimal at best, and her understanding of the role of monarch needed sharpening. Whenever she grew too frustrated, which was often, Aviama would toss her books aside, raid Frigibar's cabinets for dried meat, cheese, or wine, or write in a blank page booklet Frigibar had found for her.

Sometimes, when Aviama thought Frigibar and Semra were far enough away not to hear her, the soaring free refrains of singing would escape the broken window down to Semra's training, the sound clear as crystal, either sad enough to make one cry, or joyful enough to inspire the hope she needed to finish her daily training. Semra wasn't musical herself at all, but she quietly marveled at Aviama. How had she not known this about her before?

Semra had managed to summon the smoke several times, but never with fire, and never more than a few wisps. Frigibar had only shook his head, voicing the thought constantly replaying in her own mind: "It's not enough. It's not enough."

Two weeks had passed this way. Frigibar sometimes summarized their strategy when Semra grew tired.

"The smoke comes more easily to you when you are emotional. When you touch the boy you love, when you're afraid for yourself and people you care about. So we manipulate your emotional state. Poke at you to give you practice. If you were in control of yourself, you could control your magic, but you're not. You're unstable."

Many thanks, genius. Semra sighed. She knew the strategy. What she didn't know was why she wasn't *getting* anywhere. When she kissed or touched Zephan, it was easier to bring out the smoke at will. Even when she wasn't afraid.

Semra stared down at her obstinate, useless fingertips, the ones housing great power but refusing to give it up, betraying her each and every day. The heat in her body simmered as she reached for it, reminding her in some small way of the raging flame of fever she'd had when the magic of the dragon's kiss had first broken out into her bloodstream and taken her over. It had felt like her blood was boiling and her skin burning from the inside out.

The fever was gone, and the ache and pain no longer beset her bones, but a subdued version of that heat had remained. It was always there, like the sun above the clouds. But what caused one moment to feel blocked and clouded, and another, like those spent with Zephan, to be so clear?

Imminent danger of death seemed to clear things up a bit, but only brought out smoke, never fire, and was too risky to simulate repeatedly. Closeness with someone she cared about seemed to help too, and even frustration or any loss of temper would sometimes release a curl of smoke from her fingers. Why would a soft emotion bring about the same result as a harsh one?

Frigibar tilted his head and eyed her from across the clearing. "Relax. You're trying too hard. You need to *feel* it instead of thinking it."

"Scourge." Semra dropped her hands and squeezed her eyes shut. She pinched the bridge of her nose and let out a sigh. When she opened her eyes again, Frigibar was surveying her like a builder assessing his flawed design, unsure of just how to fix it. "I've *tried* feeling it. And I do. More than before, anyway. It's there—the heat, the energy. But it's not enough. I feel like it's playing a game with me, that every time I almost reach it, it dances away again."

Frigibar folded his arms. "You're tired."

Semra's shoulders drooped and a sliver of warmth filled her chest. He understood her exasperation. "Yes."

"You want a break?"

She pursed her lips, but there was no use arguing the obvious. "Yes."

"Well, I wish you had time for one. Is this how you trained as an assassin? Our fainting lily told me you were top of your class. Not like this you weren't. Did you hang up your hat then too, whenever you got winded?"

Semra rolled her eyes. She was in no mood for his games today. Zezura lifted her head from her place on the ground and puffed out two trails of smoke from her nostrils.

Not you too, Zez. I'm worn down enough as it is.

Zezura blew out a short blast of flame and bobbed her head up and down.

Defeat lined the edges of her mind, threatening to take her over. Two weeks, and nothing. Nothing to show for their insane venture into Nowheresville, far from the castle, far from Zephan, hopeless to stop Azi and Avaya. Semra glared at Zezura. *How is it so easy for you? What does it feel like?*

Quick as a flash, Zezura jutted her nose forward toward Semra and responded through the mark as clearly as if she had spoken aloud:

I am not in the fire. The fire is in me. It is mine. Are you your arm, or is your arm a part of you? Does it control you, or do you control it? How much energy does it take to lift your arm?

Semra stared at her. They'd communicated before, but never as vividly, as clearly as this. Semra's communication to the dragon had always been more articulate than Zezura's back to Semra. Had Zezura always been capable of it, and it was Semra's ability that was changing? Or their bond, deepening?

She replayed the message in her mind. *Does it control you, or do you control it?* Well, right now, the magic controlled her. She was unstable, like Frigibar said. And yet it was meant to be as easy as commanding any other part of her body—only a thought, a desire?

"You're afraid of it." Frigibar sounded surprised, as if he'd stumbled upon the discovery by mistake. "Why are you afraid of your magic?"

Semra's jaw tensed, and she frowned. "I'm not afraid of it."

Frigibar folded his arms. "You're not treating this like assassin training. You leaned into that—you must have, to do as well as you did. The art of the kill gave you life."

Her pulse ticked up a notch. Of course it gave her life! She was good at something. Praised for something. The feel of a blade in her hand was like honey on her tongue, salve to a wound, warmth in the cold of night. A smooth execution was poetry in motion. But now ...

A knot formed in her stomach, and Semra swallowed. "The art of the kill destroyed everything, and the man who taught it to me murdered my parents, sic'd my mentor on me, and then tried to kill me himself when Ramas failed. The art of the kill destroys kingdoms from the inside out when no one walking the streets in the cities below have any clue. The art of the kill gives power to anyone who wields it, and no one wields it but evil, blood-soaked irredeemables."

Frigibar's eyes narrowed. He leaned against a tree trunk and shook his head slowly. "You don't believe that."

Didn't she? A lump rose in her throat, and she blinked back traitor tears threatening to escape. No, she knew better. If she really believed they were irredeemable, she wouldn't have gone to such lengths to protect Pidge or the other assassins, to give them a chance at a new life. She wouldn't have stayed at Shamaran Castle as long as she did—somewhere inside she knew she was capable of good. She hadn't always believed it, but she'd forgiven herself for her past.

Probably.

Almost.

Hadn't she?

Semra rubbed the back of her neck. Her eyes stung, and her face flushed. Ramas, the commander who trained her, the voice of her childhood, filled her mind. *I always hated you.*

Next came the voice of the Framatar, the name the mountain children knew Azi by. The dragonlord, the father figure of the bulk of her life. *Everything you are is because of me. You are nothing without me!*

It was true, of course. Everything she was, everything she knew, began with that fateful day when Rotokas kidnapped her at four years old. All the memorable years of her life had revolved around the occupation and mindset of an assassin.

There was never any hope for her innocence. But Zephan had shown her that she was more than her training, more than what she'd been made to do. A part of her still came alive at using her skills, but another part wished she could have other talents. Another life.

Being pardoned for her past was one thing. Being made a noble against all reason was quite another.

Forgiving herself had been one thing. But setting herself up as some sort of thing to be emulated? To become not just an accidental dragonlord to a beast she once despised, but a powerful symbol of Jannemar—a representation of the kingdom, like the emblems that had cropped up all over Belvidore of the blue dragon against the black, like the dragon depicted on the Jannemari flag? To be welcomed to walk the halls of royalty, presume authority, even *become* royalty if Zephan really did ask her to marry him?

Doing this ... becoming this. Was she to be trusted with so much power? Authority should be stripped from those who have abused it, who have murdered with it, played at being gods with it. Not handed out like candy.

It felt wrong.

It *was* wrong.

Even if she *could* learn it. Which was quite possibly not in the cards.

Semra backed away and struck her hand out to steady herself against a tree, a rough snag of bark biting into the flesh of her palm. Dread settled over her like dense fog, and smoke baited her emotions once again as it oozed from her trembling fingers. Her head swam, and a bead of sweat ran down her face.

It wasn't right. She wouldn't do it.

But someone had to, or Azi would win. And he could not be allowed to win.

Semra snapped her head up, chest heaving, eyes wild, drilling Frigibar with a desperate plea. "You take it," she rasped. "You know about magic. You said the ancient melders could store their magic in artifacts and others not blessed with magic could access it. We'll do that."

Yes! Now that she'd thought of it, the idea took hold in earnest. It would solve everything! Frigibar was experienced, knowledgeable, and unexpected. He knew more about magic and its use than anyone alive. He had no desire to rule kingdoms, had no claim to any throne, and Garbane trusted him. Who better to wield her magic than him?

Frigibar stilled. Hunger lit his eyes for a fraction of a second before an icy shadow enveloped it. Frigibar pushed off the tree and crept forward with the unblinking intensity of a serpent, boring into her soul, hand outstretched toward her chest.

Semra drew back, and a shiver flew up her spine.

"You would so easily pass off this burden, this gift, this power," he mused, slithering forward still. "Does it feel self-less, to pass it on to another, righteous, to hand it away? Or does the danger sing to you?"

Frigibar's palm pressed against the opal on her chest as it draped over her collarbone, and pushed her back against the tree. His voice began as a low hiss and curled into a rumbling snarl as the words came forth. "You love a reckless peril."

Semra flinched and cringed away, her hair matted up against the mark of the tree at her back, her body as far from Frigibar as she could manage. His words sliced to the bone like a dagger, and a chill beset her heart. But just as her hands itched for the blade, Frigibar dropped his hand and stumbled back, shaking his head.

"Promise me." He raised his finger to point at her, rasping out his words with effort, as though fully exhausted. "Promise me you will never offer your magic to another. Promise me you will never encapsulate it in any object for as long as you live."

Semra gaped at him, her heart bashing against her rib cage, the heat of her flame roiling beneath her skin like a horse champing at the bit, begging for freedom. She could nearly taste it, but she knew she was unstable. Out of control. For the first time she thought perhaps she could release it, but what might happen if she did? There was something raving and barbarian about this fire, a fear-fire, not targeted at anything in particular, desperate only to be free. Would such a flame consume her, and Frigibar, and the whole of the wood?

Semra's chest seized with confusion, fear, and guilt—for whatever thing she had clearly done wrong, without understanding why. She did not trust herself to speak. She jerked her head forward once in a quick nod.

Frigibar dipped his head and heaved a long sigh. "Good. Good ..."

The old man's broad frame seemed to shrink, his shoulders falling forward, the wrinkles of his face deepening so that he appeared to age a decade or more in the space of that moment. He turned away and strode to the house. "The lesson is over."

Semra stared after him as he disappeared around the bend of the house, and collapsed to the base of the tree trunk the moment he was out of sight.

29

Semra's mind whirred, anxiety splintering from one thought to the next. Her perfect solution, giving her power to a more capable and deserving ally, had turned Frigibar into a crazy power-hungry enemy and back again, all in the blink of an eye. He'd been drawn to her power. That much she thought was real. But even more real was his insistence against it.

Why? What was so wrong with him having it over her? Was there a problem with the infusing process of magic into artifacts? Did he not want to bear the burden, as he'd so aptly called it?

She thought again of his observation, the one that had thrown her for a loop and sent her head spinning. *You're afraid of your magic.*

Semra slowly gathered her feet under her and approached Frigibar's tree.

Zez, a boost?

Zezura reared a drowsy head, scooped Semra up with her nose, and swung her head round toward the second-floor broken window. Frigibar had yet to show them the entrance he himself used, and recommended they simply continue entering and exiting through the window, with the help of a rope or a dragon. Semra patted the dragon's nose and slipped inside.

The grizzly reality was that the art of the kill *did* give her life, and Semra wasn't convinced anyone who thrived off adrenaline should be handed such a treacherous weapon as fire magic. And based off their evening research, fire magic was the most dangerous of them all—even forbidden, in ancient times.

And if she couldn't be trusted to have magic, why should she be trusted with an earldom, let alone a kingdom? But every joyous dream in her life now included Zephan. She would have no happy retirement to a lonely cave, and nothing but misery would follow any attempt at a secondary occupation. She could play at being a dragonlord earl, but to what end?

It all felt empty without him. And anything *with* him felt wrong. Because Zephan Shamaran *was* the crown now. And Semra Myansara, for all her atonements and Turian's generous bestowing of the surname and a title, was no noble.

Semra climbed the ladder up to the third level and paused at the top. Aviama was in the room they shared. A sweet, pure melody lilted through the door.

> *The beauty of a land with you*
> *Is lovely not with one, but two*
> *Through every shadow, you're my shield*
> *A song of love in every field*

Semra eased onto the floor beside the ladder, her feet still dangling down over the opening to the room below. What must it be like to be able to create such sounds? The tune climbed high and dropped low, playing along the scale, and something in Semra's chest swelled and ached at once to hear it.

A love song, to both a lover and a land—but what was the land without the lover? She could relate to the conundrum.

The notes floated like birds on the wing, and Semra wondered if singing them felt as free as riding a dragon did to her. If it did, she wished Aviama would sing more often.

It might do them both good.

Semra crept to the door and eased it open. Aviama lay on her back on the bed on top of the pile of blankets Frigibar had provided, staring up at the knotted ceiling, twirling an empty ink pen in her hands. Inkblots stained her fingertips, and a few papers were half-stuffed into books to one side.

The floor gave a gentle creak, and Aviama yelped, the song chopped off mid-phrase. "How long have you been standing there?"

Semra's heart warmed at the sight of her. Fainting lily, Frigibar called her. The girl was easily startled and effortlessly beautiful, so that much was right. And she needed to work on gaining a keen ear if she hoped to survive without her entourage. Semra smiled at her friend and came to sink down on the end of the bed. "Not long. How long have you been singing?"

Aviama sat up and grimaced at the books and papers beside her. "I don't know. An hour. I'm sick of books. The words got all swimmy, and I swear there isn't a thing in there I haven't read three times already. And if it *is* new, I don't under-stand it."

Semra's gaze followed hers to the books, but her mind was on something else. Frigibar. Magic. Failure.

Authority she shouldn't have. Influence she didn't deserve.

A happy life she shouldn't accept, even if Zephan ignored his court's most likely advice and offered it to her.

"If you like to sing, I think you should do it more." A lump stuck in her throat, and her mouth went dry.

Aviama's eyes widened, and then she sighed. "I do like it. I wish I was better at it. But I sound the way I sound, and there's nothing more to that. I'm so ... tired." She twisted one of the rings on her fingers. After they'd made it to Frigibar's, she'd put them back on, saying her hands felt weird without them. Semra thought they brought her comfort, something normal in her strange new circumstances.

She glanced up at Semra. "I think I sound better here, almost. Clearer. When I'm totally exhausted, in particular. Isn't that weird? I think since I've heard such amazing singers perform for us at home, sometimes I try too hard to mimic them, and it restricts the sound. When I'm too exhausted to focus so hard on being perfect, the sound just ... floats."

Something niggled at Semra, hearing that description. It sounded like Frigibar. What had he said? *You're trying too hard.* Hmm. What was it about trying too hard? Was she supposed to not care? With everything on the line as it was?

You're scared of it.

A shiver ran up her spine, and Semra's focus snapped to Aviama's face. When she spoke, her voice was hardly a whisper, husky in her throat. "Avs ... how can I accept him?"

Aviama leaned forward, searching her face. "What are you talking about?"

"Zephan. If he asks. How could I accept him?"

"If ... if he asks you to marry him?" Aviama stared at her, and her mouth twitched. "Um well, how about you say, 'Zephan, I love you, and I would do anything to be Aviama's sister-in-law. I accept your hand in marriage.' And then maybe you hug and kiss and stuff. But I don't need to see that part." She grinned.

Semra laughed in spite of herself and blinked back tears. "No, I mean ... I would accept *Zephan* if he asked, if it were only him asking, you know? But he can't ask just for himself. He can't ask me just to be his wife. When Zephan proposes to a woman, he proposes marriage to both himself and to the crown. I wouldn't be able to quietly live life with the man I've come to love. I would be putting him and all his life's work at risk by cheapening the monarchy with a murderer on the throne."

Aviama's face fell, and all levity dropped away into the grim thoughtfulness of a gravesite guest. "You're not him."

"Who?"

"Azi."

Semra's breath caught, and her chest hitched. The room seemed to close in around her, as the child of the two lives she carried most weight for losing poured tenderness on a gaping, festering wound. "I couldn't do what Sharsi did. I may be common, but I'm not her."

"Semra ..."

Semra shook her head and struck the blankets beside her with a fist. "No, see, your mother was *good*. Rats and rot, her only sin, in the eyes of the court, was not being born noble. But me? Not only am I a guttersnipe nobody raised in the mountains, but my *only* accomplishments are lists of people I've killed to serve someone else's agenda. Someone truly evil. I might not be him, but I might as well be."

Aviama shook her head, her bright-green eyes glinting in the evening light of the window. "That's ridiculous. You've been pardoned for what you did back then, before you knew what you were doing. And since then, you've saved Zephan, exposed Azi's actions and underground indoctrination program to my father, saved Lesala and all those other children and other assassin people you knew—how many did you say were in Mount Hara? No don't tell me, I know it—one hundred! You saved those people, even if some of them didn't know enough to appreciate it.

"Children. Little kids. They're in families again because of you. And when Avaya was kidnapped, you were the one that found out about her scheming, that she kidnapped herself and wanted to rule Belvidore. You were the one who encouraged Zephan and kept him going when my mother died, and again when Father died. You kept me going too. You've been the backbone for all of us. And with Zezura, you protected Jannemar and ended the battle with Belvidore at the Surion Strip. Semra, you were a huge part of stopping a *war*."

Aviama threw her hands up. "What else do you need? Should I make up some sort of penance ritual? Maybe we can dance around in a circle and burn stuff. I've heard there are people in the outlands who do that. Should we give that a go? Because I'll do it! Not to mention you saved father the first time he was threatened—you know, when Pidge was supposed to kill him. She told me. You saved him, and you saved her. You even warned father about Tymetin trying to kill him, and in the end, you stopped Tymetin—Zezura killed him before he had the chance to ruin any more lives."

Semra stared out the window at the greenery of the trees waving gently in the breeze, hints of yellow on their leaves. Snatches of azure sky melted into purple through their branches. Zephan had told her the same thing about her heart, her motives, long before she'd done anything to stop Azi. Back when she was only a runaway hoping to stop his evil before it was too late. His voice came to her now, and the sound of it was a salve to her soul.

Your job, as you call it, may be death ... but your inclination is life.

He was right. She knew that now. And everything sounded so reasonable when Aviama said it. So why did it still *feel* so wrong? Her heart bucked at the truth even when her head knew it all logically fit.

Semra thought of Tymetin, and what Aviama had said. She'd stopped him from ruining any more lives ... "But he did ruin yours. I didn't stop him in time."

Aviama winced, then shrugged it off as if the gesture would keep Semra from noticing the pain. She spun the rings on her fingers and tapped the tip of the pen against her palm. "My life is ... dark. The music is like pinpricks in a bucket. The air feels thick, and a song can lift the fog, if only for a moment. But for as heavy as my life has been, and as empty as I feel without my parents, holding on to you and my brother has given me such hope. You've grounded me. You're not just keeping me alive. You're keeping me *alive*. I can't ask you for anything more than that."

Semra hadn't considered that before. She hadn't been trying, exactly, to lift spirits. Semra had never been described as an encourager before, and it certainly wasn't praised in the mountain when she'd tried it. For all her failures, maybe she had eased the suffering she couldn't prevent.

Aviama reached forward and gripped Semra's hand. Semra looked up, into Aviama's emerald eyes, intense and solemn. "But ... but if I *were* to ask you. For anything more, that is. I would ask you to do what only you can. For whatever reason, *you* are the one with the dragon's kiss. *You* are the one with the dragon, the magic, and *your* magic isn't sifal. It's natural. It's tabeun. Your magic is natural, and your bond with Zezura is deep. You have every advantage he has, but better.

"I'm no military strategist, and these stupid books make

my head spin. But I think ... I think what I've learned is that good people often feel like they have to lay down and die in order to stay good. And I think the fact that you're starting to believe it too, means your thoughts have changed. You aren't the same person you were when you were under Azi's thumb.

"But I also think those people are wrong. Laying down and dying isn't noble. It isn't selfless. It's cowardly. And Semra Myansara, *I* am afraid of many things, but *you* are not. The only way to stop someone strong and evil is not to lay aside your power but to be just as strong as he is, and stronger, but keep yourself good. And the challenge, I think, is to keep yourself good while in possession of such power."

Semra searched Aviama's earnest features for a long moment. How had the young bouncing teenager Semra remembered meeting become such a wise soul? Perhaps sorrow was a fork in the road, an opportunity for destruction or for discernment. Once the two sisters had stood together at that fork, and while Avaya turned to chaos, Aviama had chosen the path that matured the heart. What a marvel she was! If only Aviama could see it.

Her friend's words sank deep into her mind. Semra pursed her lips, but a warmth spread through her chest, and the tension in her shoulders eased. The breath she drew next was deep and settling, and a slow smile crept over her face. "Thank you. You're really something, you know that?"

"Hmm? What? No, I don't think so. I just sit on my hands and cry my troubles away while everybody else goes off and does the real work." Aviama folded her hands in her lap and flopped back against a pillow.

Semra almost didn't hear her. Aviama's point about the greatest challenge was niggling in her mind. "So if I learn to harness this power ... how do I do keep myself good?"

Aviama shrugged. "I don't know. But I think going it alone

makes you vulnerable. It lets your head run away with all kinds of crazy thoughts, and who's to tell you how insane they are when you're by yourself? Maybe that's Azi's weakness. Maybe he's been on his own, listening to nothing but his own brain for too long. I don't think I'd last three days alone with myself and no one else to talk to."

Semra nodded and let her gaze drift out the window once more. She thought of the mountains at their backs and wondered if they had any caves. Home. What was a home? She'd called Mount Hara home for most of her life, the familiar surroundings where she ate and slept and trained and was punished. The people there were harsh and hurt, but the breeze, the rocks, the cold of the pools within its craggy depths, these had been her respite.

And now, it was two of the three Shamaran children that felt most like home to Semra. People rather than a place. The castle might be made of stone like the mountain—a rock of sorts—but it felt like confinement, a veiled harshness in judgmental glances and underhanded cuts from court. The polarity had reversed, first with the people a threat and the place a comfort, and then the place a threat and the people a comfort. Specific people. Even Garbane and Saeb made the list. And Gaulen, that infuriating self-righteous soldier.

Good men did indeed remain.

Who was she if she left them now?

Lean in. Here in a tree at the urging of the chandler, you are home—with a mountain at your back and a friend by your side. Magic courses through your veins, and for better or for worse, it is yours to steward.

Lean in. How many dragonlords do you see rising up to challenge Rotokas? How many magicians have you found to thwart Avaya? How many assassins have the mind to meet Azi face to face, and the wherewithal to win?

She might not win, but if she failed, there was no hope for any of them. Semra was weaker than Azi, but if she could conquer her magic, if she could accept her past and whatever lot in life she had left, she just might have a fighting chance.

A chance to stop Azi once and for all. A chance to save Jannemar. To save Zephan.

Lean in.

And she did. Fatigue fell over her like a blanket, and she surrendered to the energy rolling beneath her skin. It felt so close, so warm, so alive. At last she reached for it, too worn to bother straining, and a small fire the size of a candlelight flame leaped to her fingers.

30

Aviama squealed, and Semra's jaw dropped. She'd done it. She controlled fire.

Semra danced the little candlelight flame along her fingertips and back, mesmerized by the light of the flame, *her* flame, casting its miniature orange glow.

And then the light went out.

Not her light. The light from the window. A dark swathe blotted out the afternoon sun through the trees, and Semra's own little fire vanished. A chill ran up her spine, and the hairs on the back of her neck stood on end.

"Wha—"

Semra clamped her hand over Aviama's mouth and shook her head. *Don't say a word.*

The shadow rolled through, then swept by again a moment later. Had he found her so quickly? How did he know where she'd gone? Her heart stopped. They had Garbane.

That, or Siler had betrayed her again. No, he wouldn't. Not like this. He'd been done with Avaya ... hadn't he? And even if not with Avaya, he'd been wanting to escape Azi even longer than Semra. He would never feed Azi information. He skimmed money from him for years to fund an escape plan and only left earlier than planned when Semra provided the opportunity.

Semra searched out Zezura through the mark.

Are you hidden? Are you safe? What do you see?

Zezura pulled her in, and Semra fell into the dragon's seat of consciousness. Trees thirty feet wide hid the beast's large frame, and she peered her massive serpentine head around a trunk and up through a web of heavy foliage. A flying object obscured the sun, then banked and angled back toward Jannemar with a roar.

The sight of that obsidian serpent set Semra's teeth on edge, but the figure on Rotokas' back made her skin crawl. Azi.

She snapped back to her body with a low moan. *He's gone. He's gone. He hasn't found me.*

Or had he? Had Rotokas spotted the unique color of Frigibar's house, that only reptiles could see? Or did daylight and the thick trees keep him from noticing? Would he wheel back around for her, bait her to come out, or was he here for some other reason?

But the answer rocked her to the core. *We're in the middle of nowhere. There's nothing here. He knows.*

Aviama shook her. "Semra?" she hissed. "Are you okay?"

Zezura stood sentry outside, watching Rotokas' northwestern progress. *He hasn't turned,* the dragon assured her. *On he flies.*

Movement at the door caught Semra's eye, and she spun, knife blade in hand in a fraction of a second.

Frigibar peered round the corner, bushy eyebrows furrowed, face drawn. He flattened his lips, and his long mustache twitched against his beard. "I'd rather you didn't kill me, thanks. Leastways, not yet. Is he gone?"

Semra let out a rush of air at Frigibar's familiar stern

frame. "I think so. For now. But he must know I'm here, and it doesn't make sense for him to leave so quickly without finding me. He must have a plan."

"Intelligent people generally do have plans, and I don't take the man for a fool." Frigibar spoke in hushed tones and beckoned the girls to the door. "But who's to say he left quickly? Did you see his coming, or only his going?"

She blinked. "How long has he been here?"

Frigibar pulled two hooded mantles off the back of the door and tossed them to the women. "How should I know? Don't dawdle. We have a long way to go tonight, and we can't take the dragon."

Aviama fumbled with the fastener on her mantle and smoothed her skirts. "Where are we going?"

Semra returned her blade to its sheath on her pant leg and tilted her head toward their host. "Do you think he's coming back?"

"We aren't running away, sparky," Frigibar said. "We have a task, and I'll tell you what it is soon enough. Though, getting away from a house dragons can pinpoint doesn't sound like such a bad idea."

Aviama tugged the covers taut and smoothed the bed with a hand before turning to the door. "You didn't think slathering your house in something might make it stand out?"

"Nobody cared to study invisible colors in my day." Frigibar disappeared through the opening, and Semra and Aviama followed him down the ladder to the second floor. "Never expected dragons either. Or an old friend sending high-profile assassins and princesses to bash in the windows of my private, peaceful cabin."

Semra's mouth twitched. Aviama's face paled, but Semra caught her glance and rolled her eyes. She leaned into her friend as Frigibar marched around the bend and into the kitchen. She dropped her voice low. "He doesn't hate us near so much as he lets on."

"Don't be so sure of that, sparky." Frigibar swapped two pots on hooks on the wall—the small one where the large one was, and the large one where the small one was—then placed his hand on one of the hoops holding together a large barrel and paused. "And if either of you breathe so much as a whisper of what you're about to see to any living soul, you'll regret it."

Just before Semra considered asking the man if he'd lost his mind, Frigibar pressed along the side of the barrel and half of the cask split open on the opposite side to reveal a narrow staircase leading down into the dark.

Aviama's eyes bulged. "No way."

Frigibar snatched a knapsack from along the wall and descended the stairs. Semra ushered Aviama down the passage after him, mentally working through the possibilities. How did he do it? Weights and pulleys? Artifact magic? Gears and knobs? Surely the hooks were levers, connected to—

"Keep up, sparky, and tell the dragon to stay out of sight. We've got another hour of daylight."

Semra hurried down the stairs, reached back to tug the barrel shut, and enveloped them all in blackness.

"This would be a great time for somebody with magic to figure out how to produce fire," Frigibar grumbled.

Was he insulting her or joking with her? She took a wild guess and hoped he wouldn't stab her for it. "If you'd taken me up on my offer, maybe *somebody* could make some."

The silence that followed stifled her. Maybe he'd just been insulting her after all. Maybe he was allergic to jokes.

Aviama's skirts rustled as she shifted her weight beside Semra. "The tunnel was *your* idea, Frig."

"What did you just call me?"

"Um, Frig. It's one of the names I've decided to call you. Since you've given us names, I thought it only fair."

For all Aviama's talk of being afraid of things, she didn't have much of a filter. Semra stifled a laugh, and to her surprise, a deep throaty chuckle echoed from the older man.

"Fair enough, little lily, fair enough. This way, let's go."

Frigibar started off down the narrow passage in the dark, and Semra and Aviama fumbled after him. Semra reached for the fire within, but her connection to it seemed to have dwindled. She received back only a fizzle and elusive tingling, but no light.

They proceeded for half an hour in silence. To Semra's surprise, it was Frigibar, not Aviama, to speak first.

"You must understand, Semra, why I cannot take your magic. Why you must never put your magic in an artifact."

Semra's gut twisted, but her interest was piqued. He'd reacted so strongly to her offer, but now his voice was calm and stern, teaching rather than rebuking.

"Power is dangerous. It always has been and always will be, and though you may relieve yourself of the burden, you would more than likely pass it on to someone even less knowledgeable, even less stable than you, even if you did not intend it. You would want to give it to someone safe, but even if you started well, and it began in the right hands ... people die. Of old age or the struggle for power that such artifacts create. Artifacts can be lost or stolen. But most importantly, it is for *balance* that you must retain your magic.

"Listen to me, sparky, and don't you dare forget my words, because all of the world depends upon them."

All of the world? Semra swallowed and nodded, then remembered nobody could see anything, and cleared her throat. "Okay."

Frigibar barked out the next sentence in a sudden burst of

volume that made Aviama gasp beside Semra. *"Balance!* You threaten the fabric of the universe by throwing everything out of balance! It was for *balance* that the Aurin, Dru, Garjan, and Raisa set out on a deadly quest that no one asked them for, that no one wanted them on. It was for balance that they risked their lives and every human entanglement to restore.

"Back before The Crumbling, people thought fire magic was evil, but it is necessary as part of the cycle. Without it, the currents of the air are polluted with excess magic and no way to return to the beginning. There is no cycle, only an arrow, pointing to a contaminated world and sick and dying people. Do not think that because your magic is different, that you are not beholden to the same responsibilities.

"Housing artifacts are not meant to be used on a whim, used to become a bigger bully than one's enemy. They were meant to reverse the decision. A fail-safe. Wise beyond their years, they designed the artifacts with the understanding that man is flawed, and their own understanding of the solution to the plight of their own era might not be enough for all time.

"Using a housing artifact infused with someone else's magic is in itself a form of sifal. It is unnatural for an unmagical entity to use it, and anyone who engages in extended use of it is at risk of siphon poisoning. It's dangerous. The cells in my body would reject it, and though it might not show its effects at first, it would build up with no natural way to expel that foreign energy.

"To stop Azi and Avaya, you need great power. They will go to *any* lengths to get what they want, which means it will take everything you've got to stop them. Maybe more. The truth is that artifact magic is muted, finite, and dangerous."

Semra chewed on his words, mulling them over in the cool of the dark underground. "Thank you for telling me. I didn't know."

Frigibar grunted. "Yes, well, that's why I had to tell you. Now you do."

The passage turned upward, so steep that at times they climbed on hands and knees, and finally leveled out again. The soft dirt underfoot turned rocky, and Semra tripped over a root reaching out across the path.

Pinpricks of light appeared ahead, until they found themselves rounding a final corner and running straight into a vertical metal grate blocking the way. Dimness now interrupted the blackness behind them, and Semra could just make out Frigibar pulling out a single key, fumbling along the grate, and opening a narrow door that she hadn't noticed before.

Frigibar led the way through the gate, locking it behind them, and out to a craggy place on the mountain beyond the wood. Semra followed, blinking in the dusk, the scant light bright to her eyes after the deep dark.

Aviama dusted herself off from the tunnel and spun a ring on her finger. "Is the thing we're going off to do related to Azi and the black dragon?"

Frigibar scanned the scene before them, Ellix barely visible to the northeast, the vast lake stretching out before them on the other side of giant towering trees, the mountain high above them at their backs. "What word from the blue dragon, sparky?"

Semra paused, and checked with Zezura. "Nothing. No sign of them."

Frigibar dipped his head and peered at Aviama from beneath a shroud of brows. "I don't think your uncle was here for either of you."

Aviama frowned. "Don't call him my uncle. He's not part of *my* family."

The elder man pursed his lips. "Even so. There is something more valuable here than the two of you. And it is my responsibility to ensure he didn't take it. Though if he did, there's jolly little I could do about it but die in a failed attempt to stop him."

What could be more—

Semra stopped, and Aviama bumped into her. Her stomach dropped. "It's here? It's been in your *backyard* the whole time, and you didn't think that was appropriate to tell us?"

Frigibar only shrugged and angled up the mountain. "I'm sworn not to hand out the precise location, but I was surprised you didn't guess it, honestly. The origin of the Dezapi and Surion rivers are well documented as being in this area."

"Okay, what are we talking about?"

Aviama's voice sounded far away as Semra's mind whirled with the possibilities. Did he already have it? Would Zephan be dead by morning? What would Azi do with that kind of power, after he had the kingdom by the throat?

"A little help please." Aviama waved a hand in front of her face. "Hello? I'm here too!"

Semra ran a hand over her face. "Aurin's spear. Frigibar is taking us to the place Aurin plunged his spear into the Origin Wellspring, the day he ended magic and set off The Crumbling. We knew Azi and Avaya were looking for it, and now we know Azi knows where it is, and he might even have it."

Aviama's lips parted. "You mean ... we ... we're going ..."

"Yes, yes." Frigibar nodded solemnly, and his next words sent goosebumps up Semra's arms.

"We're going to the origin of the world."

31

The moon was high by the time Frigibar signaled them to stop. A night breeze wafted through Semra's hair, and she tugged her mantle closer. She breathed in deep and marveled at the older man's good shape for the steep hike they'd taken over the past several hours. Aviama doubled at the waist and put her hands on her knees, gasping for air.

"How far?" Aviama squeaked.

Frigibar quirked an eyebrow. "Not far."

Aviama groaned. "That's what you said an hour ago."

"Come along, little lily. You can rest on the boat."

Semra's lips parted. "Did you say *boat?*"

Frigibar dipped his head, allowed Aviama three minutes to catch her breath, and ushered them forward into a hole about five feet wide. The burble of running water somewhere caught Semra's ear as she descended into the blackness, and as she hopped the last few feet into the cavern, the sound gave a hollow echo.

Aviama slipped on the rock behind Semra, and Semra

reached a hand up to help her down. "Can we ever have daytime adventures?" Aviama asked, taking Semra's hand and skidding down the rock wall to the ground. "Maybe disguise ourselves as minstrels and disappear in a crowd, or join a caravan, and skip the underground tunnels and caves? We could even still do boats. You know, maybe we flee from bad guys on a ship, during the day?"

Frigibar chuckled. "Maybe one day you will, but not with me. This way."

Semra grinned and squeezed Aviama's hand. She turned back to Frigibar, carefully picking out solid footing in the dark and drawing Aviama along behind her. "Do all the mountains in this range have caves?"

"No, but you certainly seem to find yourself in a lot of caverns, don't you? Then again, I suppose someone with a dragon would be more apt to wind up in them than the average person."

Semra tracked Frigibar's movements as he picked his away across the cave floor with the sound of his brisk tread bouncing off walls closing in around them. Their footfalls emanated through the passage together, joined shortly by a faint dripping sound.

A bittersweetness swept over Semra, memories of Mount Hara filtering through her mind, some comforting, some painful. The winding corridors to the induction specialist, Adis, a kindly white-haired woman in charge of stabilizing new children in the mountain. The descent down to the river where the icy waters would wash away the grime of the road, clear her head, and bring escape from watching eyes. The trepidation of being summoned across narrow bridges over the deepest chasm to meet with Azi in Rotokas' lair.

"It's so eerie," Aviama hissed. "Can we ... can we talk about something?"

Frigibar's footfalls took a quick turn; the echo reached out across a great expanse, and the soft sound of lazy water grew. Semra struck her hand out to protect herself from the carbonate walls, and when she turned the corner, the sight took her breath away.

Bright blue-green lights glowed softly on a soaring ceiling, coating it like a blanket of numberless stars, and reflected up again from beneath in the ripples of an underground river. The gleam was enough to illuminate Frigibar off to one side, tugging a small canoe and oars from behind a faux cave wall and down to the water's edge.

Semra's heart swelled at the vastness of raw, untouched beauty, so hidden from the world. It shone not for praise or accolades, but simply for the glory of being—not for the eyes of intruders but for the sake of itself. Semra had been in caves, but never like this. This was a spectacle beyond her imagining, and she got the sense that she didn't belong in such sacred space.

"How ... how is this possible?" Semra stammered. So close to the beginning of the world ... could it be some remnant of its making? "Is it magic?"

"Glowworms. Stunning, isn't it?" Frigibar beckoned them to the canoe, and Semra tripped her way to it, unwilling to drag her eyes away from the captivating glimmer around her. Remarkable.

Aviama's eyes grew round as saucers. "Why have I never heard of this?"

Frigibar helped Semra and Aviama into the little boat, pushed off from shore, and floated them out into the river. "Because the cave system is significant, and few know their way to this side. And because after The Crumbling, people flocked to find Aurin's spear and did not return. People stopped coming. They say the mountain is accursed."

Semra cocked her head. "Why didn't they return?"

"The spear tip is embedded in the stream of the essence of magic, the core of the world. That kind of current is dangerous. Touching it can kill a man."

Semra's jaw dropped. That would have been a handy tidbit of information to know.

"Then why are we worried anyone can take it?" Aviama asked in a half-mumble as she stared about them at the radiant scene. "Wouldn't they die, and the problem be solved? And why are we going *toward* it instead of staying very, very far away?"

"We know there is a way to remove the spear." Frigibar dipped an oar into the water, and the canoe lolled side to side beneath a canopy of electric-blue stars. "The prophecy of the architect speaks of it, for example, and even the mere fact that Azi believes it is further evidence. He's no moron, and he doesn't strike me as a man who goes about a thing without due research—mad as he may be. I am responsible to ensure the spear not fall into the wrong hands, and to track changes in magical activity in the region. You are now beholden to do the same. Weighty knowledge often implores an obligation."

Semra's chest tightened. She'd gained unusual knowledge in her relatively short life—a look behind the curtain. Governors, nobles, commoners, kings. The world held a sort of smallness, where families were broken and friendships torn asunder in every social status under the sun. Grief ripped out the heart of the poor man just the same as the rich, and death brought the same coldness under wood as under thatch.

The canoe rocked as Frigibar's oar hit a shallower depth than he expected, and Aviama pitched forward and seized Semra's fingers. Semra smiled at her reassuringly and squeezed her hand, still half lost in thought.

Perhaps it all worked the other direction too—the bonds of closeness between souls could be seen whether both had money, or neither, or one had much and the other naught. A chandler might pity a prince. An assassin might be saved by a housekeeper's alliance. And a princess and a guttersnipe might float hand in hand down a strange glowing river.

Aviama tilted her head back, gazing overhead. "If the spring is the origin of the Dezapi and Surion rivers, why haven't they dried up?"

"Good question." Frigibar dipped the oar in again. "The Origin Wellspring itself is dry as bone. But after The Crumbling, water spurted from several lower places in the mountain, speeding to feed those rivers. The water has been tested time and again since, but there is no magic in them. Where it comes from precisely, and why the particular point of the origin makes the difference in the water, is unknown."

Semra watched the glimmering lights in the ripples of the water and thought of Frigibar's statement—*knowledge implores obligation*. It changed a person. No, Semra would never live in a quiet little village. She wouldn't thrive in a bustling city as somebody's demure wife, or nobody's busybody businesswoman. Who could understand her, she who had seen so much evil, *been* so much evil, fought so much evil, when they lived all their lives on the other side of the curtain—the side people like Semra created through cover ups and blood and sweat, the side they were meant to see?

Semra had knowledge of kingdoms, dragons, poisons, and the darkness of bright halls. She'd seen the destructive nature of power itself. Did she even want to toy with whatever raced even now through her veins?

But her magic was not quite like the elemental melder magic of old, the sort they'd read about in Frigibar's books—

she wasn't born with it, and it wasn't originally human. It was dragon magic, similar in kind to the fire melders, but not identical. Her magic came from Zezura. And Zezura was good, wasn't she? Surely she could trust Zez's magic more than she might trust her own.

Though now, it had become just that. And she must learn to lean in.

The tenor of the dragon's words rang in her mind.

Does it control you, or do you control it?

I am not in the fire. The fire is in me. It is mine.

Yes, she had been outfitted, beyond her choosing, with unique knowledge and power. Semra would never atone for what she'd done under Azi's thumb. But what she knew that others did not demanded that she *do* what others *could* not. She was obligated to serve, in her own way.

Her perspective was different now than it once was. With a wrench of her chest, Semra returned to the heart-to-heart she'd had with King Turian—the same one in which she'd promised to stay out of trouble, and then she'd launched herself into it within moments of saying the words.

Zephan's father had spoken to her of Semra's closeness with Zephan, and warned her of what a future with him would be like.

"In the union of a monarch, the kingdom is a third person in the relationship. It must always come first."

But of course it must. Knowledge implored obligation. And a king, responsible for so many, knew what others did not —and had the authority to act on it in ways others could not. Being a king, a good king, a *true* king, was no small task. It was why the office crumbled lesser men, and why Turian had admitted to Semra that it was sometimes lonely.

"And those who love us most," Turian had said, fervent eyes fixed on Semra's, *"must come alongside us or release us to our*

duty. Entanglements with those incapable of taking on the weight of the kingdom are dangerous."

Kings and queens were not free to do what they pleased, no matter how deeply they might wish it. Silk bedlinens and platters of meat were of little consolation to the sleepless nights and loss of appetite that accompanied the job done well.

What had Frigibar said? *It will take everything you've got to stop them. Maybe more.*

Semra dipped her fingers into the cool of the water and watched it curl, swirling about where her skin interrupted the flow of the river. Perhaps it would soon be time to see just how much it would take.

What knowledge had she, what power, that others did not? It would lead her to a door she did not want to open. A door where a little girl kidnapped from home would stand before a man ten times her strength, ten times her wickedness, an orphan nobody against a rejected royal—to stand in the gap between an empire of death and the children on the other side of the curtain, the Lesalas, Pidges, and Aviamas of the world. Hope for their futures.

And as difficult as it was to foster hope, it was harder to kill. She would not allow that flame to go out. The fire of the dragon rolled beneath her skin as resolve hardened in Semra's heart. She'd made a mistake in the throne room, in the battle of kings and dragons where Azi had locked up his nieces Avaya and Aviama, chained his brother Turian and his nephew Zephan, and planned to slaughter them with dramatic flair—the day Azi had slit the throat of Semra's best friend before her eyes and told her she was worthless.

It had been over seven months ago now since Semra's world had nearly ended, and for all her *inclination for life,* the mistake she'd made that day with Azi had been mercy. If she had the chance, she would not let him live again.

Even if it killed her.

It was her duty.

Frigibar's rumbling voice rocked her from her thoughts. "We're here."

32

———

Semra swung one leg over the side of the boat and held out a hand to Aviama, her mind still coursing with thoughts of Azi and her failure to kill him. If she'd taken him out when she had the chance, Turian and Zephan would've been beyond blame, and Jannemar would've been safe. The story would've been of the rogue assassin who turned on her mentor, not the king who executed his brother.

It would have been safer for the royal family. For everyone.

But instead, Turian had stuck him in the dungeon to rot. Except that Azi hadn't rotted. He had networked and weaseled his way out and to the top, using Turian's own daughter to do it. And Turian had been the one to die.

Semra swallowed hard against the lump that rose in her throat and blinked back tears in the blue-green glow of the cave. What if Azi *had* found a way to take the spear? Would the spear be a more powerful siphon than any other housing artifact, or would magic spill back out into the world? Would it be immediate or gradual? Stable or chaotic?

Frigibar pulled the canoe up onto the carbonate and waved them after him. "This way. It's right through here."

The glowworm ceiling of stars ended abruptly as they left the river behind them, and the openness of the cavern closed into a tunnel only three feet wide and five feet tall. Semra ducked her head to pass through it, Frigibar ahead of her and Aviama behind, and trudged steeply upward for several minutes in the cramped passage. When she reached the end and straightened in the wider space beyond, her jaw dropped for the second time that night.

The tunnel broke out into a natural circular chamber with a small opening perhaps thirty feet overhead. Rays of silver moonbeams sone down on a glistening spear shaft driven deep into the carbonate.

The dark steel gray of the shaft gave off glints of cobalt, and as Semra approached, she noticed veins of royal blue running the length of the spear. The base of the spearhead was only barely visible, a hint of bronze before being swallowed up by the ground. Fragmented carbonate fled from the point of impact in a burst of cracks flowing outward from its center, the cave floor formed almost like a black wave, smooth as glass, hard as flint.

Semra edged closer, fixated on the spear. There was no dust, perhaps owing to occasional rain, and no visible rust or aging. The only evidence that the weapon had been there longer than half an hour was the presence of cobwebs framing the hilt at its base.

Aurin's spear, the instrument of that famous elemental melder, untouched by time. Was her heart normally this electric, or was the energy at the source of the world lighting the air? Something about it felt like danger and home at once—a comfort and a thrill, in one alluring draw.

"It's still here," Aviama said. "It's safe. So everything is okay, right? We can keep training?"

The sleek, lustrous wyronite called to Semra as she circled

the spear. It was in too deep to be knocked free. Could she wrap her hands in something, protect herself from contact, and still gain enough of a hold to rip it free?

Had Azi failed to locate it, or had he not been strong enough to remove it? If she could take it from its place, hide it from Azi and Avaya ... maybe that would be enough. Maybe their power would be forever limited, their plans foiled without the promise of the spear. Maybe Zephan could overcome them if only it was removed.

Maybe she'd be okay. Maybe the magic in her blood ... It had saved her twice before, against snake poison. But a snake was another reptile, like the dragon itself was. This was a metal object sunken into the source of everything.

Frigibar's stern voice called from somewhere behind her. "Semra, stay away from it." A warning lined his tone.

Semra stepped closer and squatted down to examine its base. So embedded was the spearhead that the carbonate seemed almost smelted together with its bronze and wyronite. But the cracks splintering off from it in every direction might allow some air in, some wiggle room.

She cocked her head. "Have you ever tried to remove it?"

"No. And nor should you." Frigibar crouched down on the other side of the spear at a more respectful distance and caught Semra's eye. "The skeletons have decomposed by now. But make no mistake, they were here. The bodies of those who came before."

Semra pressed her lips together. "Azi didn't die."

"He might not have touched it."

"But he believes he can get it and live." Semra ran her hand along the carbonate floor just inches from the spearhead. Frigibar flinched.

Aviama gasped. "Semra, please back up. You're making me nervous."

Semra stared at the spearhead. So close. Had anyone tried it recently? Was there a way to make it inert? "They know a way. They must, or Azi wouldn't be flying out here already."

"Maybe that's what Avaya is for—to get it free and die in the effort, leaving him the mourning beneficiary of two kingdoms when the time is right." Frigibar stood, never taking his eyes off Semra.

Avaya as a sacrifice was absolutely reasonable. Avaya wouldn't agree to it, of course, but she was so taken by the idea of her loving uncle that she'd never have to know. Not until it was far too late. But even if that were the case, was it merely the prophecy that gave her the ability to remove it? Or was there a strategy?

Could prophecies be broken?

Semra rocked back on her heels and sighed, her shoulders sagging forward. Her head ached. Still, being here with the spear—in this place, like a step back in time—was like nothing she'd experienced. Had the cavern looked any different the day Aurin himself stood in this very place?

Was it her imagination, or did life itself pulse from this spot?

Frigibar circled slowly toward Semra.

Irritation dug needles into her chest. As long as she didn't touch it, she'd be fine. He didn't have to hover. Semra resisted the urge to roll her eyes, and returned her focus to the splinters. Maybe she could find a crack large enough to see further down.

Aviama's voice came out strained, almost a whisper. "You think he'll really kill Avaya?"

Frigibar dipped his head once. "He doesn't keep her around for sentiment. If he takes care of the king of Jannemar and the queen of Belvidore and returns bearing Aurin's spear, he'll be an emperor overnight."

But *how* would he take hold of it? *How* would Avaya remove it? Semra racked her brain, searching her memory of pages upon pages of research, books upon books of their evening candlelight reading, for something—anything—to solve the riddle.

The handle was too smooth for her to wrap her hands around. She doubted she'd have the strength to yank it out with her bare hands even if touching the thing *didn't* kill her. There must be some rule, some principle, to release it ...

Semra leaned forward, resting her chin on her hands and her elbows on the cave floor, staring at the moonlight playing along the silken strings of a spider's handiwork spilling off the bronze of the spearhead. "How did the melders create the housing artifacts?"

Frigibar shook his head. "I told you, it's too dangerous. It's sifal magic, and it weakens the potency."

"No, no, I mean ... if they removed magic at The Crumbling, how did they put magic into the artifacts? Was there a remnant of magic, some way to draw it out afterward?"

"All housing artifacts in the world today were created before The Crumbling."

Semra and Frigibar glanced up, startled, at Aviama. She shrugged. "I've had little to do but read. Magic was sometimes infused into ordinary objects for various purposes, though frowned upon by those considering it unnatural sifal magic. When Aurin drove the spear into the Origin Wellspring, the magic of the world was sucked back into its source, but magic trapped inside housing objects could not escape, providing the only magic left on this side of the spear."

Frigibar arched an eyebrow. "Not bad."

Semra pursed her lips. The only magic left ... "Except for dragons." She looked up. "Dragon magic remained in them, so there are a few exceptions."

"A few *rare* exceptions in species that hardly exist," Frigibar corrected.

Semra nodded, waving him off. And yet, the melders had created housing artifacts of their elemental power before destroying magic. Why? Wait, Frigibar had told her once. What had he said? *They were meant to reverse the decision.*

Her lips parted. Aurin and his friends knew that their solution to the problem of their time might not be enough for all time. A fail-safe, Frigibar had called it.

That was it. Avaya's necklace.

Semra lurched to her feet. "I've got it! Avaya's artifact. She *wears* it. That's why she doesn't have to hold anything to use her magic—she's still in contact with it—and that's why when I wrestled with her, the wind stopped. She was doubled over, and the necklace dangled off her neck. She lost contact."

Frigibar and Aviama blinked back at her.

"That ... makes sense," Frigibar said slowly.

Makes sense! That was all he could say? She'd solved it! Semra turned on her heel and paced the length of the cavern and back, heart pounding, face flushed with excitement. "That's their plan. That's how they'll do it.

"You have to have magic to remove Aurin's spear, and because no one had any powers anymore, everyone who tried failed and the power of the spear killed them. But the melders put their powers into artifacts in case one of them needed to reverse the decision and take it out again."

A chill ran down her spine, and her breath caught. This was it. It had to be. Semra spun to Frigibar. "It's just like you said. Putting power in an object is dangerous, because it can be stolen and fought over and fall into the wrong hands. People die. People like the original melders, who kept their powers close as a last resort. They died, and their objects were lost for hundreds of years, until one of them turned up in Belvidore around Avaya's neck."

Had Avaya known the artifact was there? How long had Avaya been chasing magic? Did Azi put her up to it, promising power of untold measure, or had she stumbled upon it while chasing aspirations of sitting on Belvidore's throne?

But Azi knew the use of the artifact would hurt whoever used it. It wasn't healthy to use someone else's magic. And that was why …

Aviama was two steps ahead of her. "He's letting Avaya take on the risk of siphon poisoning, letting her get the spear. He came to make sure he knew where it was, and next he'll bring Avaya and make her get it out."

Frigibar stroked his beard thoughtfully.

Semra stared at him breathlessly. "Well?"

"That's quite possible," he said at last.

Warmth flooded her chest at the validation of her theory. It was more than possible. It was true. She was sure of it.

Which meant they were out of time. Azi had already scoped out the spear. Avaya would be back, and she clearly knew how to use the housing artifact. Her wind was like nothing Semra had felt before.

And if it was time to get Avaya to the spear, it was time to clear the path to the throne. Zephan would be forced to surrender or die.

And he would never surrender.

Semra's chest tightened and her stomach dropped like a stone. Tears stung the corners of her eyes, and she raked a shaking hand through her hair. A curl of smoke emanated up from her fingertips.

She stilled, paralyzed by the sight as the ebony whisp wafted up into the deepness of night, the last of moonlight beginning to wane.

What had she said?

You have to have magic to remove Aurin's spear.

The prophecy was all lined up. Whoever wrote it knew Avaya would become the crimson queen, that she would find a way to break the spear free, that she and Azi of the same strong Shamaran name would aspire to taking over the region together in a great clash of kingdoms and dragons.

But Frigibar had told her that natural, tabeun magic was more powerful than sifal magic. Semra had natural magic within her, with Zezura's tabeun power flowing in her veins. Perhaps the architect did not expect an orphan assassin girl to accidentally save the life of a dragon and form the bond of the dragon's kiss, or to survive an assassination attempt through venomous snakes that would reconfigure her bloodstream and adapt her body to magical essence.

Honestly, Semra couldn't blame them, whoever they were. How could they have seen that coming?

Perhaps she was the key to the destruction of the prophecy. It was time to break the foretelling and make her own fate.

Only she was truly, *naturally*, qualified to remove the spear —even more so than Aurin or his friends would have been after The Crumbling took their powers.

Semra turned back toward Aurin's spear, and a tremor rocked her body. Her breathing quickened, the gleam of the wyronite daring her to try it. If she was right, she'd have the chance to protect everyone she loved, to kill off Azi for good, and to secure the kingdom of Jannemar.

If she was wrong, she'd be dead—but without another solution, Avaya would get the spear, and everything good would die anyway.

She lunged for the spear.

33

Frigibar and Aviama's panicked shouts roared in Semra's ears as she lurched forward to seize the spear at the heart of the world. Her hands hit the spear shaft and her body was hurled backward by a mighty pulse of power. The force of the blow tossed Semra up into the air and against the carbonate wall; she hit it like a rag doll and crumbled to the ground.

Her muscles screamed in pain, and her lungs burned for air. She couldn't breathe. She couldn't move. Semra clutched at her chest, reeling from the impact.

She'd been wrong. So, so wrong. Having tabeun magic wasn't enough to remove the spear. Semra had taken a gamble, and lost.

It was a miracle she was alive.

"Semra!"

Aviama and Frigibar flew to her side. Aviama struck her on the back and Frigibar reached for her wrist, checking her pulse.

"Semra, Semra! Are you okay? And to think I was *just* thinking what a genius you are, and you went and did something so stupid!" Aviama clipped her on the back of the head with her hand, then snatched it back. "Sorry, sorry. That was harder than I meant."

With a desperate gasp, breath returned, shocking Semra's system and racking her body with coughs. Semra planted her palms on the coolness of the cave floor, sucking in ragged breaths.

She glanced up at the wyronite spear. Its silhouette was dim in the remaining starlight after the moon passed by, but there it stood, resolute, unchanged, unchallenged.

Her theory had been sound. Even Frigibar had said so.

"I have tabeun magic," Semra rasped. "Why didn't it work? It should have worked." Semra buried her face in her hands as hot tears bled down her cheeks. Her body began to regulate, but her brain was whirling.

She'd failed.

Jannemar would fall.

"You should be dead. We'll count our mercies where we can." Frigibar tugged lightly on her arm. "Come. We have to get back down the mountain and prepare for Azi's return. If he thinks he can get the spear, we can expect him to make a move as soon as he's back at the castle."

Semra raised her head and searched Frigibar's solemn face. "I just don't understand. If the artifact magic is what the melders planned to use to reverse it ..."

"You're not meant to be the one to remove it, sparky. There's nothing left for you up here. But we're not dead yet, so there's time to come up with something else. Let's go."

Aviama laid a hand on Semra's arm. "Maybe no one can break a prophesy. Maybe we need to look for loopholes instead—we'll figure out how to take it from Avaya once she has it in hand."

Semra allowed Aviama and Frigibar to pull her to her feet,

but the feeling of doom in her gut would not budge. "Once she has it, it'll be too late."

———

ZEZURA MET them at the top of the mountain and flew them down in the last strokes of night, descending beneath the canopy of the trees just as dawn broke across the lake. Semra hadn't thought she'd find anyone less excited to ride a dragon than Aviama, but Frigibar had eyed Zezura up and down and paced back and forth for ten minutes before agreeing to get on. The sun waits for no man, and at last he was convinced that the time saved in travel, and the hiding of Zezura's massive frame was worth the foray into the sky.

Semra assembled her pack and donned the cursed dress she'd gotten from Polena as soon they arrived back at the house. The skirts were forever a hindrance, but the knife-strapped trousers were too conspicuous for Qalea—and that was where she must go.

If Azi was headed to make a play for the throne and kill Zephan, Semra would be there to stop him.

And if Azi was going to bring Avaya to the mountain to take the spear, perhaps the only prophecy loophole now was to incapacitate them before they could make the trip.

Semra tried to talk Aviama into staying with Frigibar, but neither Aviama nor Frigibar were keen on the idea. Aviama demanded she would not be abandoned again in a crisis, and Frigibar noted that his location was too close to the spear to be safe for Jannemar's only heir and the supporting documents she carried. Besides, if Azi knew about housing artifacts and how to use them, he may well know about Frigibar himself.

Semra couldn't just storm Shamaran Castle, anyway. She

didn't have an army, and very soon Zephan might not either. She had to be smart.

They set out back to Qalea that same morning, and as the azure scales of the dragon melted into blue sky, Semra gritted her teeth against the wind. For once, the road ahead brought her no pleasure, no sense of adventure. Instead of gaining skills to use against Azi, she was now wasting the opportunity she should have had—having located but failed to remove the spear, having trained for a mere two weeks but failed to learn control over her magic, and now traveling over twelve hours behind Azi and Rotokas to get back to precisely where they started.

Aviama squeezed her tight around the middle. "We're going to figure it out. Let's go save my brother."

And destroy your sister.

Semra hoped it wouldn't come to that, for Aviama's sake. But she'd let an enemy live before, and it had only caused more chaos. Could she really credit herself with mercy, in not resorting to violence, when the staying of her hand allowed greater violence to prevail?

They *had* to get to Zephan before Azi did.

And Avaya could not be allowed to leave the castle.

34

ZEPHAN

Shouts erupted outside the lower throne room door. Zephan lifted his head from the pile of documents on the table before him. A guard inside the doors flinched at a sudden crash, and the sounds of a scuffle arose in stark contrast to the room's previous dead silence.

The door cracked open a hair, and a flustered guard took a message from someone in the hall and bowed low to Zephan. "Your Majesty, it appears Earl Lundoon has arrived with some urgency. He is demanding an audience."

He'd had no shortage of angry nobles in the past weeks, but they rarely created physical commotion in the halls. "About what?"

"He is raving, Your Majesty, something about General Soldan. I'm afraid we can't quite make it out."

Zephan put down his pen and glanced down at his hands. An ink smudge marked one hand next to the bruise he'd earned in the morning's sparring session. He wished he could be back outside now. The longer he stayed trapped inside the stone walls of the place he would likely die, the stuffier it felt. He slept under the same roof as the man responsible for the killing of his mother, and who trained the monster who murdered his father.

Well, *slept* was an overstatement. Fitfully tossed and turned was more accurate. He was next on Azi's list. He had to be—and Avaya would follow after her usefulness expired. If Azi was smart, Aviama would be married off to someone to strengthen ties with some other nation, but if he was vengeful, he might wipe the slate clean and only leave himself as the sole Shamaran in Qalea.

Zephan had done his best to develop fresh eyes and ears and divert resources to his covert network, create a wildly inadequate plan for Azi's inevitable return with Rotokas, keep Avaya locked in her chambers, and continue daily duties running the kingdom. The idea that he had dropped the ball and ruffled feathers on any number of things was not at all beyond his imagining.

He set the stack of papers to the side and squared his shoulders. "Show him in."

The double doors opened to reveal a finely dressed older man with well-kept gray beard and hair, an odd contradiction to the savage look in his deep brown eyes.

Zephan arched an eyebrow and leaned back in his chair. "Lord Lundoon, are you quite well?"

"Not at all, Your Majesty!" Lundoon dropped into a curt, hasty bow and jolted upright. "Forgive my frankness but how *dare* you remove General Soldan from his position at a time like this! How dare you remove him at all, after everything he has done for your family and this great country! And what exactly are your intentions in—"

Zephan jerked upright, jaw clenched, throat tight. "You are mistaken. I've done nothing of the sort."

"—cutting off your highest court from reporting procedures regarding the allocation of military ..." Lundoon paused midbreath and eyed him skeptically. "What did you say?"

Heat flushed Zephan's face, and he smoothed a snarl from his expression with effort. "I have not removed, nor would I ever remove General Soldan from his esteemed position. I would caution you to not to insult me by listening to whatever capricious rumors my sister has been circulating from her place of imprisonment."

Lundoon snapped his mouth shut, then flattened his lips. "Your Majesty, I speak of no mere rumor. I watched two squads escort him from the castle grounds just this morning. Not supposing to make assumptions, I went immediately to the captain of the guard and was shown the order in person, with your signature and signet seal."

Rage boiled in Zephan's chest, but he clamped it down. No, he must be sensible. He knew this would come. But Azi's copy of the signet ring had gotten to him sooner than Zephan expected, and he wasn't even here to use it. Avaya must be doing it all herself, and surprisingly well.

How did one discipline a sister with unbridled power over air? Her crimes deserved execution. Was Zephan really ready to go that far? Or was there a middleman holed up somewhere with the signet ring, prepared to take the fall?

"So." Zephan stood and leaned onto his knuckles on the table. "This is how it starts. They remove my most trusted general. It's smart—he'd never back them, and he'll never buckle to blackmail."

Lundoon's eyes grew wide. "Your Majesty, it was signed by you. You're saying ..."

Zephan couldn't help it; he glared daggers at the man. "Most honorable Lord Lundoon, do you really think I would have shot myself in the foot in my hour of need? I rely on him! I rely on all of my court!"

"If that's true ... you did not, in fact, restrict my access to military reports?"

Zephan ran a hand over his face. "I want to be doing *less* work right now, not more. I'm drowning as it is, and you do fine work on that front."

"Your Majesty. This is subterfuge. Treason of the highest order. The culprit must be caught and put to death."

Yes, but what if the culprit has magic?

"We'll start with a list of everyone who has been in contact with Avaya today, and a list of every *object* that's come in or out of those chambers. I want the names of everyone who interacted with anything that came in or out—those preparing food, those who took empty trays out from under the slot beneath the door. And I want to see the order I supposedly signed."

The double doors to the lower throne room flew open, and Lundoon jumped. Zephan's heart dropped. Monac stood panting in the opening with a hand on the frame of each door, sweat running down his face.

"She's out," he rasped. "She's in the throne room, and she has soldiers. The doors are shut; there are bodies in the hall, and no one goes in or out."

Zephan stiffened, and a chill ran down his spine. No, this wasn't just the beginning. She'd leaped straight to the point. What had changed? Why now? This was not the diplomatic approach he'd anticipated they take. They needed an actual claim to the throne before reaching out their slimy fingers for it. Even with magic, it made no sense.

Using fear as a weapon would hold up on the front end, but it wasn't enough to maintain a kingdom and quiet rebellion in the long run. Was it?

Zephan's fingers flew to the hilt of his sword, the coolness of the metal his only salvation. He would receive more than a few bruises today. Would he still be alive by sundown?

It was the king they needed now. One who honored his office with unyielding strength and a willingness to sacrifice by whatever means necessary to protect his kingdom.

An ache set deep in his chest, constricting around him as pain melded with the tremble in his bones. For a moment he was transported back to a day in the conservatory with his father, as Turian had summoned him to talk about his relationship with Semra. Back before Avaya kidnapped herself to Belvidore, when the war was escalating and tensions with the court were a primary concern.

When the world was better because Zephan was a prince and not a king, and the king was the most honorable man he'd ever known. When he could be a son, and Turian his father, discussing things a son and father might.

"You're thinking like a schoolboy. Think like a politician. What does winning look like?"

"The court leaving us alone and giving their support."

"Who wins in the best negotiations?"

Zephan had steeled himself and took a deep breath. "Everyone."

"Correct. Which is why your us versus them attitude will destroy your reign before it begins. You can't afford to get offended. Taking offense is for lesser men with fewer responsibilities. You need to be smart."

Zephan had been thrust into shoes too big for him when his father died too soon, but the time for tripping over his feet was over. He must be what his nation needed—calm, decisive, strong. He must think like a politician. And he must not operate on an island.

What was the other thing his father had said?

"I would urge you to think of the crown. It is your first love, and you must never be unfaithful to it."

How his father would be grieved to know his son and daughter were tearing each other apart, with Aviama hanging in the balance! But today, Avaya was not his sister. She was a threat to his first love.

Zephan strode forward, clapped Lundoon on the shoulder and pulled him in to speak low into his ear as they moved out to the corridor. "Go to Firfell and get me those reports. Say nothing to anyone else, and tell him you need them by *mark of sundown.*"

Lundoon dipped his head and disappeared out a side door to the courtyard, and Zephan marched down the corridor with Monac at his side. "How many does she have?"

Monac snapped his fingers and motioned to several other guards; two disappeared, and four fell into formation around their king. "I'm not sure. But Soldan was escorted out publicly, and there are at least three confirmed dead upstairs and two more in the infirmary."

"How did this happen?"

"No one seems to know. No one is talking. She was in her rooms, the tray was taken inside, and then she was gone."

Zephan clenched his hands into fists as they walked. "I'd bet you anything Teriv is the one who took the tray. They found a way to get her in, and she posed as Avaya knowing she's been hold up and no one sees her face. Avaya could have been gone from her rooms all last night."

Monac and Zephan coursed down toward the feasting hall, where knights, guards, and others often gathered. They'd need more than a handful for a decent show of force. The doors were shut, and a document with Zephan's signature and seal was nailed to its surface.

Zephan scanned it and ripped the paper from the nail, gritting his teeth. It was an edict outlining a change to the line of succession—the eldest child of any gender would henceforth be permitted to rule, rather than the eldest male, reverting back to Avaya as the rightful heir.

Of course, Zephan had planned on making this change already, and had already written it up. But the edict to remove Avaya and Azi Shamaran from the family line must be produced first, and that document was with Aviama.

He squinted at the seal, and spotted what he was looking for. A slight imperfection in the lower left corner. This was the fake, the replacement his jeweler was ordered to make for Azi. Bless him for the courage to add the flaw. If they both came out of this alive, Zephan would see to it the man was rewarded for his faithfulness.

Zephan threw open the doors, and a shock wave rolled through the room of people beyond as they spun toward the disturbance. He held the document aloft. "How is it that I do not know about this?"

Blank stares and open mouths gaped back at him. Heat rolled through tense muscles, and his pulse pounded in his ears. Zephan's lip curled as he crumpled the paper in his hands. "How is it that not one of you came to me the moment you saw it, asking questions begging what madness had come over your king to release an edict like this supposedly opening the door to a foreign enemy? Think for yourselves! *If I wrote it, how do I not know about this?*"

One knight stood timidly from his seat at a long table and bowed. "Your Majesty, we were told you were in meetings all morning and not to be disturbed. We were meeting together even now to discuss what may have happened."

"I need you with me. I need you to *think* and *question!* Are you with your king?"

A shout went up from the men.

Zephan thrust the paper in the air and ripped it to shreds and raised his voice. *"Are you with your king?"*

A roar of assent went up from the men, and Zephan's knees nearly went out with relief to hear it.

"She has no claim!"

"Treason!"

"Long live the king!"

"To the death!"

They might not be far off. Monac shouted instructions, and the men organized themselves into squads and platoons at his order. Zephan took a deep breath and dropped his voice to a whisper in the din, turning in toward Monac. "Raise the distress signal. Take two trusted guards and don't let anyone know what you're doing until it's done. Meet me at the rendezvous. The mark of sundown is here."

Monac left without a word, and Zephan led the way out of the feasting hall and up the northwest guard stair, a rear detachment splitting off to cover the southern stair.

The familiar clank of mail and iron reverberated in the musty stairwell, and a thread of hope dared build in his breast as they crested the top. But just like that, his heart sank—a formation of armed soldiers met them at the landing, Gaulen standing in command, grim as the grave.

"Your Majesty." Gaulen inclined his head an insulting hair's breadth, squared his shoulders, and barked out his words in a clipped tone. "Her Majesty, Queen Avaya Shamaran Madensig of the double crown invites you to an audience in her formal throne room posthaste."

Zephan cocked his head and let fire burn in his eyes. "I have not heard of this queen. Perhaps there is another name I might know her by. Avaya the deceiver and traitor of two kingdoms. Disowned princess of Jannemar and widow of a husband whose blood cries out from the ground at the folly of his worst minutes of life, those few spent in union with a snake."

Gaulen's lip curled into a snarl, an expression rendering the man almost unrecognizable after so many years as a trusted soldier at the highest level. Their physical position against the stairs was not lost on him; Zephan and his men were at a disadvantage.

"The dragon returns! The dragon returns!"

The call rang out down the hall, and heads swiveled toward the windows, but Zephan could make out nothing among the throng. Had Semra returned, just in time to save the day? Or would her lifeless body lay with his as she forsook her protection of Aviama to come to his aid?

All color drained from his face at the thought, and his fingers wrapped firmly around the hilt of his sword. No, it was too soon. Surely she would not abandon her quest. Surely …

Another shout went up, asking the all-important question both sides begged to know.

"What color is it?"

A beat of silence followed, as Zephan imagined the silhouette of a dragon in the distance drawing steadily nearer. A ripple of nervous energy ran through the assembled guardsmen, and the hairs on Zephan's neck stood on end. Which color would bring him relief, and which would strike fear? He did not know.

The answer came in a panicked yell resulting in a burst of whoops, hollers, shrieks, and screams. "Black. It's black!"

Scourge.

As impossible as the situation was against Avaya's wind and whatever army of mercenaries she had amassed, it was hopeless with Azi and Rotokas at the helm.

Zephan drew his sword, and chaos erupted on the landing.

35

———

The necessity for night had been burning in Semra's chest through all the waning hours of daylight, knowing that even if they'd barreled through the last day of travel as they had the first five, they couldn't risk exposing themselves and Zezura by arriving while the sun reigned. They'd made excellent time, but whether they'd caught up to Rotokas was anybody's guess. They'd not caught sight of him on the journey.

Now at last Zezura had dropped them off on the outskirts of Qalea, and they'd picked their way through the streets of the city to the only place Semra could think to go. She squinted in the dim lanternlight of a tavern across the square, and tugged Aviama around the block and down the back alleys behind the buildings. Only two more doors, right? Or were there three?

She paused, and the light patter of feet caught her ear to one side. Semra shrank back into the shadows, an arm wrapped around Aviama, and waited, her knife resting obediently in the palm of her hand. Footfalls in the distance, receding. Whoever it was must have moved on. Or did the second set of footsteps carry a different gait?

A solid frame knocked Semra back against the building, and she gasped as the cold bite of steel pressed against the skin of her neck. Aviama let out half a squeal when a low voice cut her off.

"Don't let me catch you again, or I'll—"

The growling voice paused, and the arm against her throat relaxed. "Semra! And the other one, who shall remain nameless. Hello."

Semra breathed a sigh of relief and ran a hand across her neck as the man released her. Rats and rot, she hadn't come all this way just to let a run-of-the-mill thug jump her in an alley. At least, as consolation, it hadn't been a common criminal after all.

Siler stepped back and eyed her in the dark. "I must've gotten better at sneaking."

Semra shrugged. "I saw you."

"No you didn't."

No, she didn't. Semra pursed her lips. "Maybe I'm losing my touch."

"Don't lie. I was fantastic at it before, and I've only improved since then. But I thought you two were supposed to be out in Nowheresville staying out of trouble."

"I wish you people didn't greet so aggressively," Aviama grumbled. "It makes me nervous. And I'm already *so* tired. Can we go inside?"

Siler nodded and led them through the back door of the scribe shop and into a storage room. "I assume you're about to need something. Before we get to business, did you bring pastries for me? Croissants? Anything? I've had a terrible late-night snacking habit as of late."

"I've got half a strip of dried venison and three swigs of

two-day old water." Semra sank down on a crate and pulled her feet up after her. "Interested?"

Siler grimaced. "I've been spoiled, with business booming and the tavern next door. No thank you."

Aviama's face lit up at the mention of the tavern. "Can you get us some real food?"

"In the morning." Siler crossed his arms and leaned against the wall. "If I thought *I* was spoiled living in the city instead of a cave, I can't imagine how you haven't fallen over dead. How'd you like it out there in the real world?"

Aviama screwed her face into a thoughtful expression, as though answering such an inquiry required every muscle in her face. Semra arched an eyebrow, and Aviama lifted her head after a moment's pause. "Enlightening. I missed my bed. And I could have used something better to eat now and then. But it wasn't so bad, and I liked the wide openness of the world. I just wish I could see more of it, under better circumstances. I've spent too much time cooped up."

Semra smiled. The young orphan princess had handled the adjustments of the road and the multiple threats of death remarkably well. And somehow, she remained positive and encouraging. Semra was proud of her.

Siler blinked. "You're nothing like your sister."

"Thank you," Aviama said softly. Something in Semra's chest pinched. Aviama used to look up to Avaya.

"Someone has been spying on us." Siler shoved off the wall and rummaged in a box along the shelving. "That's who I thought you were, skulking around back there just now. I'm not sure if they're working for Avaya, or if they've caught wind of some of our ... business practices ... and been displeased."

Semra snorted. "*You*, run a business without high moral standards? I'm shocked."

"I knew you would be. And this is exactly the kind of sour

business that gives me a sweet tooth, you know? Disgruntled customers are always easier to deal with after a strawberry tart. But Avaya has been busy, and I thought you'd like to see—ah! Here it is."

Siler snatched a paper from the box and handed it over. Semra took it, and Aviama plopped down next to her on the crate to read over her shoulder.

Semra perused the parchment, and her stomach dropped as she read it. She snapped her gaze back up to Siler. "What is this? I told you to get documents *set up*, not to write any! It's a good forgery, but you had better not have released this anywhere."

Aviama's mouth dropped open. "This gives Avaya a claim to the throne. Zephan already wrote up an edict to let women into the line of ascension, but he would never do it like this."

"This wasn't us." Siler jabbed a finger at the document. "That was posted in the square just yesterday. It seems we're not the only ones forging royal documents."

But even forgers had their weaknesses. Surely their style and flaws would lead to the culprit. Semra examined the paper, the ink, the royal seal. "What imperfections have you found?"

"None. I think this came from the castle itself. Just not from Zephan, obviously."

Aviama took the document from Semra and inspected the seal. "We know this can't have been done with the real signet ring. And look, just here—the line is broken."

Semra instinctively closed her hand into a fist, the plain gold band of the back of the signet ring burning into her finger, the emblem heavy against her palm. Someone had a replica of the signet ring she wore. Semra absentmindedly ran a thumb over the smooth band. The stamp of their fake wasn't quite perfect. How had they missed that?

Siler's gaze dropped to catch the movement. "When's the big day?"

"Hmm?" Semra glanced up at him, and the storm gray of his eyes bored into hers.

He nodded toward the ring, and quirked an eyebrow upward. "Has princey made a proposal? Something you're afraid to show off?"

Semra pulled back, folding her arms and stuffing the signet ring hand under the crook of her elbow as she did. "Can you not get through a *basic* conversation without digs and nicknames? Considering he might be *dead* any day now, and I'd very much like to prevent it?"

"I was teasing." Semra glared at him, and he spread his hands. "Fine, you caught me, I wanted to see what you thought about the idea and whether it would make you squirm. And it did. But now I see it isn't just an idea. He's already proposed."

Aviama and Semra exchanged a glance. Semra shook her head. *Don't say anything. We have more important things to discuss.* And Semra didn't need Siler's ribbing. But the light in Aviama's eyes was impossible to miss.

"I see." Siler studied them a moment, and Semra's stomach flipped twice. "He hasn't proposed, but you know he will."

Semra opened her mouth, but Siler held up a hand. "Don't bother. You're queen of denial, if nothing else, but Aviama here seems very excited for a wedding. Just remember our services if such a day comes to pass. We'll mark up our marriage document prices for royalty—you understand—but still quite a reasonable price."

She rolled her eyes. "You're not even a legal business." Why did he have to be so observant, and poke and prod, and twirl the conversation to things that had nothing to do with him? And why did the thought of Zephan proposing fill her with butterflies, when she was in no position to accept?

Siler's hand flew to his mouth in mock distress. "I'm offended. Of course we are. Our officiating process is fully legal, just like all our other official services. It's the behind the scenes, bonus services you have to watch out for. The ones we generously offer our consumers that they don't always know they're getting."

Naturally. Like the *clear out overly valuable items* package, or the *sensitive information gathering for blackmail* option. No extra charge. Semra groaned.

"That"—here Siler stabbed an accusing finger at Semra's hidden hand—"is obviously not an engagement ring. The metal band is too thick and flat for women's jewelry, and when you were here before, you hinted that you needed only the paper, the wax—everything but the seal—for the forgeries. You plan to use it. And now I'll lay off on the wedding talk because I'm *very* interested in knowing precisely what you plan to do with the king's signet ring."

Her friend, her saving grace getting out of the mountain, the first person to catch on to Azi's lies ... it felt strange, not telling Siler all her concerns, the way she would've six months ago. But after his betrayal with Avaya, and with the sensitivity of the information they held, it was better to play things close to the vest. Even if he'd never work for Avaya again after the abuse he suffered, even after Semra and Pidge saved him, he still had a bottomless appetite for *jemari* coin.

Semra leaned back against the wall and let her shoulders drop. What she would give to put time on hold and sleep for a day before facing the world's troubles. "You're being paid, and well, for your forgeries. We'll get to that. But right now, I need to know. Is Rotokas back?"

Siler sighed. "This morning."

She stared at him, struck by everything that small piece of information might mean. Blinked. Swallowed.

Of course he'd beat her back. They'd made excellent time, but a sixteen-hour head start, and one passenger rather than two clearly made a difference for Azi. But he'd been back *all day.*

A lot could happen in a day.

A bead of sweat ran down her forehead into her hair. "What's the word on the street from the castle?"

Aviama shifted uncomfortably next to her, but said nothing. Semra could almost feel her friend's heartbeat pick up speed, in rhythm with her own.

"The flag flew upside down for about ten minutes this morning before Rotokas landed. It's been righted now, but they've snuck out a few bodies." Siler hesitated, and Semra's mouth went dry. "No funeral palls. Nothing so public as that. Evidence would suggest things are not good up the hill."

"But ... he's alive, right?" Aviama's voice came as a whisper, and even that small sound broke as she forced out the words.

"If he was dead, they wouldn't bother forging his signature." Semra leaned her head back against the wall and stared up at the ceiling. Hot tears stung her eyes and rolled down her cheeks, and she did nothing to stop them. She was on the wrong side of the castle walls.

Zephan fought for his life, or worse, laid it down, while she served as bodyguard to Aviama and wasted time on errands with Frigibar that hadn't shown any promise. The spear was found, and Avaya would turn the tables once she had the spear in hand, but with the fake edict in the public square and bodies being smuggled out, whatever tense standoff had existed before had come to a head. And fight though he might, Zephan would lose.

While Semra sat here, doing nothing.

Her chest hitched, and she could feel the burning fire running like a current under her skin, the smoke threatening to eek its way out her fingertips and fill the small room.

No, not threatening. Asking.

It waited on the brink, like her tears as they had brimmed along her lashes, swirling in the chaos, begging for an outlet. But this time, it did not spill forth without a second thought. Barely reined in, perhaps, but reined in nonetheless.

Her skin crawled with contained energy. She had to get it out. Semra unfolded her arms and flames sprang to her fingertips, ten dancing candle lights merging into two swirling, glowing orbs of fire floating up from her palms, born aloft by a layer of smoke cradling the light in her hands.

36

Semra stared at her hands. The warmth from the flames was gentle and comforting against her skin, not as harsh as she would've expected. She was more like a conduit than anything else, simply opening or closing valves that allowed the fire forth.

Zezura's description came to mind, and for the first time, Semra understood it.

The fire is in me. It is mine.

Siler jumped backward, his eyes nearly popping out of his head. "You brought magic back. You have magic. How did ... how ..."

Aviama clapped her hands. "Look! You did it; you did it! You relaxed, didn't you? You let go. Before, it had found you, but now *you* have found *it!*"

A small smile tugged at the corner of her lips at Siler's astonishment and Aviama's praise. Semra passed the fire from one hand to the other, balancing two swirling spheres in one hand like a juggler and wiping tears from her face with the other.

"It's not what you're thinking," Semra said to Siler. "Magic isn't back in the world. But it *is* in me, to whatever small degree. Like it's in Zezura."

A brisk knock sounded at the door, and the knob turned. Semra dismissed the fire with a wave of her hand, but they did not recede or return to her. Her heart leaped into her throat, even as the answer struck her: *does a dragon's fire go in and out, or only out? The flames don't return to you.*

Semra reached desperately for Zezura through the mark. *Help! What do I do? The fire won't go away ...*

Matter never disappears. Fire magic restores balance to the earth, and the earth needs it. Release it to the air and let the atmosphere consume it.

Why hadn't she consulted Zezura before? Frigibar might know the most about the history of magic, but Zezura had lived with it all her life. How did a dragon know such sophisticated knowledge? Were they born with the understanding, or did they gain it from somewhere?

Push, don't pull. Semra extinguished the flames with a wave of her hand, bending her thoughts on propelling the fire forward in a burst of energy. The burning spheres burst apart as if they'd collided with a wall, and only a few lingering embers remained drifting through the air down to the floor.

Pidge gaped at her from the doorway, and the box in her hands dropped to the floor. "I ... didn't see that. I don't even know what I saw. But whatever it was, I didn't see it." Pidge collected her box and gulped. "It's good to see you, Semra, except that you have terrible timing. You can't be here. It's not even daybreak, and the shop will be ransacked by lunch. Eyes are already on it, and they may already know you're here."

Scourge. Semra's stomach twisted. "Where's Zephan?"

"Nobody knows. Word is he's still in the castle, but every

contact we have went silent. Except for this box, which I wasn't supposed to receive for another week." Pidge turned to Siler. "The mark of sundown has already begun."

Semra glanced between them. Her attention settled on the box in Pidge's hands. It was identical to the one Garbane had delivered to Pidge outside the tavern two weeks ago.

"So. Avaya has taken control." Siler grimaced. "Which means Zephan is either captured or dead, and they're delaying the news, or he's alive, and they don't want to show their hand that they *lost* the king."

Lost. Lost was good. That's the theory Semra would be going with. She might not know where he was, but as long as Azi and Avaya didn't either, that would do just fine for now.

"We have to prove that the edict posted yesterday is fake," Aviama said. "Show everyone that something is very wrong at the castle, and ruin Avaya's claim. If Zephan didn't write and seal that document and didn't authorize it, then it's not legal. And if it's not legal, Zephan remains king while he lives."

Siler shook his head. "Except for a hostile takeover, which is precisely what's happened."

"She doesn't want an uprising." Semra hopped off the crate and paced the small room. "She doesn't have the spear yet, and swinging for the fences before she has it is risky. Why now? Something went wrong. She needs a claim to the throne to convince the armies to follow her, until she's strong enough to do more damage."

Pidge set the box down on a stack of boxes by the door and swung an arm over it. "Won't that make him look weak? Out of control?"

"Not if we do it right. A clever play. Something to throw them off their game and let the people know he's still in charge, even from beyond the walls." A thrill ran down

Semra's spine. She might not have access to the castle, but she wasn't helpless. Not anymore.

Aviama spun to Siler. "How many document templates are we working on?"

Siler hesitated, then smirked. "More than you asked for."

Aviama grinned. "I have an idea."

37

Semra squeezed through the crowd, her pulse pounding in her ears. She stretched up on her toes for a glimpse of the parchment the whole city seemed to have huddled around, hung on the center fountain above the water's spray.

Three days. That's how long it had taken Siler and his team to wrap up their forgeries and post twenty documents all over Qalea. Word on the street was that two of them had even made it inside the castle, appearing one morning in the kitchens and the guard tower.

A central hub of Qalea's bustling business center, *Lady of the People* was the perfect place to focus their efforts and disseminate information to the public. The fountain was erected in Queen Sharsi's honor after her death, replacing a statue of an old general championing Jannemar's victorious exploits in years past. The talk of the town and the breeze of rumors flowed through the middle of the city where all the major roads converged, here under the supervision of the Lady.

The stone fountain depicted a female statue dressed in the

clothes of a commoner but with a leafy crown upon her head, her hair made of a cascade of nezil myansara flowers, their stems wrapping around her and winding themselves into the bodice of her dress. With one hand she held a spade over her shoulder, the hardiness of work in a farmer's household rooting her to the people's plight, and with the other she poured abundantly flowing water from a great pitcher emblazoned with the Shamaran crest.

A murmur rolled through the crowd until one man two heads taller than Semra erupted with a booming bellow. "What is the meaning of this? Have all royal edicts lost their meaning? Has the crown lost all honor?"

A small woman behind Semra piped up in a high-pitched voice, craning her neck behind a host of her taller peers. "What does it say?"

"It says whichever stableboy is able to stand on his head the longest upon the king's death shall be crowned king," someone called out. "And two streets down, there's another one that says the kingdom will be granted to whichever royal dovecote pigeon has flown the most miles in Jannemar's service!"

Semra snorted and coughed to cover it as she eased her way through the crowd toward the other side of the square. The strategy wasn't subtle, but it certainly did the job. It was Aviama's idea to release a slew of authentic-looking documents so ridiculous that they couldn't possibly be real, thereby casting Avaya's edict under suspicion. If fakes could look that good, that real, then all edicts would need verified.

Siler and Pidge had been more than happy to provide content crazy enough to cause a ruckus, getting everyone talking, and challenging the authenticity over the edict of women in the line of ascension.

"What does the bit at the bottom say?" someone yelled. "Right above the seal there?"

The tall bellowing man leaned forward to squint at the parchment. *"Coronu tabeun, collora sifal.* Blessed be the natural, cursed be the unnatural. And here, 'Let the man who thinks, think for himself.'"

"But what does it mean?"

"Isn't it obvious? They're all counterfeit! Worthless!"

Semra angled away from the crowd and slipped away, the cries of the people following her as she went.

"Can we trust nothing with the seal?"

"The seal must be false! Someone is masquerading as the king!"

"To write stupid nonsense? Why bother? It's a capital offense!"

Semra shook her head. Of course, while Avaya's edict used the authentic paper, pens, and scribe's elegant writ, the seal and signature were forged. Ironically, it was the documents about pigeons and stableboys that used the real royal seal, though on copycat paper and replicated formal script. Semra had pressed the king's signet ring into the hot wax herself.

And it had worked like a charm. The outlandish edicts were all Qalea would be talking about for days, inside the castle and out. What she wouldn't give to see Avaya's face when she heard about it!

Semra extricated herself from the throng around *Lady of the People* and into the flow of moving crowds dipping in and out of the stores to complete their various errands. Errands that no doubt they would carry on with no matter who reigned from the castle on the hill. They wouldn't feel the bite of the king's loss, not like she would, not until their backs broke under taxes of a greedy queen, or their needs were unattended to.

They weren't losing one of the only good things in their lives. They were only losing a sovereign. The people loved him, in their way. But not like Semra. They might know his smile, but they didn't *know* him.

She picked up her pace, weaving past shops with their swinging signposts, two boys chasing each other with wooden toy dragons, and a mule cart rumbling dutifully over the cobbles. Walking the streets of Qalea still felt like a mission to Semra. She'd never lived in a city, and most of her experiences in them were for training or for assignments. Crowds were camouflage, but so many people in every direction also made her nervous.

It took Semra thirty minutes to make her way to the marking she was looking for, a sunset the size of her thumb in graphite gray along a stone wall. The old homes in this section of the city were built as a long, connected strip, cutting costs to build and each home sharing walls with those on either side. It was an unusual setup for Qalea, since most dwellings were free-standing structures, but lower working-class types had squeezed into them until overflowing. Perhaps that's how it earned its nickname—The Weeds.

The setting sun cast three rays over the hill in the drawing. *Left,* Semra reminded herself. *The sun sets west.* Semra turned left and counted one, two, three doors. Yes, this was the place. She knocked three times and ducked inside.

The house was small, even smaller with seven people inside. Aviama, Pidge, and a middle-aged brunette sat in chairs to one side of a cold fireplace opposite a young man in a chair, and a middle-aged man standing next to Siler along the wall next to him. Two curly haired kids of maybe ten or eleven poked their heads around the corner on the far side of the room, but disappeared when Semra glanced their way.

"When a king teeters, servants have the power to push him

over the edge." Quern, the man of the house, furrowed his brow and tugged on the ends of his beard. "They could also stabilize him, if they so chose. The invisible dictate the prominent. The powerless direct the path of the powerful."

"Dragons and daylilies, power itself is only an illusion anyway!" Pidge set down a cup of tea and flopped back into her chair, tucking her feet up underneath her. "The most wicked dictator could be ended in a night by a well-aimed knife or uniquely prepared herbal tea. And when nothings band together, well, isn't that something?"

Semra took a seat on the floor next to Pidge's chair, and Quern's wife handed her a mug. Ironic timing given Pidge's comment about poisoning just now, but it smelled divine.

Siler turned toward her with a twinkle in his eye. "Well? How are the pigeons and stableboys faring?"

Semra grinned. "Taking the city by storm. Any word on the king?"

Quern shook his head. "Nothing. But if he's out there, he'll get the message. No two ways about it."

"And so will Avaya." Aviama wrinkled her nose, then grimaced as she caught herself. Semra had told her not to talk about anyone in her family with familiarity. She should talk about them like townspeople, and reveal her identity to as few people as possible.

Though she looked the spitting image of her sister, and a blonde version of her mother. Anybody with half a brain should be able to decode the truth about the mysterious Shamaran sympathizer who sat too straight in chairs and ate too properly at tables. Another reason Aviama couldn't stay in Qalea to wait out the results of the contest over the throne.

Semra hadn't told her yet, but it was only a matter of time. She'd have to find safekeeping for Aviama, even if she hated it, even if it made her mad. Aviama was the crown princess. The one heir to the throne with a legitimate claim who might actually do Jannemar some good.

With Azi and Avaya taking charge of the kingdom, it wouldn't be long before they cracked down on freedoms in the city to flush out dissension. Even the family they stayed with now risked endangering themselves to be part of Zephan's underground support network. Semra had been surprised to hear of the secret web of people behind him, and her heart warmed at the thought.

He wasn't alone. Maybe he did get out, and somebody was helping him and keeping him out of sight.

Semra cupped the mug and took a sip, letting it warm her straight down to her toes. "And the code hidden in the edicts —we're *sure* it indicates the Pour Man's Palace?"

Siler rolled his eyes. "Have I ever steered you wrong? You looked at it yourself. Stop worrying."

Semra nodded, but her stomach twisted into knots. What if Zephan didn't find the hidden message? What if he deciphered it, but couldn't get to the tavern to leave a message? What if Avaya deciphered it before him? What if he was already dead, and all their efforts were in vain?

Maybe a riff-raff establishment like Pour Man's bar wasn't the best option.

A heavy knock thudded against the door of the house, and a muffled voice called through the door from the street. "King's guard! Open up!"

Semra leaped to her feet and her heart dropped like a stone.

Aviama glanced up hopefully at Semra, mouthing, *Zephan?*

Semra shook her head and pulled her to her feet as Quern edged slowly toward the door. Quern's wife shooed Semra and Aviama toward the back rooms, and Siler and

Pidge moved smooth as butter into new positions. Pidge dunked her hand into her tea and dabbed the liquid along her forehead and matting the hairs around her face, and Siler plucked a blanket from before the fire, tucked it in around her in her chair, and hovered protectively nearby. He wrapped one arm wrapped around her shoulders, and Pidge tucked herself into his side as if she were a fragile, frightened little bird.

Semra cocked her head and arched an eyebrow at him, and Siler winked at her. How many times had they used this storyline? She could already see it playing out—the sick, contagious weakling keeping inquisitors at a distance, the devoted friend or husband demanding no one raise her blood pressure too high, for fear of putting her health at further risk. The excuses for having people coming and going—doctors? Friends? Which explanation would he use?

She half wished she could stay to see it all, but the guard banged on the door again, and Semra pulled Aviama into the back hall, where two bedroom doors faced each other, the curly headed boy poking his head out to stare at them from one, and the girl from the other.

As soon as they were out of sight, the front door creaked open, and a deep voice carried in through the small home.

"King's guard. We have a warrant out for the arrest of this individual, and a missing person's report on this one." A rustling of papers followed, and the wooden floorboards groaned under the weight of a large man.

"Forgive me, sir, but you've not asked me any questions, and I did not give permission for you to enter my home," Quern answered.

"Someone matching this description was seen entering this house. Mind if I look around? I know you wouldn't interfere with an investigation of this nature. Do you read, man?

This woman is charged with murder, kidnapping, multiple assaults, and conspiracy to commit treason."

Kidnapping? Rats and rot, that was ironic.

The guard's heavy footsteps crossed into the living area where Siler was rubbing Pidge's arm comfortingly. Pidge let out an overpowering string of hacking cough sounds with enough enthusiasm to alarm any casual observer. Semra shrank back against the wall, and the curly haired boy waved Semra and Aviama into his bedroom moments before the guard would have had a view of them.

"Treason! Why, I never!" Quern's wife's voice trembled, and Semra thought the fear in it was real.

"You there, what's your name? I've never seen you in The Weeds before. What's your business here?"

"Klenner Scant, sir," Siler answered, his voice more demure than Semra had ever heard it. "My wife ... she's terribly sick. The doctors haven't given her long, and we just ... we needed to see friends before ... before ... well, we've had a few visitors ..."

Aurin's spear, had he conjured *tears?* Semra shook her head, then scanned the bedroom. Small mat on the floor, chest, chair, and modest homemade table to one side. Window. *Yes.*

Semra crossed to the window, unlatched it, and swung it partway open, then snapped it shut. *Scourge.* The rear exits were covered with two more guards on the south side.

The guard's voice drifted down the hall, and the hair on Semra's arms stood on end. "There are more mugs than people. Who is the extra cup for?"

Think fast, think fast. Anything that exposed Quern's family as having protected them could get them arrested. Leaving was no good. Staying was no good. But if they were going to get caught, they were going to be *moving.*

If she could manage to keep the guards alive, that would be a bonus, but not a necessity. The safety of the heir to the throne was paramount. Semra lifted her skirt and drew two throwing knives from the trousers underneath. The boy blinked, eyes wide as saucers. Aviama swallowed.

Semra knelt next to the young boy. "After we leave, lock the window, and crawl in bed. You've been sleeping for an hour, okay? It'll help your parents."

The boy drew himself up tall and nodded. "I'm fast. Nobody will catch me!"

"Shh. Okay, good."

A wail cut through the air from the living room, and a crash and shout rang out. "Can't you see you're upsetting her? She's not been lucid for weeks! Get out! *Get out!*"

"You'll not be giving the orders here, cretin!"

Semra unlatched the window and ushered Aviama over to whisper in her ear. Her eyes widened, and she shook her head. Semra touched a finger to her own lips and nodded. *Don't dawdle. Don't doubt. Just do it.*

"But what if—"

"Shh. This is our way out." Semra gave Aviama a look, and she swallowed, then turned to the window. Semra reached out and gripped her sleeve, and the princess turned back. Semra hesitated. "Run like the wind."

38

Semra gave Aviama the signal, and for a moment she forgot to breathe as the kingdom's last hope for stability dropped from a child's bedroom window and ran for her life—alone and unguarded—straight at the two guards watching the south end.

Sweat broke out on Semra's forehead, and a chill ran down her spine. Had she just sent Aviama to her death? Would her last action be to hush her friend's concerns and send her blind into the teeth of the enemy, before Semra was arrested herself?

The guards hadn't been looking down the street at the moment Aviama jumped. Semra had made sure of it. But they saw her now, and the sound of their running feet was swallowed up by Aviama's fever-pitch cries.

"Please, please! Get me out of here, get me out! She's on the roof, I got away and slid down ..."

"You slid down the ..."

"*Help* me, *please!*"

A whistle and a shout, and the two men took up either side of Aviama, ran down the back street with her, and disappeared. Semra slipped from the window, nodded at the boy, who closed and locked it as promised, and bolted down the street, knives in hand.

Her feet flew across the dirt path, and Semra mentally blessed The Weeds for its poor upkeep. No money for roads on this side of town meant no cobblestones—only packed earth, and the sound-deadening benefit it provided.

Semra rounded the corner and skidded to a stop. She looked left, then right. Her mouth went dry. The streets were empty.

Idiot! You've lost her!

"Please, hurry! Did you see her? She was back there ..."

Semra's heart leaped at Aviama's voice, and she broke into a full tilt run down the back alley. A man's voice hushed her, but as Semra approached, she heard what he said from around the bend.

"She said make no unnecessary stops. We'll find the other one later."

"Keep your voice down. The *king* is waiting. We'll keep you safe, miss, don't you worry."

The second guard's voice was deep and stern. He might have been smart enough to play the game, but the first guard had let it slip—he *knew* he wasn't working for Zephan. He was working for a woman.

A woman with whom Semra was at war. Under the thumb of a murderous dragonlord.

As if on cue, a fire bolt blazed overhead and Rotokas' huge black frame swept overhead in a *woosh* of air that sent chills down Semra's spine. But if she called Zezura now, the ruse would be up. Everyone would know she was in Qalea.

But was it already over? Could Azi see through Rotokas' eyes the way she could with Zezura? Did he know she was here?

Aviama and the soldiers ducked on impulse as the wyvern's enormous body coursed above them and twisted around to look, turning them face to face with Semra. The guards drew their swords.

Which guard was the dumb one?

One guard stalked forward, the other gripping Aviama's arm until she winced.

Semra danced backward. "You boys like to play?"

"Not with the likes of you," the front guard growled.

Low tone. Voice match. He was the smart one, the diplomatic one. *Target lock.* Semra ran forward, sprang to the side just as her adversary lunged, spun, and threw her knife at his jugular. The man knocked her blade from the air with his sword, an impressive feat.

The front guard slashed his sword at Semra, grazing the side of her dress, and shouted back at his companion. "Take her and go!"

It was then that Rotokas did her a favor for the first time in his long, miserable life—he made a second pass over the fight, and the guard made a fatal mistake. His gaze flicked skyward for half a second, and the black wyvern was the last thing he saw as Semra let fly with her second knife and buried it in the man's exposed neck.

The second guard yanked Aviama backward, half-carrying, half-dragging her away, sword extended and flashing wide eyes between his dead friend, his friend's killer, and the dragon making increasingly low passes overhead.

Semra dropped into a low crouch as she ran and ripped the knife free from the first guard's neck. Blood dripped down the blade and trickled down over her fingers. Rotokas made another pass, and this time a long claw extended toward her. Semra's chest squeezed tight and she threw herself into a roll.

Stabbing pain ripped across her back as the razor-sharp

edge of a talon cut through her dress and bit into her skin. *Just a graze. I should know the difference by now.* It wasn't entirely true. She was sometimes surprised by the extent of her injuries after the fact. But when she'd been whipped in the dungeons, her skin had shredded like cheese, and this was nothing like that.

Semra roared up from the ground, barreling into the second guard and slashing a deep gash into his arm as she went. The man cried out and released Aviama, and the princess threw a punch across his jaw.

Semra twisted the guard's arm behind him, jabbed the blade of her knife into his neck, and let swirling ebony smoke seep from her fingers and envelop them in total blackness.

"Nice punch," Semra lied. "Hold onto me and don't let go."

"Thanks." The princess seized her shoulder in the dark. "My hand hurts."

Obviously. Your wrist wasn't straight. Semra made a mental note to teach the girl how to throw a proper punch. She had terrible form, but a warm pride bubbled up in Semra's chest at her commitment to the blow.

Semra doubled over the guard, threw his sword to one side, and twisted the blade against his neck. "If you don't want to be dragon fodder, you'll run with me. If you get further than an inch ahead, I'll slice through your carotid and gut you like a pig."

The pulse of the guard's blood gently pressed against the pressure of the knife beneath fragile skin. She noted with some satisfaction that his heart rate was through the roof. They ran then, Semra extending out her smoke to billow out before them and up into the biggest smoke signal she'd ever created.

Subtlety was over. Azi knew she was here. And blocking Rotokas' vision was the only chance she had of getting out alive, even if it screamed her location to every guard in the city.

Two blocks flew past them underfoot, three blocks, four, the guard's hands flung out in front of him to keep them from bumping into walls. They collided several times on the way, and twice Semra's knife nearly slaughtered him as they tripped over each other running in the dark. Blazes of fire lit up the shadowy tide pressing in around them like a lantern through fog as Rotokas gave chase, searching them out in the narrow spaces below.

Rotokas' wingtip blasted them with a rush of air, and a ripple of terror flooded Semra's body at his closeness. She gritted her teeth. *I'll take out your other eye,* she thought to herself. *I'll carve out the talons from your toes and impale your eyes with them. Don't test me!*

Screams bounced off the walls of buildings ahead as shopkeepers and customers panicked at the wave of blackness swallowing the world around them. Fatigue burned in the muscles of her arms as she pushed the cloud forward. At last she found a door and shoved the guard through it, Aviama following with her hand still clamped to Semra's shoulder.

Semra pushed the smoke continuing on down the street as far as she could manage, as if they were still moving that direction, and then the murkiness ebbed, and she released the last strands of smoke to be wafted away with the rest.

The gray curls lifted from the air around them, and Semra found herself standing in a large kitchen with massive basin sinks, dishes stacked high on shelves, and an array of pots, pans, and a large wood stove in the center. They were in the back of a restaurant, though it was eerily empty. How long ago had the employees fled? Were they still in the building?

Either way, Semra didn't have long, and couldn't drag the

guard around forever. She dropped him against the wall like a sack of potatoes and twisted the knife against his trachea.

"You think you serve a magic queen." Semra's lip curled into a snarl. "Let me introduce myself. I am your worst nightmare, and I don't need any trinket to use my magic. She's not special. She's *deranged*. And unless you want to pick out a basket for your head to go in, you're going to tell me what's happening in Shamaran Castle."

39

T he guard swallowed, and winced as the movement pressed his neck into the knife. His face had drained to a ghastly white, and he clamped his injured arm with his hand. "I need a torniquet."

"Your arm will be the least of your worries if you don't tell me what I need to know." Semra squatted in front of the man, tilted her head, and opened her eyes unnaturally wide. "If you die today, it'll be because your neck was hacked halfway through, your empty head dangling awkwardly from its shreds."

"Aurin's spear," he breathed, "Jannemar is lost to a battle of witches."

Semra's lip curled and she slugged him in the stomach with her left hand, her right drawing a pinprick of blood from his throat. "I don't cast spells. Tell your *sifal* queen that what she does with tricks, I do *tabeun.*" Semra paused, and her mind went to what Frigibar had said of the long-term impact of siphon magic. Sifal magic was poisonous. "How is she feeling these days, your queen?"

The guard clenched his jaw, but his eyes darkened.

"Robust health and mighty as the sword."

Semra's lips flattened. A lie. Avaya must be showing signs of siphon poisoning and hiding it. But this guard knew something was amiss.

She glanced at Aviama, and the princess opened her hand and swept it in a welcoming gesture toward the guard. Her friend arched an eyebrow. *Go ahead. Do your thing.*

In a single smooth motion, Semra slammed the man to the floor, dug her fingers into the gash in his arm, and dropped her knee on his chest. The guard roared in pain and reached up to grab a fistful of her hair; she nicked the skin of his throat again and jerked her head at his other arm. "Aviama, if you would."

Aviama ran to the guard's other side and dropped both knees on his uninjured arm, ripping his fingers from Semra's hair. Semra's scalp burned from his grip, and she shook her head. "I need to know how long Avaya has been ruling in the castle, and where the king is."

The guard snorted. "Jannemar has no king."

Semra slashed her knife across his collarbone in a painful but superficial slice, and returned it to his throat. "A stupid thing to say, given the circumstances. How long ago did Avaya take over, and where is Zephan Shamaran?"

The guard spit in her face. Semra grimaced and dug her fingers into his arm again.

Using both arms to restrain someone was so inconvenient when they went to spitting. There was no arm free to wipe their disgusting missile from one's face. Few things were truly disgusting to her, but spittle made it on the list.

"Let's play a game." Semra glared at the guard, and Aviama shifted her weight on the man's arm. "I'll cut through your windpipe, so you bleed out with gargling and gasping but no screams, and we'll take bets on whether it takes you thirty seconds to die, or less. Or, instead, you can tell me the answer to my simple questions, and you can have the honor of living longer."

The man clenched his jaw, and hesitated. "Four days ago. Zephan's in the wind. Nobody knows where he is."

Relief washed through Semra's body, and the tension in her muscles eased. She took a deep breath to steady herself, and let it out. "Rats and rot, was that so hard?"

"He's safe." Aviama ran a hand through her hair.

"Maybe. For now."

They'd already been in the building too long. They had to move. The wound on her back burned fire as her body began to settle from the stress of the encounter. Semra needed something to cover the slash in the back of her dress, and some sort of poultice or healing ointment would be a bonus if she could find it.

How many people would be converging on the area where the smoke had disappeared? Were they already surrounded?

Zephan's in the wind. Good. Maybe he really was safe.

"But we're not." Semra raised her knife hand, and the guard let out a scream.

Aviama threw a hand out. "Wait!"

Semra groaned, but stayed her hand. "Aviama. Sometimes you just have to kill people. He's seen too much. He knows where we are. And he serves Avaya. We can't let him follow us."

Aviama drilled her with a reproachful glare. "You told him if he answered our questions, he'd live longer."

"And I'm true to my word. The first option was him living thirty seconds or less. We've been sitting here for at least a minute since then, maybe two. He has in fact lived longer, and I'll even make it quick enough that he doesn't feel much pain before the end. I'm not without mercy."

Aviama pursed her lips and laid a hand on Semra's shoulder. "With that smoke signal, everyone in Qalea already knows where we are. Let him deliver your message, and tell about what he's seen. Why should Azi think he's the only dragonlord willing to fight for Jannemar? You're back, and you're strong. Let him chew on that."

The guard glanced furtively back and forth from the assassin to the princess, and back. Semra eyed him. Aviama had a point. Secrecy was out the window anyway, so she just had to make sure he didn't follow them. And if she provided him the right message, maybe she could draw Azi's focus off Zephan.

Semra sighed. "You make an annoying amount of sense when you want to."

Aviama beamed, and Semra smothered a smile. She scanned the room and nodded to a stack of tablecloths against the wall. "Bring me one of those." Aviama sprang to her feet, and Semra pressed the knife tighter against the guard's throat. She lowered her voice, for only him to hear. "I'll humor her, but only as long as you cooperate. If you don't, I'll kill you the painful way, and sleep like a baby. Say nothing, and blink twice to agree."

The man's face flushed red, but he blinked twice. Aviama returned with the tablecloth and held it out. Semra shook her head. "I'm not moving my knife from his throat, so you're going to do this. Get one of my extra knives and cut off two long strips."

Aviama paused, then moved Semra's skirt out of the way to get a knife from Semra's pant leg, cut the tablecloth to get it started, and ripped off two long strips. At Semra's direction, she tied a torniquet around the man's arm—though the gash was big, but not so big that he would lose significant amounts of blood, the baby.

"Tell your sifal queen she knows nothing of power. Tell her she's getting sick, and it will only get worse. Ask her if she's ever been poisoned and lived, and of the two of us, which one is more famous for kidnapping? And tell her if she ever wants to see her sister again, she'll paint the dragon on the Jannemari flag blue. Because that's the only color dragon with any chance of bringing her home."

Semra snatched the second strip of tablecloth from Aviama's hands and chucked it at the guard.

He caught it with his free hand and glared up at Semra. "What's this for?"

Semra leaped off the man's chest and slashed through the tendon at the back of his heel. "For this."

Aviama screamed and clapped a hand over her mouth, and Semra whirled her around and shoved her back out the door. The screaming man left a siren to their location at their backs, and Semra flung the rest of the tablecloth around her shoulders like a mantle to cover the rips on her dress as they fled.

Cover me, Zez. Cover me now. Clear the skies.

Semra bolted with Aviama down the street, and turned onto the beginning of the cobblestone, nearly tripping over a body on the ground. Aviama stumbled over the dead man's leg, and Semra took hold of her and skidded to a stop. The man was a royal guard, but *whose* royal guard?

A torn off parchment tucked into the guard's chain mail caught her eye, and she crouched to get a better look. Semra grinned. It was a symbol of a raven. One she'd seen before.

"What is it?" Aviama hissed.

"It's Siler. These guards probably came to find us, and would have caught us if not for him and Pidge. They're clearing the way for us to escape."

"Escape *where*?"

Semra winced. It was an excellent question, but she had no answer. Except that she needed to get Aviama somewhere safe and split up from there. Semra had just practically begged Azi and Avaya to target her instead of Zephan and Aviama. Aviama wasn't going to like being set aside, but she couldn't be nearby when the next card was played. "Come on."

The streets were eerily empty, a stark contrast from the morning's busy gaggle around the *Lady of the People*. Semra glanced up, where her leftover black smoke had billowed up over the buildings, now borne along by some breeze or other, a blight against an otherwise blue sky.

Is that how people saw her? A blight?

But the smoke had saved them, hadn't it? The people had run from it, afraid of what they didn't understand, and perhaps they were right to run. Perhaps the guard was right to be terrified of her ability. But without it, Aviama would've been lost. Things need not have danger beaten out of them to be worthwhile. And if Semra wasn't herself dangerous, *she* would be the worthless one against the likes of Azi and Avaya.

Zezura was in the air, but Rotokas was nowhere to be found. Somewhere a horse whinnied as they crossed toward the wealthier part of the city. Semra jerked Aviama down a side street toward the sound.

People began trickling out and about, and Semra slowed her pace to match them. To her left, a man and woman picked up spilled produce from a donkey cart as the donkey stamped its feet. *The beekeeper!* Yes, of course. This wasn't him, but the donkey reminded her of Honey outside Garbane's house, and it was the perfect place for Aviama to hide. So long as someone went with her. Pidge would do.

Ahead, a woman yelled at her toddler for running down the street with a piece of laundry over his head, his sister chasing him with a cascade of giggles. Three doors down, two men argued over a broken saw outside a carpentry shop. Semra eyed them, but neither turned to look as they passed. And to the right, around the back corner of the carpenter's shop, two legs and feet were visible on the ground, being dragged away by some unseen person.

Semra's heartbeat sped up, and she angled quickly away from the carpentry shop and toward the residence side. Half of her desperately wanted to chase those lifeless feet and uncover the mystery, but with Aviama in tow, there was nothing for it. Either it was Siler or Pidge, in which case there was no point in bringing attention to their location, or it was an enemy, in which case she would only bring her young charge closer to danger.

Focus. Horses.

Semra slipped down a side street behind a row of homes. Aviama was nearly jogging to keep up with Semra's brisk pace, and breathing fast. Whether it was from fear or exhaustion, she didn't say, and they moved at a steady pace.

Two houses down, a clothesline dried a family's wardrobe. Semra snatched two scarves from the line and discarded the tablecloth in their place, all without slowing down. She wrapped one scarf around her shoulders to cover the rip in her dress and passed the other to Aviama. "We need a different look. Cover your hair."

Aviama dutifully wrapped her long blonde ringlets in a remarkably fashionable headscarf, and Semra handed her an empty bucket from the yard of the next house as the two of them proceeded quickly along the row.

The princess tucked the handle in the crook of her elbow and wiped her dirty hands on her filthy cotton skirts. "What's this for?"

"Appearances. We need to look different as often as possible."

The hairs on the back of her neck stood on end as they crossed the street at the end of the row and came in sight of three larger homes and a stable on the far side. Semra clutched at the fringes of her pilfered shawl, concealing her knife in its folds. There were few constants in life as reliable as the blade. A well-balanced knife was a faithful friend.

Semra darted across to the first home and rounded the back, where a small grove of trees lined a garden. It was the closest thing to genuine cover they'd had in what felt like millennia. Still, cover for her and Aviama was just as good a cover for anybody else, and they were being hunted.

Snap.

Semra whirled around, and Aviama flinched. "Sorry," she hissed.

Her chest constricted, and she clamped her jaw shut, adrenaline still whirring through every blood vessel in her body. Semra resisted the urge to slap the girl. *Stop doing loud things.* She knew Aviama didn't know any better, but the next time something was loud enough to make her jump, it had better be—

Whack!

Thud!

By the time she spun, it was too late. An archer fell from the roof of the house and landed face down in the dirt twenty paces away. And an arm wrapped around her waist and jerked her backward off her feet.

In a flash, Semra turned into her attacker and raised her knife. She threw all her weight into the plunge, but the man reached out like lightning and caught her wrist. In a smooth motion he doubled her arm behind her back, pulled her in with an arm at the small of her back, and pressed his lips to hers.

40

———

Semra gasped at the unexpected kiss and reeled backward, and to her surprise, her captor let her go. Two men blinked back at them, a broad-shouldered bear of a man holding Aviama with a hand clamped hard over her mouth, and a sandy-haired man, leaner than the other but muscular, with stubble shading his face. Both wore common garb, clunky boots, and leather farrier's aprons.

She stared into the soft tender face of Zephan Shamaran. Though not quite grasping reality, she could not deny those amber eyes. Aviama exclaimed something against Monac's hand, and he pressed a finger to his lips and let her go.

Semra's heart skipped a beat and warmed at the sight of him—her friend, her safety, and the only man she had ever truly, deeply loved. In an instant she was in his arms again, pulling his face down to hers, drinking him in.

Time slowed, and for a single heavenly minute, everything in the world was right. Zephan wasn't king, and Semra had no bloodstained, sordid past. No obstacles existed, no dragonlords, no crimson queens of enemy nations, only a man and a woman reunited at last.

Monac cleared his throat, and Semra jumped. She pulled back and felt Zephan's smile as he pulled her in for one more kiss before letting her go. Her cheeks flushed hot, and she bit her lip.

Aviama and Monac were staring at something, and it was only then that Semra noticed—hundreds of tiny embers, like glowing constellations of stars, hung suspended in the air in a ring around Semra and Zephan. Zephan's eyes popped wide as saucers, and Semra dispelled the sparks with a flick of her fingers. "Sorry."

That was new. *And kind of cool.*

Zephan shook his head in wonder, then sobered. "I know you're headed for the horses, but they've got guards that way. Could I interest you in an ox cart?"

Semra cocked her head. "You've got an ox cart hidden in your tunic somewhere?"

"Hidden, yes. This way. We ran into Pidge and Siler. They're holding off the rest of the squad."

Dispatching them, more like. But Semra only nodded, and goosebumps ran up her arms as Zephan took her hand. Aviama ran to him and he gave her a big hug with his free arm, and Monac gestured further into the grove. "Time to move."

Monac led the way, further from the residence and back to the shops district, ducking into the blacksmith shop from earlier. The lead blacksmith turned his back to them as they came in, but shifted his body out of the way as they passed him and progressed into a back room. The room was stocked with anvils, bellows, and iron tools so that hardly an inch of the wall was uncovered. Double doors, often open to the air when the workshop was active, were chained shut at the back.

Charcoal, dust, and a massive furnace captured attention in the middle of the room, and boxes of horseshoes, hinges, harnesses, and hammers boasted a long list of customers. Monac and Zephan hung their aprons on a hook along the wall, and two men Semra had never seen before materialized from the other side of the furnace.

Zephan held up a hand. "They're with me." It was unclear which party he had aimed the comment toward, but it relaxed Semra and Aviama just as much as the two bodyguards. Zephan turned to the men. "What's the news?"

"Avaya shut herself away in the king's chambers this morning," one replied. "And Azi has been carrying out all matters of state. She is said to be spending time in mourning over King Turian, and preparing herself for coronation."

Semra jerked her head up. "Has anybody seen her since then?"

The two bodyguards exchanged a glance. "Not that I know of."

Monac's eyes narrowed. "Why? What are you thinking?"

Semra's lips parted. Avaya had moved fast. Faster than fast. And Azi had done something unexpected. Could he really have done it? Was he as closely linked to Rotokas as Semra was to Zezura? She swallowed. "When is the last time anyone saw Rotokas?"

Zephan furrowed his brow. "Recently. With the smoke. He did a sweep over Qalea."

"No, obviously I know. I was there. But since then?" Semra's stomach dropped. *There's no way he was that fast. There's no way ...*

The walls of the room threatened to close in around her, and she reached out to Zezura, a desperate clutching hand grasping at straws.

Where is he?

But the dragon sent back just what Semra had feared. *Not*

in the city. Not near the castle. Not under the waterfall. Semra's chest tightened. *Gone.*

Aviama slipped her hand through Semra's arm. "Semra?"

"Rotokas is missing. He didn't give up the chase. He was called off." Semra ran a hand through her hair and turned to Zephan. "Avaya's gone. Rotokas is gone. It never occurred to me that Azi and Rotokas would split up. But they have. And they've been planning it. Setting the scene by hiding her in the castle, showing glimpses of her here and there to show she really is just holing up in her rooms. Preparing for a secret absence."

Understanding dawned, and Zephan clenched his jaw. "Did you find it?"

No need to explain. She knew he meant the spear, and there was no reason for the bodyguards to know the details, however faithful they might be. Semra nodded. "Week's dragon ride."

Monac held up a hand. "Don't you dare. I'm coming."

Aviama folded her arms. "Me too!"

Semra grimaced, and Aviama's face fell. "You're leaving me behind."

"If it makes you feel any better, we're leaving Monac too. With you. Do you still have what I gave you?" The documents. Aviama nodded, and Zephan turned to his friend. "I need you with her. Protect her with your life and keep her location absolutely secret. Protect her like you protect me, with every ounce of the same considerations. Do I make myself clear?"

Monac pressed his lips together, but dipped his head in a curt nod. "I don't like it. You don't need to go."

"It's true. I can ask Siler and Pidge. I just won't be as effective alone." Semra nearly choked on the words as they came out. Did she just say she was *less* effective alone? Rats and rot, what had happened to her?

But it was true. And without knowing the extent of Avaya's abilities, She'd need at least two teammates. Any more, and there were too many riders.

Monac folded his arms. "We don't even know for sure that anybody's going after it."

The door slid open, and four swords rang from their scabbards, each man springing to a defensive stance. Siler and Pidge ducked in and closed the door behind them. Siler whistled. "Nice party."

Pidge flicked her wrist, sending a knife spinning up in the air and snatching it by the handle with hardly a glance its direction. "Did Zezura catch up to Rotokas? I saw her heading east, but he had a head start."

Semra froze. "When?"

Pidge shrugged. "He wheeled away from the smoke toward the castle and took off from there. It can't have been long—how long ago did you end up in the back of that restaurant?"

A chill ran down her spine. No, it wasn't tremendously long ago, but Avaya was prepared for the journey. Semra gripped Zephan's arm. "Azi is running the castle. Who knows what contacts he's using. Send one of mine and one of yours with Aviama, and one of mine and one of yours with us. You can stay out of sight."

The thought of leaving him made her heart ache, but it was the smartest thing to do. Still, Zephan didn't always go for the safe, smart option.

And he didn't plan to start now. Zephan shook his head. "I'm coming. I'm spinning my wheels here, and Monac has been begging me to get out of the city—"

"This is *not* what I meant," Monac grumbled under his breath.

"—and anyway, Avaya's my sister," Zephan continued,

ignoring his friend. He brushed a lock of hair behind Semra's shoulder. "And I am quite disinclined to leave you."

Semra's cheeks flared red at his display in front of an audience, but she warmed to his touch. She allowed a small smile. *Together.*

Monac shifted his weight. "If anything happens to you—"

"Nothing's going to happen, except that we *will* get Azi and Avaya's paws off Jannemar, and the kingdom *will* be run by a *stable* Shamaran once again. My decision is final."

Aviama bit her lip, and Monac frowned. Semra knew they hadn't missed Zephan's careful wording. His assertion that nothing was going to happen was ridiculous—racing dragons, artifacts of magic, and standoffs between rival kingdoms were hardly *nothing*—but his second statement could be taken at face value, as himself returning to the throne, while also making room for a second Shamaran option. The last stable Shamaran.

A potential for a princess to rise for the first time in the nation's history to become Her Majesty, Queen Aviama Shamaran of Jannemar.

Should the worst occur, Aviama would remain. The kingdom would be safe if only they could rid the world of Azi's clutches and Avaya's magic.

Siler pursed his lips. "I don't mean to be rude, but I can't help but feeling like you've all forgotten where we are. Aurin's spear, you look like a funeral, but nobody's died yet. Well, nobody on our side, anyway. And if you want it to stay that way, we've got to move."

Pidge nudged Siler playfully, and Semra was reminded of their closeness during the sick wife ruse. Comfortable. "Do you think you can survive without me for a few weeks? I'll take the dragon and the Primary Wealthy Snoot. You can check in on Secondary Snoot, and keep things running."

Siler's mouth twitched. "They haven't us to go yet."

Pidge rolled her eyes. "Obviously she wants us to. She'd be an idiot to pass on our help, and I daresay the kingdom will fall without us. And without a kingdom, well, it's not good for business."

Siler glanced up at Semra. "How's your guilt-ridden drive to work alone?"

"Improved somewhat, thanks." Semra grinned. "We *do* need the help. Zephan already has his people. I'd like one of mine along—someone who knows the mountain. The way Azi thinks. Somebody I don't have to train on how to work with me." She shot a look toward the bodyguards. "No offense."

They shrugged, perhaps grateful not to be considered for a dragon-riding mission with the crazy assassin lady.

Siler took a breath and nodded. "Well, princey?"

Monac set a hand on his sword hilt, and Siler waved him off. "No disrespect. *Kingey* simply has no ring to it, and I simply cannot bring myself to use the titles."

Pidge was practically bouncing. "If Semra says we're in, he'll do it."

Zephan arched an eyebrow. "Am I so transparent?"

Aviama snorted. "Oh, *please!*"

Zephan spread his hands. "We'd be honored, yes. I'm sure we can work out a deal that fits both our interests."

"Splendid!" Siler clapped his hands. "I hope it includes monthly pastry deliveries and a healthy dose of *jemari*. Rookie, you'll have to catch up with Semra later. I'll take the dragon and Primary Snoot. You'll take backup Snoot and run the business."

Pidge's eyes grew wide. "You trust me to run the business?"

Siler shrugged. "You're already doing it half the time. Just don't mess it up."

Pidge beamed, and Siler grinned. Had she imagined it, or

did his eyes light up whenever hers did? Semra smiled, but when Siler caught her watching, he sobered. Siler cleared his throat, suddenly all business. "I've got a go bag, but it isn't enough for three. We'll meet back in an hour and take off from there. Semra, call Zez. We don't have time to be sneaky."

41

The group dispersed from the blacksmith's shop in three shifts, and Semra, Zephan, and Siler met as scheduled one hour later—on the roof of the tavern two doors down from Siler's scribe storefront. Semra had shed her peasant's dress with relish, clad once again in trousers and a loose tunic. The mark of the dragon's kiss on her chest reflected shards of brilliant light in every direction.

After several minutes conversing, Semra had slipped down from the roof alone, a shovel over her shoulder, and torn five blocks across Qalea in broad daylight. She garnered the attention of three teams of soldiers and half the city's civilians, and led them exactly where she wanted, soldiers and townspeople alike running from every direction for a glimpse of the king's assassin—the woman whose blue dragon had saved the kingdom from the black dragon those months ago, who had saved Jannemar soldiers on the Surion Strip as the battle waned in the effort against Belvidore, and who even now had not abandoned them as the cursed one-eyed black wyvern struck fear into their hearts once again.

She'd heard the whispers in the last few days. Had she

betrayed them? Was she a coward, hiding in the darkness? Had she ever cared about the country to begin with?

The wanted posters had surely added fuel to that fire.

If fire was what they wanted ... well, then, fire is what they would have.

Semra let curls of smoke go up like flares, marking her progress toward the city center, screaming her presence for miles around. But this time, instead of fleeing an unknown darkness, the people converged, choking off the roads until the guards were swarmed by civilians.

It had been Aviama's idea to send Semra off with fanfare. "Ignite the city with hope, with rebellion," she'd said, her eyes alight. "We've exposed coercion and hostile takeover in the monarchy. Now it's time to show them we aren't defenseless. Show them they have a choice, that they can take a stand. Zephan is in hiding, and so he should be. So give them a face to rally behind."

Despite her insistence that she wanted no part in the rule of a kingdom, Aviama was sounding more and more like a queen with each passing day. She stood a little taller, spoke a little louder, and asserted ideas that were both diplomatic and strategic. Semra wasn't sure Aviama had noticed it yet, but the others' arched eyebrows, slow smiles, and nods were enough to show Semra that the princess was gaining their respect.

Now, her leather-clad feet flying across the cobblestone, the roar of the crowd pushing her forward and drowning out the pounding of her own heart, Semra wondered if it had been such a good idea after all. What if she didn't make it to the city center?

But just as the thought entered her mind, she burst into the square, the *Lady of the People* greeting her in a stoic symbol of hope. Semra leaped up the fountain and planted her feet on the basin rim. The people flowed in from every direction, and she counted no fewer than twelve soldiers in the mix, pushing through the mass of bodies.

She cleared her throat. *Don't say it. It really won't make that big of a difference. And it's so corny.*

Three soldiers broke free from the crowd. Semra readjusted her grip on the shovel, but blunt force trauma really wasn't her preferred method of assault. A blue streak cut across the sky. Now or never.

I'd prefer never. But I did promise ...

Semra grimaced, and raised the shovel high in the air. It wasn't a spade, but was the best they could manage on short notice. As in, it's what was on hand in the blacksmith's shop when Aviama came up with the idea.

Silly. Unnecessary. Ridiculous.

But it *did* hit close enough to the target, here on the fountain, next to *Lady of the People* and her spade.

Semra silently begged Zezura to save her quickly, less from the soldiers and more from the embarrassment of this moment. "You are Jannemar," she began, her voice hardly discernible among the din.

The crowd hushed each other when they saw she was speaking, and even one of the soldiers hesitated. The closest guard reached the foot of the fountain, but a gust of wind and an aquamarine dragon dropped from the sky in the space between him and Semra.

Semra ran three long leaps along the fountain brim and up onto Zezura's back, still clutching the shovel. The guard froze, and silence fell over the crowd.

"You are Jannemar," she said again. "Not whoever runs the castle. Not power-hungry traitors unfit to rule. There is no Jannemar without its people. But a people without brains become slaves."

Not exactly the suggested wording. Semra raised her voice.

"I saw your fathers, your brothers, your sons at the Surion Strip. Brave men in a war that *Avaya* made worse. *You* are the army. So whose army are you? Avaya's? Or Jannemar's? Who do you trust to protect our borders, to wage wars and fight enemies?"

Semra threw the shovel into the crowd and ripped the folded wanted poster from her belt, shaking it out and holding it up. "It's my face, but Avaya's offenses. Kidnapping, murder. Assault, treason. And yet Her *Majesty* will demand you bow! The soldiers know. The rumors are out. She'll make her claim public soon."

She tore the poster in two and tossed the pieces to the ground. "Let the man who thinks, think for himself."

The crowd erupted, and Zezura took to the air. Semra gulped. Had that just gone ... *well?*

It was hard to say how much of the uproar was agreement or fury. But one way or another, she'd given her little speech and survived it. Her chest swelled as a smattering of fists pounded the air as the dragon did a low sweep over the square before pulling away and banking south.

Mere minutes later, Zezura sped beyond the crowd's sight and dropped to the roof where Siler and Zephan waited.

Zephan smiled at the sight of her, and she couldn't help but grin back as he clambered up the dragon's side and settled in behind her. "How'd it go? It sounded like success from here."

"I did it. Huge crowd. I hope it spoils Azi's day."

Siler quirked an eyebrow. "Did you throw the shovel?"

Semra reddened. "Yeah."

He laughed and shook his head. "Aurin's spear."

"Aurin's spear indeed." Semra lifted her face to the wind as Zezura angled toward the sun. "Let's go get it."

42

"Going and getting" the spear was a bit of an oversimplification, of course. No one could get the spear. Not without dying. That is, no *normal* people.

Semra could apparently attempt the feat and live, but her last try had made it obvious she would not be removing it from its place in the origin spring. So why did Azi and Avaya think they could take it? Did they expect Avaya's wind to be strong enough to loosen it? Was there some other magical loophole they'd discovered? Or had Azi decided simply to dispatch Avaya in a rather creative way?

Little talking happened on the way, the wind of the ride snatching away any hope of conversation, and each of them sank into their own anxious thoughts. At least, that's what she assumed—how could the situation bring any other thoughts besides anxious ones?

At best, Avaya had a couple hours' head start. Rotokas was an older dragon than Zezura. Semra thought Zezura was faster in sprints—and Zezura was adamant that she was—but Rotokas' experience may have provided him with more long-term endurance and better adeptness at taking advantage of air currents. Zezura carried three people, and Rotokas carried one, but the beasts were so large it might make no tremendous difference. The race would be a close one.

They ate dried meats and bread on the way and landed in the woods east of the Dezapi River several hours after nightfall. Siler pulled out more of the same dried meat, tossed portions to Zephan and Semra, and plunked down with his back against a tree trunk. Semra stretched out the sore muscles of her legs and settled next to Zephan. He put his arm around her shoulders, and Semra let out a contented sigh.

Her person was safe. Her people were safe.

For now.

Siler faked a gag and rolled his eyes. "I'd say I'm glad you two aren't denying the obvious anymore, but I'm not sure I can stand a week of this."

Semra stiffened, and her cheeks flushed, but Zephan only pulled her closer. He tore off a chunk of jerky with his teeth and grinned. "We appreciate your sacrifice."

She leaned her head on Zephan's shoulder and let her tension ease. It was weird letting someone see their closeness, but it was just Siler, and they were in the woods. It's not like they were parading through the throne room like lovesick kids in front of court. And they'd been apart too long for her to care.

Semra swallowed a bite of meat and raised an eyebrow at Siler. "Are you saying you have no romantic interests of your own?"

Siler jerked his head back, too quickly, before returning his attention to his meal—if it could be called a meal. "I don't know what you're talking about."

Semra bit her lip to stifle a laugh and composed herself. "Pidge is nice. You work well together."

"She's been a great help to the shop," Siler hedged. Did his face just turn a shade of red? "She's sharp, and a quick learner, and a surprisingly good actress. All critical for a business like ours."

Zephan laughed. "Scourge, who's in denial now?"

Siler glared at him, and something in Semra's chest warmed. She liked seeing him this way, ruffled by a few light jabs over a girl. A different girl than her. Someone that fit him better—more similar lifestyle goals and values, but still challenging. Pidge liked coin as much as anyone, and she would positively adore frolicking through an expansive villa. But if she really cared about him, she wouldn't put up with Siler forfeiting whatever softness remained in his soul for a job.

Semra thought of the two of them at the underground network house, Siler hovering protectively nearby, and the way Pidge looked into his eyes in the blacksmith's shop. Semra smiled. Maybe Pidge could bring something out of him that was good for them both.

Siler clenched his jaw and threw a pebble at Semra's shoe. "What are you smiling at?"

She clamped her lips together to stifle an ear-splitting grin, and shook her head. "Nothing. I like seeing you happy."

"I'm not happy. I'm grumpy." Siler's eyes narrowed, and he crossed his arms. "And I'm going to need princey to send me a mountain of pastries in a trunk made of solid gold to make up for the misery that this trip is likely to entail."

This time Semra did laugh. "Do mountains fit in trunks?"

"This one will. He'll need a *lot* of gold." Siler glanced at Zephan and smirked

Zephan chuckled.

For the beginning of the end of the world, it felt a little bit like bliss. Semra wanted good things for Siler, sometimes things he didn't seem to want for himself. Despite what he may have believed in months past, Siler and Semra wouldn't have been happy together as a couple. But their shared childhood and experience—their time escaping the mountain, saving a child, and executing their biggest mission to date, fighting their mentor—it was a bond not easily forgotten, no matter what had happened since.

Zephan shifted beside her, and Semra barely caught sight of Siler glancing up at him before Siler stood with a grunt and sauntered off into the woods, mumbling something about a perimeter.

Semra started to sit up, but Zephan pulled her in, and she lay her head on his chest. Zephan captured her hand and turned it this way and that in the moonlight, the two of them watching soft silver rays play against the gold band on her finger.

She twisted it around to set the signet mold on top of her finger instead of in toward her palm. "It's time you had it back."

"No. Hold onto it a little longer. Besides, it's come in handy so far."

A weight dragged at her heart. Was he still so unsure of his survival? The spear was far from in hand, and Azi carried out the duties of the crown while Zephan sat here in the dirt, twirling a leaf in his fingers under a canopy of trees.

Semra swallowed. "Aviama doesn't think she'll ever be queen. She would do it, if it came down to it, but she doesn't think she'll need to."

"She's an optimist, but I'd like to think maybe she's right. She certainly does have plans for the next queen though." Zephan stopped suddenly, and gently raised her from his chest. Semra's throat tightened. He searched her face. "As do I."

It was the boldest he had ever been. Could she? Dare she?

Semra's mouth went dry. Those amber pools of earnestness, tenderness, would beg her to consider it.

She looked away. "I think ... I think all that needs to wait until we get the spear and stop Azi and Avaya."

Zephan tipped her face up toward his with a thumb, and her stomach flopped. He brought his nose to hers, and she waited for his kiss, but his lips only brushed hers, and he paused. "Why? Why wait?"

Zephan ran a hand up her arm, and he smiled as goosebumps followed the trail of his fingers. She tried to remember what they were talking about. It was important, wasn't it? Rats and rot, had he almost proposed?

Semra's breaths came quickly in the circle of his arms, and she steeled herself. *Focus.*

"For the same reason you won't take back the signet ring," she said at last, her voice only just above a whisper. "It won't matter if we're dead. And we have other priorities right now. You finding a queen won't matter so much if you're not king. You *have* to be king."

Zephan slipped a hand around the back of her neck and kissed her deeply, a desert drinking in its first taste of summer rains. Her breath caught, and her heart exploded in a cascade of fluttering butterflies. Semra reached up to twine her fingers in his hair and drew him closer.

He ran his lips along her jaw to her ear. "Why do I have to be king?"

Semra froze, and her sudden stillness caused Zephan to pull back, studying her in the dark. Would he really try to give it up? Did he know the court would reject her, or was he so beaten down by his short reign that he was ready to throw in the towel?

A sadness lined his handsome face, and it struck Semra then how similar he looked to his father. She saw it even clearer now with the stubble on his face, since Turian always had a beard. Turian had looked this sad once, when he talked to her about kingship. *Sometimes it's terribly lonely.*

He had spoken of marriage and wisdom, too, and that his own marriage to Queen Sharsi had been against the court's wishes and caused friction early in his reign. What was it he had said?

Love is not enough for a king. Love is not enough for a prince. I have tried to tell my son this.

The crown came first. Always and forever. A marriage was never just a marriage for a monarch.

But without Zephan, Jannemar would fall.

Semra cursed herself as she said it, but the words tumbled out all the same. "You must."

Zephan groaned and leaned his head back against the tree trunk, staring up at the stars through the tree branches. "I know. Because if it isn't me, it's Aviama, and I could never do that to her. And if it isn't one of the two of us, I hand my people over to tyrants. And so we have remaining only two options—fight and win or fight and die. But it's nice to pretend, even for a few moments, that life might be different."

"A comforting illusion," Semra agreed, "But an illusion nonetheless."

They sat there together for some time before either spoke again. Semra's heart felt as if a constant pressure bore down on it, threatening to burst it at the core. The weight was unshakable. Nothing could be done to lift it, not for herself, not for Zephan.

"Why haven't you told me you love me?"

Semra snapped her head up toward him, mouth agape. "What?"

Zephan stared down at his fingers and started shredding a

leaf. "Aviama told me. You said it to her in passing. You said you loved me."

A squirmy feeling turned her insides upside down, and Semra bit her lip. "Um ... because ..." She racked her brain for a good reason, but came up empty.

"You're waiting to see if I die." He said it softly, matter-of-factly, like the answer to a puzzle he'd finally discovered. "You're closer to me than you've ever been to someone. It freaks you out. You won't go further until you know I won't leave you."

Semra's chest hitched. She'd never thought of it that way before. She wanted to challenge him, tell him he was wrong. But if he was wrong, why were hot tears spilling down her cheeks, and why had her lip started to quiver?

She barked out an unconvincing laugh, and a restrained sob choked off the sound. "You haven't said it to me either."

Immediately Zephan sat up and twisted to face her squarely. "Semra." He tugged on a tendril of her hair, took her hands in his, and lifted them to his lips. "Your fire, your spunk, those faces you make when you think I'm being stupid, they light my life. Your tenacity, resilience, and hope in a goodness worth fighting for, your faithfulness to those you care for, are a sight to behold. And you are the most stunning creature I have ever laid eyes on."

Semra stared at him, speechless. A thousand thoughts raced circles round her head, but she didn't bother catching any of them. All she could focus on was Zephan, and the ridiculous, beautiful words coming out of his mouth.

He took a deep breath and let it out, his amber eyes holding her steady, commanding her attention. "I dream of a life where I wake up to you as often as the sun rises, and kiss you good night as often as it sets. Semra. Semra Myansara. I love you."

Something like an unrefined squeak made it out Semra's mouth before Zephan kissed her again and drew back, his face gentle, but solemn. "Don't say it now. Even if you were going to. I don't want it to be just because I said it, or because you think you should. But know now that *I* love *you*. And I always will."

With that Zephan pulled her into his arms, as every wall she'd ever built crumbled down in an avalanche of tears.

43

When Semra awoke, trails of dried tears streaked through the dirt on her face. Zezura's body curled around her, her aquamarine tail draped over Semra's legs, and Zephan and Siler spoke in hushed tones off to one side. Semra sat up, poured a dash of canteen water into her hands, and scrubbed her face with it before clearing her throat and suggesting they take off.

The week passed quickly, the days spent flying, the nights spent sleeping, with strategy brainstorming sessions over scant dinners. Zephan didn't bring up marriage again, and Semra skirted any topic too close to it. Siler watched her closer than usual, but said nothing.

You're waiting to see if I die.

Zephan's words haunted her, and their power convinced Semra that he was exactly right. There were other concerns with accepting a proposal, were he ever to officially offer one —the responsibility of the crown, his late father's warnings about the weight it brings and the damage done when the court is opposed to the union, and Semra's obvious bloodstained history. She may have been pardoned, and she was grateful to serve, but she was unfit to rule.

But those weren't reasons to avoid broaching the topic at all. Talking meant there was hope. Hope was dangerous. They were far from safe.

Azi's voice floated through her mind, and bile rose in her throat at the sound of it: *My dear, my dear ... you know I am the only one who has never left you.*

It was almost true. And though Semra had come to have confidence that Zephan would never abandon her of his own volition, that didn't mean he couldn't abandon her in other ways.

The list of threats was long. And if Avaya got her hands on that spear, somehow able to remove and wield it, the likelihood of Zephan's imminent assassination leaped to a hair's breadth away from one hundred percent.

The week wore on, and they were no closer to a plan for keeping Avaya from the spear. Siler suggested gathering konnolan to use against Rotokas, the chemical that Belvidore had used against Zezura. While effective, the substance deadened magical essence and acted essentially as a poison. It was inert to nonmagical entities, but Zezura and Semra would both be affected if they were nearby. After seeing how sick Semra became after her last exposure, Zephan was unwilling to risk it. Semra had noted they didn't have time to get any, since Belvidore was the closest place with a supply of the stuff, and they certainly wouldn't be open to trade.

Direct confrontation seemed the only option, cutting Avaya off and getting the necklace off her before she got to the spear. Splitting up for the element of surprise was the only chance of getting close enough to remove the housing artifact. Being the only one with any experience in the cave system at the origin of the world, but having hardly explored it herself,

Semra could only recommend an entrance by the river for Siler and Zephan, and a direct onslaught from above by Semra.

Dragons against dragons were enough to draw one's attention from just about anything. Semra grimaced at the memory of Zezura and Rotokas, thrashing about in the Shalladin. Zezura was up for a fight, but Semra hated to pit them against each other again, knowing how close a call it was last time. But there was no scenario Semra could imagine in which Zezura and Rotokas *didn't* face off.

No one had ideas for what to do if they were too late, and Avaya got to the spear first. Perhaps then they could only hope for a swift end.

The terrain shifted from forest to mountains, and as they approached, their aerial position offered a view of the Dezapi and Surion rivers spilling out from Frigibar's mountain and splitting off in different directions. The town of Ellix nestled into the western side of the mountain range cradle as it wrapped around the lake, its waters lapping against a bank feeding the legendary trees Semra had spent two weeks in with Aviama.

It was early afternoon by the time they descended. Semra angled Zezura around the far side of the mountain and around the side beneath its peak, but these were meager efforts. Rotokas would have seen them as they crested the horizon a few miles off, but with a fifty-foot dragon and seventy-foot wingspan, even human eyes would clock their arrival if they were paying attention.

Semra wondered if Rotokas might drop Avaya off someplace and attack while Zezura was in the air with precious cargo—after all, Rotokas killing off the king *and* Azi's two most successful and rebellious assassins would be a dream come true for Azi and his ambitions. And Zezura would be less agile with three passengers to protect. But the skies were suspiciously clear as they glided in on a southeast wind and landed in broad daylight.

The gate in the pathway they'd taken with Frigibar was a problem, and there wasn't time to misremember what turns to take in the dark. There was only one way to find out if Avaya was in there already. So Semra led them on foot directly to the pinnacle of the mountain, toward the natural skylight opening shining down on the spear.

Zezura folded her wings with a huff and a click of her jaw, but acquiesced to walking—*like a common jackrabbit,* she complained. A cool breeze wafted through Semra's hair, but there was no comfort in it—only a reminder of Avaya's power, and a question of whether she would be able to stand up against it this time.

"Remember, she needs physical contact with the necklace to use it." Semra drew a knife and flipped it in her palm. "Zephan … if it comes down to it …"

Zephan's lips flattened, and his features hardened. He gave a curt nod, and swallowed. "Only if there's no other way."

Siler glanced at her, and Semra grimaced. She hadn't intended to ask permission, exactly. She didn't want to put guilt on Zephan for Avaya's death, if she had to take her out, but she also didn't want Zephan to hate her if she killed his sister. But if Avaya decided someone was going to die today, well, Semra would do everything in her power to ensure it wasn't one of them.

No matter the cost.

Siler stepped behind Zephan, out of his view, and shook his head. He tapped his own chest. *I'll do it.*

But Semra knew better. If worst came to worst, whoever could, would. There was no other choice.

Her jaw clenched, and she turned back up the slope.

Zezura nosed her shoulder as they moved up the slope, and Semra ran a finger down the smooth scales of the dragon's face. Her muscles relaxed a tad at Zezura's touch. No one else literally felt what Semra was feeling. Zezura's acceptance and understanding were on a whole new level.

Siler picked his way across the rock, dropping his voice low next to Semra. "Why hasn't she made a move on us yet?"

Semra shrugged. "Maybe we overtook her, and got here first. Or maybe she beat us, and has the spear, and doesn't care about us much."

"She'll always care," Zephan muttered. "She can't stop."

Semra winced. Azi was the same way.

The breeze played with the ends of Semra's hair, lightly wafting them behind her. The sky was too blue for what was about to happen, if they found Avaya at all. Too often after a tragedy, the world kept on turning, the sun kept on shining, and grass kept on growing. The world held no visible wounds of the loss, and the birds even dared to sing. But Semra knew more than anyone that the invisible pains were often the worst ones.

The breeze reversed, and Semra's hair blew across her face in the gust. She froze. *Avaya. She's here.*

Up head, the skylight opening to the cavern looked only like a small hole in the craggy mountain peak. It was wide enough for a person, but certainly too small for a dragon. The mountain pass narrowed here, falling steeply down on either side. Semra glanced over the side, and regretted it. A fall from this height could kill.

Zephan nodded to Siler, and Siler pulled a rope from his pack. He looped it around a boulder, knotted it, and tugged. He gave a thumbs up. As long as they watched their footing, the rope should get them across the narrow portion and most of the way down into the cavern before they ran out of coil.

Semra caught his eye and tapped the inside of her wrist with two fingers. He pursed his lips and did the same. This mission wouldn't be fun, or well planned, or likely even end well. Avaya was the woman who Siler had been hired and then betrayed by, Zephan and Aviama's sister, Turian's daughter, the woman who blamed Semra for her parents' deaths—a lady of many faces. A person who would do anything for power. A person willing to ally with the most evil individual Semra ever met.

Woosh.

Another surge of wind, and the impact knocked Semra clean off her feet. She gasped and flung her arms out, but instead of rough rock, her fingers found smooth scales. Obsidian black.

Clawed feet seized her around the waist, and dragon fire cut the cloudless sky with furious orange and red. Semra's stomach dropped, and her mouth went dry, and for an instant she was a four-year-old child snatched from her small village home in Rotokas' grip. *I'm sorry, Mother. I didn't mean to go so far. The ball rolled outside, and I would only be a moment ...*

The men shouted, and Rotokas' flight took a tumble as Zezura barreled into him in midair. Rotokas' hold on Semra's midsection weakened, and she slid several inches toward doom before the wyvern clamped down once again. Semra struggled to retrieve a knife from her thigh, but even as she did, she realized there was nothing she could do with it. If she didn't get free, Rotokas would kill her, but if Rotokas dropped her, the fall would save him the trouble and she would die anyway.

Zezura flew at Rotokas, latching onto him and herding him back up the mountain, where Zephan and Siler ran along the narrow footbridge like ants on a log in the distance. Rotokas thrashed back at Zezura with his wingspurs, breaking his flight pattern and smashing Semra into the rocky mountainside. Throbbing pain radiated up her arm and leg.

Semra dug for her knife again, but her hands found only Rotokas' talons and the edge of her trousers as she was tossed about. Her fingertips grazed the knife handle. *So close.* Semra twisted over Rotokas' talons with a grunt and seized the edge of the knife. She loosed it from its sheath, but fumbled it, and the blade fell.

Rotokas sank his teeth into Zezura's neck, and Zezura roared in pain. *Aim for his eyes,* Semra said to Zezura. *He's sensitive about his last eye. Let's make him terrified to lose it.*

Zezura dug her front talons at Rotokas' face, and Semra unleashed curls of black smoke. *Let the darkness remind him of his future—a vision as black as his scales.*

Rotokas reared back, and Zezura smashed him into the footbridge, breaking off the top and destroying the path for ten feet across. The black wyvern's hold loosened on impact. Semra dropped to the dusty ground with a grunt, rolling to her feet until there was no more ground to roll on. Her feet slipped and her scream caught in her throat as she tumbled off the ledge.

Hands seized her wrists, stopping her descent with a jolt, and her legs crashed into the rocky wall below. She snapped her head up and saw Zephan and Siler each grasping one of her wrists. They hauled her up and ran with her toward the skylight, Zephan covering her body with his own as they left their backs exposed to the battling dragons.

Semra twisted around to see blue and black scales barrel by in a whir. Her heart twisted, and she hesitated. What if Zezura got hurt?

A second, more frustrating question followed. What could she do about it?

Zezura sensed Semra's doubt, and sent the same word

Zephan and Siler were hissing at her as they angled for the skylight: *Go.*

Semra spun and sprinted for the skylight. Siler passed her the rope, and she took it without question. The plan was always for Semra to go first, as the only person Avaya should be expecting to accompany the dragon. But with Rotokas and Zezura tearing each other apart on the mountaintop, and Avaya potentially inside with her sifal magic, it was hard to say which place was safer. Semra scooted through the opening and dropped down the hole to the cavern below.

Avaya stood on the cavern floor below, dressed head to toe in a flowing scarlet gown. No, not scarlet—blood red. Crimson.

Semra's pulse pounded in her ears. The crimson queen strode forward with one hand clutching her necklace and the other outstretched toward Aurin's spear.

44

Bile rose in Semra's throat, and she thought she might be sick. Avaya came with all the trappings of the architect prophecy, even wearing a crown out in the mountains of Nowheresville, with nothing and nobody to notice but the spear itself.

Rushing wind filled Semra's ears as it answered Avaya's call, spilling into the cavern and swirling in a great arc. The dragons fighting outside were forgotten. Any screams Siler or Zephan may utter were silenced.

Two things occurred to Semra. First, the wind was so loud that Avaya may not have heard the incredible ruckus they'd made on the mountaintop. And second, Avaya was gathering the wind strength to rip the spear from the origin of the world. Which meant Semra would be dangling in the midst of a cyclone thirty feet high, before being dashed to bits against the cave walls.

The rope swayed in the air currents, and even as Semra lowered herself carefully down, the force of the wind swept her sideways. The length of the rope ran out fifteen feet above the ground, leaving another fifteen beneath her.

Child's play. Semra waited for Avaya to take three more steps toward the spear, and dropped to the ground behind her, rolling forward and springing to her feet with two knives in her hands by the time she popped up again.

Now was her chance to kill Avaya. She saw her window to end it all, and her fingers itched on the knife.

How many times had she done it before? She'd held the keys of life and death in a blade, or even bare hands, and turned the lock forever. Yet now she faltered.

Weakness.

That's what Azi would say. What he *did* say, in the king's chambers that day. He'd seen her pass up the opportunity then. And that supposed loving uncle, that caring mentor, did nothing but cluck his tongue. *Pity,* he'd said. A pity that his former student would not kill his current mentee. A disappointment that the child he'd stolen and trained would not slit the throat of his latest protégé.

But that's not what Semra was anymore. She'd thrown off the Bandaka name and embraced a new one. Her inclination was no longer death, but life.

Only if there's no other way.

Four paces separated Avaya from Aurin's spear. The winds rose, and the rushing grew to a great roar. Semra bolted forward and launched herself at Avaya.

Avaya twisted at the last minute, throwing her hands up to protect herself as they collided. The two of them sprawled to the ground, and the wind broke apart. Siler and Zephan dropped through the opening with the rope, and Semra wondered briefly how long the strength of the wind had prevented their entrance.

Semra rolled to her feet and spun, but Avaya had already recovered. She threw out a hand, blasting Semra back against the wall.

Avaya's emerald eyes darkened to a moody reptilian green. Her typically rosy cheeks had turned sallow, and the bags under her eyes did nothing to strengthen her impression.

Semra strained against the force of Avaya's wind, but she could barely move her fingers. "The spear will kill you."

Avaya's gaze flicked to Semra's hands. Her lip curled, and the blades in Semra's fingers ripped from her hold and skittered to the ground. "Wouldn't that please you?"

"No, it wouldn't." *Convenient, yes. Pleasant, no.* Semra didn't want Avaya to die. But the threat could not remain. "Look at you. The siphon poisoning is already setting in. How've you been feeling lately?"

Avaya sidestepped toward the spear. "It doesn't matter. It's a sacrifice. For the kingdom. With more power, I can reverse its effects."

Siler stalked slowly toward Avaya's other side. "You're smarter than this. You're acting like the brainless princess, the one everyone thought you were. I thought you were going to prove them wrong. He's using you."

The crimson queen eyed his movement and threw him back with a blast of air. "*You* don't understand. We're going to make Jannemar and Belvidore strong, together. A historic unity. Our father was *weak*."

Semra winced at the insult of Turian. She glanced at Zephan. His face was etched with pain, and his upper lip twitched in the smallest hint of a snarl. The next moment, it was gone. He reached a hand toward his sister as he edged along the cavern wall.

"Come on, Avs. This is enough. We can make Jannemar and Belvidore strong together, but not like this."

Avaya's jaw clenched, and the strength of the wind against Semra ebbed as she stared at him. "Together," she whispered. "I wish you meant it."

The wind dropped away altogether, and Semra took a deep breath. Had she stopped the wind on purpose, or forgotten to maintain it?

Avaya's eyes glistened with tears, and she shook her head at Zephan. "I wish you were as much family to me as Azi is. I wish you could listen and care the way he does. You've always looked down on me."

"*Family*?" Zephan gaped at her in open wonder, and the rage seeped in like rain on cracked, dry ground. His nostrils flared, and his hands tightened to fists. *No,* Semra silently begged. *Delicately, oh so delicately.* He opened his mouth, fury lighting his amber eyes aflame, and Semra cleared her throat, keeping her voice as steady as she could manage.

"Avaya. I know this man. I know him *well.*" Semra dared not move, not yet, lest Avaya remember she had abandoned her wind restraints. She checked on Zephan. Aside from the heat in his cheeks, he had snapped his mouth shut and seemed to be controlling himself. Semra looked back at Avaya. "He will let you poison yourself with sifal magic, let you take the fall if things go wrong, send you to retrieve a weapon that will kill you if you touch it—all without getting his own hands dirty."

"Not that he's against getting his own hands dirty," Siler muttered. "He'll do it when the time is right. He's conning you."

"You were nothing to him, *nothing,*" Avaya snapped. "Means to an end. I *am* the end. A place at the table. A chance to be what he was born to be, a royal family member taking the kingdom to new heights."

Zephan jabbed a finger at the weapon lodged in the carbonate at the center of the room. "If you touch that spear, you will die. Everyone who touches it does. You're driving the kingdom into the ground."

Siler edged a little too close, and Avaya threw a gust of wind at them all, plastering all three of them back against the wall again. Siler and Zephan were tossed to the far side, separated from Semra. Her chest tightened.

A throaty laugh filled the cavern, a dark contrast to Avaya's graceful exterior. "That shows how much you know. Azi is smarter than you. There is a way to take the spear and survive."

It was almost true. Semra had *touched* the spear and survived. But she had tabeun magic, not sifal. Was it the use of *any* magic that kept someone alive? Did magical energy somehow absorb the excess power, to keep the blast from being fatal?

Semra groaned against the strength of Avaya's wind. Had Azi really found a loophole?

"Stop!" Zephan yelled. "You're destroying our family, our home! You could *never* rule! I knew you were selfish, but I never took you for a traitor."

Avaya blanched. With a twist of her palms she threw them to the floor, and Semra's ribs ached at the impact. Her heart weighed heavy, pulling her down into the onyx black of the cave floor. There was no reasoning with an unreasonable person. She snaked her hand down her trousers toward her next pair of knives. A tear escaped down her cheek. She knew what she must do.

Forgive me, Zephan.

Avaya lifted her chin, drilling her brother with an ice-cold glare. "I told you before. Jannemar is a kingdom of burning bridges, in a war quickly depleting the kingdom's coffers. The country is weak. Radha is an enormous power with an unrivaled navy force. If it were not for their own civil war, they would have descended long ago. I know what they want and how to buy their alliance."

Semra's fingers grazed the hilt of her knife. Slowly, slowly, she snuck the handle into her palm. Avaya continued.

"If Belvidore aligns with Radha, Jannemar doesn't stand a chance. But if Belvidore and Jannemar unify, we will strengthen each other, and become a mighty powerhouse in our own right once again. We can make alliances with Radha, offering access to our mines to rebuild our financial stability. We can defend against enemies as we see fit. We will be respected in the world as a military power."

Siler caught Semra's eye across the room, and his gaze flitted to Semra's hidden hand. He inclined his head in the smallest of nods. *It's time. Do it.*

Zephan pressed his lips together. "As if Belvidore doesn't have enough troubles of its own. You need the pressure off Belvidore. And you need Jannemar not to ally with Radha against you."

Semra dragged herself along the floor. Avaya stalked toward Zephan. Was he keeping her attention on purpose, to distract her, or had he lost himself in the argument?

Would she kill him?

For all her betrayals, for all her evils, Avaya had never threatened to kill Zephan. Not directly. But watching her now, Semra wasn't so sure.

Avaya cocked her head. "Belvidore isn't the one in trouble. Our army is alive and well, and marching into Jannemar as we speak. A processional, you could say. Did you hear? There's going to be a coronation. The first double crown *queen*."

Semra's blood ran cold. Avaya didn't need the loyalty of Jannemar's army to secure the throne. Not if Azi threw open the gates from the inside and invited enemies in, attacking from a place of advantage. With no army commander to direct Jannemar's forces.

"Do you know who this belonged to?" Avaya lifted the

shell pendant on her necklace and ran a thumb over its smooth surface. "This belonged to Aurin's friend, Raisa the windcaller. One of the four elemental melders at The Crumbling. This necklace was here when magic died. It's only fitting it be here when magic returns."

Avaya threw her hands in the air, lifting her face toward the sky. Light glinted off Avaya's golden crown as a great gale swept through the cavern ceiling opening. The windstorm swept the chamber, building in power as it swirled round, summoned by the housing artifact of Raisa, the elemental melder, and directed by the crimson queen.

The flowing red of her gown whipped around her body, and the thinness of her arms seemed strong again as she commanded the squall.

Semra's stomach dropped. A knife throw would be useless now. It would be just as likely to hit Zephan or Siler as Avaya, with gusts this forceful.

She had to make it to the eye of the storm, the one place where there was no wind. Avaya. Zephan braced himself against the wall, staying low to the ground, and pushed against Siler's feet as he stretched along the floor toward Avaya. Semra strained against the winds blowing her hair back and beating against her face, inching forward on her stomach.

But Avaya paid them no mind. She strode forward to Aurin's spear, placing one hand on Raisa's necklace and summoning all the power of the storm in the other. Crimson skirts billowed out behind her as she reached for it.

With a loud cry, Avaya seized Aurin's spear.

45

———

A great crackling sound exploded through the chamber. The mountain shook, and a shadow passed over the skylight of the cavern. Dragons roared outside in a distant, bone-chilling din.

Semra squinted through the barrage of wind just as Aurin's spear flung Avaya backward. She hit the wall and crumpled in a heap. The wind vanished.

Boom.

CRACKKKK!

The cavern broke apart and an avalanche of rock filled the gap. Semra's heart lurched to her throat, and she flew across the carbonate toward Zephan. Zephan gathered his feet under him and lunged for her, but Siler yanked him back with a yell as a boulder twice his size plunged into the space he had occupied moments before.

"*Nooo!*" Semra's scream left a ringing in her ears, and she raked a shaking hand through her hair.

The new rock wall settled across the cavern, splitting it in two—Siler and Zephan on one side, and Avaya and Semra on the other. *No, no, no.* This couldn't be. They'd only just found each other again.

Semra struck the rock with a feral cry. Her knuckles screamed at her, but she welcomed the pain. A soft breeze played across her cheek, and her blood ran cold. Semra spun to Avaya, but it was too late. Not only was she alive—she'd gathered enough wind for an upward boost and launched herself up to the rope fifteen feet overhead.

Avaya disappeared out the skylight without a trace, pulling the rope up with her. Semra was alone in the cave. In a *fraction* of the cave. With Aurin's vengeful spear still lodged in the floor.

Her mouth went dry. Avaya hadn't gotten the spear. That much was a mercy. But why hadn't it killed her? Was sifal magic enough to protect her? What of the prophecy? Was the timing wrong? Would she be back? Or would Azi secure her throne and himself as successor, and kill her swiftly for failing?

Had Azi found Aviama? If he had, she may already be dead.

Belvidore marched on Qalea. Had they infiltrated the south, sneaking in through the mountain pass? Would they make themselves known, or slowly travel through and pop up unexpectedly?

If Avaya made it back to Qalea, she would strike quite the scene leading her people into Shamaran Castle. Semra felt sick. *Avaya's* people. The ones she kidnapped herself to. The ones belonging to the husband she murdered. Not the ones she was born to serve.

She could never serve. She was weak-minded and selfish. Nothing like Zephan.

Zephan.

Semra flew to the wall of cascaded rock and threw her

weight against it, earning nothing but a bruised rib. Her chest tightened, and she searched the wall for cracks, openings, anything along the avalanche divide. "Zephan? *ZEPHAN!*"

Fingers shot out and seized Semra's wrist, and she screamed. Looking down, she saw a narrow space between three larger boulders. No other chinks seemed to exist along the collapsed wall, and this one was just large enough for an arm to snake through.

"I'm here, I'm here!"

Semra gripped his hand, and her tense shoulders dropped at the sound of his voice. "Why didn't you say anything?"

Zephan's voice sounded hollow from the encapsulated chamber beyond. "I did. I was calling for you, but you didn't say anything. And then you started screaming, and couldn't hear me. Is Avaya there?"

Semra shook her head, then remembered he couldn't see her. "No. No, she's alive, she's fine, but she got up the rope and took it with her. She's gone."

Silence settled over them. She squeezed his hand and leaned against the wall. A lump rose in her throat.

"I'm fine too, thanks for asking." Siler. "Feeling right at home back here."

He sounded far too chipper for the scenario, but her lips twisted into a thin smile just the same. She cleared her throat, but her voice was rough when she spoke. "I'm glad you're okay."

"We've been having heart-to-hearts," Siler continued. "Did you know princey gets his pastries imported?"

She rolled her eyes. "No he doesn't. There's a contract with several bakeries."

Zephan laughed. It warmed her soul.

"Aurin's spear, why do you know that?" Siler exclaimed. He hesitated. "Ugh, that expression is so *awkward* now."

Why *did* she know that? In her line of work, useless information today could be critical tomorrow. Perhaps that's all it was. She knew the inner workings of the castle better than most, by now.

Zephan squeezed her hand and pulled away. It was an awkward position to maintain. "Why didn't the spear kill her?"

Semra sank down against the wall with her back against the carbonate. "I don't know. I think the magic absorbed some of the excess energy. Frigibar thinks it was my magic that kept me alive when I tried to remove it, and that it only killed people without any. Avaya only has sifal magic, but she used a lot of it."

"I guess all she can do now is head back to Qalea and take charge of the Belvidorian army," Siler said. "Take over Jannemar the old-fashioned way."

"But with a dragon." Zephan let out a sigh from the other side of the wall. "And sifal magic. It might be poisoning her, but it *feels* strong enough."

Semra reached out to Zezura. *Where are you?*

Nothing. Semra's pulse ticked up a notch. She sent another message through the mark of their bond, an urgent alert tugging at her heart. *Are you okay? Are you safe? What happened?*

But no answer came. Tears pricked at her eyes, and she swallowed against the lump in her throat. It didn't budge. Her chest hitched in a sob. Had Rotokas killed her? Was everything she loved doomed to die?

"What now?" she squeaked. *Squeaked.* Were dragonlords supposed to squeak?

Maybe she wasn't a dragonlord anymore. Maybe there was no dragon. Semra gritted her teeth as tears poured down her face. No, until she got out of here, she couldn't know for sure.

"Can you make it out?" Zephan asked.

Semra snorted. "Have you ever seen me fly? I have a decent jump, but not thirty-feet-high decent."

Siler clicked his tongue. "Pity. No wonder you need a dragon."

Even Zephan laughed. "Okay, it's okay. We're going to be fine. Can Zezura fit her tail through the opening, or something?"

Semra choked on another sob. "She's not answering me."

Zephan swore.

"Is there a passage behind you? There should be a narrow opening leading to an underground river. I sort of remember how far to go before turning for the exit. I think."

Zephan's voice came again. "With that vote of confidence, what could possibly go wrong?" A pause. "If there was an opening, it's caved in now. We're in a small pocket, maybe twenty feet long, ten feet wide."

"Nothing but a mountain and claustrophobia to remind me of home," Siler chirped. But this time even he sounded a little deflated.

Semra leaned her head back against the wall and closed her eyes. Azi on the throne. Avaya flying toward the army. Without Zezura, they'd be a week behind Rotokas even if they got out now and found horses. As it was, the king was trapped, Siler was trapped, Aviama was hidden—for now—and Zezura might be dead.

Wind seemed like an excellently helpful magic to have. Smoke wouldn't do her any good in here, and fire would be a pretty distraction if anything. It didn't move mountains or lift her toward the sky. And it was useless against rock.

"Do you think your treehouse friend will come investigate?" Zephan asked.

Semra considered this. Frigibar would definitely check on the spear, and the landslide would absolutely have caught his attention. It was probably even loud enough to cause a ruckus across the valley to Ellix. "Yes. But I'm not sure if his way in is safe now, or passable."

"I'm sure Zezura's fine," Siler said. "Maybe she's knocked out. If we wait it out, she'll come to. Send up a smoke signal for Frigibar, and one of the two of them will come."

Semra uncurled her hands and let onyx smoke billow up from her fingertips and out through the skylight of the cavern high overhead. It was a hopeful thought, but even if Frigibar could come, they'd be waiting hours. If he brought rope, he could get Semra out, but what about Zephan and Siler?

A melancholy stillness settled over the cavern, and afternoon light softened toward evening. Semra reached out to Zezura frequently, hoping to rouse her —to hear something, anything—but time stretched on, and still there was no reply.

An hour passed, maybe two. It was hard to tell in a space where exhaustion and sadness mingled. Semra wept silent tears, her shoulders shaking with sobs, and let them ebb at their own pace. The ache in her core was all too familiar. Terrible things were par for the course in her life so far, and she'd been waiting for the next one to drop. But it hurt all the same.

And this time, she had more to lose than ever.

Zephan broke the quiet with a soft word. "Semra?"

She opened her eyes, staring vacantly up at the sliver of sky she could see through the cavern opening. It had the audacity to be blue. "Hmm?"

"Why do you avoid me when I talk about the future? Are you really just waiting to see if I die, or is there something else?"

Semra's gut twisted. There *was* something. There were multiple somethings. And as Semra cycled through them now in her mind, she identified exactly zero that she wanted to discuss. "Umm, I mean, I think you were right before. About the ... leaving thing. It's possible I have some abandonment issues."

A heavy pause stretched between them, and anxiety flipped her stomach inside out. But when he did speak, his words did nothing to calm her. "And if you knew I would live, and we made it out of our latest scrape, then what? Would you say yes?"

Semra's pulse raced, and her chest tightened. Long fearful fingers seemed to reach up her insides like vines, strangling her. Her lips parted, but no sound came.

Would she say yes? *Could* she say yes?

She knew what she wanted to say. She'd known for a while now, and could no longer deny it. But this wasn't Dahyu, and she was no diplomatic treasure. If she told him, would she ruin the scraps of what they had?

Could there be any scraps, if she kept leaving him in the dark?

She swallowed. "I'm not good at this."

Zephan laughed, and Semra pictured an eyeroll going along with it. "You're *terrible* at having these conversations. When I first told you, outright, that I liked you—*more* than liked you—you looked like you were about to kiss me. And then you punched me and ran away. Literally fled. And, you know, right now, there's a wall between us, but we're also trapped in here. So, no punching *and* no running. It's an opportunity I can't pass up."

Semra took a breath. "The only tolerable futures I can envision have you in it. The only happy ones are with us together." *But I can't accept.*

Siler groaned. "I'm living my nightmare. Seriously, this is worse than torture. Semra, none of us are idiots, so stop beating around the bush and tell the man why you refuse to marry him."

Whack.

"Ow! Semra, princey punches people too! Unprovoked!"

Semra squeezed her eyes shut and wrapped her arms around her knees, dropping her head forward. Her chest ached from deep within, a place that used to be empty, dark, and cold. Was it worse to have something to lose?

No. Having something to lose meant she'd experienced something beautiful. That love, hope, and loyalty were not ancient fables. And they'd given her something to be alive *for*.

A tear slipped down her cheek, and she lifted her chin to wipe it away. "I would love ..." She sniffled and tried again. "Zephan Shamaran, I would love nothing more than to be your wife and trap you to me forever. But I can't be a queen. Crowns aren't meant for people like me. The court knows it. The people know it. It's possible that everyone but you knows it." She hesitated, searching for the answer that would make most sense to him. The response that would sound the least like an excuse. She grimaced. "Your father knew it."

46

A beat of silence filled the cavern, and Semra's pulse pounded in her ears. When he spoke again, Zephan's voice was solemn, an edge lining its tone. "This is about my father?"

Semra flinched. Wrong choice of words? What else was she supposed to say?

A deep sigh came through the hold in the wall, but this time, his voice was soft. "What did he say?"

She closed her eyes, transporting herself back to the bench in the garden where the best father figure she'd ever seen had scolded her and counseled her at once. His brown eyes were kind, but firm. Understanding, yet unyielding. "He married your mother against the advice of many, telling him it was unwise, and it caused issues with the court. He said a king *has* to have support from the gentry, and play the game of politics, even when he hates it."

Semra swallowed, the ache in her heart growing as she spoke. "He said love is not enough for a king. That the crown must always come first. Those who love you must come alongside you or release you to your duty. He said" —she paused, thinking back—"Entanglements with people who can't take on the weight of the kingdom are dangerous."

What would Zephan think of that? Who had he trusted more in life than his own father? She leaned her head back, and a tear slipped down her cheek.

Quiet lived on for another minute, but the question he raised next surprised her. "When was this?"

Semra threw her hands up, a sudden burst of heat flaring in her chest. "Why does it matter? Isn't it enough? He told me he'd tried to get through to you. But isn't it obvious? I'm the entanglement. I'm the danger. And even if Turian hadn't said a thing, don't we know enough to know that you marrying me puts a nail in the coffin of your reign? Your reputation and your father's legacy would be forever marred by a connection with an assassin. Not just a connection. A *union*. That's insane. It was bad enough for your father to marry your mother. But your mother was a commoner, not a killer. I'm both."

Semra swatted at an angry tear and took a breath. "Aside from your father, you are the best king Jannemar could hope for. Without you, the kingdom falls. Anything to interfere with that would be selfish. Aviama isn't strong like you. The tough calls, the warrior mindset, she doesn't have it. She's the best second option you've got, and more queenly by the day, but it's *you* that Jannemar needs. It would be ungrateful of me, ungrateful to your father, to accept a position in the monarchy. And that's what a proposal of marriage is from you, isn't it? It's not a casual, hey there, I love you, you love me, let's get married and spend forever together. It's a job offer. For life. To one of the hardest jobs in existence. And I'm wildly unqualified. Not just unqualified. I'm *unfit*. And for you to—"

"Stop." The anger in his voice surprised her. She stopped.

Zephan snaked his arm through the hole in the wall and held it out to her. "Take my hand."

Semra stared at it, suddenly unsure of herself.

"Take it." Again, his voice was strong. Commanding.

She took it.

His voice was calm and even. "We're going to address everything you just said. Because there's a lot of lies in there. But first, you need to trust me that I don't ask stupid questions for no reason." Semra heard him take a deep inhale. "The conversation you had with my father. *When was it?*"

Semra bit her lip. "I was on house arrest, accused of killing King Arnevon. I was sick and taking the tonic Coanor made for me. Siler had already sent me messages that people knew I was unwell, and there were threats to my life. I just didn't know they were from him yet. Turian told me he wanted to help me, but couldn't if I kept getting myself into trouble. He wanted me to keep my head down. I promised I would, and I escaped on Zezura within minutes of leaving our conversation."

"He was trying to keep you safe and clear your name. He wanted to prove to the court that you weren't the culprit by creating an alibi through house arrest, and letting the real killer expose himself. But you were right—the castle wasn't safe. He couldn't protect you from assassins of your caliber. If you had stayed, you would be dead."

Semra's voice was small. "I know. I so wished I could have kept my promise to him."

"Semra. If my father gave his blessing, what would be your objection then?"

"He's dead." She hated saying it so flatly, but there was nothing for it. It was true.

Zephan was unfazed. "Go with me. If we *did* have his blessing, what would be your objection?"

The answer was obvious. "That I am unfit."

"And if you were deemed fit for office?" Zephan pressed.

"I'm not."

"But if you were."

Semra hesitated. A bittersweetness blossomed in her chest, warmth mingling with pain at the thought, a tender sprig of hope checked by the cold, wet blanket of realism. "I would say yes."

Zephan's hand gripped hers, and he seemed to freeze. "You—you would say yes?" he stammered.

Semra smiled. "I would say yes."

Nobody said anything for a long moment, and Semra bit her lip. "Zephan?"

Siler snorted, and Semra jumped. She'd nearly forgotten he was there. "He's grinning like a big doofus. Give him a minute to get his brain back."

"Sorry. I—right, okay." Zephan cleared his throat. "My father spoke to me also. *After* he spoke to you. You're right—he was worried about my closeness to you. He told me I need to think like a politician. He told me the crown is my first love, and I must always be faithful to it. *Just as you would never be unfaithful to your wife, and you would desire the best for her, protect and love her, so too your crown.*"

Semra considered his words. So far, everything made sense. What *didn't* make sense was the idea of Zephan marrying her, in light of such advice. There was no approach to marrying her that would salvage her past.

"He quizzed me about you. Interrogated, more like." Zephan laughed. "First, he addressed how being with you impacted me personally—not just my happiness, but my character. He asked me if you make me a better man. If you challenge me to grow, or to stoop to unwise choices."

Semra tried to imagine how that conversation might have gone. She itched to know what he'd said.

Zephan continued. "Second, he addressed the diplomatic implications of our marriage. He asked if the relationship between us could be spun to an angle that wins the people's approval and connects them to the monarchy. Something strong enough to sway the court. He urged me that whoever I marry *must* make political sense. My father never regretted marrying my mother, commoner though she was. He regretted *how* he went about it. There is a huge difference.

"And third, Father questioned me about your happiness. If you could be happy in a cage like ours. I am certain of the answer to his first question, and confident we could effectively handle the second. But only you can answer the third. And I admit, I'm anxious over your answer."

Semra twined her fingers with his against the rockslide wall, tracing her thumb along his hand and palm. She wondered for the hundredth time what it might have been like to grow up with a father like Turian. Firm, but loving. Gentle, but challenging. It was nothing like the so-called "love" she had from Azi, where weakness was beaten out of them *for their good,* and for the cause he made up for them to champion.

Turian had seen her, really seen her, and taken the time to try to protect her. Such humility from a man surrounded by schmoozing and false praise was rare. But Sharsi had been his anchor, his grounding. And what if ... what if she could be that for Zephan?

Her heart swelled with fresh flutters. Could she really allow herself a future of happiness?

Siler groaned. "This is the wildest romantic tryst I've ever been a part of."

Smack.

"Ow! Don't be bitter, princey. By now, even *I'm* rooting for you. I've just never heard a pair of lovebirds debate themselves to marriage with logical treatise. It's a very weird experience. If we ever get out of here, I'll tell all the boys with girl troubles to create a presentation for their sweethearts."

Semra ignored him, her mind too taken by the possibilities before her. "I would be happy anywhere I was with you." She paused, thinking of the stuffiness of the castle, how the walls caved in around her when she was on house arrest. "I would need regular dragon rides. And excursions, to anywhere. But if I could be of use, having something valuable to do, and could be with you—well, that's the dream I haven't let myself dream. But aren't you worried you'll be run out of Qalea? The laughingstock of surrounding nations, with a court full of suspicious side-eyes and neighboring kings undermining your leadership and sanity for having chosen me? Would I really make you happy, or am I a nice distraction?"

"Semra Myansara." She could almost see Zephan shaking his head at her as he said it. "Anything *else* feels like the distraction. You, my dearest love, are a deeper joy than fleeting happiness. You push me. Challenge me. You are the strongest, most incredible woman I've ever met. Probably the most stubborn and independent, too, which has nearly killed you on multiple occasions. But we sand each other's rough edges, and together we're stronger than we ever were apart.

"You said you wanted to trap me to you, but being with you isn't a trap. It's as free as I've ever been. When I am stifled in the castle, you're my fresh air. When I'm lassoed to this or that responsibility and the weight of it all pulls me down, you are my sanity. You keep me going. There's nowhere else I would ever rather be than by your side.

"If you're afraid to keep me from Jannemar, you should know—you make me a better ruler. And as angry as the court might be if I marry you, they'll be much more infuriated to learn that I plan to marry you or no one at all. I will die a bachelor and create innumerable succession issues in our fragile nation should they deny me."

Semra's cheeks flushed. She tilted her face up toward the evening light spilling down into the cavern, and a warmth spread out from her chest throughout her body. Her heart raced. Her stomach flopped. And there in the cave of their tomb, exits blocked, hope cut off, a smile split across her face.

Oh, how she loved him! Who fought for her like he did? Who had ever dared to love her so completely, like he did?

But even as the door to a future with Zephan began to crack open, a force seemed to hold it there, not quite ready to let go. Semra bit her lip.

"And your father's blessing? He liked me enough as a person, but that's not good enough for the monarchy. I thought he only gave warnings and worries about us being together."

"Not true. He may not have verbally handed out a blessing, but *after* you were cleared, he gave you the title of earl." Zephan squeezed her hand. "Not countess. *Earl*. He didn't just give you land to look after; he gave you military responsibilities among the gentry and invited you to court. It was his last act as king before his death, and the closest we'll get to an obvious blessing. My father removed the obstacle of common birth by elevating you to nobility. He even gave you a surname affiliated with the queens of Jannemar, a symbol of resilience in our kingdom: Myansara. He was waiting for you to catch up, but that *was* his blessing."

Semra's jaw dropped. Turian had waited until her name was cleared, pardoned her past sins, and paved the way for her marriage to Zephan. He'd removed any complaint the nobles could publicly bring against her birth, and bestowed virtue on her by the name Myansara. The symbol, the inheritance of Jannemar queens.

It was the first poem Zephan had ever mentioned to her, explaining why the gates of the castle were named Dragon Gate, Spearhead Gate, and Nezzi Gate. Back when he was Dahyu. But it meant so much more now, coming from Zephan. She hadn't known the verse he'd recited came from the architect prophecy. Maybe he hadn't either.

But after staring at it countless times in the last several weeks, the words came to her easily. The flower *nezil myansara* that grew at heights of ten-thousand feet, up in the mountains, a solace of beauty in harsh environments. Unmatched resilience and grace. The legacy of royalty.

Turian had marked her for queenship. And she'd hardly noticed.

"But ... my history ... I still dream of the faces of people I've killed. I am stained with blood. Child of the mountain. I don't deserve authority over other people, better people."

The twist in her gut drew her back down to earth. *I'm unfit.*

"That's enough of that." Siler's tone was matter of fact, and she pictured him crossing his arms and somehow sprawling out in the confined space beyond. "The only virtue you allow yourself is a guilty conscience, and I'm not convinced it's as admirable as you seem to think it is.

"You may have been a child of the mountain, but you're the least like us. You won't take contract work with your skills. If you don't marry princey, what are you going to do? Nothing, that's what. You're going to go find a mountain hole to rot in with Zezura. I know because you told me. Though I think really, you would end up helping people some other way. Trouble may follow you, but projects find you too.

"Lesala was your first one. You took care of her and gave her a family. You gave who knows how many other kidnapped kids back to their parents, or found them new homes. Pidge is obsessed with you. She talks about little else, some days. She wants to *be* you. Let me ask you something. Is there any hope for Pidge? Can she make something of her life? Or should she just give up and end everything?"

Semra's lips parted. It was true, before Avaya's kidnapping, she'd planned on disappearing for good. And she never anticipated any of the ways she'd helped her fellow children of the mountain. They were so like children, after all. The idea of Pidge being ruined for life because of Azi's influence set her teeth on edge. She clenched her jaw. "Don't be stupid. Pidge is smart and funny and can pick up new skills as easily as she picks pockets. She's got a good heart. She can do anything she puts her mind to."

"Yes. She can." The unyielding firmness in Siler's voice sent a chill down her spine. "She's brilliant. I wish she'd see herself the way we see her. It's so obvious, isn't it, that she deserves good things? Should she feel guilty for overcoming evil, and working her tail off to heal, and finding something worth living for?

"You fought for the children of the mountain to have a future. You got Turian to sign the deal and offer free apprenticeships and new lives. You believed in them. You even believed in me. I think I'm your only failed project, really. You've done a number on anyone you've encountered since leaving Mount Hara.

"If you go hide in a hole, what does that show them? But if you've turned your life around, and rise from the ashes of the mountain to a queen with the influence to save countless more, what then? How dare you throw that away, all so you can feel sorry for yourself in a pit, rocking back and forth, saying, 'Well, at least I didn't accidentally become happy.' Stop punishing yourself for your past. It doesn't mean what you did was okay. But what's done is done. You've made your penance. Learn from it. Release it. And live better tomorrow."

Semra reeled. What a pitiful hypocrite she was! He was right, of course. That's precisely what she was doing. Wallowing. She grimaced. Nothing was more ridiculous than a helpless, wallowing worm. And that's what she was. Did it matter if she deserved the authority? She couldn't cover over her past with new good deeds. There weren't enough good deeds in the world.

But if she could do something good, and *not* doing it caused *more* pain—if punishing herself was pointless and only hurt the people she loved—and leaning into her future brought joy and freshness, hope and healing, then what had possessed her to decline it?

The question wasn't whether she deserved it but whether she could carry the weight responsibly. She was acquainted with weight. It had been her lifelong companion. But for once in her life, she might carry the weight of the world with a companion, a love that was not weakness but encouragement and strength. A thrill ran through her.

Could her heart's desire be acceptable?

She glanced down at Zephan's hand. His fingers were white. Semra squealed and released him. How long had she been cutting off his circulation?

Siler gasped. "The ashes! The architect thing, what did it say? It said something about ashes ..."

Semra furrowed her brow, trying to remember. "Ashes, ashes, something about plants ... leaves?"

Zephan snapped his fingers and pulled his arm back through the hole. "I've studied this far too many times recently!" He recited the verse in question:

Blooming in adversity, nobility she claims;

Despite the soot upon her roots, she's called to greater aims.
Ashes, ashes, hail her coming, magic in her leaves,
Her solemn strength is weathered wild even as she grieves

"Scourge!" Siler clapped his hands. "I know why Avaya couldn't get the spear. She isn't the crimson queen. *You* are."

47

Semra's heart stopped. "What?"

"It's you," Siler said. "It's always been you. We've all been morons."

Semra stared across the cavern to the place Aurin's spear still stood, rooted in carbonate. Mocking her. "No. I tried to take it out before. It blasted me backward, just like it did to Avaya."

"You weren't queen before." Zephan's voice was soft.

"That's got to be it," Siler said. "The prophecy is for the crimson queen. That's you. You're right, your history will always be a part of you. You'll never shake off the blood in your ledger. But it's also spurring you on to a new chapter. Only you can do this."

Semra lurched unsteadily to her feet, her eyes fixed on the spear shaft. Hints of cobalt blue beckoned to her from the splintered veins embedded in the deep wyronite gray. The bronze peeking out at her at the base of the spear head reminded her of the rose gold patterning along Zezura's shimmering aquamarine scales.

Could a prophecy written so long ago have known everything in her life that would come to pass? She took a step closer. Could it somehow be meant for her?

"Stop. Semra? Semra, don't touch it. Stop."

Semra stopped. "Zephan?"

"Forget the spear. Forget Jannemar. Forget it all. I've told you how I feel. What my father said. Even Siler told you his thoughts, which were strangely genuine. It felt weird." Zephan hesitated, and Semra twisted back toward the rockslide between them. "I won't marry you for any other reason than love. I can't marry *just* for love, but I think we have a lot more between us than that. This is one of those beautiful times when what I want and what is wise overlap. But I have to know that you marrying me isn't another self-sacrifice. If you say yes, you'd better not say it for the spear. Or for Jannemar. Or to spare Aviama the throne. Say it for me, or don't say it at all."

Her stomach dropped. How could he think that? Semra's heart went out to him, and she realized how little of her thoughts she'd shared. It wasn't right. Zephan's openness with her should be rewarded with reciprocation. He deserved the world. If all he wanted was a piece of her mind, that should be easy.

Slowly she pivoted and strode for the wall. Semra knelt in front of the hole. "Look at me."

Zephan shifted on the other side, and though it was dark, a faint silhouette of familiar features came into view as he dropped his face down to look for her.

Semra's gut wrenched, and her chest threatened to tear in two. A burning constricted her throat, and she swallowed. "I love you. I'm sorry it's taken me this long to say it. But I do. I love you more than anything in the world, and I will live and die by your side, if you'll have me."

Zephan grinned, and the twinkle in his eyes lit the darkness beyond with hope. "We'll hope for the living part."

She laughed. "I think you're a fool for loving me, Zephan Shamaran. But I'm so grateful that you do. Be sure this is what you want, because if I marry you, you'll never get rid of me."

"I expect nothing less. I'm counting on it."

"Aren't you going to ask her?" Siler pressed from behind the wall.

"To marry me?" Zephan pulled back and glanced in Siler's direction. "But didn't she just say yes?"

"No. She didn't. You said how getting married was a great idea, but she can't marry you for bad reasons. Then *she* said she loved you, and some other mushy stuff. Nobody actually asked. And as the symbol of our society, I would hate such traditions of clear communication to fall by the wayside."

Semra pursed her lips to hide a smirk, and Zephan arched an eyebrow.

"I can't ask her from back here. It's boring. There's no romantic flair at all."

"I'm afraid you can't afford to wait. We need the crimson queen, and if you don't ask her, she can't be a queen."

Semra shook her head. "It doesn't matter. First off, being engaged doesn't make me a queen. And second, we're still trapped in here."

"Ah, but what if you *could* get married here and now?" Siler asked. "And then you became queen, and then you got the spear, and then you used it to get us all out? That sounds rather promising, wouldn't you say?"

Zephan and Semra exchanged glances through the hole in the wall. She cocked her head. "We can't get married up here. Not for real."

"Why not? Because as it turns out—yes, see, here we are ..." A rustle of papers followed, and Siler let out a breath. "It just so happens that I often carry marriage certificate paperwork around with me for scribe work. I had three weddings to officiate just last week. I also carry some basic contract forms, but I don't think any of those apply today."

"You … you carry …" Semra furrowed her brow.

Zephan's mouth fell open. "You're saying we could actually legally get married. By you. Right now."

"Correct." The jovial nonchalance was back in Siler's voice. "I've never been more in favor of a wedding. But then again, weddings don't usually save my life. This one very well might, so can we get on with it?"

Zephan peered back down the hole at Semra. Semra blinked back at him. "This is insane."

He shrugged. "That seems to be our specialty. Listen, if we get out of here alive, I'll marry you one way or another. If we kick everybody off my throne and take back the castle, we'll have to have a wedding ceremony there anyway. But if we're going to get married one way or another … well …"

Zephan held up a finger and rummaged along his pockets and sword belt. The hole in the wall was so narrow, Semra could only see vague movements. She leaned forward and stuck her eye against the hole, but her head blocked out what little light they had.

"I spend enough of my life in the dark as it is," Siler grumbled. "Can we get that sliver back in here?"

"Sorry."

Semra rocked back on her heels. Was she really about to marry Zephan? Minutes ago, it was an impossible thought. But now …

Now, hope sprung alive, and once planted, it grew, refusing to be put out. A smile split wide across her face. The arms she'd come to love could surround her forever.

If only they stayed alive long enough.

"Semra?"

It was Zephan's voice. Semra's attention snapped back to the hole, and she leaned forward. "Yes?" Her heart thundered in her chest, her pulse pounding in her ears.

"Can I have my signet ring back?"

Semra gaped at the hole, then shook off the absurdity and handed the item back to him through the narrow space. "Right, yes. Of course."

"I have something for you," Zephan said. "When I gave you the signet ring, I told you it wasn't the ring I wanted to give you. And the truth is, the moment I was alone after that happened, I got the ring I'd dreamed of offering you and kept it on my person. It gave me hope, something to fight for. That one day I might give it to you, and you might accept it.

"Semra Myansara. You are the most stubborn woman I have ever met. You're often right, which is obnoxious, and you've become someone I lean on." Zephan cleared his throat. "Ugh, this isn't how I meant to say it. I had things planned to say. But um ... my mind went blank and I'm kind of nervous and I forgot them all."

A new smile crept slowly over Semra's face, but she clamped her mouth shut and waited. Zephan took a deep breath. "I am a king, with a kingdom and people under me that do what I tell them. I am responsible for the wellbeing of just about everyone and everything, which at times feels too great a load to bear.

"Taking care of you, protecting you, even when you can protect yourself, is my greatest honor. Having someone by my side who dares disagree with me, loudly, and challenges me, is a blessing that few have. I hoped one day to have a marriage like my parents had, but now I know: we will build on their foundation and create a love that grows deeper by the day.

The pressures of the world don't threaten us. They've proved to bring us closer.

"You are the most beautiful woman I've ever seen. You're the most intelligent woman I've ever known. And you pair it with a love for people and drive to help them that is unmatched. Loving you and being loved by you is the greatest adventure of my life. I would rather live a thousand adventures with you than a safe boring life with anyone else. So, here it is. Officially. Will you marry me?"

A lump lodged in Semra's throat. Her chest tightened, and she blinked back tears. Semra let out a short laugh. If this was his backup speech, he'd done just fine! She bit her lip. "Yes. Yes, I will marry you."

Zephan reached through the narrow space and held out his hand. Semra reached out a trembling hand, and Zephan drew her arm through and slid something smooth and cold onto her finger. He ran his thumb over her fingers, brushing across the ring. He released her, and she pulled her hand back and gasped at the sight. The last of the evening light glanced off a large sapphire in the middle, set with resplendent diamond on either side.

"It was Mother's," he said softly. "I'd hoped you would wear it. Do you like it?"

Semra stared at it. "It's much too nice for me. I've never owned anything like this. But it's beautiful."

"I'm not convinced anything is quite nice *enough*," Zephan said. "But it seemed fitting that you have this one. It means a lot to me."

She tilted her hand this way and that in the light, watching the blue and rainbow reflections bounce off the stones on her finger. Absolutely mesmerizing. "Thank you."

"Right, well done. Step one complete," Siler chirped. "Here

we go. I've got the certificate filled out. I just need your signatures, and we'll have you two married in no time."

Zephan took the paper, and a rustle and a light scratching filled the silence. A moment later, the paper and pen were passed through the hole, and Semra uncrumpled the parchment and spread it out on the carbonate floor.

A strange feeling settled over her. Her future, the mark of a new era, in a few dark lines on paper. Siler had filled out all the boxes except the signature lines. The witness box was signed *Sinan Ravenbrand.*

Semra laughed. "Ravenbrand? *Raven?* A little on the nose, isn't it?"

"Ehh, maybe." Siler chuckled. "I couldn't help myself. Most people who know that name and would cause problems are dead."

"Is the certificate legal with an alias?" Zephan asked.

"Oh, Sinan Ravenbrand is more real than I am. I've been Siler to the people in the mountain all my life, but kidnapped kids raised as assassins by psychopaths don't usually get registered anywhere. I was taken from a small village. There's no record of a Siler anywhere, and there *is* record of Sinan. He's more real than Siler anyway, so this is as legal as anything."

Semra grinned. It figured that if she were ever to get married, it would be like this. Trapped in a cave, death on the horizon, an uncharacteristically massive gemstone shimmering on her finger, and an assassin's alias to officiate. She wouldn't have it any other way.

She touched the pen to paper and scrawled her name. But not the surname of a bondservant, Azi's lackey, Semra Bandaka. The name given to her by a king, the name of queens, the symbol of strength. *Semra Myansara.*

Semra passed the certificate back through the hole, and Zephan captured her hand and slipped a second band onto her finger. "I have the wedding band too. I had them set it with diamond and opal, because ...well, I think of you whenever I see opal. And I thought it made sense to include Zezura. She's stuck with me now too, in a way."

The mark of the dragon's kiss. The thought of Zezura stung, and she sent out another desperate message to the dragon. *Be alive. Be safe.*

Semra withdrew her hand, and her lips parted. Next to the sapphire ring was a second band lined with small diamonds on the ends, and a crown of opals nestling perfectly against the sapphire in the center. "It's ... stunning. It doesn't seem to belong with a dirty tunic and trousers."

"Maybe you'll have to raid Aviama's closet."

"I'm not giving up trousers! I can do the compromise we had before, *sometimes.* The one that includes trousers underneath."

Zephan laughed. "I'm kidding. You can wear a sack for all I care. The ring is perfect on your finger, and you're absolutely gorgeous in anything."

A warm tingling spread through her body, a blanket of peace and some deeper contentment than mere happiness. Here in the tomb of their confinement, she was the safest she had ever been. Secure. Found. Loved.

"I love you," she said.

"I love you too."

Siler cleared his throat. "And I love pastries. But if we don't get out of here, the last thing I'll have had to eat is dried jerky."

Semra turned toward Aurin's spear. The memory of the blast struck her like a slug to the stomach. Such power! Enough to kill any natural human. Enough to maim or render unconscious any magical person, should they land less than favorably.

Was the prophecy enough? Could she remove the spear and save them?

Semra's breath caught. She gathered her feet under her, stood, and squared her shoulders.

There was only one way to find out.

"Be careful."

A ridiculous suggestion by her new husband. There was no *careful* or *not careful*. There was nothing for it but to reach out and take the spear. It would either accept her as the answer to prophecy, or smash her against the cavern.

Husband.

Did she just get married? She didn't feel any different. Happy, excited, warm and fuzzy, but not different as in *entered into lifetime commitment, accepted a role in the monarchy, forever begun a new chapter in life and kingdom* different.

Was there a particular feeling she was supposed to feel? Would it hit her later?

But the mission came first. It must always come first, even as the crown must now come first for her and Zephan together. Avaya was on her way back to Qalea, on a healthy dragon, with the Belvidorian army marching their way to the capital. The spear had rejected her. Would it reject the rightful queen of Jannemar?

A chill ran down her spine, and she shook off the thought.

There would be time to deal with that weirdness later. At this moment, she was a knife-strapped, trouser-wearing dragonlord facing off against a six-hundred-year-old weapon buried in the origin of the world, the wellspring of magic.

Semra stalked toward the spear, the hum of fire magic coming alive in her blood. The closer she got, the louder the hum, like lightning flooding the surface of her skin, begging to be let free. *We are alike, you and I,* Semra mused, half to herself, half to the spear. *Tabeun. Natural. The same.*

Her pulse pounded in her ears and she sprinted across the cavern, covering the distance at a run, overpowering any hesitation yet pulling at her mind. Semra threw her hands out and captured the spear shaft with both hands. A current bubbled up from the spearhead and hit her like a wave, the weight of its power a hundred times stronger than any gale Avaya could dream up.

The might of it was greater than before, and for a moment the world flew by in slow motion. The ground was ripped away like a rug snatched from under her, and she toppled in a backward spin through the air. The wind of the blast knocked all breath from her body, and her lungs burned for air. Her hands filled with crackling flame she did not remember summoning, and she threw out her arms to break her fall.

A great thundering *boom* rocked the mountain, and the cavern shook as Semra hit the ground. Ringing filled her ears, and she squinted up toward the spear. Her vision swam, but Aurin's spear remained. Was the thunder still rumbling, or was her mind playing tricks?

Lay your head down. It'll be okay … just rest a moment …

Semra groaned and fought against heavy eyelids. Pain radiated up and down every inch of her body. She tensed her muscles to stand, but they refused her commands.

The ringing continued, but so did the thunder, and this

time when she looked up, she saw the rock wall shift and tumble.

Crackkkk!

CRASH.

Zephan. Siler.

Semra cried out and lurched toward the collapsing wall, her body barely responding to her desperate orders. She winced against the throbbing in her head and crawled on raw arms and elbows, scraping her stomach over the cavern floor.

A deep *boom* sounded somewhere in the mountain, and the muffled roar of rolling rock and boulder haunted her every movement. Semra dragged herself inch by inch toward the resettling, shifting wall. The narrow gap through which Zephan had given her his mother's ring and passed a marriage certificate just moments before was gone.

Semra threw a ball of fire at the wall, but the flame hit the rock and was extinguished. She hurled another, and another, and as she regained control of her body, she rose from the ground and ran at the wall with a scream.

"Zephan! Siler! Talk to me!"

The rumbling stopped, and Semra sagged against the rubble partition between them.

"We're here! We're here."

Semra slid to the ground, her shoulders falling forward, and buried her face in her hands. They were safe. As safe as they were before, anyway. With no way out.

"Are you both okay?"

"Yes. I guess the spear doesn't think much of prophecies," Zephan said. "Are you hurt?"

Semra glanced down at her arms. Scrapes, bruises, and redness covered her forearms where she landed, and a laceration decorated her left arm along the bone. Her head still hurt, but her vision had stabilized. "I'm fine."

"There's something here. I think there's a tunnel." Zephan's voice grew more distant, and Siler let out a shout.

"Ho! What did you say about the way you got in with Frigibar? Is this it?"

Semra jerked her head up. "West side? Narrow? You might have to duck?"

"Yes!" Siler's voice.

A shuffle and echoing, running footfalls followed, moving further away, and then returned. "The passage looks clear. It leads to a fork. One side has collapsed. The other opens up to a crazy glowing river. You've got to see this!"

Semra let out a sigh of relief. "I have. They're glowworms. That's the way out."

"Downriver?" Zephan asked.

Semra nodded, then remembered he couldn't see her. "Yes. The caverns were wide open on that side. If there aren't any more cave ins beneath the surface on that end, you should be able to get out." She quickly told them what to look for and what she remembered of the way in, and how to find Frigibar once they were free. If they got free. "I just don't know how deep the river is or how steep the bank. We had a canoe when we came in. You'll have to swim out, and hopefully there are enough places to rest that you'll be good to go."

"We'll send Siler out. I'll wait with you."

"There's no time. Avaya's already miles ahead, and we might not be able to rely on a dragon." Semra swallowed against the lump in her throat. "Besides, if Siler comes back with a rope for me, it won't do *you* any good on that side of the wall. Get some horses and send Frigibar up to me with a rope. I'll be fine. But swear to me you'll go straight to Qalea and let Frigibar come back for me."

As much as she'd love the company, Semra was accustomed to being alone. It made no sense for Zephan to waste time here, and if they ran into any obstacles, it would be advantageous to have Zephan and Siler working together. She knew it; he knew it.

Silenced followed, and she knew she'd won. Zephan grunted. "This isn't how I pictured our wedding day."

Semra laughed. "This isn't your dream honeymoon?"

"Avaya's running, and she has Rotokas," Siler said. "If we want you two lovebirds to have a kingdom to rule over, we've got to go."

"Semra?" Zephan's voice shook.

"Go. I'll find you."

His voice hardened. "I can come back with Frigibar."

Semra let out a breath. Her chest hitched, and her tired muscles sagged. "Do you think that's the wisest move for the crown? The crown that must always come first?"

A beat of silence.

"I won't leave until we've found Frigibar and he's on his way, *with* a rope."

Semra dipped her head. "Deal."

"And I'll get the necklace from Avaya."

She grimaced. "Please don't do anything stupid."

He laughed softly. "I love you."

"I love you too."

"I'll see you soon."

Receding footsteps. Echoing sounds.

The last of the evening light twinkled into night, a soft moon setting the scene for a melancholy mood. The stars mourned the absence of day, and the moon bemoaned the sun, sending forth only shadows of the glory of those mighty rays.

Zez? Zezura, are you there?

Nothing.

She was alone.

49

Hours passed. Twilight descended into the deepness of darkest hours. Semra glared at Aurin's spear, the glistening wyronite almost disappearing into the shadows. It wasn't possible. No one could remove it. The prophecy was a farce. The elemental melders meant to end magic, and they had done so. Soundly.

What if the prophecy was only a bit of children's story, a confusing batch of poetry someone had mistaken to be important? Someone's nighttime half-conscious musings, or a writing of what they hoped might come to pass. The desires of a land bereft of magic, aching for the conveniences and normalcy The Crumbling left behind.

The gash on her arm was small, but still bleeding, and worth cleaning. Semra reached for her magic that came so easily here, at the origin of the world, and jumped in surprise at how quickly the fire leaped to her hand. She brought the fire to the cut, and flinched as the flame licked at her skin, but did not pull away. Semra ran it along the length of the gash until the wound cauterized and dropped her hand.

An unexpected positive of her magic.

She needed more positives, didn't she? Because Zephan and Siler might not make it out of the mountain at all. And the rockslides might settle in ways that would cause new avalanches before they made it out—or even after, when they were exposed to the elements on the side of the mountain.

And if they made it out, they needed horses. And if they found horses, they'd have a two-week travel time. Which was a week later than Avaya would get there on Rotokas. And if they made it, they would have to take control of whatever army remained, and find a way to get close to Avaya, and fight off Belvidorian forces.

All from inside the castle.

Without Zezura, when Azi had Rotokas.

Without Semra. Because even if all those things happened, and Zephan and Siler got out, and found Frigibar, and he came and saved her—if she had no dragon, she'd be traveling to Qalea by horse. Again, something she didn't have. A *slow* something.

Semra had felt Avaya's power. It certainly was poisoning her, but the sifal magic grew stronger even as Avaya's body weakened. With a dragon, magic, the Belvidorian army, and Azi at the helm with his untold network of resources ...

Zephan and Siler were both going to die.

"My dear, my dear ... you know I am the only one who has never left you."

Semra's blood ran cold at the sound of his voice. It was no less frightening than if he'd been there in the flesh. Azi had needled his way into her mind once again.

She'd fought this battle before and won it. Hadn't she? But if she had, why was he back? Perhaps she wasn't as grown as she thought. Even still, her mind gave him power.

And it was true, wasn't it? For all her denials, everyone else had left her. Her closest friend from the mountain, Brens, had betrayed her. And when Brens finally came to herself again, Azi slit her throat. The rest of the mountain children, her colleagues, people she'd known all her life, tried to kill her when she fought to expose Azi. Her colleagues framed her for murdering Queen Sharsi, and her mentor from childhood attempted to murder her when she was thrown in the dungeon.

She could see Ramas' face even now, his lip curled in a snarl, his eyes alight with hate. *I always hated you.* He'd said it with such conviction, such malice. *No one will remember your failings. No one will think of you at all.*

Ramas had paid for his own failure when the mark of the dragon's kiss on Semra's chest absorbed the venom, and she chased him down the dungeon hall and killed him with his own asps. But his words weren't far off, were they? Who was she to be remembered? And what did she care if she was remembered, if she was dead?

Even the one assassin colleague who had escaped with her had betrayed her. Semra would always care for Siler, but in a moment when she needed him, he let Avaya's purse strings lead him by the gullet. They had reconciled, but she could never shake that knowledge.

Turian was the best, most loving father she'd ever seen. To have had him care for her and to have disappointed him was crushing. And then he was assassinated. And she couldn't stop it. And she lost someone else, again.

Zezura. Bonded by the deepest connection Semra could fathom, the mark of the dragon's kiss, saving the dragon's life had turned her own life on its head. They shared emotions and deep loyalty in an incomprehensible, indescribable way. Semra never imagined that the dragon could leave her too. A dragon should live longer than a human.

Semra's bottom lip trembled, and she clutched at her

chest. Azi was laughing at her in her mind's eye, holding a knife around Avaya's throat as she served him with glee. A snarl eased into Semra's features at the vision. *Fool. I would have saved you if only you had let me.*

Her body collapsed in on itself, doubling her over, and her shoulders bowed. Semra moaned. Her body ached, and her chest hurt. A chill ran down her spine, and Azi's voice assaulted her mind again.

My dear, my dear ... you know I am the only one who has never left you.

Yes. Because try as she might, she could never be free of that despicable snake of a man. It was perhaps the only promise to her he hadn't broken. Azi, *the Framatar* as he had so pretentiously demanded to title himself, was attached to her soul like a ball and chain. And it seemed he was resolved to stay there until death parted them.

But whose death?

You did fine against your playmates in the mountain, my dear, but you've never been a match for me.

Angry tears spilled down her cheeks. Her nostrils flared, and she slammed a fist into the cold hard cavern floor. Forgotten in the dark, desolate in a lonely, invisible grief, Semra's muscles strained against the growing feeling that the walls of her mountain prison might press in, press in, press in all around her until she suffocated.

Some queen she was. Ha! Zephan married her, but for what? His arms may never encircle her again. His lips may never find hers again. And their bodies may well never draw breath again by week's end.

Semra stumbled toward Aurin's spear, seething at the bane of her captivity. But it wasn't the spear's fault, was it? It wasn't the spear's fault that she was alone, and helpless, and hopeless, once again.

Once and for all.

Her pulse pounded in her ears as she staggered forward. She fell to her knees before the incandescent wyronite weapon, gentle moonbeams drifting down to settle on a mighty thing of legend. And what was she against legends and prophecies and battles of old?

Semra welcomed the bite of the harsh rocky floor. One of the few signs left that she was alive, for however short a time, and the only experience in that wretched hole that accurately fit the anguish of her soul. Semra threw her head back, lifted up her voice, and screamed at the sky.

The echo of that chamber was as hollow as she felt at her core.

Zephan and Siler would be dead soon if they weren't already. Rotokas had finally taken out his revenge on Zezura. No one was coming.

And even if they did, she'd have nothing left to live for.

What a sham queen she was, daring to lead the Jannemar people as a murderer! Queen of blood, queen of nothing. *Crimson queen.*

But she'd owned her sin, she'd seen the truth of what she was doing under Azi's thumb and fought against it. Even still the red was not removed from her, her victims no less dead than they'd been before. But the king pardoned her and gave her a noble title. Turian had chosen to accept and care for her, despite everything.

Aviama was clueless without her. She'd lost both parents and a sister, in a sense, and still came to Semra for comfort. Pidge was too reckless and mountain-oriented to see the need for diplomacy and mediation. She was explosives in a can, ready to blow—but now she had Siler to keep in check and him to watch over her. Zephan often knew exactly what to do but needed support and help seeing perspectives outside his experience.

Semra loved him. And now she knew that though she didn't deserve a title, that didn't mean she wouldn't make a good queen. No, she didn't deserve to be queen, but she would wear the authority confidently and use it in the service of others.

Perhaps she would die trying, but she would not abandon her kingdom and her people to the cruelty of Azi and Avaya.

Her kingdom.

Her people.

Semra shook her head in wonder. And just like that, she belonged again—first with Zephan, and then to a kingdom, a culture, a context. She had a home, and the mountains, and caves, and rivers were a part of it.

Hail, Crimson Queen.

It was a half-mocking sentiment, and it rocked her. The thought felt *other,* somehow, but filled her mind nevertheless. Semra stilled.

Then pain rocketed through her like a sledgehammer, head to toe. Semra screamed and fell to the ground, the agony of a dragon condensed in her small frame.

Zezura.

Semra felt her pull away, and the pain eased. But Semra chased after her, unwilling to fully break their connection. *Where are you? Are you safe?*

The dragon sent her a flash of trees by the lake. She was alone. Her enormous frame reverberated with exhaustion and hurt, mostly in an injured wing.

Zezura was alive. Semra's tense muscles nearly melted into the ground in relief. Hope sprang alive again. She was not abandoned. She was not alone.

But she couldn't fly.

Semra had to get out of the cavern without the dragon's help. It was time for Semra to help Zezura, not the other way around. She glanced around the darkness of the empty hole.

Twinkling stars cast only dim luminescence through the opening thirty feet overhead. The cascade of rock and boulder seemed to have settled. If she took hold of the spear again, could she cause another one and break apart the mountain? Would she die in the attempt? She'd been lucky to land decently so far, but luck could run out.

Semra racked her brain searching for everything she knew about Aurin's spear, about magic. One thing still didn't make sense. Why hadn't the spear killed Avaya?

Frigibar had told them that the spear killed anyone who touched it. Anyone without magic. Therefore, Semra's tabeun magic must weaken the strength of the blow somehow, from whatever it normally doled out. Avaya's sifal magic was a poor substitute for natural magic, though apparently substitutionary enough to save her life.

Semra sat up. How did it work? Why would magic weaken magic? And even if that's what was happening, how could small magic like theirs—sifal, tabeun, or otherwise—make an impact on the powers at the heart of the world?

She pursed her lips and crawled to the base of the spear, squinting at the place where it embedded into the cavern floor. The bronze of the spearhead peeked out just a little before being swallowed into the carbonate. Something was carved there, but it was too dark to decipher the markings.

Semra leaned forward, crouching on the ground to get a better look. She called for the fire, and it came to her hand. Orange-yellow light filled her palm, and the shadows fled from her fingers. The marking on the bronze was three rocks collected together, symbolizing earth. Fire was engraved in a wider circle around it, the rest of the shape disappearing into the ground.

Where had she seen that before?

Zezura blasted into her vision with the memory of Zephan in the bedchamber window, holding up the sketch of Aurin's spear. Semra shook her head to clear it. *Got it. Thanks.*

Yes, that was it, wasn't it? Except the engraving was incomplete, mostly submerged in the rock of the cavern floor. Semra thought back to the sketch again. Aurin was one of four elemental melders that brought about The Crumbling. One fireblood, one crestbreaker, one quakemaker, one windcaller. Fire, water, earth, air.

Aurin was the fireblood, carrying the spear. Dru the crestbreaker. Garjan the quakemaker. Raisa was the windcaller, whose necklace turned housing artifact Avaya now carried. Frigibar had told them how firebloods were once outlawed, thought of as lesser melders, and despised. For years they were banned from the Tabeun Tournaments.

What was it Frigibar had said about magic? *It formed the world, fueled the world, was thrown out of balance and sickened the world, and finally was laid to rest by Aurin at the origin of the world.*

Semra froze. The magic wasn't the problem. It was not the *presence* of magic but the lack of *balance* within it that had sickened the world. And fire magic was the balance keeper.

Water, earth, and air formed the triangle on the spear's carving, according to the sketch; but fire encircled them all to hold them in balance. Without fire, magic from the Origin Wellspring poured into the rivers, filled the soil from which all plant life grew, and filled the air, but became too concentrated.

Without fire to burn off the excess, the atmosphere was polluted. Sickness struck humanity. It was their prejudice and narrow sightedness that struck them with disease all those years ago.

Semra stared at the flame in her hand and twisted it around her fingers. *Fireblood.* There were no elemental melders anymore. Semra's dragon-born magic was as close to human firebloods as anyone could be.

Fire dealt with excess magic. Fire created balance ...

The royal-blue veins in the wyronite spear shaft glowed brighter than she'd remembered from just moments ago. Currents of magic at the deep inner workings of the world swirled up and down its length, the cork to a wine bottle turned upside down.

And how could one remove a cork without spilling wine everywhere?

The answer was obvious. Control the excess. The wine in the bottle's neck.

Semra's skin hummed with the magical energy in the air. Her magic sprang to her command so easily in this place, as if her very nearness to the spear—or to the spring?—amplified the power in her blood.

Magic saved her life when she touched the spear before, absorbing energy from the spear. What if she could absorb more? No, not absorb. Burn.

Semra's heart raced. The hairs on her arms and the back of her neck stood on end as she gathered her feet, stood, and took a deep breath. Slowly, she lifted her hands and summoned the flame.

50

———

Semra's mouth went dry, but her body came alive with the adrenaline flooding her veins. Her hands trembled as she lifted them up and called forth the flame. Fire leaped to her palms, but it wasn't enough.

How would she know what would be enough? She didn't know, but two meager balls of fire wasn't going to take the edge off at the origin of the world. Semra closed her eyes. Her pulse pounded in her ears as she reached out to the dragon.

My fire is your fire. How do you call your magic?

Zezura huffed a great spiral of smoke from her nostrils. *You call it magic because it is unfamiliar. I call it part of me.*

Semra didn't have time to think it out. She had to feel it. Feel the how. *Show me.*

Zezura's body blazed with pain, and the feeling nearly knocked Semra to the ground as their connection deepened. The dragon roused herself with an effort, lifting her head toward the moonlit lake. Heat built first in her chest, building, building, the light glowing at her throat with a warm, electric tingling.

Fire is as magical as the rising sun—you might not know how it works, but that doesn't mean there isn't a reason. Zezura opened her mouth, and the energy she'd built up inside swirled at her core, just waiting to be set free. A massive torrent of flame spewed forth in a torrent, lighting the night as it flew across the water. *Command what is yours. The fire is in me. It is mine.*

Semra let Zephan's face suspend in her mind before her, a sadness funneling into rage at the thought of Azi's destruction. Her lip curled, and with the urgency of her mission gripping her chest, she balled her hands into fists.

This time, she did not reach for the fire. She did not invite it. She commanded it, and the flame of her blood dared not disobey. *The fire is in me. It is mine.*

Semra threw her hands out to either side, and as the heat built in her small frame, she bade it hold ... hold ... and released the blaze in a burst of light.

Fire crackled in the air and showered the cavern with flying embers. Night gave way to the flash of inferno leaping from her hands across the open space, her silhouette harsh against the brightness of a white-hot burn.

In that moment, Semra was struck by the fraction of power she held in contrast with the wellspring beneath her feet. What smallness of might she channeled compared to the powers that melded the very world in which she lived. What obscure inkling she claimed to understand, when the dragonborne magic was a fraction of the spring's power, and Semra's magic a fraction of Zezura's.

And yet the spring invited her to treat with it. Played with her, as a parent and child. *Come to me.*

Semra stepped up to the spear, letting the fire lick at the air, burning, burning, burning.

Something in her soul gave a small nudge, setting in her mind only one word: *now.*

Semra raked her hands through the air, a trail of flame in

their wake, and took hold of the Aurin's spear. A jolt ran through her body. Her muscles seized, rippling with tremor after tremor, frozen to the birthplace of all created matter. And then her body returned to her control, the excess magic burned away by the fire in her blood and the flame in the air.

On instinct she shot her own magic down through the shaft, the heat of it mixing and bubbling through the floor, melting through the prison where the spearhead had been confined for the last six hundred years. Cobalt blue lit along the veins of the wyronite spear like lightning. The cracks running like spiders from the point of impact in the floor widened, and a distant rumble and rushing sound emanated up from their depths.

A shiver ran down Semra's spine. She gripped the spear with all her might and pulled. Her muscles strained, fire and sparks flying from her hands in every direction. A guttural groan rose from her throat and up through the air in a scream, mingling with the smoke up through the opening far above.

The spearhead shifted. First a centimeter, then an inch. And then, as her taut muscles cried out for relief, Aurin's spear slid free.

A deep *CRACK* sounded below. Song clear as crystal, light as the sun, mournful as the dirge of the dove filled the chamber:

Never, never, never again
Reign of terror now will end

Semra gasped and stumbled backward, the spear still in her hands. She glanced around, whirling the spear in front of her, but she was alone. The haunting song was louder than a natural voice, carried by a wind that swirled the cavern and lifted the ends of her hair with its breeze as it sought its escape, up and out through the opening to the night sky.

Water erupted from the cavity at her feet where Aurin's spear had been lodged. The cork was free. Blood drained from her face. She tripped over her feet in her hurry to escape the deluge, but the strength of the current knocked her down. Semra wiped her face with one hand, the other still clutching at the spear.

In a powerful gush, Semra's fire extinguished. The river burst to freedom from its underground confinement, sweeping her away and stealing her breath. Raging waters lapped and surged against the walls of the cave as more and more water shot up from beneath and rocked the surface into powerful swells.

A wave took her under. Semra tumbled through the water and kicked as hard as she could, but which way was up? She opened her eyes, but saw nothing but darkness. In desperation she called for fire, but all that came were boiling bubbles swallowed in a roiling flood.

Lungs burning, eyes stinging, Semra kicked again and again, unsure if she drove herself closer or further from salvation. Her chest caved in under the weight of the water, her body starving for air. Her foot struck rock.

Semra flailed along the side of the rock, following it as it curved. There, that was the jutting portion of the ceiling she'd remembered seeing from below. But if she was on the ceiling, and immersed in water...

No air remained in the cavern.

She fought panic as it closed in on the fringes of her mind. It took all her focus to bend her energy toward a careful search of the cave ceiling. Time was running out. She was going to drown.

Her fingers scraped along the rough cavern. Semra's head

pounded with the rushing of water and the sound of her own erratic heartbeat. A jagged edge sliced her finger, but she hardly noticed against the burning of her starving lungs.

The ceiling ended. Abruptly, as she searched, her hand shot upward into nothingness—a blessed, *dry* nothingness. The cavern opening!

Semra scrambled for it and thrust herself through the hole and up into the chill night air. The river burst out the hole and down the mountain, carrying Semra along in its mighty current. She gasped in ragged pulls of air as the water tugged her down the mountain. Something hard struck her as she tumbled down in the cold water, and pain radiated through her body.

She struggled to right herself in the water just in time to see the outline of passive trees up ahead, the silhouette of the forest dark as pitch against the moonlight. If she hit one, it would all be over, spear or no spear.

Her foot caught on a root or rock and sent her spinning underwater. When she came up again, the mountain still rushed by her, the trees were only fifty paces off, and a dark hooded figure crouched in the branches of the first great tree.

A lasso flew from the man's hand and landed uselessly in the water before her as she rocketed forward toward twenty-foot-wide trunks solid enough to smash her to bits. Semra yelped, throwing a hand up in the air. "Here! I'm here!"

The wind and water swallowed her voice. The rope came again, and this time, it landed around her torso. Semra threw an arm through the loop just in time before it cinched tight and yanked her back against the rolling tide. The rope bit into her trapped arm, and she swallowed a mouthful of river water as she dipped beneath the surface.

The figure in the tree strained to hold her weight, the rope wrapping around the trunk and holding her there against the bark as the river rushed past. Beyond her, an army of enormous trees stood stoic, unconcerned by the human missile so nearly headed their way. Beyond them down the mountain, a glimmer of the lake reflected the moon through the branches, the twinkle of Ellix just barely visible across the valley.

Behind her, the mountainside was unrecognizable with rockslides and formations she had no memory of. Water still spewed from the top of the cavern, a powerhouse of unchecked rage breaking free. Semra held out a hand against the tree trunk and used her legs to push herself further up in the water. The rope grew taut to hold her progress, and she pushed again to get a better view around the side of the tree at the man who had saved her life.

His arms bulged in the effort to hold her there, a flowing white beard whipping in the night wind, the wrinkles of his furrowed brow deeper than she'd ever seen them. Frigibar. He was older somehow, yet stronger, than she remembered, and something in the resoluteness of his flint-gray eyes sent a sliver of warm hope in the freezing, rushing waters around her.

Her muscles sagged and her eyelids drooped. Strength left her. The dim twinkling of the stars went out, and the fight in her body gave way to exhaustion.

51

Semra eased awake, blinking in the sunlight streaming in from the treehouse window. She knew Frigibar hated anyone calling it a treehouse, but Semra hadn't discovered a more reasonable thing to call the place where he lived. With a jolt she lurched upright, the memory of recent events flooding back.

Daylight. She'd slept all night? Semra glanced out the window. The sun was high. *And* all morning? No, no, no ...

Semra flung the covers back and swung her legs over the side of the bed. The movement sent shooting pains through every fiber of her body. Her sore muscles protested at even small actions, and she winced as her feet hit the wooden floor.

She ran a hand over her face, and drew it back to stare at it. Bandages wrapped her forearms, and her hand had wrappings tight around it also. Every piece of that hand ached, more than any other part of her. Why couldn't she stop its shaking?

Ice shot down her spine, and she froze. *The spear.* That hand had been holding the spear. Had she lost it? After everything, if it was gone ...

Semra threw back the blankets, scanned the small, bare room, and spun back to the wall where her bed jutted up against it. Her pounding heart skipped a beat, then slowed. Aurin's spear lay in the bed with her, the ornate, carved bronze spearhead half-under her pillow, as if it were a doll comforting a child for bed.

"It was frozen to your hand last night."

Semra jumped and whirled to see Frigibar in the doorway, arms crossed, observing her. He nodded at the spear. "Or rather, you were frozen to it. You'd gripped it so tight, and the water was so cold, your fist locked up around it and wouldn't let it go. Even with you asleep, you wouldn't let go, and I haven't been particularly inclined to touch it."

Well, that explained the soreness. Semra looked down at her hand and winced as she stretched it out. "Thank you. For saving me."

Zezura, are you there?

The snappy response was groggy and more sour than usual, but hit Semra clear as a bell. *I didn't hear from you for a while either, but did I let you sleep? Yes, yes I did.*

Semra pursed her lips, but couldn't help the smile that took over her face. Her dragon was safe, and feeling better.

Frigibar jerked his head toward the window. "Yes, she's here. Battered and bruised, stiff, but I got her a few sheep for breakfast and patched up her wing. She's lucky the limb was only bruised and not broken. Still, she won't be healthy enough for endurance flight for at least a week. Maybe two."

Semra's stomach dropped. She swallowed. "A week isn't good enough."

"It's going to have to be. Whining about it won't heal her any faster. And you could use some recovery time too." Frigibar shoved off the wall, disappeared in the hall, and reappeared with a tray.

The smell of fresh bread, cooked meat, and cheese filled the small room. Steam rose from the meat. Semra tried to remember her last hot meal. Her mouth watered.

But Avaya was on her way to Qalea *now*. Zephan and Siler were on their way to their deaths *now*. "Did you see Zephan?"

Frigibar set the tray down on the bed next to her. A cup of tea and a vase of nezil myansara flowers accompanied the plate. Semra's jaw dropped. She quirked an eyebrow, but he pretended not to notice and only shrugged. "I saw your man, yes. Or, husband, I should say. Congratulations, by the way."

Husband. What an odd, foreign word! She glanced down at her left hand and marveled at the massively conspicuous ring sparkling there. His mother's sapphire, with a crown of opals for the mark on her chest and the dragon bond it represented. It was so like Zephan to make everything an event, a meaningful token. A ring could never just be a ring. If he lived long enough to *be* her husband, Semra thought it might become her favorite word in all the world.

"When? Where are they? Were they hurt at all?"

Frigibar wagged a finger at her and pointed at the plate.

Semra snatched a piece of meat and popped it in her mouth, only barely regretting it when it burned her tongue. It tasted like heaven.

Frigibar nodded, satisfied. "They're fine, and headed to Qalea with the best horses I could wrangle up. He wanted to stay, but Siler made him go, as you'd told him. And he made me promise to come get you from the mountain, which of course I set out to do at once."

Semra stuffed a piece of cheese in her mouth and ripped a chunk of bread off the roll. "You wrangled up horses? I thought they'd have to go to Ellix. There's nothing between here and there."

"Truth be told, I wrangled them a couple of weeks ago. Receiving more visitors seemed rather likely after your last departure, and I thought it advantageous to keep a few steeds around for myself and anyone with me that might need a hasty getaway."

Smart. Semra swallowed the bread and cheese together, then bit into another chunk of beef. "Do you still have an extra?"

Frigibar grimaced. "It's not best to leave in your condition anyway."

"My condition is fine." So what if she could hardly move? Semra set her jaw.

"Your dragon's isn't. But she will be soon, and on a good day, she flies twice as fast as any horse. You'll make up time."

On a good day. Semra bit her lip. Her eyes stung with unshed tears. "Frigibar, if they die while I'm lying on this bed ..."

Frigibar held up a hand and shook his head. "Then they will die while you were doing every best possible thing to be there. Because, as slow as it may *feel,* resting here is the fastest way to get to them. Leaving now and overworking yourself, or causing Zezura to tear her injury and ruining any chance of being strong when it comes time to face your enemies, would be foolish."

Semra's tears betrayed her, snaking down her cheeks in hot trails. Her chest hitched. "I hate doing nothing," she whispered.

Frigibar's shoulders fell forward, and he came and knelt beside her bed. He lifted a single white nezzi flower from the vase and twirled it in his fingers. His deep gray eyes found hers. "The most resilient living things grow in shadow. In obscurity. Roots are established underground, and the shoot of a seed must mature alone and unappreciated before reaching the surface. Harshness is familiar to resilient things. It needs very little to thrive."

He lifted the flower. "These have been cut, but still they last a week or two before any signs of wilting. The strongest people know how to take what little resources we have and turn it into advantage. *'Resilient is the flame within the shoot that sprung of stone. Harshness is her home, yet wise would make her friend of throne.'* And see, by the ring on your finger, it seems our bright young king has begun his reign with wisdom."

Semra took the bloom and sniffed it, forcing herself to slow down and notice the sweet, honey-like aroma. So now even Frigibar agreed—Semra was the crimson queen of prophecy. But Semra had read the prophecy of the architect too many times. The beginning sounded hopeful, but two lines stood out to haunt her as she sank back against her pillow:

Home among the mountains, plucked and left to battle dread:
Uprooted Myansara must be planted, or be dead.

52

ZEPHAN

Zephan patted his horse's neck and adjusted the breastplate of his armor. The Jannemar emblem shone on his chest in the blazing sun, a spear with the wings of a dragon, shrouded by nezil myansara flowers. A helmet and breastplate were the only pieces of his normal attire for war that the network had been able to smuggle out, and he was grateful to have them. If he was to die today, he would do it under the crest of his beloved kingdom.

His thoughts wandered back to Semra, as they had a thousand times in the last hour. Had Frigibar gotten her out of the cavern? Would she be chasing him now on horseback, only a day or two behind? Was Zezura dead? If Zezura was alive, they would have overtaken Zephan by now and beaten him to Qalea.

It had taken all his effort to engage meaningfully in the morning's strategy meeting with Monac, Soldan, and other key allies. The trek with Siler had been melancholy, dark, and purposeful—every step away from Semra was a knife to his chest, but every mile closer to home was a mile closer to Avaya and the necklace.

The only hope of victory was in removing the necklace from Avaya's neck. Even so, Rotokas presented a tremendous problem. Konnolan wasn't common in Jannemar. One of Zephan's teams had been assembling explosives to help offer options, but there was no way to know how effective they might be—and they couldn't risk harming civilians if Rotokas outsmarted them and the bomb missed its target.

Only Zephan and his inner circle knew about the necklace. And only Zephan knew he planned not only to steal it, but to use it against Avaya and Azi to secure the kingdom. Maybe the siphon poisoning wouldn't take hold if he only used it for today and then destroyed the artifact.

Or maybe the effects would set in, and he would slowly, eventually die of it. But Semra, Aviama, and his people would be saved. He might even get to live a year or two with Semra as his wife. Zephan swallowed hard against the lump in his throat. It was an exchange he could live with. He just had to get to Avaya and snatch the pendant.

Before him, a motley crew of militia in farmer and trades-men's garb shifted their weight in the town square and shielded their eyes against the bright afternoon. A few wore armor under larger tunics, but they were off-duty guards and soldiers—or soldiers who had deserted the service of a traitor queen to follow their true ruler. Their loyalty would reward them with position, or with death. Only time would tell.

And it was their loyalty to *him* that placed them in such danger. Zephan set his jaw and squared his shoulders. No, he couldn't afford to think that way. Being weighed down by guilt wouldn't keep his men alive. He, Zephan Shamaran, was more than an individual. He represented the crown, his father's legacy, and the vision of Jannemar they all shared.

"Warriors of Jannemar." His voice caught in his throat, and Monac straightened in the saddle beside him. Zephan steeled himself and took the hint. He cleared his throat. "Warriors of Jannemar! Today we fight the greatest battle of our time. Today we fight, not against a neighboring rival, not over land, not merely for resources or borders. We raise our swords against the highest form of tyranny, against traitors who would set a heavy yoke around your shoulders."

The way all dictators were wont to do. The way Azi had, beating his supposed children for displeasing him, but indoctrinating them effectively enough that they begged for forgiveness rather than take out their revenge and break free. He had done it to Semra. And he did it to Avaya even now. Would his destruction never end?

But Zephan knew the answer. No. It would not end. Not as long as the man drew breath.

"These impostors live detached from you in high places, having nothing in common with you but the crops they would take from your fields, the money from the mouths of your children, and the freedoms you've so long enjoyed. We know the sort, don't we? You've seen them all your lives. The sort of men and women who swindle and cheat with no regard for others, who cause pain wherever they go without remorse. They use weighted scales in the marketplaces, and their dice always roll to their benefit."

A figure moved at the far side of the crowd. He turned his back to Zephan and made a marking on the side of a shop, then disappeared. The drawing showed a setting sun over a hill, and a moon rising in the sky above it. Zephan's chest tightened. It was done. His latest decree was finalized and duplicated. If he died today, Semra would reign in his stead.

He hoped she would not hate him for it.

Zephan returned his focus to the crowd. "Imagine a man and a woman like that in your own life, but of higher ambitions—ambitions that harm not just their neighbors, but a nation. Goals not for prosperity of their people but for luxury for themselves, power for the sake of power paid for by *our* blood and the money to fuel it from your broken backs.

"My father died in the service of Jannemar. We may live up on the hill, but our gates open and our ears incline to hear you. My father knew the ways of the crown, and my mother the ways of the people—their marriage was a union of ideas that prospered a kingdom, and I will always seek to honor them both. This man Azi is a murderer and a thief! My sister Avaya listens to his every poisonous whisper, driving the kingdom into the ground!

"Was it the black dragon, or the blue, that gave you comfort in its presence? Was it the black dragon, or the blue, that saved Jannemar at the Surion Strip?" Zephan ripped his sword from the scabbard and thrust it in the air. "To arms! For your children! For your land! For Jannemar!"

The people roared their approval. Steel rang out in the square as swords, daggers, and axes joined his blade in the air. Their voices came together as one, shaking the air with their fervor: "For Jannemar!"

For Aviama. For Semra, and the abuse she suffered at Azi's hand. For every child that she saved from his clutches. Never again.

Resolve hardened in Zephan's heart as he turned toward his childhood home and kicked his horse into a canter, the militia falling in around him as he led the way. He would lead, or he would die. But he would not stand idly by.

Zephan raised his sword and let out a shout, and as they crossed the bridge, the Nezzi Gate opened and Belvidorian troops poured out. A horn blew, and the Spearhead and Dragon Gates flew open, more fresh, well-armored men spilling down to meet them. A hideous shriek shook the sky, and the shadow of the ebony Atas Mountain Wyvern of Mount Hara appeared on the battlement.

Perhaps this is what it was like for a mouse looking up at an eagle's nest. If they were lucky, the eagle would show off, and the cat would play with its food before the final blow, buying him time.

The impossible battle had begun.

53

The sun warmed Semra's cheeks as she flew down to rolling hills on the outskirts of Qalea. Zezura's aquamarine scales shimmered in the brilliant light, almost matching the sapphire on Semra's finger. She had spent a full week at Frigibar's waiting for Zezura's wing to heal. Every moment of the waiting was torture, and she'd been itching to fly. But Frigibar was a skilled healer, and whatever concoction he'd used in his poultice seemed to do the dragon good.

The air seemed brighter somehow, the hum of magic filling the mountainside and spilling down into the lake. Semra wondered if the wellspring water was more concentrated with magic somehow, and if exposure to it speeded healing. But maybe dragons simply healed quickly, or Frigibar's methods were particularly effective.

One way or another, Semra's deadline of leaving in seven days had been met—barely. Frigibar cautioned her that she couldn't push Zezura too hard or she could reinjure the wing. With Zezura's fragile recovery, any confrontation with Rotokas now was doubly dangerous. And there was another catch—

Zephan had told Frigibar that Semra had to make a stop on the way to the battle.

Eight days of travel, eight days of useless, mindless flight and sleep, flight and sleep, and at last they descended to a small farm dotting the landscape below. Knots multiplied in Semra's stomach as the wind blew her hair behind her and the grass rushed up to meet them. Did Zephan really think they'd have critical strategies to impart before she made a beeline for Shamaran Castle, or was he trying to delay her, keep her out of harm's way? He had to know he was doomed without her. Zephan was a capable fighter and an effective leader, but a remarkable swordsman was still in danger against an unstable sifal melder.

The farmhouse was precisely where Frigibar had said it would be, surrounded by several other buildings, pastureland, and a small forest of short tree trunks cut off and topped with straw like a house. Zezura landed heavy on her feet, and Semra threw her hands forward to stabilize herself on the dragon's neck. Still, it was smoother than the last few landings had been. She was improving.

From the ground Semra saw the trees with straw toppers were carved and painted, with an opening on one side. The buzz of bees busying themselves around the hives was enough to keep her at a distance. She grimaced and hurried toward the house. No time to waste.

A shriek came from inside, and Aviama ran from the house. Semra's heart leaped. She was safe.

"Get back in the house!" yelled a gruff voice. "It's broad daylight!"

Aviama ignored the voice and Semra ran to meet her. Aviama threw her arms around her, and Semra clutched her tight. "Are you okay? What's happening? Where's Zephan?"

Aviama released her and pulled back, tears in her eyes.

"I'm fine. Yeppuli is a good man. You're the one all scratched up. But—oh!"

Her friend's eyes scanned the bandages still wrapping one of Semra's arms and hand, her mother's sapphire ring sparkling on Semra's finger, and the wyronite spear firmly attached to her pack. Aviama's lips parted. "Wow."

The beekeeper yelled again from the doorway of the house, holding the door open and gesturing them inside. "I'm not going to ask again. Don't make me come out there! It doesn't matter what side catches me—you're risking my neck!"

Aviama ran for the house, and Semra hurried after her, Zezura loping along the grass at their backs. Semra wanted to point out that the dragon gave away their position, but decided not to bother. She was here for messages from Zephan and hoped to take off again in five minutes or less.

Semra dipped her head at Yeppuli, the large beekeeper she remembered from the square. She wondered briefly if Honey had a supply of flowers on the property here, or if those were a delicacy the donkey only enjoyed at Garbane's house. She turned to Aviama. "I can't stay. I need to know if there are messages for me."

Aviama nodded. "Zephan has an inside man on Avaya's guard, but he doesn't know if he's still alive. They've got explosives, but no konnolan. They're assaulting the gates, and Zephan will be heading underground to get access to the castle and try to get to Avaya."

Semra's heart sank. A frontal assault was a terrible idea. How many men would he lose in the distraction to get to Avaya? What if he never made it? Honestly, what were the odds he even got close?

Aviama scanned Semra's face. "A lot of the men left Avaya's army to serve their true king. The militia isn't just farmers. They're soldiers. And once the rest see that Zephan is alive and well, and what's really going on with Azi and Avaya, they'll turn." She bit her lip, weakening the confidence of her words. "They need you to pull focus, distract, and weaken Belvidorian reinforcements. Zephan is still hopeful that some of the Jannemari soldiers supporting Azi and Avaya will come to their senses."

Semra nodded, but her mind was on battle. She turned to go. "I've got to get there. I'll see you when it's over." *I hope.*

Aviama grabbed her hand. "I have something for you."

"It can wait. We'll have time later." Or not, if they all died, of course. But the sooner she left, the better chance she had of helping.

Aviama shook her head. "It has to be now. Please? It's for the fight. Zephan signed off on it."

Semra grimaced, but steeled herself when hurt stole over her friend's face. Her skin crawled with the knowledge of every wasted moment. As good as it was to see Aviama, there was no information here. The trip was a useless delay.

The princess didn't bother waiting for a reply. She grabbed Semra's hand and yanked her to a side room in the house. Three small beds lined one wall. A basket of clothes and a whittled wooden dragon spilled onto the floor in the corner. And the trunk Semra assumed Aviama had been living out of stood open at the foot of the first bed. Aviama reached in and pulled out a box.

"I had it made on rush order while I was stuck here waiting for everybody else to do things." Her cheeks flushed. "It's the only thing I could do. Please wear it. You and Zezura have been a symbol of hope for our people ever since you fought Azi in the throne room and took up residence at the castle with us. When you left for the spear and made the speech in the town square, they latched onto your words, your face, your inspiration. But then you dropped off the map for a couple of weeks when they felt they needed you most. We don't have numbers on our side. We need intimidation. We need focus on you so that Zephan can get the necklace. And this" —Aviama lifted the box and handed it to Semra—"will give you that."

Semra's stomach twisted, and her heart ached. What if she wasn't worthy of their hope? What if they looked to her, and she only led them into more death and destruction and misery than before?

Carefully, Semra lifted the lid off the box. She gasped. Glistening-white folded cloth greeted her, intricate inlaid gold along the neckline.

"I know what you're thinking. It looks like a dress, and you can't fight in it. But it's not—it's like the outfits we made custom for you before. A skirt-like style from behind but it splits open in the front to show the pants, see?"

Aviama pulled the article of clothing from the box and let the bottom of it roll down to the floor. The fitted bodice looked like any of the exquisite gowns Aviama would wear. A belt of alternating aquamarine, sapphire, and opal sparkled at the waist. But below the waist, trousers replaced a traditional skirt, with built-in sheaths for throwing knives to boot. The flowing skirt in the back had slits running along it—she'd be able to move unencumbered.

"Helmet?" Aviama pulled a big clunky silver thing from the trunk, and Semra wrinkled her nose.

"I'm not wearing that. It looks like a prison for my head, and it'll kill my peripheral vision."

"I figured you'd say that. No worries, it would totally ruin your look anyway. Just don't get shot in the head." Aviama tossed the helmet aside. "There's a breastplate too. It's light and only protects your heart and torso, but it's better than nothing. I figured you weren't going to want to wear one at all, but this is better than nothing."

Semra arched an eyebrow. Aviama had been been busy.

She dug into the trunk and pulled out a shining metal breastplate custom-fit for a woman just Semra's size. Aviama grinned sheepishly. "Polena still had your measurements. It should be perfect for you."

Semra stared at it. She reached out and touched the Jannemar emblem on the chest. *Her* kingdom. *Her* people.

The crown, forever first, forevermore.

Semra's chest hitched. "Thank you."

"No problem. Hurry up and put it on."

Semra shrugged out of her pack and set the spear on the bed. Aviama ogled it, then paused, her gaze captured by the flowers sticking out of Semra's pack.

"Are those what I think they are?" she asked, pointing.

Semra's cheeks flushed. Flowers were such an odd thing for a killer to carry. "Frigibar made me bring them. 'A reminder,' he said."

Aviama's eyes hardened and her lips flattened as the brightness of her face fell into a staunch determined expression. "All your life, Azi taught you to fear him. Today, we'll teach *him* to fear *you*. No longer does he frighten you with a snap of his fingers. Azi uses a dragon to bully people, but that doesn't work on you. You have a dragon too. Azi wants the throne. You have it. Today, Azi faces his worst fear—his greatest student, his greatest achievement, taking everything he's ever wanted." She dropped into a curtsy and plucked the white flowers from Semra's travel bag. "Your Majesty. It's time you looked the part."

54

———

Shamaran Castle rose against the horizon, the sun glancing off its white limestone in every direction. Zezura caught an air current and glided in from high overhead. With her wing only freshly recovered, saving the dragon's energy was important. They'd climbed higher than they otherwise would have, making it easier for Zezura's camouflage to disappear against the clouds. They would hold off their descent and ride the currents until the last possible moment.

Wind rushed past Semra's ears, a vague distraction from the pounding of her heart. The castle grew nearer, and soldiers spread out like angry ants down below, spilling from the outer bastion down to the gates. Archers in the towers released a volley of arrows into a mismatch of militia launching grappling hooks up the gate. A *boom* rocked the defense over Spearhead Gate on the east, and a man fell from the guard tower.

Semra's breath caught. Rotokas swept out from the cleft in the cliff and dove down on the tower, spewing flame from his onyx mouth to the screams of his victims. Militia hopefuls staggered back. The portcullis slammed shut, locking out all the progress they'd made on that side.

The numbers of Zephan's men were abysmal. Avaya wasn't even out using her magic—they could easily win without it. But if Azi and Avaya stayed holed up inside, getting the necklace would be impossible.

Semra urged Zezura into an arc and made a loop over the castle. Her throat tightened. Three or four men had broken through the northwest door in the wall by the cliff, leaving ten bodies in their wake. Rotokas turned from the tower and took off toward the outer ward in their direction.

The time had come. Semra took a breath and adjusted her grip on Aurin's spear. Fire hummed along the surface of her skin as she commanded the power in her blood. Zezura hovered, high above the battlement, then plunged straight down into the fray.

55

ZEPHAN

Another explosion rocked the air, and Zephan swore under his breath. Munitions were limited, and he preferred they be used on Rotokas and not on blowing up his home. Repairs were expensive. It would be hard to care about repairs if he was dead, but he'd given the militia leaders precise instructions for the bombs. Military leaders were mixed with civilians, and organization had been a nightmare. Slipping away from the battlefront had been no easy task.

Zephan stole across the outer ward, Monac and two other guards at his side. Woolen cloaks concealed their armor, piecemealed from what had been smuggled out over the last several weeks. The door across the yard led into the castle keep and dumped out next to the northwest guard tower and the stair going down to the dungeon.

His heart thundered in his chest. Forty paces to go.

A roar split the air over the distant din of battle, and Zephan snapped his head skyward. The enormous frame of the black wyvern hurtled toward him. Monac swept Zephan behind him and raised his sword, but brave as he was, Monac was no match for Rotokas.

Ahead of them, the door of the keep swung open. Three Belvidorian soldiers charged out, and Zephan burst forward to meet them. Mercy was not an option. If the Belvidorian soldiers didn't get out of the doorway in the next four seconds, Rotokas would eat Zephan and his three men for lunch.

Zephan swung high, and the soldier met him steel to steel; he danced forward, sliced his sword through the man's gullet, and shoved the body backward. Two seconds. He was out of time.

A lightning-fast motion captured his eye in the sky over the black wyvern, and a gush of fire like nothing he'd ever seen poured down on Rotokas from above. Rotokas crashed into the side of the keep and skidded to a halt six paces from Zephan's feet. His heart leaped to his throat and goosebumps ran up his arms at the sight plunging down from the heavens.

The great blue dragon divebombed straight down into the thick of battle, her shimmering scales greater protection than the finest shields in all the world. A glorious shout went up from Jannemari forces at the gates together, rippling through the fighters in a mighty wave. But it was not the dragon that stole their hearts and inspired hope from the dregs of a losing battle. It was the woman on its back.

Zephan couldn't take his eyes off her. He'd never seen anything as captivating, as dazzling as Semra was at that moment. Her lithe body perched atop the fifty-foot dragon, her dark hair flowing behind her, dotted with white flowers. The mark of the dragon's kiss glittered on her chest, framed by the white satin fitted to her frame from head to toe.

Muscles taut, expression flint, chin high, Semra lifted an arm overhead, and Zephan's heart nearly failed. Aurin's spear, last held six hundred years ago by Aurin himself, shone in the light of the sun. Not a sound escaped her scarlet lips as fire wrapped around the spear shaft like vines and exploded from the spear's tip in a powerful deluge.

Could it be that this splendid creature was the same he had held tight in the woods, had danced with in the stables of Madensig Fortress?

"She's come for us," the Belvidorian man hissed, eyes bulging as he gaped at the sky. "The dragon witch!"

Zephan's lip curled and he slugged the man in the temple. He dropped like a stone, and Zephan slit his throat. "That's my wife, imbecile."

Wife. A spectacular word! He hoped to use it every day for the rest of his life.

Gaulen blinked at him from the doorway and arched an eyebrow. "You've been busier than I thought." He spun back into the keep and thrust his sword into the armpit of an approaching adversary, then swept his arm in a welcoming gesture inside the castle. "Your Majesty."

Zephan grinned, reluctantly tearing his focus from the magnificent woman in the air to the loyal bodyguard on the ground. He clapped the man on the shoulder and slipped inside. "Very soon, Gaulen. I'll tell you everything. Now show me the dungeons."

Gaulen led the way down to the dungeons, Zephan, Monac, and the last two Jannemari guards trailing behind. The dank, dark cold of underground hit Zephan in the face as they reached the landing and sprinted down the final steps to the long stone hall. Gaulen whistled in two low blasts and was rewarded with answering whistles. He tossed Zephan a key, and Zephan flew to the aide of those most trusted advisers, leaders, and bodyguards that hadn't managed to escape in time.

The last cell door swung free, and forty men dropped to their knee before their king.

Zephan shook his head. "Thank you, but there's time for that later. It's you who is owed the greater debt between us. We go to the guard tower, and we don't stop until the castle is secure. Watch your backs—and keep a weather eye at the sky."

The guards took up a formation around Zephan, and Gaulen led them up the stair to the ground level. Pounding feet flew this way and that on the floor above them. Screams emanated through the walls.

Boom.

The ring of steel and clash of bodies filled the air, louder than before.

Boom.

Were those his explosives or Azi's? What if Rotokas killed Zezura? What if the spear was too powerful to wield, and it killed Semra? The idea of never holding her again, never looking into those eyes ...

Zephan shook his head to clear it. *Concentrate. Step one, weapons. Step two, Avaya. Step three—defeat Azi, reclaim the throne, and give Semra the wedding, honeymoon, and life she deserves.*

A blast of wind knocked him off his feet, and he fell in a heap amid the writhing bodies of his companions as they struggled to right themselves. Zephan looked up. Avaya leaned heavily on the doorway, white knuckles desperately clutching at the pendant at her neck with one had, the other outstretched toward Zephan and his men. Already the pits under her eyes had deepened since he'd seen her in the mountain at the wellspring. Her face, once the envy of all Jannemar, was gaunt and flat. But it was the soulless absence about her lifeless green eyes that arrested his heart.

Where was the sassy sister, the lively renegade? Had she known what would happen to her since the outset or only realized when it was too late?

Azi clucked his tongue and wagged a finger as he materialized out of one of the ground-floor meeting rooms. "Such a shame you couldn't die with honor. Your father could have died with a sword in his hand like a man, but instead he fled from danger surrounded by bodyguards."

Heat flared in Zephan's chest and his muscles tensed, but he said nothing. His father was following appropriate safety protocols when fire broke out in his chambers and his bodyguards escorted him out. His sword was at his side when the explosive hit. The one thrown by one of Azi's best lackeys.

Zephan cursed under his breath. He'd forgotten step one-and-a-half of his plan—avoid Azi until *after* Zephan had the necklace. Of course, not letting Avaya see him until he had the drop on her would have been better too.

"Not to worry," Azi said, examining his cuticles. "Nothing will happen to you yet. I'll make sure my ungrateful ward watches you die."

Avaya bristled. "I'm not a ward. I'm a queen."

"Not *you*, idiot." Azi dismissed her with a wave of his hand. "The one I raised and trained and poured endless resources into. The one who betrayed me after I fed her, clothed her, and taught her to survive and thrive in this life. My ungrateful mountain child."

Avaya looked like she'd been slapped. She opened her mouth, then closed it. Something pinched in Zephan's stomach. Azi rolled his eyes.

"Avaya still has weaknesses. She has insisted her weakness remain alive for the time being. I told her I'd acquiesce as long as it made sense, but I can only abide such glaring shortcomings for so long."

How had Semra survived in the care of this man for so many years? Zephan looked Azi up and down. The man was strong, there was no question about that. Though more slender than Zephan's father, his arms were all muscle and sinew. The mark of the dragon's kiss stood out on his temple, and he carried himself with unmatched, unconcerned confidence.

Azi signaled Avaya, and with a rotation of wrist a gale of wind hit Zephan in the back. He sprawled to the floor with a grunt. Azi glided forward. Zephan swung for him, but his sword arm hit an invisible wall. He gritted his teeth.

The dragonlord plucked Zephan's sword from his fingers and whirled it in a low arc. The men plastered against the wall behind him yelled obscenities at their own powerlessness, but what were they to do?

Zephan ignored Azi and drilled Avaya with a cool glare. His hands curled to fists, but he checked himself. *What do I want to happen next?* She always bristled when he challenged her authority, her power. She was defensive about her capabilities and her rule. About the way she believed she'd been overlooked.

He bit his tongue and softened his face. "Avs. I don't want anything bad to happen to you. You're already being poisoned. Don't you see it? It started with our family, killed and torn apart. We should have stuck together. I should have relied on you more. I wish I had."

The moment he said it, it was true. He'd been so caught up with his own grief, he hadn't checked on Avaya at all. After their mother died, Zephan had thrown his energies into saving Semra, helping alleviate his father's duties while he grieved, and working to expose Azi. He'd consoled Aviama some, but usually when she sought him out, not the other way around. By the time he thought about his older, self-righteous sister, she had completely shut down and pushed him away. And by the time their father was assassinated, Avaya had already gone rogue, kidnapping herself to Belvidore, waging war, and nurturing the bitterness and fury between them.

Avaya's jaw clenched, but her sifal magic did not abate. Zephan swallowed, and his breath caught. Was his sister in there at all? Or had his neglect already killed her? "I'm sorry."

She looked away, and Azi arched an eyebrow. "A slow start for all the apologies she requires. Abandoned by her father to sit on sofas in pretty dresses instead of military council meetings and appropriate training for a successful reign. Without me, she'll have no idea how to keep things running. Because she was never taught."

Fire flashed behind her eyes, but she said nothing. Zephan eyed her, but she avoided his gaze.

"And then you continue his folly, keeping her to her rooms, blocked from anything important, never consulted, never considered. How women have been mistreated by your family for generations! A woman with a mind as bright as hers! You brought this on yourself. You created it. You deserve it." Azi whirled the sword through the air again.

As if Zephan had locked Avaya in her room! Zephan tilted his head at Azi. "You're the better man, aren't you? *You* would never discriminate. You use men and women alike, disposing of one as easy as the other when their usefulness runs out."

Azi's lip curled. "Yours is frightfully limited." He jerked his head at Avaya. "Let's go."

Avaya grimaced. "I can't bring Zephan with us and keep the other men here. It's too much."

Azi seized Zephan by the arm and dragged him forward, the cool steel of Zephan's own sword pressing against his neck. "You, with me. Leave the men. Just push them back outside and barricade the door. Rotokas is having trouble holding off the blue one, and we're losing men on the gates."

Zephan's heart soared at Azi's disgruntled report. Semra and Zezura were doing damage.

"Is it really wise to leave us behind?" Monac shouted.

Azi turned back, and Zephan's chest tightened. He shook his head. "Let the sun set."

Monac clamped his jaw, but his eyes followed his king's every movement. Had he gotten the message? More important work remained. Keeping Azi's attention now would only get them killed. *Stick to the plan.* His men had to get to the tunnels.

Azi smirked. "Giving up so soon? Such a pity. I'd hoped for more of a show."

Zephan flinched as Azi nicked his neck, and as one every man against the wall blanched with him. Azi clucked his tongue. "So sensitive. Avaya, my dear, open the door and throw them out."

Avaya did as instructed, opening the door at the end of the corridor and stepping back to let her powerful wind sweep them back out to the outer ward. The sounds of their protest muffled against the door as it swung shut. Azi snapped his fingers, and two Belvidorian guards ran around the corner to barricade the door.

Zephan lifted his chin and called to the soldiers. "Which of these two is your monarch? I thought your king was dead. But it seems you have a king again."

Azi struck him on the side of the face, and Zephan's head snapped back. The coppery taste of blood trickled into his mouth from the cut along his cheekbone. Azi wrung his hand, and Zephan laughed.

"Did my face dirty your knuckles? If only your dragon could help you now. Scourge, he usually does all your work for you, doesn't he? When he's not busy losing to Zezura, that is. You know what they say about younger models. Younger dragons, younger dragonlords ... your time is ended, old man."

Azi kneed him in the small of the back and shoved him forward. The blade bit into his neck as they hurried along the corridor, through the wall surrounding the courtyard, and out onto the top of the wall over the carriage road, over the Nezzi Gate. But it was worth it. And he'd found Azi's pain point.

Stifling heat slammed into Zephan as they stepped out into the blazing light of the afternoon sun. The sounds of battle raged around him—the screams of men mixed with sword and shield, the whistle of arrows, the stamp of running feet under heavy armor.

To his left, forest cropped up beside the castle, grappling hooks latching onto the wall toward Spearhead Gate. Belvidorian men fought hand to hand with Zephan's militia and deserters at the base of the towers, at the gates, and along the walls where his men had broken through. Qalea stretched out before him, and the countryside beyond it, filled with plains, rolling hills, forest, and rivers—the land of his father, the legacy of his ancestors, the responsibility on his shoulders.

A team of militia scaled the wall on the east side, and a Belvidorian squad ran past a charred, useless catapult to meet them. Zezura swept up the wall and engulfed the squad in flame. Semra spun Aurin's spear in the air from the dragon's back and thrust a tunnel of fire down on the enemy defending the portcullis below.

Zephan's heart skipped a beat, and his lips parted at the sight of her. Dressed in white, myansara flowers cascading with her hair—she was magnificent. He almost laughed when he realized Aviama must have planned for it as soon as they left her. She'd orchestrated Semra's motivational speech to the people at the town square, and she'd arranged for Semra to show up as the queen she was. How different his sisters were!

Azi stiffened and dragged him backward. "Do something!" he screamed at Avaya. "For once in your miserable life, make yourself useful!"

Semra turned in her seat on the dragon, and in that moment, her gaze latched onto Zephan. She froze, fire still rolling from her fingers down the shaft of the spear and shooting down at the base of the gate below.

Hello, beautiful. Whatever you're thinking, don't do it.

A massive black beast streaked through the air and collided with Zezura.

Semra fell.

56

Semra plummeted to the ground in a vortex of flame. A solid, scaly tail knocked her from the air, and she hit the side of the battlement and dropped like a rock. The trees of the east side rushed up toward her. Branches knocked her this way and that. Warm blood ran down her arm.

Don't lose the spear.

An arrow pierced the tree trunk just below her, and the shaft snapped as her body crashed through it. She landed with a jolt on a wide branch and pitched sideways. Semra flung her arm out, and the spear caught on two branches over her head as the rest of her body continued to fall. Semra kicked her legs in the air, dangling from the spear in the top of the tree.

Rats and rot. Another arrow whistled up through the leaves, a hair's breadth from her ear. A chorus of angry shouts went up at the base of the tree. Semra gritted her teeth and swung herself up to the opposite branch, pulling the spear free and whirling it in the air, knocking another arrow from its path toward her head.

Zephan. He was just above her, up on the bastion, right now. Semra had meant to draw Azi and Avaya out, but she hadn't imagined Zephan would be in their clutches. Her mouth went dry. She had to get up there.

"People of Jannemar!"

A wave of nausea rolled through her at Azi's voice. The sound boomed unnaturally loud, carrying over the battlement and down to the fighters at the gates and beyond. "People of Jannemar, what do you fight for? What do you die for? What does any people want, but economic prosperity, safety from enemies, and the freedom to live and move about as they please? You fought for the Surion River decades ago, and for what? Under Turian you lived on the brink of war for decades, and you find yourselves armed once again with swords and martyrdom for another man's ambition. But what of *your* ambition? What of *your* safety, *your* desires? Did you see Turian on the battlefield with you? No!"

Semra's throat constricted. Turian was putting out fires at home, but Zephan *did* fight on the front lines. Another arrow flew up past her face, and she pressed herself tight against the trunk of the tree.

"Jannemar is the laughingstock of our neighbors! A nation destroying itself with expensive war, failing to take advantage of resources and alliances that might refill our coffers, and vulnerable to attack. And now know this, that Turian not only failed you in this, but was a traitor to the rightful king, for he was the second of two sons.

"But even though I have rights to the throne by blood, for the sake of family and for the sake of you, my people, I will place on the throne a queen of not one kingdom but two—rival nations united for the first time. Safety, security, and sharing of resources will strengthen both kingdoms under one throne. Zephan Shamaran is a liar and a traitor. You deserve better, and I will see that he pays for his crimes."

Semra's tongue stuck to the roof of her mouth and the pit in her stomach opened up into an endless chasm.

"Zephan Shamaran, you are hereby publicly charged with oppression, false imprisonment, inciting a riot, attempted murder, assault on peaceful dignitaries, abuse of power, and high treason. The penalty for such reckless lawlessness is, regrettably, death."

Semra's chest caved in. Her head swam, and she swayed. She squeezed her eyes shut. *No.* Zephan couldn't die. Not like this. He couldn't leave her, after everything they'd been through. A scraping and *clunk* drew her from her thoughts, and her eyes snapped open. A grappling hook bit into the bark of the branch next to her. If the soldiers couldn't bring her down, they would come up. She gritted her teeth. Fire didn't mix well with wood.

Get me up the wall, Zez.

A thundering crash answered her as the two dragons rolled through the woods far below. Screams paved the way for them along the forest floor, and a flash of fire burst through the brush, and was gone.

Crash.

Snappp.

The tree Semra was perched in cracked and swayed. Semra's stomach lurched, and she braced herself among the branches. The castle wall rose beside her, the top of the branches only brushing the stone beneath the wall.

"With this cleansing, we shall raise up an empire built on truth, prosperity, and security. We will establish the double kingdom of Jannemar and Belvidore, as the crimson queen of old takes her place at the helm, the rightful ruler at her side. It is time for you to have true leadership again. It is time for a new age."

The tree fell. Semra's arms and legs were moving before she had a chance to think. She ran up the trunk of the tree as it dropped away, planted the spear on the descending bark, and launched herself at the wall. At her command, obsidian smoke billowed forth from her fingers, covering the wall in a thick darkness.

She clawed at the wall, but misjudged the distance in the blackness. Aurin's spear hit the stone at an angle and flew from her hands over the battlement. Semra's fingers found purchase on the rough sandstone edges of the crenel, her full bodyweight bearing down on her hand strength on the wall.

Semra pulled herself up with a grunt. Every muscle strained in the effort. Her hands burned with the scuff of the stone. But her focus had already moved on—to the man who had destroyed her, the man who helped to heal her, and the woman who rolled a wrecking ball in every salvaged piece of her life.

A strong breeze wafted through the smoke, dispelling whisps of dark haze. Semra dropped low, covering herself with fresh black billows, and scrambled along the floor, throwing her hands out in a vain search for the spear. Time was running out. The breeze kicked up to a gale, and there would be no more hiding. Avaya's power was fixated on Semra.

Semra would keep Avaya's attention trained on her, then remove Azi's greatest weapon. Avaya had to die first. Then Semra would reclaim the spear, and Azi would be next.

She called to the fire.

I am the fire. It is mine to command.

A heatwave swept beneath her skin, leaping to her word. *Come to me.*

Semra held the flame, hold, hold, and then launched forward out of the void. Fire licked at the smoke, burning it away like melted wax. Azi held Zephan fast, thirty paces off, blade to his neck. Avaya stood closer, only twenty paces away, bent like a wizened old woman with her hands directing the wind through the smoke. Tears streaked her face, and her green eyes met Semra's with a haunted, hunted expression.

Against all reason, Semra's heart went out to what could have been a kindred tortured soul. But Zephan's life was on the edge of a knife, and the power in her hands could not be dispelled.

Azi hesitated, and Zephan took advantage. In a flash, he wrenched Azi's sword hand away from his throat, spun, and delivered an elbow strike to the dragonlord's jaw. Azi stumbled back, and Zephan wrenched his sword free.

Semra's attention diverted, and she rained down fire on her childhood mentor. Avaya lunged for the spear, just now visible under the abating smoke. Zephan flew across the open space and tackled his sister to the ground.

A shadow blocked out the sun overhead, and Semra spun to protect herself from an aerial attack. Rotokas opened wide his mouth, and the glow of the fire lit the back of his throat an instant before it poured down on her. She threw up her hands and met fire with fire, the stream connecting in the middle and sending sparks flying in every direction. Zezura rocketed up over the wall and crashed into the black wyvern. Semra ducked beneath a shower of embers and twisted back to the scene on the wall.

Her heart stopped, and the sounds of battle seemed to fade under the overpowering rush of Semra's heartbeat in her ears. Zephan ripped the necklace from Avaya's neck, but she lifted one hand beyond his reach, the pendant secure in her clutches. And on the other side of the clash of the dragons, the dark figure of Azi Shamaran, the Framatar of the mountain, strode toward her. A spear held in his hand.

57

The blast of wind from the pendant in Avaya's hand knocked Semra off her feet and sent her tumbling over the wall. Her scream caught in her throat, and the whirl of thoughts spun too fast to catch as she hurtled through the air toward the mass of bloodshed below. She crashed hard onto a blue blur, catching her just in time.

Semra snatched a knife from its sheath and adjusted her seat on Zezura's back as the dragon climbed back up above the wall. Rotokas dipped his head to the stone of the castle wall, and Azi ran up his neck and took his place astride the beast. Below them, men merely fulfilling their assigned duties, their sworn commissions, struck each other down at the word of their monarchs. She gritted her teeth.

"Is this what you wanted?" Semra shouted, dodging a fireball from the wyvern's throat. "Is this how you thought power would come?"

Azi whirled the spear over his head and flashed her a leering grin. "I have always had power, my dear. It's in my blood. The question is, now that you've become weak, how many people will you let die before you come home?"

Semra leaned low over her dragon's neck as Zezura lunged for Rotokas. Her teeth raked against the wyvern's throat, and Rotokas struck at Zezura's underbelly with razor-sharp talons. Semra and Azi clung to their mounts, and the two broke apart. Semra threw a fiery stream down on Azi, and Rotokas rotated into the blow.

"I'm not your bondservant, and you were never home. Semra Bandaka is dead."

Azi laughed. "If you've sunk so low to deny reason, it won't matter what your name is. You'll be just another body stinking up my ditches."

Rotokas launched after Zezura, and Semra pulled her away and down over the raging battle breaking through the gates. *Show them the meaning of speed.*

Zezura wheeled through the air with expert agility, the tip of her wing brushing the soldier's helmets as dragon and rider alike poured out fire from above. Belvidorian men shrieked, Jannemar opponents roared, and the Belvidorian soldiers at the Nezzi Gate portcullis toppled into a scalded heap.

A blast of fire singed her arm, and Semra twisted away from the edge of the flame. Azi aimed the spear in her direction again, fire bursting from its tip and hitting Zezura in the shoulder just in front of where Semra perched. Her chest constricted, and her body tensed. What if Aurin's spear wasn't a housing artifact like Raisa's necklace? What if it housed the very magic at the origin of the world? Her magic came so easily when the spear in hand. Without it, it still came, but with less strength. But she hadn't drawn from the power within it. She had dared only to rely on her own tabeun magic, letting the spear hyperfuel the energy as her fire traveled down its length. But what damage could Azi do by siphoning the magic inside the spear itself?

Semra blasted a ball of fire back toward Azi, rotated

Zezura into a spin, and waited for Rotokas' mouth to open. His jaws split wide, and she sent a torrent of flame to the back of his throat just as it began to glow. Whole body shudders rippled through the wyvern's enormous frame. He sputtered and jerked, but Azi knocked Zezura clean off her trajectory with a mighty surge from Aurin's spear.

The courtyard rushed up toward them, the fall snatching Semra's breath away even as Zezura caught their descent and leveled off up over the throne room. *No, not there. If we live, and we have to restore the throne room again, Zephan will kill me.*

The restorations overseen by Turian, whom Azi had sent Tymetin to assassinate. The marble floors were still stained by Brens' blood, Semra's friend from the mountain, whose throat Azi had ordered slit in front of her. A flash of memory from the cavern of Mount Hara hit her like a ton of bricks—Azi, feeding a sniveling man to Rotokas after being disappointed by him. Azi, beating Brens for her supposed weakness, when she came to give report on a botched mission.

Semra's face screwed into a disgusted glower, heat rising in her chest. Zezura swept over the cliff and banked hard, dropping beneath Rotokas and bursting upward for an underbelly strike. Semra braced for impact, but the power of their collision was too much. The hit knocked her off balance, and the smooth scales of the dragon's hide slipped away. Semra's heart lurched into her throat as she slid off Zezura's back and down her side.

Her hands flailed in the air. One hand caught Zezura's talons, and she dangled there, holding on for dear life to two dragon toes as they coursed through the air. Rotokas dove after them, and as Zezura twisted away, Semra's hand slipped. She swung her other arm up, but to no avail.

Drop me off somewhere. Anywhere. I can't hold on.

Zezura dropped altitude back over the south bastion,

where Avaya and Zephan now fought. Zephan had Avaya in a death grip, restraining her and at the same time making it impossible for her to get a clean hit with her magic. Avaya writhed in his grasp, the pendant still clutched in her fist, throwing haphazard blasts and gales where she could.

There. Drop me there and keep Rotokas busy and Azi away from the wall.

A dragonlord was only a man, after all. He had no wings of his own—so if Zezura kept Rotokas in the air, Azi would be unable to land. Zezura roared her answer and angled for the wall. Azi lifted Aurin's spear, aiming for Semra's one hand on Zezura's claws, as she swung with the wind beneath the dragon.

Semra forced her body to relax. Tense legs could be broken legs if she landed wrong. Fire blasted from the tip of the spear. Azi lifted a horn from his waist and blew, loud and clear.

Boom.

Something hit her then. Not hot, but a tug, like a puff of air. A cloud of powder exploded around her, and the air seemed to ignite as Azi's fire strike lit the cloud.

Muscle strength left her body, and her hand slipped free.

58

Semra's pulse pounded and her head throbbed as she tumbled through the air. A wave of nausea rocked her. Somewhere above the din of the battle, Zephan's familiar voice was shouting.

Above her, the dragons fell.

Rotokas.

Zezura.

Falling.

She rotated in the air, and a blur rushed under her just before her skull would have crashed into stone. Eerie shrieks sliced through the air, and soldiers screamed on the carriage road below as two fifty-foot dragons plummeted down on them.

Semra's muscles ached, and she nearly threw up at the ricochet of her body as she jolted to a stop. She winced, then squinted up into the perfect face of Zephan Shamaran. Warmth eased the ache in her bones, and she slackened in his arms.

"Hellooo, handsome man I married," she slurred. "At least, I think I did." She furrowed her brow. Her head hurt.

Zephan grinned. "You did. And you better not forget it, either, because you're stuck with me." He cradled her head in his lap and lifted a shield against a blast of wind pushing them both up against the castle wall. Had he had a shield before? Where had he gotten one?

Semra lolled her head to one side. Several fallen corpses littered the stone around them. Had there been bodies on the bastion before? No, it had been clear. She'd missed some sort of scuffle in her brief absence.

She grimaced as a dizzy spell washed over her. "He used konnolan ... on his own dragon."

Zephan nodded. "I know. Avaya must have had it brought in from Belvidore. Their magic is sifal, and konnolan only deadens magical *essence.* I'm not sure how it effects the artifacts, but Azi and Avaya will feel fine. He took out the dragons just to take you out of commission."

The wind cut off abruptly, and Zephan lowered his shield. Avaya pulled her hand in, clutching the pendant to her chest, and collapsed to the stone. Red eyes set deep in the gauntness of her tear-streaked face, her once-glorious hair an unkempt matte of golden tangles.

Thump.

Semra struggled to sit up. The wooziness began to ebb, but her weakened body still refused to follow directions. A stabbing pain twisted in her gut. Azi straightened on the edge of the battlement wall where he had landed and leaped down ten paces off. He swung the spear in a flourish.

Zephan drew Semra tight against him with one arm and lifted his shield toward the dragonlord with the other. A numbness settled over her, as if the scene on the south bastion of the castle was only another nightmare in a sea of gnawing griefs. At least here, helpless though she was, she was with Zephan.

Azi pursed his lips and heaved a heavy sigh. "I thought a sparring match of this scale would be more interesting. Didn't I set the scene well enough?" He gestured toward the gates, the fighting soldiers, the capital down below, and twirled the spear in his hand. "I filled the arena to watch. I provided a stage for all to see. I so hate to let down the people. What a disappointment."

Zephan shifted out from under Semra, sliding his hand from around her shoulders and brushing her leg as he propped her against the wall. He turned to face Azi. Semra tried to reach for him, but a wave of queasiness washed over her again, and the weakness pulled at her like long icy fingers.

Zephan could have been made of steel, and it wouldn't have mattered. Azi thrust him back with a flick of his wrist and a torrent of sifal flame. Zephan raised the shield just in time, but his feet slid backward even as he leaned into the onslaught. Molten metal dripped down the base of the shield, glittering in the sun on the stone walkway.

Semra groaned. The stone was cold beneath her cheek. It was a fight just to work her hands up under her face to push herself up. Her head spun, and the burning in her chest did nothing to help the racing thoughts.

Only two things remained: to disarm Avaya of the pendant, and to send Azi to the grave once and for all. Avaya would be nothing without Raisa's artifact. Zephan could be restored to the head of his army, and even with the odds against him, his resourcefulness might just see him through.

If only Semra could get the pendant from Avaya.

And kill Azi.

Azi leaned into the spear, eyes flashing with delighted reverie as magical red-orange tongues of fire shoved Zephan backward and licked at the edges of his shield. Zephan dropped to his knee with a grunt and threw his shoulder into the barrier.

"No!" Avaya's lip trembled, and she reached an empty hand toward her brother. Her eyes filled with hatred as she twisted to glare up at her uncle. "This isn't what I wanted."

Azi laughed. "Just because you've decided you don't like it, now that it's here?" He dropped the fiery onslaught and knocked Zephan to the ground, then turned and spat in Avaya's face. "Halfwit! Weakling! This is *exactly* what you wanted. Power, fame, a chance to impact history. Well, you're welcome, darling, because that's what you've gotten. Consumed, obsessed, and blind—the makings of half the leaders in your history books. But not all leaders live to tell their tale. Give me the necklace."

Avaya set her jaw and shook her head. She tightened her fist. Azi's lip curled. He slapped her across the face, sending her sprawling, and ripped the pendant from her grip.

"Look at this pathetic opposition," Azi sneered, sweeping his hand over the three young people on the ground before him. He clucked his tongue, whirling Aurin's spear in one hand and running his thumb over Raisa's pendant in the other. "My royal niece, who showed such promise, is now even more worthless than before. My mountain daughter, who betrayed me, has the strength of a mouse. And my nephew, the only able-bodied numbskull left, the impostor *king*. You have no magic, boy. All you have is a half-dead orphan girl and a greedy sell-out sister."

The king of Jannemar gathered his feet under him and took his stand, holding nothing but a battered shield. The emblem of Jannemar shone on his breastplate, and against all hope he charged the dragonlord of the mountain—the killer of both his parents—while his enemy held all known magic in his hands.

Rats and rot, how she loved and hated him for it! How he stared death in the face, and launched into its open jaws, heart unending, spirit undampened. He could not hope to win. But Zephan Shamaran would go down with the ship, fighting to his last breath.

Azi stalked forward. His eyes were fixed on Zephan, and a cruel smile twisted his lips. Semra screamed and threw her hands outward, begging her fire to answer. Sleepy embers crackled at her fingertips, but fell harmlessly to the stone.

Zephan's muscles strained as he threw all his might into a forceful one-handed blow, using the shield as a blunt force weapon. Azi's smile hardened, and raised Raisa's pendant. Semra slid her hand to her thigh to draw a knife into her palm. She had no magic, and little strength, but what she did have? She—Semra's fingers stilled. The first two sheaths were empty. She'd only remembered using one.

Zephan's other hand twitched. Had Semra been at any other angle, she would have missed it.

Azi blasted Zephan to the ground, and a howl of rage split the air. Semra snapped her head back up to Zephan, checking him over, looking for injuries. He moaned on the ground, and the gale from the pendant sent him skidding across the stone to the wall ten paces over. She turned to Azi then, and saw it— one of her throwing knives buried in the forearm holding Aurin's spear.

That handsome sneak had stolen a throwing knife and outwitted the dragonlord. Semra's lips parted. She'd hardly been more in love with him than at that moment.

Azi's face contorted into a grotesque, snarling glare. He adjusted his grip on the spear and sent a stream of fire down on Zephan, not bothering to attend to the knife handle jutting from his arm.

Semra shot upright, her heart in her throat, but the

sudden movement pitched her to the ground again in a dizzy spiral. Azi shot Zephan with blast upon blast of wind and fire, bashing his body from one side of the bastion to the other, his lips drawn back in a grimace. A cat with a mouse, playing with its dinner.

Avaya was shouting, but Semra couldn't hear. All her focus was bent on a slow crawl, dragging her weak body toward Azi, an inch at a time. Her muscles cried out in protest. She could taste the bile forcing its way up her esophagus. But if Zephan refused to go out in a heap on the ground, so would she.

Azi hit Zephan with another burst of flame, and his tunic caught fire. Avaya lurched forward on scraped hands and knees, but Azi swung the spear and knocked her back. Azi kicked Zephan's body. It did not move.

A chill washed down Semra's spine. Her chest caved in, ripped apart and collapsing all at once, an open-mouthed scream filling the air with the agony of a thousand tortured souls.

"Leave him alone!" Her throat was hoarse, her mouth dry, and she choked on the words. "Leave him alone. I'm the one you want, aren't I? Your best student, your failed project." Semra's head swam, and she gritted her teeth as the sensation passed. Could Zephan be alive? She had to get Azi away from the body. She licked dry lips. "One of the lucky ones. So few of us got the chance to take revenge for our own kidnapping and indoctrination. So few of us remember anything about our parents—but I remember they loved me, and I know you are the one who butchered them on the mountain you made me call home."

A sob hitched in her chest, but the moment she felt it, it was gone. Evolved. A grief attended to might one day bring peace, but long-hidden injustices brought vehement wrath.

Somewhere deep in her core, beneath the weakness of her

outer frame, a fevered hatred brewed. Her fists clenched. Her breathing rose. Every thought rushing by in a river of panic dimmed to a singular focus.

Do what you were made to do. He wanted you to kill, and so he made you a killer. Make him proud—one more time.

Darkness hovered over her mind like a storm cloud of fury just waiting to rain. She summoned her flame, and it simmered beneath the surface of her skin. Muted. Useless. Just like her. What was she without her strength? What was her skill, without the body to use it?

She clenched her teeth. Azi stood over Zephan, peering down at him in a long gaze, showing no signs that he'd even heard her. Nothing could have incensed her more.

Had he not also destroyed her mind? And what consumed *his* mind? Her next words poured out in a rush. "The people will never acknowledge you. They'll never love you. You will only ever be the lesser son, a tantruming child in dress up."

Azi ripped his attention from the boy king at his feet to the troublesome girl at his back. He strode for her then, and seized her by the throat. In her weakened state, each finger seemed to hold the strength of an army, pressing in against the soft flesh of her neck.

He threw her against the low battlement wall, and her body wrenched backward at the waist, the limestone cutting into her back. His iron grip clamped down on her throat. Pain radiated from every indent of his iron fingers as he cut off her air supply and brought his nose to hers.

"I don't care if they love me. They need only to fear me. And after today, I'll have their fear in spades."

59

Semra gasped for air as Azi's hand released her throat. In a single smooth motion, he spun her around and shoved her head down over the edge of the battlement wall. She squeezed her eyes shut against a dizzy spell, and Azi slapped her in the face. The sting in her cheek was hardly noticeable against the ache in her bones, the sway in her knees. She forced herself to focus, to open her eyes to whatever scene might await her down below.

The Belvidorian soldiers held the towers and fortified spaces, and had pushed back the militia. Only the carriage road to Nezzi Gate still held Zephan's men, and the road was blocked by a black wyvern and blue dragon. Both lay motionless.

Could the fall have killed them? Shouldn't the konnolan start wearing off? But then, it hadn't worn off Semra yet—and the dragons carried far more magic in their blood, and had much harder of a fall.

Men tore at each other with the bite of steel and the iron of arrows. Blood stained the base of the portcullis far below and to her right, and as two soldiers locked in combat spun out of the way, she could just make out the top half of a man buried under its weight. The spikes at the bottom of the gate would have impaled him with no hope of escape.

Semra shuddered, remembering a time when she risked such a fate herself, flying under the gate on horseback. In hopes of saving Avaya, as it happened. It was all so ironic now.

Meanwhile, lives continued to be lost. Did the corpse with portcullis spikes through his organs have a family? Children? Semra felt sick.

It was all for nothing. Because they were losing.

A tear slipped down her cheek as she stared down at Azi's shadow cast far below, whirling the legendary weapon over her head with practiced ease. The knife still jutted from his arm, though he seemed not to feel it.

She couldn't beat him. Maybe at full strength, she could hold a candle to the man who taught her all the tactics of death, but not now. Now, she could hardly stand.

Her dragon was poisoned or dead. Physical strength eluded her. Skill fell short against a man twice her size with three times as much experience. What was left against such reckless evil?

The answer hit her square in the chest. Maybe she didn't have to win. She'd been coming at this all wrong, assuming she had to bring defeat crashing down around Azi's ears, and stand victorious over her oppressor. But hadn't she learned —hadn't she learned that it was enough to escape the oppression by freeing her soul, stretching her wings after being clipped so long, and opening the door for other caged birds?

Anger ruled Azi all his days. Power fueled his every capricious thought. And was she so different than he if the same motivation took control of her own heart?

He could not be allowed to live. But she could not be

allowed to become him or he would live on, even though he died.

As long as Azi was out of the way.

Dragon to dragon, lord to lord.

A movement far to one side caught her eye. A roar went up, and a rush of fresh reinforcements poured onto the towers controlling the Dragon Gate portcullis. It looked to be an entire platoon, and the man at the front struck the Belvidorian guardsman at the pulley with such force that he flew right over the wall. Semra held her breath as the man turned around. Gaulen.

Azi spun Semra around and seized her throat again. "You are my greatest failure."

Semra looked back at him, and she wondered how many people had seen this expression in his eyes—the murderous one he gave right before snuffing out another life. How many people had seen it in her own eyes? How easy it was to turn to violence. How easy to play to the whims of a wicked heart. Dead men created few problems.

She gripped at the meat of his hand, digging her fingers in, trying to break his hold, but it was iron. She could almost feel the fire in her blood burning away the konnolan, trying to fight off its effects. Semra's lungs burned. She gagged.

Semra slipped one hand down toward her thigh, but Azi caught the movement and captured her hand. "I taught you *everything*." His voice came in a coarse hiss, spittle flying from his teeth. "You don't think I know you?"

Over Azi's shoulder, Semra could see Avaya bent over Zephan's body. His foot twitched. Semra froze. He was alive.

Something pulled her gaze far down the west wall, and she almost laughed at the sight of it. A man and a woman led a platoon of their own, a ragtag team with a formation that was neither military nor civilian. It looked like the mountains.

The group was armed with all manner of weaponry—grappling hooks, rope, bows and arrows, axes, and a large black satchel carried carefully between two men. And they set themselves at the wall right over the mass of the Belvidorian troops gathered down below.

Her heart thumped wildly, and the tingle of irrational hope spread through her body. A wave of nausea took her then, and she wavered. But as the dizzy spell cleared, so too did the weakness.

Azi threw her down at his feet and raised Aurin's spear over his head, sifal magic running along the wyronite in a spiral of waiting flame, waiting only for the command of a master. Semra hit the stone with a force that reverberated through her body in a ripple of pain. She twisted up to face him, his boot in her back, a flood of next steps running through her brain.

The sacrifice of the elemental melders played at the fringes of her mind, then grew and narrowed into a singular focus. Surely it was the voice of one of these four that was captured in the wellspring at the death of magic, released again after six hundred years. The song played, a poignant, haunting melody underpinning the heart of that legendary mission all those years ago:

Never, never, never again
Reign of terror now will end

A curious camaraderie with these ancient strangers settled over her, bringing with it an unexplainable calm. The crown must always come first. The kingdom before the individual. Zephan would understand—how many times had he put himself in harm's way, willing to die for the same?

But what if this time his sacrifice wasn't to die but to live in her wake? Perhaps when the darkest of agonies came, life was the harder choice.

She'd never wanted so badly to stay alive than in these past months with Zephan. *Perhaps your job, as you call it, is death... but your inclination is life.*

And so it was for life that she would die. For Zephan, for Aviama, for the people under her stewardship, for however short a time. If she could stay close to Azi, get a good grip on him, and take them over the wall—well, a dragonlord was only human after all.

She looked at Zephan, and even as she watched, he sat up. His eyes latched onto hers. His face was bruised, his armor scuffed, but his eyes—those amber eyes bored into her like the white hot of a knife snatched fresh from the blacksmith's forge.

He knew. Somehow, he knew.

If she bade him farewell, if she touched him, she would never leave him. But she must.

Azi flung fire down on Semra, and she threw up her hands just in time. Fire met fire in a powerful red-orange stream, enveloping the dragonlords in a shower of sparks. Azi's eyes lit with pleasure, obsessed with his new toy.

Semra pulled her hands in toward herself, grimacing as if her magic was buckling to his. His lip curled and he pressed the spear further and further down over her chest, still reveling in his newfound power.

But old tried-and-true worked just as well. The instant he was close enough, Semra hooked his ankle with one leg, shoved her other foot against Azi's hip to control his fall, and swept his feet out from under him. Zephan ran forward and looped his arm around Semra's waist, dragging her backward.

Panic welled in her chest. *I have to stay close. Distance is his advantage.* Semra pulled away, but Zephan's grip held her fast, and he whirled his body to place himself between Semra and Azi. "Don't do anything stupid," he murmured. "Together. Promise me."

His breath tickled her ear, and a tingling sensation sent a shiver down her spine. Suddenly she turned into him, pulled him into her, and kissed him. His lips parted in surprise, and he staggered back a step. She pressed into him, memorizing the feel of his arms, the touch of his lips, if only for a moment.

Zephan's arms loosened. Behind him, Azi gathered his feet.

"Forgive me," she whispered. And she slipped from his grasp and launched herself through the air at Azi.

60

———

Semra hit Azi like an arrow from the string, and they toppled over the castle wall in a tangle of arms and legs. A blast of fire shot uselessly up into the air over their heads from the spear. The battle below spun up toward them as if in slow motion—the men in combat, the bodies underfoot, Gaulen and his men capturing the Belvidorians between his troop and the militia on their other side. Rotokas stirred on the carriage road, a puff of smoke going up from his nostrils.

A blue blur interrupted the white of the sandstone wall, and a pang of guilt slugged Semra in the stomach as she realized Zezura was climbing the wall to get to her up on the bastion. The joint of her wing was bent and bleeding, yet she hoisted her massive body up the battlement tooth and claw.

I'm sorry, Zez. It was all she could manage, as they spun to their deaths down below.

A gale of wind burst up from below, catching them and rocketing them back up and over the wall. Azi smashed the shaft of the spear into her back, writhing in his effort to extricate himself from her body. She locked her legs around his waist, summoned fire to her palms, and smashed her hands into both sides of his face.

His open-mouthed scream shattered the air, and the wind broke. Azi and Semra dropped back down to the bastion, and Aurin's spear clattered to the ground and rolled away. The two dragonlords whirled apart, but even without the spear, Azi still held Raisa's pendant. He lifted it up, and Semra braced for the impact that would throw her over the edge for good.

A high-pitched shriek cut through the gathering wind, and Azi jerked upright—a sword blade protruded through his torso. Avaya stumbled back, eyes wide, mouth agape. Her hands trembled.

The wound running through Azi's body glowed cobalt blue. He gripped the pendant in frozen fingers, his knuckles white, his eyes black with a seething hate. But he did not fall.

He rotated in a tight circle, his arms thrown to the sky, and the air around them surged to his will. A mighty windstorm twisted around Azi's body, enveloping him in unbreakable currents of air. Semra and Zephan exchanged a terrified glance, just as Zezura's great blue head swung over the top of the wall. The dragon's voice filled Semra's mind like a single clear bell.

Take from me. This kind of magic requires more than you have.

Semra's chest hitched as puzzle pieces locked into place. *A dragon-blooded stroke.*

Her gaze fell on Aurin's spear, slowly rolling away in the buffet of the wind on her enemy's other side. Avaya followed her glance and dove for the spear. She yelped as she touched it, and cast it low toward Semra, beneath the bulk of the storm.

Semra caught it in her fist and dipped the spear tip into Zezura's wound. The dragon roared, pulling herself up over the battlement wall and spreading her wings behind the couple on the bastion. The sun glinted against the Jannemar crest on the king's chest as he turned to his queen.

Zephan held out a hand. "Together?"

Semra dipped her head. "Together."

The two of them seized Aurin's spear from either side and ran forward into the gale, the spear tip cutting through the sifal magic of the hurricane, dividing the wind to its right and left. In a single stroke, the spear plunged through the dragonlord's stomach just above where Zephan's sword still lodged. The blue glow flew out his mouth and up his hands, and Raisa's pendant fell from his fingers.

Azi Shamaran stiffened and collapsed. A knife protruded from his arm, a sword impaled him through the middle, and his vacant eyes bore the glaze of death.

Avaya caught the pendant as it fell, and straightened. She bit her quivering lip and chewed a nail, then raised her eyes to Zephan. Her red dress hung in tatters from her shoulders, and her gaunt face was lined with exhaustion. But even in her shame, when she lifted her chin, she somehow looked the part of a queen.

"Will you accept my surrender, on the condition that my men are granted safe passage back to their homeland? They only answered the call of their queen—just as yours answered the call of their king."

Semra and Zephan stood side by side, each still holding Aurin's spear between them. Azi lay dead at their feet, and Avaya stood before them with her petition. Zephan's hand slid up over Semra's as she gripped the spear, and her tense muscles relaxed under his touch. She sidestepped into him until her hip brushed his, and their arms touched. Warmth flooded her body.

Zephan swallowed and squeezed her hand. He lifted his

chin as he looked at his sister. "Are you making a formal request of surrender?"

Avaya pursed her lips and gave a curt nod.

Zephan took a deep breath. "It doesn't look like it."

Semra looked up at him, but his gaze remained fixed on his sister. He had never looked more like a king, or more like his father, as he did in that moment. The authority of Turian sitting in the throne room mixed with the weighty sigh of bearing a heavy crown. She found herself examining the cut of his jaw, the soft firmness of his face.

There was no eagerness in his expression, no desire to rub Avaya's nose in her defeat. Semra wondered if, as a brother, he might almost be tempted to release her to her sorrow. But as king, he could never make such a reckless allowance.

Avaya clenched her jaw and gave her brother a long, hard look. But as she glared at him, and he stared back with no animosity, but only a willingness to wait, the fire went out and she knelt before him. "I, Queen Avaya of Belvidore, surrender to King Zephan of Jannemar. I and my people are at your mercy."

Zephan dipped his head. "I accept your surrender. On condition that you surrender not only this fight but also the throne of Belvidore. We will appoint another ruler in your stead, see that the nation is stabilized, and bring you home to Jannemar under my supervision. You will accept whatever consequences of your actions we choose in high court—but if you accept, and maintain your men on the journey back to their country, I will see that your life is spared."

She let out a shuddering breath and nodded. Avaya rose, strode to the edge of the wall, and grimaced as the sifal magic of Raisa's artifact stole her energy one last time. As she lifted up her voice, it carried loud as thunder over the battle down below. "Men of Belvidore, surrender your arms. Your service has been valiant, and your safety is granted. Your bravery and loyalty will be rewarded, and the time may come when we call you again to fight for in the name of your monarch, but today —today two rival kingdoms stand at peace. The king of Jannemar and I have come to an agreement."

Zephan walked Semra over to stand beside Avaya and lifted Aurin's spear over their heads, their hands still connected over the spear. The sounds of combat halted, and a shout went up.

Avaya stepped back from the wall. Her shoulders slumped, and her eyes misted. In the space of that moment, she seemed to age ten years. But her lip curled and her green eyes flashed as she glared down at her uncle's corpse. "They're not your men. They're mine."

Zephan held his hand out, palm up, to his sister. Avaya eyed him for a moment. Her fingers lingering over Raisa's pendant, and her thumb ran over its ridges. After a moment, she swallowed, and handed it over.

Semra turned to the dragon curled up in the sun on the castle wall, her injured wing held gingerly against her huge serpentine body. "You okay, Zez?"

The dragon coughed and snorted a whisp of smoke, and Semra ran a hand down her nose. "We'll get you taken care of. Thank you. What would we do without you?"

The dragon snorted again. *Jump off high buildings, apparently.*

Semra's mouth twitched.

Zephan seized her hand, spun her into a twirl, and caught her in a low dip. Her cheeks flushed and butterflies exploded in her stomach. He brought her upright again, slipped one hand to the nape of her neck and one to the small of her back, and pulled her close.

Semra reached for him. He kissed her on the neck and

brushed her nose with his, letting his lips pause as they grazed hers. "Hello, wife."

Joy like the blossom of spring flooded her chest, and she could hardly help the huge, beaming smile that broke across her face. "Hello, husband."

Semra pressed herself into his chest and stretched on her toes to kiss him. He tasted like sunshine, though she hadn't a clue what that meant. His arms tightened around her, and the world faded away until all that existed was the orphan girl who had become a queen, and the boy she'd met in the woods who had become a king.

Castle or cave, peace or war—decadent cakes, or stale bread on a long road—here in his arms, she was home.

The doors of the towers from the keep flew open, and three platoons of Jannemar royal guard, soldiers, and militia spilled out onto the bastion. Semra didn't recognize the first platoon leader, but Monac led the second, and Siler and Pidge led the third—though *platoon* was too formal a word for the group of outlaws they seemed to have assembled.

Semra blushed at such an audience to their kiss, but when she moved to pull away, Zephan's arm around her waist tugged her close again. A swirl of glowing embers had encircled them, a burst of magic Semra had no conscious memory of making. Zephan grinned at her as the sparks dissipated into the air along a gentle, natural breeze.

Zephan signaled to Monac, and Monac strode forward to take Avaya into custody, his platoon taking up positions around them. Castle staff slipped out onto the wall and filled in the spaces behind the platoons, craning their necks past the soldiers for a glimpse of their king and his dragonlord assassin.

A broad-shouldered woman at the back clapped her hands with a delighted squeal. Semra laughed. She should have known Saeb, the persnickety housekeeper, wouldn't bear waiting behind the scenes for long.

"Long live the king!" Saeb shouted. "And long live the countess, Lady Myansara!"

"Countess?" Siler shook his head. He stepped forward and scooped up a nezil myansara blossom, fallen from Semra's hair sometime during the fight. Siler twirled it in his fingers and winked. "Long live the crimson queen!"

Semra's chest tightened, and her heart raced. She scanned the faces of the people. How would they take such news?

Zephan lifted Semra's hand so the gems of his mother's ring sparkled in the light, and kissed it.

Pidge grinned and dropped to her knee. She yanked Siler down beside her, and the two platoons and staff beyond them fell to their knees in a wave. Gaping mouths and smiling faces stared back at Semra and Zephan.

And then the shout went up, as a single voice into the sky:

"Long live the king! Long live the queen!"

Semra and Zephan sat in the conservatory, morning light glinting softly off sparkling marble floors. The greenery along the walls and curated miniature garden set in the middle of the low stone table in front of them rustled with the whisper of a gentle breeze flowing in through the open doors of the balcony.

Semra smiled. Her first memory of this room was of dangling over the edge of that balcony, barely hanging on. Zephan had come to save her then—before she'd known he was a prince. Before she'd known much of anything really. She'd known nothing of trust, security, or true loyalty back then. Even if she had, Semra never would've dreamed that *she* might have all those things one day.

Nevertheless, that day had come. And it was time now to extend another hand of friendship, offering peace to another soul who never expected to see it.

Through the glass panels of the door, Semra could see two figures approaching down the walkway over the Great Hall: a castle guard and a woman. The guard posted at the door opened it and bowed.

"Her Royal Highness, Princess Blaise."

Semra thumbed the hilt of her knife as her pulse ticked up a notch. Why was she nervous? And why was it so against protocol to clean knives during official meetings?

Zephan gave a nod, and the guard stepped aside to let in their guest.

Blaise glided into the conservatory like a spindly underfed fawn—furtive and wide-eyed, bony, and haggard, but with a curious light in her eye. Her skin was pale, but with more color than Semra remembered, and a simple braid fell down the back of a pale-blue silk gown. The light trill of a bird sounded outside the window, completely overpowering the minuscule patter of her feet on the marble floor.

The princess curtsied low and rose—silently, expectantly awaiting whatever fate might have for her here. Zephan and Semra had not exposed much of their intentions when they'd sent their envoy and summoned her from Belvidore. They'd sent a gift to ease her mind that they meant no harm and given her three days to depart on the trip. She'd arrived just yesterday and been allowed to settle into her guest quarters and rest from the journey.

"Good morning." Zephan smiled warmly.

Blaise answered with a thin, high-pitched voice, and her own nervous smile. "Good morning, Your Majesty."

Zephan nudged Semra, and she cleared her throat. "We're so glad you're here." She gestured at the seat set out across from them for the princess. "Please, sit."

Blaise perched on the edge of the seat and folded her hands neatly in her lap, her back straight as a board as she eyed the monarch pair. Semra wondered what the poor girl was expecting. Imprisonment? Banishment? But no, why would they have invited her so far and hosted her as they had if it were one of those?

Semra cleared her throat. "I'm not sure you remember me, but I—"

"I remember you." The confidence and clarity in Blaise's tone surprised Semra. Blaise tilted her head. "You were dressed as a servant and looking for Avaya. I told you I had reservations about her and that no one ever listened to me."

Zephan and Semra exchanged a glance.

Blaise shifted in her chair. "I never forget a face. Very good with names, too, but you didn't give me one then. It's just as well. It wouldn't have been a real one, so I'm glad I waited."

Semra nearly laughed aloud. Yes, she'd do. "You're sharp. Observant, smart. We've asked around—no one in the castle has a bad word to say about you." An *odd* word, sure, but not a *bad* word. "You've educated yourself on diplomacy and matters of state, you disapproved of the actions of both your father and your brother, and your health, though limiting, is improving in their absence. Not to mention, you were the only person in Madensig who seemed to catch on that Avaya was not what she claimed to be."

Zephan leaned back in his chair and folded his arms. "We want you to rule Belvidore as steward. I'm not interested in conquest for conquest's sake. The region needs stability, and your people deserve it, after all this time. Belvidore will become a territory of Jannemar, but distinct, preserving your culture and traditions, and cared for by someone they know —you."

Blaise blinked back at them. She didn't move.

Semra furrowed her brow and leaned forward. "We know your health is up and down. But the fact that you made the trip here at all is testimony to your improvement, and as steward, we could surround you with much more help. You could retain your residence in Madensig, and would agree to quarterly reviews and regular meetings and updates on how things are progressing."

The frail woman before them tapped her foot on the floor and worried her lip. The tapping quickened from a mild rhythm to an overanxious frenzy. Her hands trembled. She sat on them. "You want me to rule?"

Zephan nodded. "You don't have to. But we would help you. Belvidore would be under Jannemar's supervision in all the broad strokes, but the day-to-day business would be yours, to whatever extent you're able."

Blaise ripped her hands from under her seat and clapped them over her mouth, her big eyes bugging out. "Yes! Yes, I will! Oh, I thought I was on trial, or going to be sent far away, or you were going to hide me very kindly in a hole."

Semra's mouth twitched. Zephan laughed. "I think we have a long future ahead of us, collaborating for the sake of our people's peace and stability. Make me a list of what *you* think Belvidore's greatest strengths and weaknesses are, and the greatest points of concern in light of the power transition ahead. We'll meet next week with the full court. For now" — here Zephan took Semra's hand, sending a tingle running up her arm—"we have a wedding to prepare for."

Blaise frowned. "I thought you were already married."

Zephan waved a hand. "We are. But as it turns out, legally eloping through a collapsed wall in a faraway cave is neither traditional nor helpful for kingdom morale, formally welcoming a new queen, or any of the other benefits of an actual ceremony."

Semra wrinkled her nose and leaned in toward Blaise. "He's making me wear a dress."

Zephan gave her a shove and wagged his finger. "Don't misrepresent me. I *persuaded* you to wear a dress. It's going to be spectacular. And you'll be such a ravishing vision in it that not a single soul will dare say no to you, and it'll be good practice for us all, for the rest of our lives."

Semra flushed, undoubtably beet red, and her heart squeezed uncomfortably at his effusive praise. Though he hadn't stopped slipping compliments into daily conversations every chance he got, she was still getting used to it.

A knock came at the door, and though the guard stepped forward to introduce the intruder, Aviama bounced in anyway without waiting for his announcement. "I've come for Semra! You told me I could steal her and keep her with me for girly wedding things *all* day today, and, well, it's daytime, and it's today! Hand her over!"

Blaise jerked to her feet, fighting a grin, and Zephan tackled Semra into her chair. "No! I take it back! She's staying with me!"

Semra kicked him off, equal parts laughter and embarrassment taking her over at his display in front of Blaise.

Zephan straightened and gave a short bow to Blaise. "Forgive us. Newlyweds, you know." He laughed again. "You'll be escorted back to your quarters, and we'll see you at the wedding. And I look forward to our meeting next week."

Blaise gave three awkward curtsies and stumbled out of the room toward the guest chambers. Aviama clapped her hands.

"Can you believe it?! A whole day of wedding plans and flowers and dresses and—finally, it's time for parties, after the year we've had, don't you think? Oh, we *will* have parties! The wedding is just the beginning, though it will certainly be the best one. Will you let me dress you up for your birthday?" Aviama hesitated. "When *is* your birthday?"

Semra shrugged. "I don't have one. I mean, I obviously *had* one, but nobody knows when we were born. We all just age up at the new year." The thought of still being connected to

Bandaka traditions soured her stomach. "Maybe ... maybe I could pick a new one?"

Aviama squealed. "Yes! Yes, please do! How does one choose a birthday, when it isn't the day they were born?"

Zephan slipped his arms around Semra's waist. She jumped, and he grinned. "I've been thinking about the birthday thing. I wondered if ... well, you're a Jannemar queen now, and there are so many sad anniversary days. I wondered if you would take my mother's birthday as yours. Sort of sweeten it again."

Semra twisted to face him and scanned his expression. She already wore his mother's ring—was it right to take her birthday as well? "Are you sure?"

Zephan nodded. "I'd like you to. Avs?"

Aviama's eyes misted, and she nodded. "I like it."

Something in Semra's chest pinched, and she bit her lip. But as kind as it was, it wasn't quite right. "What if I take the day after? I don't think stuffing happy things onto sad things makes them any less sad, and now that the nation is stable, we can afford to breathe a bit and remember our dead. Let her birthday still be for her, for mourning, remembering, telling sweet memories. And the day after, we can have a happy celebration day."

Zephan pulled her in and kissed her. "Thank you. Yes, let's do that."

Aviama wrinkled her nose and stuck out her tongue. "Yuck. Enough of that. I'm stealing her away now."

The princess pulled Semra away and dragged her to the door. She jabbed her finger at Zephan as she shoved Semra out the door. "You promised I'd have the whole day, so interruptions! And *no peeking!*"

No ruffles. No drapey sleeves to get caught on things. Nothing unreasonably heavy.

Semra blinked at her reflection in the mirror. Aviama had hit all of her requirements for the dress. Yet still, somehow, the woman staring back at her wasn't a guttersnipe assassin but a lady. A noblewoman.

A queen.

The makeup was natural, but beautiful, with a brush of rose along her cheekbones, glittering golds and browns on her eyes, and lips painted crimson red. The flowing skirts, tragically, had no slits or modifications for easy knife access—but that was no surprise. Aviama had sworn up and down that she if anyone touched the glorious skirts of the wedding gown, it would be over her dead body.

The castle had seen enough dead bodies. No one dared cross her.

Shimmering white swathed Semra's body, long sleeves filmy and comfortable but tapered at the wrist. Delicate gold encircled her waist, and trails of gold fell down her skirt like the embers of an exploding star. The neckline dipped just enough to reveal the opal dragon's kiss on her chest, and her dark hair swept over one shoulder in cascading curls and interwoven nezil myansara pins. Semra turned and twisted to look over one shoulder, where the back of the dress dropped low to reveal her whip-lashed scars.

That last bit was Zephan's one request—*Let the people trust that in the service of Jannemar, their crimson queen first shed not others' blood, but her own.*

Semra never would've dreamed that her beatings in the dungeon of Shamaran Castle, falsely imprisoned for the murder of Queen Sharsi, would land her here, putting those scars on display for the kingdom.

Zephan had always seen further into her than she had seen in herself. When she'd seen a despicable weapon for death, he'd seen a protector of life. Two sides of a single coin —the same skills required for each, but one was drawn to darkness, and one fought for the light.

Her heart soared, and, for once, she didn't resist it but let it fly. Aviama stood to one side, beaming. She ran forward and hugged her, and Semra hugged her back. Semra didn't know what it was like to have a real sister, but if she were to have one, Aviama was the kind she would want.

Today she gained not only a husband—again, really, since they were technically already married—but the kingdom, a sister, a family, a home.

The weight of the crown.

A purpose.

A calling.

Aviama drew back, tears glistening in her eyes. She sniffed. "I think you're the most beautiful thing I've ever seen."

A lump lodged in Semra's throat, and she swallowed hard against it. "Thank you."

A knock and a grunt called their attention to door. The

gruff bearded face of Garbane greeted her, his frame dressed in simple but fine wardrobe. The man's hair was as maintained as she'd ever seen it, and his rough hands tugged uncomfortably at the edges of his vest. "Ready?"

Semra nodded, and the chandler offered her his arm.

Aviama gave her another quick hug and kiss and ran down the back stairs to walk in at the assigned time. Four guards followed Semra and Garbane at a respectful distance as they made their way down the hall.

Garbane patted her hand as they walked. "You look good."

Semra flushed red. "Thanks." She cleared her throat. "How much do you hate me for making you dress up?"

He chuckled. "No more than you hate Aviama, I'd guess."

Semra's breathing quickened as they descended the stairs, entered the Great Hall, and came to the doors leading out to the courtyard. Never in the history of the Shamaran royal line had a wedding been held outdoors. But never in their history had a dragonlord been a monarch, either, so Semra and Zephan agreed it was time for a change. Nothing stuffy. No cold confining walls, no matter how ornate those walls might be.

Guards opened the double doors and stood sentry on either side. Music played in light, lilting tones. A mass of people crowded the courtyard and spilled into the expansive gardens down the steps. Free-standing archways lined the aisle at intervals, wooden frames set with flowers and wispy sheer cloth gently billowing in the wind.

Beside her, Garbane drew his shoulders back and straightened. Semra followed suit, lifting her chin and letting the chandler set their pace. Select servants and staff had been allowed to enjoy the ceremony without running its minutiae, and they filled out the chairs nearest her—Saeb, Belon, and

Murin among their number. Every one of them gasped and smiled as she passed.

Semra smiled back, her heart hammering in her chest. The aisle curved down the steps and into the heart of the gardens, passing lines upon lines of people. Nobles, dignitaries, counts, and earls. With some satisfaction Semra noticed a man in a ridiculously large-plumed hat among the nobles. Isra, one of her friendlier assassin colleagues, had invited himself to the ceremony.

But as they made the turn around the bend, all thoughts of the people around her dropped away. Because there, at the end of the aisle, was Zephan.

He stood in all the shining regalia befitting his station. Medals glittered on his chest; a ceremonial sword hung on his belt, and a crown adorned his golden head. He was unquestionably handsome. But Semra's favorite part was the wonder in his eyes when he saw her, the glisten of tears as emotion flew to the surface, and the blissful grin that took over his face.

Semra set her eyes on her future, standing there, waiting for her, and choked on a nervous laugh. He caught the movement, and the two of them stifled laughs at each other from across the way. At the end of the aisle, Garbane bowed at Zephan and passed her from his own arm onto Zephan's, and the traditions that followed passed in a blur.

The officiant said something. Lots of somethings. Zephan gave his oath to love, honor, and protect her until the end of their days, and Semra gave hers. She stumbled through it, but she meant every word, and at the end of the day they would be bound together in an unbreakable bond whether she repeated herself three times or not.

Their oaths were made, their union affirmed, and Semra knelt before her king. Zephan placed a glittering crown on her head, and drew her up as queen and kissed her. Embers flew from her fingers in a gentle swirl, to the awe of the crowd; but the more amazing thing to Semra was not the dragon magic in her blood, but the wholeness of her heart—once empty and shattered, now full to bursting.

Gasps and murmurs went up as a great aquamarine dragon swooped overhead, arced, and dipped low over the crowd. Something hit Semra in the head, and she pulled away as Zephan pulled a stick from her hair. Semra arched an eyebrow and looked up.

Zezura had a flower bush in her mouth and was shaking it as she flew, flowers falling like rain on the distinguished people down below—and twigs, and sticks, and leaves. Semra laughed and held out her hand, and the great blue dragon landed behind them and dropped the bush to nudge her fingers with her nose. Zephan patted her on the neck.

"What do you think, Zez? Do you approve?"

The dragon gave her well-pleased huffing snort, and shot a short burst of flame down the sides of the aisle, lighting a line of torches leading back to the Great Hall.

Applause broke out throughout the garden and up through the courtyard, and Zephan and Semra led the way back up the aisle to the Great Hall for feasting and dancing. She'd never seen the hall so elaborate or so full of people. But with her colleagues taking up positions in shifts, the royal guard having undergone fresh training, and knives still close on the thighs beneath her skirts, she'd also never felt so safe in a crowd.

And she'd never felt safer to be herself.

Siler snatched a pastry from a servant's tray and spun to intercept them with an over-exaggerated, flourished bow. "Congratulations. This might be nice and all, but remember, I'm the one who officiated the real one." He took a bite of the pastry and licked his lips, and for an instant, his mocking exterior dropped to sincerity. "Today, I'm almost proud to be from Jannemar."

Semra's eyebrows rose. "I thought all monarchs were bad and kings were all the same."

Siler shrugged. "Yes, well, I've never respected a monarch before. So this will be a new experience for me." He glanced between the two of them, king and queen standing together, and let out a breath. "You're good for the kingdom. The two of you. And I think I've decided that caring about the kingdom and the people in it is worth doing."

His gaze strayed somewhere beyond them, and Semra twisted to see Pidge dancing with Lesala, the little girl Semra and Siler had first saved from Azi's mountain all those months ago. Shafii and Tinat Rinab, the healer and his wife from Ryden who had adopted her, clapped and egged them on from the sidelines. Pidge glanced up, laughing, and waved at them.

A warm feeling spread from the top of Semra's head to the tips of her toes. She wrapped her arm around Zephan's waist and leaned her head on his shoulder. She'd so badly wanted good things for Siler. It hadn't been with her. It wasn't meant to be. But seeing him with Pidge, and the softening in him as he looked at her, did her heart good.

Siler dipped his head and disappeared into the crowd, and a large, framed man with a flowing beard took his place before them. "Your Majesties."

Semra smiled. "Frigibar! I'm surprised you came."

"Hey, sparky." The older man pressed his lips. "I haven't come to the capital in decades. When I got your invitation, I thought now was the time ... and we have something time-sensitive to discuss. There will be fallout from removing Aurin's spear from the wellspring. Magic has been released into the world again after six hundred years, and its effects have already started popping up. Those impacts will slowly spread from the origin point throughout the surrounding areas and the world."

Semra grimaced. They'd known removing the spear would not be without consequences. But there was no way to know exactly what those consequences would be. Without a plan in place, with the last keeper of knowledge on the use of magic standing in front of her, the aftermath of the spear debacle could be disastrous. She nodded. "I'll see to it you're hosted in the castle. We'll set up a meet."

He bowed. "I won't stay in the castle. But I will come to a meeting."

Zephan reached out to clasp the man's forearm in welcome. "We look forward to it. I imagine there is much to discuss. Don't leave tonight until we've set an appointment."

Frigibar gave a stiff nod and melted away. The musicians struck up a new song, and Zephan held out a hand. "We're technically supposed to be the ones to open the dance floor, though I'll give Pidge and Lesala a pass."

Semra took his hand and let him lead her out onto the dance floor. The masses of people split before them, and the buzz of conversation dropped to a hush as all heads turned toward the couple in the center of the room.

How many times had they danced like this? Semra shook her head, marveling at how far they'd come. A dance lesson in the woods with a healer's apprentice named Dahyu. A dance at the gala in this very room, right before the queen was killed. Another dance in the woods. A dance among the haybales in the loft of an enemy's stable.

It may have seemed haphazard to anyone else, but to Semra, it was the progression of their relationship. It was the building of trust, to catch her when she fell, to be there when she turned around, that in stables, or forest, cave, or castle, the constant was never their surroundings and always, instead, each other.

Forever she would be at his side.

Forever, he would be at hers.

And when the music subsided, and Zephan took her to the head of the room where two ornate thrones had been set, shame did not cripple her to approach such an authoritative seat. Pain did not riddle her belly at the hypocrisy of her blood-soaked ledger.

She didn't deserve the crown. She didn't deserve her husband.

But it wasn't about deserving it. None of that mattered.

She was pardoned, and the sun still shone, and the people still needed caring for, despite any marks on her record.

The court stood witness to their wedding. The kingdom welcomed her as their queen. And a dragonlord girl from nowhere had bloomed in adversity, claimed nobility, and taken her place in history.

Semra turned toward her husband, and found him watching her already, his eyes drifting over her and returning to gaze softly into hers, a gentle smile at his lips. She held out her hand, and he kissed it.

Unable to help herself, she leaned in and kissed him again.

Home.

And with that, hand in hand, the king and queen of Jannemar took their thrones.

COMING SOON: MELDERBLOOD

Find out what happens after magic is unleashed into Jannemar, with book one of a brand new series coming December 2023.

Princess Aviama's world has been steeped in chaos ever since long-dormant magic returned to the world – and came alive in her blood.

Click here to learn more on Amazon!

THANK YOU FOR READING!

Thank you so much for reading *Crimson Queen,* book 4 of *The Blood and Flame Saga*! I hope you enjoyed reading it as much as I enjoyed writing it.

If you did, would you be willing to leave a review? Reviews help enable authors to continue doing what they do, and help other readers to find books best suited to them.

If you'd like to leave a review on Amazon, **click here.**

ABOUT THE AUTHOR

Author of *The Forgotten Stone* and the *Blood and Flame Saga*, E.A. Winters loves pouring herself a cup of hot chocolate with a mountain of marshmallows and delving into creating epic fantasy worlds for you to enjoy.

Erin lives in Virginia with her husband and two boys. When she's not writing, Erin is spending her time with her family. She loves playing board games and reading, whenever the elusive "free time" opportunity arises.

ALSO BY E.A. WINTERS

Blood & Flame Saga

Book 1: Dragon's Kiss

Book 2: Broken Bonds

Book 3: Noble Claims

Book 4: Crimson Queen

Stand Alones

The Forgotten Stone

www.ingramcontent.com/pod-product-compliance
Lightning Source LLC
Chambersburg PA
CBHW050953210726

48287CB00004B/1206